ALSO BY SILVIA MORENO-GARCIA

The Beautiful Ones
Mexican Gothic
Gods of Jade and Shadow
Untamed Shore
Signal to Noise
Velvet Was the Night

CERTAIN DARK THINGS

SILVIA MORENO-GARCIA

Jo Fletcher
BOOKS

First published in Great Britain in 2021 by

Jo Fletcher Books
an imprint of
Quercus Editions Ltd
Carmelite House
50 Victoria Embankment
London EC4Y 0DZ

An Hachette UK company

Published by arrangement with TOR Books,
an imprint of Macmillan Publishing LLC, New York.
First published in the United States in 2017.

A CIP catalogue record for this book is available
from the British Library

HB ISBN 978 15294 1 560 5
TPB ISBN 978 15294 1 561 2

10 9 8 7 6 5 4 3 2 1

Printed and bound in Great Britain by Clays Ltd, Elcograf S.p.A.

Papers used by Jo Fletcher Books are from well-managed forests and other responsible sources.

To the vampire: Germán Robles

ACKNOWLEDGMENTS

Thanks to my agent, Eddie Schneider, and the editor who originally purchased this manuscript, Quressa Robinson, for helping bring this book to life. Thanks to Kelly Lonesome and the Nightfire team who brought it back from the dead.

Thanks to David Bowles for correcting the Nahuatl employed in the novel.

Thanks also to my mother for letting me watch horror movies late at night, thanks to my great-grandmother for narrating horror movies to me, thanks to my children for bearing with me when I write and drift far away.

Thanks finally to my husband, who is my first reader and for whom I write. He is the salt in every dish I taste.

NOTE TO THE READER

You are holding in your hands a book with a strange genesis, that came back from the dead.

In 2011, my short story "A Puddle of Blood" appeared in a Canadian anthology called *Evolve Two: Vampire Stories of the Future Undead*. It starred Domingo, a garbage collector, and Atl, a vampire. I had toyed with the idea of both characters for a while and brought them together for this short meeting. Afterwards, I became interested in using the story as the springboard for a novel and wrote *Certain Dark Things*.

Twilight had been a big hit in 2005, but by the time *Certain Dark Things* made the rounds with editors, the market had been bled dry. To make things worse, it was a weird book. It was a noir—I call it a neon-noir—set in an alternate Mexico City. Editors were puzzled. We found a young, energetic editor who liked it and the novel sold to Thomas Dunne Books, and was published in 2016.

Just around the time it was going to be released, Thomas Dunne was reorganized and downsized. *Certain Dark Things* and my other novel under contract were orphaned. They quickly went out of print.

Then the book seemed to acquire an odd second life. It kept appearing in lists of recommended books. People emailed me each week asking where they could find a copy. A friend told me the hardcover was going for $150 on eBay. It seemed like I was witnessing the birth of a cult book, something that might be spoken about in years to come but never reprinted.

But an odd thing was happening at the same time my book disappeared. Horror seemed to be making a comeback. Nightfire was announced. It was, wonder of wonders, a horror imprint from a large publisher. And suddenly, *Certain Dark Things*, which had been quietly put in its coffin and packed away, was alive again.

Something else happened while I wrote this book: Germán Robles, to whom I dedicated this book, died. Robles played the Count Karol de Lavud in a couple of Mexican horror films. In the 1990s, he was acting in the play *The Lady in Black*. I saw him on stage and got his autograph afterwards. Robles inspired several characters in my short stories, including the vampire in "Stories with Happy Endings," and the vampire Bernardino in *Certain Dark Things*.

As a child, I spent a lot of time watching black-and-white Mexican movies. Everything from comedies to noirs showed up and I'd marathon through four or five flicks over a weekend. I liked Christopher Lee and Peter Cushing and Vincent Price, but I loved Robles.

My high school friends say that when I was a teenager I'd tell them I was going to become a vampire. I don't remember it, but I believe it. I was a weirdo. I blasted Bauhaus, carried Truman Capote under my arm, tried to teach myself French because of Baudelaire, and I was in love with Robles. Not in a romantic, *Twilight* way, but in love with the black-and-white world he inhabited. They don't make movies like they did then. And you don't fall in love with silver nitrate anymore, but I did. I loved the oh-so-fake-looking sets of his movies, the shadows and the shots of him staring disdainfully at the camera.

If there was a celebrity I always wanted to meet, it was Robles.

My husband used to live near a cafe where Robles often had supper with his friends. I could have, I suppose, waited for him there, but that just seemed stalkery. And I didn't want to do it because there's a difference between the performer and the character they give flesh to. I understood the separation.

I dedicated the book to Robles after asking my husband if that seemed like too much of a fangirl thing. My thought process was that I'd write, "To Robles, the vampire," and when the book was out I'd mail him a copy. Maybe he wouldn't be able to read it (I didn't know if he spoke English), or maybe he wouldn't care.

"He's eighty-something," I told my husband. "I should finish the book quick, what if he dies?"

And then, of course, he did die. Before the book was out.

I've only cried over one celebrity's death. It was Robles.

Certain Dark Things is back and it's still dedicated to Germán Robles. I like to think he had something to do with its revival, seeing as he was never able to stay in his coffin.

If you look in the back of this book, you will find some new extra content created for this edition. I hope you enjoy the return of the vampires.

Silvia Moreno-Garcia
August 14, 2020

CERTAIN DARK THINGS

Collecting garbage sharpens the senses. It allows us to notice what others do not see. Where most people would spy a pile of junk, the rag-and-bone man sees treasure: empty bottles that might be dragged to the recycling center, computer innards that can be reused, furniture in decent shape. The garbage collector is alert. After all, this is a profession.

Domingo was always looking for garbage and he was always looking at people. It was his hobby. The people were, not the garbage. He would walk around Mexico City in his long, yellow plastic jacket with its dozen pockets, head bobbed down, peeking up to stare at a random passerby.

Domingo tossed a bottle into a plastic bag, then paused to observe the patrons eating at a restaurant. He gazed at the maids as they rose with the dawn and purchased bread at the bakery. He saw the people with shiny cars zoom by and the people without any cash jump onto the back of the bus, hanging with their nails and their grit to the metallic shell of the moving vehicle.

That day, Domingo spent hours outside, pushing a shopping cart with his findings, listening to his portable music player. It got dark and he bought himself dinner at a taco stand. Then it started to rain, so he headed into the subway station.

He was a big fan of the subway system. He used to sleep in the subway cars when he first left home. Those days were behind. He had a proper place to sleep now, and lately he collected junk for an important rag-and-bone man, focusing on gathering used thermoplastic clothing. It was a bit harder to work the streets than it was to work a big landfill or ride the rumbling garbage trucks, sorting garbage as people stepped outside their houses and handed the collectors their plastic bags. A bit harder but not impossible, because there were small public trash bins downtown, because the restaurants left their garbage in the alleys behind them, and because people also littered the streets, not caring to chase the garbage trucks that made the rounds every other Monday. A person with enough brains could make a living downtown, scavenging.

Domingo didn't think himself very smart, but he got by. He was well fed and he had enough money to buy tokens for the public baths once a week. He felt like he was really going places, but entertainment was still out of his reach. He had his comic books and graphic novels to keep him company, but most of the time, when he was bored, he would watch people as they walked around the subway lines.

It was easy because few of them paid attention to the teenager leaning against the wall, backpack dangling from his left shoulder. Domingo, on the other hand, paid attention to everything. He constructed lives for the passengers who shuffled in front of him as he listened to his music. This one looked like a man who worked selling life insurance, a man who opened and closed his briefcase dozens of times during the day, handing out pamphlets and explanations. That one was a secretary, but she was not with a good firm because her shoes were worn and cheap. Here came a con artist and there went a lovelorn housewife.

Sometimes Domingo saw people and things that were a bit scarier. There were gangs roaming the subway lines, gangs of kids about his age, with their tight jeans and baseball caps, rowdy and loud and for the most part dedicated to petty crimes. He looked down when those boys went by, his hair falling over his face, and they didn't see him, because nobody saw him. It was just like with the regular passengers; Domingo melted into the tiles, the grime, the shadows.

After an hour of people watching, Domingo went to look at the large TV screens in the concourse. There were six of them, displaying different shows. He spent fifteen minutes staring at Japanese music videos before it switched to the news.

**SIX DISMEMBERED BODIES FOUND IN CIUDAD JUÁREZ.
VAMPIRE DRUG WARS RAGE ON.**

Domingo read the headline slowly. Images flashed on the video screen of the station. Cops. Long shots of the bodies. The images dissolved, then showed a beautiful woman holding a can of soda in her hands. She winked at him.

Domingo leaned against his cart and waited to see if the news show would expand on the drug war story. He was fond of yellow journalism. He also liked stories and comic books about vampires; they seemed exotic. There were no vampires in Mexico City: their kind had been a no-no for the past thirty years, ever since the old Federal District became a city-state, walling itself from the rest of the country. He still didn't understand what a city-state was exactly, but it sounded important and the vampires stayed out.

The next story was of a pop star, the singing sensation of the month, and then there was another ad, this one for a shoulder-bag computer. Domingo sulked and changed the tune on his music player. He looked at another screen with pictures of blue butterflies fluttering around. Domingo took a chocolate from his pocket and tore the wrapper.

He wondered if he shouldn't head to Quinto's party. Quinto lived nearby, and though his home was a small apartment, they were throwing an all-night party on the roof, where there was plenty of space. But Quinto was friends with the Jackal, and Domingo didn't want to see that guy. Besides, he'd probably have to contribute to the beer budget. It was the end of the month. Domingo was short on cash.

A young woman wearing a black vinyl jacket walked by him. She was holding a leash with a genetically modified Doberman. It had to be genetically modified because it was too damn large to be a regular dog. The animal looked mean and had a green bioluminescent tattoo running down the left side of its head, the kind of decoration that was all the rage among the hip and young urbanites. Or so the screens in the subway concourse had informed Domingo, fashion shows and news reels always eager to reveal what was hot and what was not. That she'd tattooed her dog struck him as cute, although perhaps it was expected: if you had a genetically modified dog you wanted people to notice it.

Domingo recognized her. He'd seen her twice before, walking around the concourse late at night, both times with her dog. The way she moved, heavy boots upon the white tiles, bob-cut black hair, with a regal stance, it made him think of water. Like she was gliding on water.

She turned her head a small fraction, glancing at him. It was only a glance, but the way she did it made Domingo feel like he'd been doused with a bucket of ice. Domingo stuffed the remaining chocolate back in his pocket, took off his headphones, and pushed his cart, boarding her subway car.

He sat across from the girl and was able to get a better look at her. She was about his age, with dark eyes and a full, stern mouth. She possessed high cheekbones and sharp features. Overall, her face was imposing and aquiline. There was a striking quality about her, but her beauty was rather cutting compared to the faces of the models he'd viewed in the ads. And she was a beauty, with that black hair and the dark eyes and the way she stood, so damn graceful.

He noticed her gloves. Black vinyl that matched the jacket. She wasn't wearing a fancy outfit, but it fit her well; the clothes were of good quality, he could tell as much. The subway car stopped and Domingo fidgeted, wondering where she was headed, trying to build an imaginary biography for her and failing, distracted by her nearness.

The young woman patted the dog's head.

He was looking at her discreetly, and he knew how to do discreet, so he was a bit surprised when she turned and stared right back at him.

Domingo froze and then swallowed. He found his tongue with some effort.

"Hey," he said, smiling. "How are you doing tonight?"

She did not smile back. Her lips were pressed together in a precise, unyielding line. He hoped she wasn't thinking of letting the dog loose on him for staring at her.

The subway car was almost deserted, and when she spoke her voice seemed to echo around them even though she spoke very softly.

"Should you be out by yourself at this time of the night?" she asked.

"What do you mean?"

"How old are you?"

"Seventeen," he replied. "It's early. It's just before midnight."

"No curfew?"

"No," he scoffed. "I live on my own."

"Ah, a man about town."

There was laughter in her voice even though she didn't laugh. It made Domingo feel stupid. He stood up, ready to push his shopping cart to the other side of the subway car, to leave her alone. This had been a terrible idea, what was he thinking talking to her.

Her gaze drifted, skipped him, and he assumed this was goodbye. Goodnight. Go to hell. Which was the only reasonable response from such a girl.

"I'm looking for a friend," she said unexpectedly.

Domingo blinked. He agreed, uncertain.

"Would you like to be my friend? I can pay you."

Domingo wasn't in the habit of prostituting himself. He'd done it once when he was in a pinch, after he'd left the circle of street kids. Times had been hard, and one did what he could to survive. He'd been cold, hungry, desperate for a few pesos. He wasn't any of those things now.

"Sorry, I'm not sure I understand," he said. "Did you—?"

"I'm getting off at the next station. Would you like to come with me?"

Domingo looked at the woman. He'd seen her walk by those other nights and he'd never thought she'd speak to him. When he'd tried to talk to a girl on the subway the previous year, she'd recoiled. Domingo couldn't blame her. He did look grubby. And now this beautiful woman was chatting him up. Who was he to imagine a babe of that sort was gonna give him the time of day?

He nodded. He'd never been a lucky guy, but maybe he was in luck today.

Her apartment building was located just a few blocks from a busy intersection. It looked rather run down, a box of bricks built in the '50s that had not been updated. The tiles that had once decorated its façade might have been green and lively in the beginning, but they were now a muddled brown. Many of them had slid off, revealing the naked cement beneath. The apartment's name was written on a plaque by the entrance, but someone had defaced it.

Though he was reluctant to part with it, Domingo left his shopping cart near the front door of the building. People stole your shit if you didn't keep an eye on it. Garbage pickers were notorious for it. You could spend hours gathering glass bottles only to come back and discover they'd disappeared. That's why you kept your stuff close. Domingo didn't think he could ask her if they could take the cart into her apartment, so he hid it behind the stairs and prayed nobody chucked it out.

They climbed the stairs and he noticed that the building was in better shape inside; there were tiles with cracks here and there, but some retained their original coloring. There were potted plants running down the hallway and he realized the apartments were organized around a center square. He leaned against a railing and peered down, spying the laundry area below, which had stone sinks and several clotheslines.

"Hey, you haven't told me your name," he said when they reached the fourth floor.

"Atl," she replied, taking out her keys.

"Is that foreign? What does that mean?"

"No. It's Nahuatl." When he looked befuddled she elaborated, "You know. As in the language spoken by the Nahua? Ok, what they call Aztec, I suppose. It means 'water.'"

Ah, he did know about the Aztec having read the display around Templo Mayor, near the station there. It was an odd name but it was pretty. It suited her. He thought her voice sounded like water, like a stream filled with pebbles, though he'd never seen a real stream in his life. All he'd had were the periodic floods in Mexico City during the rainy season, when the garbage gets stuck in the sewers and the water overflows the drainage system, creating little rivers full of debris, rotten fruit, and dog shit. The door swung open and she turned on the light. The apartment was small and empty. Atl owned a rug with some cushions on top of it, but had no couch, no television, and no table. She didn't even have a calendar on the wall. A very big window sported garish, tattered curtains, further spoiling the place.

He thought girls had more of an interest in decorating their apartments. He pictured nice living rooms with pink curtains and neat furniture. A stuffed animal, perhaps. That's how it looked like in the magazines, with rooms like museums. And the ads, the ads had told him to expect color coordination, scented candles on tiny tables.

The apartment did have a heavy smell, animal-like, probably courtesy of the dog. Perhaps she kept more than one pet.

"You haven't lived here long, have you?" he asked.

She stared at him and for a moment he worried that he'd offended her. Maybe she didn't have a lot of cash after all, and couldn't furnish the place. He was no one to judge.

"I'm passing through. Do you want tea?" she asked. Her voice carried a soft indifference.

Domingo would have preferred soda or a beer, but the girl seemed classy and he thought he ought to go with whatever she preferred.

"Sure," he said.

Atl took off her jacket and threw it on the floor. Her blouse was pale cream; it showed off her bony shoulders. She didn't bother taking off her gloves. Looking at her, he thought of smoke, of incense and altars, and the painting of a girl he'd seen in a discarded museum catalogue.

He followed her into the kitchen. She lit a match and placed the kettle on a burner.

"I'm Domingo," he told her.

Her gloved hands moved carefully, pulling out two cups, two teaspoons, and a box filled with tiny sugar cubes.

The dog padded into the kitchen. Atl leaned down, whispered something in its ear, and then it walked out.

She opened a tin decorated with pictures of orange blossoms. It was filled with white tea bags.

"I'm going to pay you a certain amount, just for coming here. If you agree to stay, I'll double it," she said.

"Listen," Domingo said, rubbing the back of his head, "you don't really need to pay me nothing. I mean, you're cute. I should be paying you. Not . . . um . . . not that I think you work that kind of gig. If you do that's all right too," he added quickly.

"I'm not what you think I am."

Atl looked at him as she fished out two tea bags and closed the tin. She grabbed a pad of lined notepaper that was attached to the refrigerator. It had smiley kittens on it. He knew it wasn't hers; it was probably the relic of a previous tenant. She wasn't a smiley kitten girl, that was for sure.

"No, man, no, I wasn't saying, you know. Just . . . in case, I—"

"I'm a Tlāhuihpochtli."

That's not a word he expected to hear. Domingo blinked. "You can't be. That's a type of vampire, isn't it?"

"Yes."

Domingo had heard about vampires. He'd seen the stories about them on the television. He'd read about them in old comic books and graphic novels. He'd never thought he would meet one, not here.

For the first time, he noticed a certain redness to her eyes, as though she had been awake for a long time, as well as dark circles faintly visible beneath her makeup.

"It's vampire-free territory in Mexico City," he mumbled.

How'd she gotten in the city? Sanitation should have nabbed her. Those Apostles of Health who were supposed to stop whatever new disease was going around, but who didn't do jack shit except harass people in the poor neighborhoods. What was it Quinto had said? Something about how the human species was self-destructing at a bacteriological level but sanitation in Mexico was too busy fining people to care. But they would have noticed her, wouldn't they? And if not them, then the cops.

Maybe she wasn't a vampire. Could just be a wealthy, crazy girl playing dress-up. But he didn't think so. He felt he was staring at the real thing.

"I know," she said, scribbling a number on the pad of paper and holding it up for him to see. "How would you like to not have to work for a whole week?"

Domingo leaned against the wall, arms crossed.

"That's more like five for me," he said.

He should have been more worried. He wasn't sure if vampires really did have mind powers or if he'd simply been lulled into a sense of comfort by the woman's appearance; either way, he didn't feel scared. He felt a bit giddy and nervous, but there was none of the true fear that should punctuate this moment. It was a good moment, like that time when he found a new pair of fancy sneakers in a trash bin, box and all.

Atl nodded. "I need young blood. You'll do."

"Wait. I'm not going to turn into a vampire, am I?" he asked, because you can never be too sure—and he wasn't sure of anything. Vampire comic books and shit, they contradicted themselves.

"No," she said, sounding affronted. "We are born like this."

"Cool."

The kettle whistled. Atl removed it from the burner and poured hot water into the two cups. She placed the tea bags in the cups and offered one to him, pointing to the sugar.

"Help yourself."

He grabbed a sugar cube. She tossed six into her cup. Atl's spoon rattled against the cup's sides as she stirred.

Vampire. Like in *Crypt of Darkness*. Something both strange and awesome and intimidating. She was pretty. She had money. She was cool. He didn't hang out with cool people. He didn't hang out with much of anyone.

Domingo placed his hands around the cup and took a sip.

"It won't hurt much. What do you think?" she asked.

"I don't know. I mean, do I still get to . . . you know . . . sleep with you?"

She let out a sigh and shook her head.

"No, and don't try anything. Cualli will bite your leg off if you do."

Domingo took another sip. He was disappointed. But then he wondered if he might not get a small kiss as a token of affection. A tiny smile. A brief hug. Any of those things would make him happy. Disappointment turned to hope. And there was, of course, the money. "How do we do this?" Domingo asked, setting down his cup.

Atl removed her gloves. Her fingers were long and beautiful. But the nails were sharp and black. It was not nail polish. These were her natural nails. These were a bird's talons.

She raised those long hands and placed them on either side of his face. Domingo thought his previous idea about vampire powers might have been right, because he didn't flinch. He just stared at her as her hair turned into feathers and her hands seemed to grow more talonlike.

She craned her neck.

"Don't worry, this won't take long," she said. "And don't move."

Atl was part bird of prey, yet he did not move a muscle. She leaned down; her lips brushed his neck. It did not hurt . . . much. It was a quick stab of pain that burned down his neck and through his body. After a few minutes he did try to move as the pain slowly seemed to wake up a part of his brain that had been shut down, but it was too late. She held him in place, her strong, wicked talons digging into his shoulders.

It became enjoyable rather quickly. One moment he was flinching and the next there was a slow, sweet wave that dragged him down. It wasn't like drinking booze or sniffing paint thinner, though he had tried both and discarded them as useless pursuits. It was a haze. The haze you experience when your eyes are heavy and you are about to fall asleep, where your limbs feel tired, your whole body is weighed down, and there is this soft, pleasant sensation as you surrender to exhaustion.

Domingo closed his eyes. Geometrical patterns exploded behind his eyelids, shifting from yellow to orange to crimson until they turned black and there was nothing but a heavy, inky blackness around him.

He felt his knees buckle. The velvet darkness cushioned him. It held him tight in its embrace. He felt himself sliding down and the darkness helped him, sliding down with him.

He lay in this velvet blackness for a while before drifting into a dream.

Domingo awoke with a blanket against his cheek. He raised his head. He was still in Atl's kitchen, on the floor, and the blanket was wrapped snug around him.

Atl was leaning against the refrigerator. She had her cup pressed against her lips. Her eyes were closed.

He wiped his mouth with the back of his hand.

"Don't try to stand up yet or you might vomit. I'll help you in a few minutes," she said.

Domingo touched his neck. He felt a bump, but it didn't seem like a big wound. Good. He'd half-feared she'd torn a chunk of flesh off when she first bit him . . . or whatever she did. He felt light-headed and his extremities were jumbled. He waited quietly, not knowing if he was allowed to speak.

"My legs feel funny," he said at last. "It's like they've fallen asleep."

"Mmm. Think of it as an anesthetic."

"Is it gonna hurt later?"

"No. Your neck might itch a bit, but that will pass in a day or two. It's like a mosquito bite."

"Do you always do that?" he asked.

"What?" she replied.

"Do you change?"

Atl opened her eyes and nodded. She took out a container with orange juice from the refrigerator. She filled a glass with the juice.

"You can't tell anyone. You understand?"

"I wouldn't," he said.

"Because I'd hurt you if you did," she said.

Her voice held no obvious threat, but he knew she meant it. It was in her face, which had no blunt edges. A smart man might have been intimidated. He was curious.

"Do you think you can stand up?" she asked.

"Yes."

She reached into a cupboard and grabbed a plastic box, pulling out a handful of pills, which she dumped over the kitchen table. Then she turned

to him and lifted him up with such ease—as though he were a rag doll—
that it made him gasp.

"Are you all right?" she asked.

"Yes," he said.

"You need to eat well. You need to pick foods rich in iron. I have a few
iron supplement pills for you. If you drink them with orange juice they'll
be more effective."

She walked him to the table. Domingo had to lean against her. His
hands trembled, but he managed to pop the pills into his mouth. He drank
the whole glass of juice.

They stood together, Atl propping him up, for what seemed like a long
while. The feeling had returned to his legs and the slight light-headedness
that was plaguing him had vanished.

"Are you ready to go home?" she asked.

"Yeah."

She walked him to the door, holding it open for him. He attempted to
say goodbye, but she closed the door before he could speak.

CHAPTER 2

She ought to have killed him. She should have drained him whole, broken his neck.

And then what would I do with a corpse, stuff it in the refrigerator?

It's not like she knew the first thing about disposing of a body.

Izel would have known. Ocoxochitl Izel Iztac, First-Daughter, Lady of the Fragrant Flowers. The bright promise of their clan. They all called her Izel because she was "the only one," the precious child. Atl had been a secondary consideration from the day she was born. Atl of the Iztac. Atl Second-Born.

Atl who couldn't do anything right.

She wasn't Izel and she couldn't dwell on this. She'd done what she'd done. The boy would live. Let it be. No murder. It would not have been honorable anyway, he was no armed foe, nor the member of an enemy clan. Perhaps, considering that, Izel would have agreed it was best to let him go.

But you have no honor, a nagging voice that sounded like Izel whispered in her ear. Guilt spoke with her sister's voice.

Atl stopped scratching the dog's head and opened the bedroom window, letting in the night air. She felt strong. Alert. Giddy and brimming with energy. She thought about stretching her wings, sneaking along the rooftops.

It was too dangerous. Everything was too dangerous in this city. She missed the North and the desert with its endless dark skies, the coldness of its nights against her skin.

The Tlāhuihpochtin had moved around Mexico through the centuries, up and down the country, restless, likely nomadic in the beginning. Their exact place of origin was vague. Perhaps they'd roamed Baja California, by the sea, but the Bolsón de Mapimí also hid traces of her kin. In time they'd come in contact with the Aztecs, long before the foundation of Tenochtitlán and the establishment of their empire. But though the city of canals, with its mountains and volcanoes, had been a comfortable abode for a few centuries, they returned to the desert, went back North. And though they might stray from their ancestral lands, the memory of the cirio trees and the yucca and the pitch-black sky above the arid land did not abandon them. Atl's mother was born in Sinaloa in 1895, and though she lived in Mexico City for several decades, she never forgot the North. Neither could Atl, ever, no matter what happened.

Atl sat by the window, trying to remain still, holding her cup of tea between her hands. She took a sip and grimaced. It wasn't right. She headed back into the kitchen, in search of sugar cubes. She found them and discovered that the ants from the other day had returned and were eating the cubes she had left out in the open.

She crushed the ants with the palm of her hand, even though it would likely do little good. If they had found their way in once, they'd find their way in again.

She popped two sugar cubes into her mouth and wondered what she'd do about this pest. Ant repellent. What was a good ant repellent? Vinegar? Perhaps. Cinnamon. She didn't like the smell of it. Pepper? She thought ants didn't like pepper. Except for sugar cubes, some drinks, her tea satchels, and a bag of dog food, her kitchen was empty.

Atl supposed she ought to stop by the supermarket to buy pepper. She could also buy food. Cans of tuna and vegetables. Cereal. She would not eat it. It was for show. In case she had visitors, as she'd had tonight. Not that she planned to have many visitors. She wasn't staying in the most elegant of buildings. But that meant more sanitation sweeps. If a sweep did take place, they would look around, either to make sure she wasn't harboring illicit substances or to see if they could steal something. She could see a curious sanitation worker going through the kitchen drawers and finding them empty, a bit fishy, that. She could picture the worker staring at her. A young woman, alone, no ID papers and no food. Northern accent. Let me check . . . my, this woman's body temperature is not right.

Maybe they wouldn't peg her for a vampire. Maybe the curious sanitation worker would think she was a junkie or a Croneng. There were tons of people with Croneng's disease running around these days. It was a virus that made humans hemorrhage from the nose and gave them sores, spoiling the blood supply so that now on top of cancers, STDs, AIDS, and tuberculosis, vampires had to also watch their food to make sure it wasn't tainted with this new disease. Vomiting dirty blood was no fun.

She'd heard people blaming vampires for this, saying they had caused it, which was ridiculous, but humans had a way of blaming vampires for everything these days. Back in the Middle Ages—back when her kind was still half-hidden behind myth and superstition—some people thought vampires caused the plague. They did not, though the bubonic plague did help to expand the reach and power of the Necros. Necros, just like the German Nachzehrers, when in a pinch, could feed off carrion, something unthinkable to other vampires. They found a plentiful supply of corpses in Europe while other vampires starved, deprived of a clean blood supply. The old wives' tale that vampires liked nubile virgins perhaps had some root in the sensitivity of vampires to tainted blood. If you had a virgin on your hands then you could avoid drinking the blood of a syphilitic. But since STDs were not the only awful diseases humans carried, that did not provide much protection against anything.

The boy had remarked about her lack of furniture. The furniture could be explained by a recent move, but the lack of food . . . yes, she must do something about that.

Atl sighed and put away the sugar cubes.

It was hard to think about those things. She wasn't used to keeping up appearances. She hadn't needed to. Back north, Atl had her mother and her sister and a host of servants to take care of her. The North was like a great oozing wound, and the vampires drank from it freely. Mexico City . . . it was not friendly to her kind. But she'd run out of options.

This was it. Her safe haven.

She hated the apartment, though. She hated the color of its walls and the scratches on the kitchen counters, the ancient dirt staining the bathroom tiles and the way the pipes rattled. She hated the smell of it, the smell of the whole city. Dirty. When it rained, it smelled like wet garbage—and it rained constantly. The stench was worse in the subway, but she forced herself to take it. She lacked a license and ID papers, no way she could drive. Taxis were an option, but she was afraid of getting in an unknown vehicle. No place to run, there. It was better to brave the subway, to walk down the filthy streets with her umbrella. And she'd found *him* in the subway, at any rate, so good things did come from that place.

Domingo.

Atl again wondered if she had made the right choice. Her instinct and her upbringing compelled her to drag her food to her lair, but she still did not know if this was wise, if the way she'd handled him was foolish or efficient. And yet, what other alternative did she have? If she had fed in the streets, someone could have seen her. The same went for the cheap motels that charged by the hour. Too many nosy people, both cops and criminals.

There were other problems. A willing donor, for example. Procuring a sex worker from the streets meant dealing with a pimp, and Atl did not want to pick a fight with a brute who thought she was bruising the merchandise.

No, too much trouble there. That narrowed the options. Young blood . . . Twice before she had found street kids sleeping in alleys. They were both out stone cold. She fed from them: no pimp, though she feared the eyes of vagrants upon her.

It was risky. Besides, the blood of the street kids was bitter from the cheap drugs and booze running through their veins. It gave Atl a headache and cramps. It almost made it worse than starving.

Atl had decided to change her tactics. Domingo had looked clean and nice enough. No telltale signs of drug use. He smelled healthy, too. His blood, when she tasted it, was warm and sweet. Old blood, sick blood, drugged blood: that was like feasting on carrion. Finally she had found a fresh, delicious meal.

She must make it last. She must conserve her energy. Atl drummed her fingers against the ceramic cup. There was plenty of time before sunrise. Unlike European vampires, Atl could handle the sun, though it weakened her. It required too much energy to move through the city in the daytime. She must save her strength. This meant sleeping longer.

Sleep had its dangers, however. Cualli could guard her but he was not infallible. Between staying up and wasting energy or sleeping and being vulnerable, Atl picked sleeping. She closed the window and slid open the closet's door. Inside were a sleeping bag, a pillow, a blanket, and scraps of paper. She had been nesting there. It was a big departure from her mother's luxurious home, with its Aztec artifacts and expensive furnishings. All that had been left behind. Atl had only her wits, some money, and the vague hope she would be able to find Verónica Montealban, and she wasn't exactly sure how she might manage that. What she had to go by were a few old papers her mother had held on to.

Atl got in the closet and reached beneath the pillow. She stared at the photograph. It was a Polaroid, one corner bent. The image showed her mother, and next to her, a young woman, whose hair was parted in the middle. It had been decades since the photo was taken.

Verónica Montealban was much older now. Very likely she did not resemble the young woman she was looking at. She might have left the city. She might even be dead. If she was alive, she wasn't making it easy for Atl to find her. Why would she? But she had been mother's companion, her tlapalēhuiāni, for a number of years—Atl refused to use the word "Renfield" to describe her; it was such a coarse term foisted upon them by Anglo pop culture.

Mother spoke of the human girl. She had been loyal, efficient. The adult Verónica had smuggled certain items for her mother, years after she had left her mother's side. She could be trusted, Mother said. If she found Verónica, Atl might be able to figure a way out of this mess. She couldn't stay in Mexico City forever, but leaving its limits meant certain death.

Guatemala. There had to be a way to get into Guatemala. Crossing into the States was out of the question; the northern border zone was too militarized. God, she needed papers, a smuggler, a damn weapon that packed a bigger punch than her switchblade knife.

Well, you have to stop kidding yourself, that voice that sounded like Izel's said. *You can't get to Verónica without Bernardino.*

He'd know where to find Verónica. But there was no assurance she could trust him, and since he was . . . since he was a Revenant and that particular type of European vampire could gobble *other* vampires, well . . . they were a bit like boogeymen for the average vampire. There was also the issue of their customs. Vampires were incredibly territorial. They used envoys to communicate. She had none and could not imagine showing up at his place, dashing protocol. Although he'd been somewhat of a friend to her mother when she'd been much younger, Mother said he'd turned on her in later years. Bernardino was dangerous. Paranoid. Still. There had been mention of certain debts owed by him, but these were vague allusions. All Atl had to bank on then was the value of her deceased mother's name, and she wasn't sure how far that might go. Her sister would have marched into Bernardino's house. Atl was too much of a coward.

Atl placed the photograph under the pillow. Cualli whined. She knew he wanted to sleep next to her, but she needed the dog to guard her.

"Cualli, sit," she ordered.

She slid the closet door shut, and then buried her face against the pillow. Atl gained control of her breathing, slowing it down. Sleep, when it came, was like plunging underwater. She sank into darkness, her breath slowing so much her chest was barely rising and falling.

The following evening, Atl decided to go shopping. It was a chance for a much-needed walk, but she was afraid of going outside. Each time she ventured into the city streets, it was an opportunity for a sly cop to ask for her ID. Staying inside the apartment, however, could be just as bad. Cabin fever would not be productive.

To hell with it. She needed to stretch her legs. She wasn't made for stillness. She'd heard of vampires who could happily burrow into the earth and spend their time quiet in their damp mounds of dirt. But those were other breeds. Atl put on her jacket and grabbed her dog's leash. It was raining, only a drizzle, so she pulled her hood up and did not bother with the umbrella. The all-night mini-supermarket was only three blocks from her place. Its sign glowed orange, then white. She told her dog to wait outside.

When she walked in an annoying bell rang to announce her arrival. She looked around, carefully scanning the place.

There was a tired man in an orange uniform behind the counter, protected by an acrylic partition. He was mesmerized by a small television set and did not even lift his eyes to look at her as she walked by. Three teenagers dressed in neon jackets were hanging in the store, busy chatting with each other. She could hear the music from one of the kids' headphones. Heavy metal.

She hated that music. It had no . . . symmetry.

Atl grabbed a plastic basket. She walked down one aisle, looking at the labels. She had never paid much attention to human food. She wondered what she should buy. Atl grabbed two cans of beans and tossed them into the basket. She located the pepper and bought more sugar cubes. She stopped to look at an area that had potato chips and candy on display. The lists of ingredients were alien to her. It wasn't like she ate this shit. Godoy's kind, the fuckers who called themselves Necros, could. She wasn't sure if Bernardino's type could stomach it.

Atl gritted her teeth and threw a bag of potato chips into her basket. Maybe she should get more of those iron supplements she'd grabbed the other day. She didn't know if they actually worked, but what did she know in the end? Barely nothing.

She should not be in this situation, second-born and still woefully young. She was twenty-three in a family that could span centuries, the baby of the clan. Twenty-three and spoiled, because she had not cared much for anything that wasn't fun and blood. She remembered Izel chiding her a few months ago for her disinterest in the family business, for gallivanting around the city on her new motorcycle. But Mother hadn't cared.

Atl smirked. Why would she? Mother had preferred Izel. Izel was the strong one. Izel was the heir. Izel was everything. Atl was just the spare.

Now Izel was dead. And Atl couldn't do a thing on her own.

The bell rang again, startling her. Two cops walked into the joint.

Atl's hand tightened around the plastic handle of the basket. God damn luck. She steeled herself, shifting toward the back of the store, closer to the refrigerators.

The teenagers were laughing raucously. They were popping chocolates into their mouths.

"Hey, whose idea was it to park a car and take two whole spaces out front, huh?" one of the cops yelled.

The teenagers turned their heads. One of them tripped and spilled dozens of bright, colorful chocolates onto the floor. They scattered wildly upon the white tiles.

Atl felt the immediate desire to throw herself to her knees and start counting them. It was a nervous tic, a thing about her kind. She closed her eyes and rested a hand against one of the refrigerators.

"It's, like, for two minutes, man," one of the teens said.

"Two minutes. Okay, you fucker, show me your license. All of you, IDs and licenses."

One of the cops had lit a cigarette. She smelled it as if he were standing next to her. But he wasn't. He was on the other side of the store. He wasn't close. Everything was normal. She was just a normal person going out for a normal walk. Buying groceries. People did that.

"You going to give me a fine?" one of the teenagers said. "Are you?"

"What are you high on, kid?"

Shoes squeaked upon the floor. The stench of the cigarette drifted closer to her.

A cop was heading her way.

She would be fine. She looked perfectly normal. She'd fed recently. Her eyes weren't red, her cheeks were not too hollow.

She would be fine.

Atl looked down, staring at the prices stuck inside the refrigerator. Her lips moved silently, mouthing the numbers.

The cop stopped next to her. She didn't look at him.

"Show me your license and ID," he said.

"I'm not with them," Atl said. "You can ask them."

He paused to look at her. His gaze lingered.

"Hey you, why are you handcuffing me, motherfucker? My dad is a lawyer, you dick!" one of the teenagers yelled.

The cop next to Atl turned his head and yelled to the teenager.

"Shut your mouth!" he said, then sighed and looked at her again. He seemed tired. "Damn kids, probably going out clubbing, you know?"

She nodded, wishing he'd leave her be.

The policeman opened the refrigerator door and pulled out an energy drink, then walked back to the front of the store. The teenagers were muttering to each other, the one who had been handcuffed still repeating the bit about his lawyer father. The policeman who had spoken to her told them they were headed to the station. They protested, and then came the expected bribery. Once they had their money the cops undid the teen's handcuffs, bringing to an end the evening's performance.

The cashier, sitting behind the partition, returned to his TV watching as soon as the policemen and the teenagers left the store.

Atl waited for a couple of minutes, grabbed an energy drink, and dumped it in her shopping basket before standing in front of the cashier and shoving a few bills beneath the opening in his partition. She didn't bother waiting for him to give her her change.

She walked outside, rubbed Cualli's head, and glanced around her. The street was empty. She was fine.

But she needed to make a damn move before she ended up like Mother and Izel. Now.

"Come on," she told the dog.

CHAPTER 3

Rodrigo walked faster, scanning the lines outside the Zona Rosa's night-clubs. It was close to midnight, he had a headache, and he needed a cigarette.

It was the kid's fault.

Rodrigo had never felt like a stereotypical Renfield—or, the way the low-class assholes who couldn't speak English pronounced it, *Renfil*. Yes, he'd seen how the young vampires treated their assistants and no, not all of them were nice to them. But Godoy was classy, he did things properly. And yet . . . Rodrigo was educated, refined, effective, and still Mr. Godoy felt the burning need to send his son with him, a vampire who had more teeth than he had common sense. Godoy trusted Rodrigo. But maybe not *that* much.

Mr. Godoy insisted that someone from the family needed to go with the crew, making it sound like Rodrigo was a toddler instead of a grown-ass man. And when things turned sour in Guadalajara, Junior would not be left behind. Rodrigo had not wanted to bring Nicolás, El Nick, to Mexico City, not only because it was a pickle to smuggle a vampire into Mexico City, but also because he found the little prick insufferable.

Then, to top it off, La Bola—who was huge, but not too bright, one of the younger goons who got along well with Nick—had not been watching the boy as he'd been told and now Nick was roaming around the Zona Rosa on his own. Ten vampire subspecies and Rodrigo had one of the most dangerous in his hands. Not to mention Nick was young. He could get into all forms of trouble. He often did. But they weren't on their home turf; the rules of the game were different.

Rodrigo bumped into a man handing out leaflets advertising "seven dancing semi-virgins" onstage, and pushed him aside. The Zona Rosa had been famous as a gay area and many gay clubs still remained, but since the late '90s a good chunk of it had transformed into Little Seoul, with a multitude of internet cafés, restaurants, and clubs geared toward Koreans, dominating streets around Florencia. There were also a few men's clubs, some fancier than others, and a lot of nightclubs, both Korean and Mexican, several of them adorned with a rainbow flag, which identified them as LGBT-friendly zones. It was fashionable for certain heterosexual

Mexico City youths to dance at the LGBT clubs, though the Korean ones were not popular with outsiders.

The Zona always looked a bit in decline, ever since the '80s, its luster lost when massage parlors began replacing art galleries. The wealthier, more fashionable people danced in Polanco or Santa Fe, and they gave these old clubs—which were frankly a bit seedy—a wide berth. But the kids from nearby colonias did not know any better, other clubs were far away, and they couldn't have gotten into El Congo even if they wanted to, so they lined up for the clubs at the Zona, where few bouncers checked IDs, merry and ready for a night of partying.

Neon signs burned bright, flashing white and red and green. The themes of the clubs were wildly different. One going for the Wild West, another attempting a spaceship, the third a kitsch pink. Rodrigo crossed a street, avoiding two Cronengs who were asking for spare change. He elbowed through a gaggle of teens.

Rodrigo finally spotted him. Nick was chatting with a girl who was standing in line outside a cheap club called Bananas, complete with a glowing neon blinking banana to signal its location.

"Nick," Rodrigo said.

The boy turned his head, looking bored. He had the easy looks, easy swagger of his type, and the bad attitude to match. His clothes were neat and expensive. He sported sunglasses and a knowing smirk, always sharp at the edges.

A handsome kid. His family were beautiful. Too beautiful. He'd heard about the uncanny valley. That sensation people got when they looked at computer-generated faces that approximate realistic human features, though imperfectly, causing a deep-seated sense of revulsion because the slight imperfection signals there is something amiss. That's exactly what Nick's type inspired. The feeling that something was very *wrong*. It was that tiny fraction of the human brain trying to warn you, yelling flee! But it was a split-second thing, like a flash frame, and then you were subdued by the charm and the smile of the vampires.

"Time to go."

For a moment Rodrigo doubted Nick was going to come, but then the boy whirled away from the girl and walked to his side, removing his sunglasses. Christ, it was the eyes that did it for him. Rodrigo wasn't scared of vampires. He'd been working for them for years and they—barring a couple of species—looked similar to humans, at least most of the time and for the most part. And the feeling, the nagging feeling of danger that came with them, he'd grown used to that. But the eyes, it was the eyes that bothered him with boys like Nick, the eyes he could never get used to. They were very large, their pupils dilating until it seemed like the vampire had just returned from a visit to the optometrist. It was a small detail, to be sure, something most people might not catch, but boy did those eyes with those dilated pupils give Rodrigo a bad feeling.

He swallowed his dismay, as he always did, pushed it down and away. "What do you think you're doing?" Rodrigo asked.

"Nothing," Nick said.

"You can't hunt here."

Not with sanitation crews sweeping the city. Bribes could buy almost anything back north, but this was not the North. This was good old Mexico City, which had fallen to the Spaniards but would not yield to vampires. Rodrigo had no time to bury a corpse for this spoiled kid. And if Nick didn't mean to drink and kill, if he meant to drink and gain control of a human—that nasty trick the Necros loved to play—well, that wasn't going to happen either. It was too fucking risky.

"Who said anything about hunting?"

"Don't bullshit me, pretty boy," Rodrigo said.

The neon banana sign blinked from yellow to green and then back to yellow. Nick flashed him a smile that was all teeth.

"What if I was hunting? These people are nobody."

"Nobody can still call the cops. If you're hungry we'll head back to the apartment and open one of those blood packs," Rodrigo reminded the kid.

"Drinking that blood is like drinking piss."

"Nothing I can do about it."

"We should be hunting that bitch down," Nick said as he fiddled with his sunglasses, thought it over, and put them on again.

"I might do that if you hadn't left the apartment without an escort. It's Mexico City."

"I don't need an escort. Give me a cigarette," Nick said, snapping his fingers.

Damn twat, Rodrigo thought, but he took out his cigarettes. Gauloises. He never smoked anything else. Lighter, American-style cigarettes were for pansies. You either smoked dark or went home. Rodrigo smoked dark, and he smoked a lot.

He took out two cigarettes and struck a match, lighting both and handing one to Nick. Nick took a puff, gave the line of young people one last look, and shrugged.

"Fine, let's head back to the apartment," Nick said.

They had to walk several blocks, back in the direction of Parque España. They stopped at a liquor store because Nick wanted booze. Nick's kind—Necros, though jokers called them "Necros nacos," the trashy vampires—drank like it was going out of fashion. Something to do with endophenotypes, but Rodrigo was no biologist.

True to his heritage, Nick put half a dozen bottles of vodka into a green shopping basket. He also wanted absinthe. Not just any absinthe. Czech absinthe, using the original formula, with authentic wormwood. They did not have any and Nick looked like he was going to pitch a fit. Rodrigo convinced him to take two bottles of whiskey and said he'd find him absinthe later.

When they walked into the apartment they found La Bola eating fried chicken and playing video games. He sucked his fingers and waved at them.

"Where are Colima and Nacho?" Rodrigo asked as soon as he closed the door.

"They've gone to find those cousins they mentioned. To help with the job."

Rodrigo had brought only three operatives with him. He needed a few extra hands to help out. It would not be difficult to recruit a few more guns. Nacho and Colima had relatives here, eager for a break, for a ticket back north. These thugs were cheap and easy to come by. He might have been able to play it with just the lot he had, but Rodrigo didn't want to take chances. Although Atl was alone, she was still a vampire and she'd already given them a run for their money. Of course, Rodrigo had Nick, but Nick was young and hardly well trained for such a task. He'd lost the girl when they were in Jalisco; she'd slipped from his fingers despite his macho posturing. It hardly mattered how big your fangs were if your prey could outwit you, and land a mighty good punch in your face, breaking a few of those sharp teeth. He healed fast—vampires like Nick were like sharks and there was always a tooth behind the one that just fell out. When they were angry, their maws were a scary sight—but facts were facts. Nick had been outwitted by a girl.

"I wonder what they'll bring," Nick said. "Colima and Nacho are vermin. I liked Justiniano."

"Justiniano's dead and vermin serves its purpose."

Nick grabbed one of the bottles and opened it. He sat down on the couch and began drinking it straight from the bottle, vodka dribbling down his chin.

"Come," Rodrigo said, motioning to La Bola.

They headed from the living room to the studio. Rodrigo kept two places, one in Sinaloa and this other one. Of the two, the Mexico City apartment was the grander place even if he visited it sparingly. It had more style, more things, more of him. The apartment was large, with tall ceilings. There was a monochromatic look about the furniture, everything black and white, though he added dashes of color with several paintings of vast sizes hanging from the walls.

The studio was very much the same. A huge desk, a couple of comfortable chairs, and his rare books on display. Electronic books might be easy to purchase, but Rodrigo was a collector, not a consumer. This, he thought, was what differentiated him from the vampire lords—God, the affront of these drug pushers to call themselves lords—who splashed their cash with no taste. Rodrigo had taste. He had style.

He couldn't say the same for everyone else.

"Sit," Rodrigo ordered.

La Bola sat on one of his fine leather chairs. While Rodrigo was short and skinny, La Bola was a tall, beefy man. Despite their difference in bulk, La Bola looked at Rodrigo meekly.

As soon as La Bola sat, Rodrigo approached him and punched him in the face.

"You moron, didn't I tell you to keep an eye on the kid?"

"I was, Rodrigo! But this is Mr. Godoy's son. I can't just—"

"Lock him in the bedroom if that's what it takes. What do you think Mr. Godoy will say if his son gets picked up by sanitation?"

"He said he was just going to get himself some tail," La Bola babbled.

"Wake up, you moron. How long have you been around vamps, huh? Three years?"

La Bola raised a couple of fingers. "Two."

"You should know better, shithead. Tail ain't ever just tail. Not for Nick. I shouldn't have talked your dad into letting you work for me."

"I'm sorry, Rodrigo."

"Just watch him, properly."

"I will," La Bola muttered as he rubbed his face. "Um . . . Rodrigo, did your contact know anything about the girl?"

"No," Rodrigo said, irritated. "But she was in Toluca. I confirmed as much. Which means she's here. Somewhere."

"Hey, Rodrigo! I want pizza!"

Nick. He was probably guzzling his second bottle and aching for greasy food.

"Go take care of him," Rodrigo told La Bola in a low voice.

La Bola dipped his head, hurrying back to the living room.

Rodrigo stretched his arms and smoothed his suit, pausing to check his black enamel cuff links. He glanced at himself in the great floor-to-ceiling gilded mirror that adorned the south wall of the office. Gray, thinning hair, parted in the middle. A web of wrinkles etched on his face. Teeth slowly yellowing. Yes, he was getting old. Maybe too old for these games. Even a vampire's goon deserves a pension and a peaceful retirement.

He'd go live somewhere sunny. Somewhere where he'd never have to stare another bloodsucker in the face. He'd killed enough of them for Godoy.

Just one more, he thought. *Just that blasted girl. How long can she run, anyway?*

CHAPTER 4

Domingo woke late. He stretched his arms, propped himself up on his elbows, and reached for the hand-crank lantern. He wound it up and then lit an oil lamp and a candle for good measure.

There was no electricity in the web of narrow underground tunnels that ran downtown, but it was a free space to hang out and he didn't mind having to maintain a mountain of lanterns on hand. Besides, Domingo did not need electricity, not when he had his comic books. He raised the lantern and looked at his special pile of vampire comic books. He owned a big stash of them.

Domingo stared at the colorful panels. Eventually he turned his attention to the wall he had plastered with magazine and book covers. He ran a hand over an image of a vampire woman in a long white dress, a misty forest behind her.

Vampires. Danger. Adventure. He'd met one and she was damn pretty.

Domingo looked at the pile of hybrid personal protective clothing he was putting together for the rag-and-bone man. He should do some work, collect more clothes, take empty bottles to the recycling center. But he did not need to. He had money. He had a whole fortune.

Domingo did not know how to spend all that cash. After careful consideration he decided he needed breakfast. He exited the tunnel and walked into a fast-food joint, where he purchased an egg-and-sausage combo. It didn't taste the way it looked in the picture, but he wolfed it down and bought a large orange juice at a stand outside. He drank it in a few quick gulps, then went back for a milk shake.

Afterward, he headed to an internet café. It was one of the large ones, with many rows of booths squeezed next to each other. Each booth had a door with a latch that would open only after you tossed tokens into a slot. Domingo bought a handful of tokens from an attendant at the front counter, then squeezed himself into an empty booth.

Domingo sat in a ratty fake leather chair that had been patched one too many times. The computer screen was hidden behind a partition, and Domingo had to insert more tokens into a slot before the partition opened. He scooted closer to the computer screen, clumsily thumbing it until a few options showed up. He chose keyboard input, and a compartment beneath the screen slid open. He pulled out the keyboard.

The breathy moans of a woman spilled into Domingo's narrow space. He frowned. The woman panted and moaned again. The guy in the next cubicle must be watching porn.

Domingo pulled out his frayed headphones, carefully wrapped with insulating tape, and pushed the play button on the music player. Depeche Mode began to sing about a personal Jesus. Domingo didn't know a whole lot about music, but when he'd first found his player it was filled with '80s songs and he'd listened to mixtures of Soda Stereo and Duran Duran with fascination. He'd asked Quinto about the bands, because Quinto knew all kinds of weird things. Quinto had taken him to an internet café much like the one he was in now. They'd downloaded more tracks and Quinto had talked about a new wave, but Domingo told him he'd never seen the ocean.

Domingo did a search for the word "Tlāhuihpochtli." Stories about gangs, murders, and drugs filled the view screen, images quickly superimposing until they formed a large mosaic. Domingo tugged at the images, running his fingers across the screen.

He scrolled through an article about the history of the Tlahuelpocmimi, pausing to look at the images that accompanied the text. They were black-and-white illustrations that looked very old, but were nothing like the pictures of the European vampires in the graphic novels. No one was wearing a cape, for one.

"Mexico's native vampire species, with roots that go back to the time of the Aztecs," he whispered.

The article had lots of information but it used very big words he didn't know, such as "hematophagy," "endemic," "anticoagulants," and "matrilineal stratified sept." Domingo could read well enough, but these words and sentences were much harder than the ones in the mags. He gave up on the article, preferring to stare at the bold headlines and colorful pictures of the vampire gangsters. Those resembled the comic books he kept at his place; he was comfortable with this stuff.

Domingo opened another page and read the headline twice.

CHILD KILLERS.

"The Tlahuelpocmimi have a specialized diet. They consume only the blood of the young."

The accompanying illustration showed a drawing of three hags huddled together. One of them was holding a baby up by its foot, dangling it above her grotesquely, impossibly large mouth. The other two were rubbing their hands together, waiting their turn.

But no. Atl had not killed him. Atl was not an ugly, old woman.

A countdown number blinked on the screen. If Domingo wished to stay inside the booth, he would need to dump more tokens into the slot. Instead, he stood up and left. The attendant was banging on the door next to Domingo's, urging the bum who had fallen asleep inside to get out.

It was raining when Domingo stepped out. He pulled up his jacket's hood and walked up the street, hands in his pockets. He went back to the tunnels, lit a couple of candles, and fell upon his old mattress, thinking about Atl. He knew plenty of assholes. One didn't get to be his age and live in the streets without bumping into a few of them. Atl didn't strike him as one of the bad guys. And she was beautiful. And he hadn't been with a girl in a while.

Domingo wondered what it might be like to date someone as beautiful and special as Atl. He had never really dated. There were hurried copulations in back alleys, the sort street kids manage. The rest he could only imagine, the stuff of commercials for wedding dresses and tuxedo rentals.

Domingo placed a hand beneath his head.

He remembered Belén and there was a sour taste in his mouth.

Belén liked to wear her hair braided with plastic beads. She had a gap-toothed smile but she was nice. They'd snuggled together in the park, her head resting on his shoulder. Then Belén had gone off with the Jackal and he couldn't even talk to her after that.

Domingo blew out the candles, turned on his music player, and the happy beats of '80s pop music lulled him to sleep.

He went to the public baths the next morning. He bought a ticket for a public bath with a tub instead of the communal showers and purchased two hours of bath time with unlimited use of water. He made a point to purchase the expensive shampoo and soap. He also bought a shaving kit.

Domingo usually brought laundry to wash at the baths, but not this day. He filled the tub with warm water and slipped in, soaking until his fingers were wrinkled. He washed his hair with lots of shampoo. Two years before he'd had lice. It had been very annoying. He had to buy a soap that smelled bad and a lice comb to get rid of the infestation. It might have been easier to shave his hair off, but Domingo thought that his hair was one of his best features.

Once he was done with his bath, Domingo stepped out of the tub and wrapped the towel he had brought with him, tying it around his waist. He did not shave often. It was not like he had a lot of facial hair, merely some incipient whiskers. But he wanted to appear well groomed. He lathered his face and shaved.

After his bath, Domingo went clothes shopping. He had never bought new clothes in his entire life. When he was still living at home, before his stepdad kicked him out, he'd enjoyed the hand-me-downs of his older brothers. On the streets, when he was washing car windows, there was little chance of new clothes. Now that he gathered garbage he found enough stuff among the rubbish to wear. Shoes, hats, jackets. If the rag-and-bone man didn't want them, Domingo kept them. But that day he had money and he ventured into a department store.

He tried on fancy jeans, peered curiously into the full-length mirror. He'd looked at his reflection in the rearview mirror of cars and in bathrooms. Not like this, under so many lights, three mirrors angled and repeating his image.

Domingo observed himself critically. His hair was longish and a rich, pleasant brown. His mouth, when he opened it, revealed ugly, crooked teeth. He had bushy eyebrows, a broad nose. He was not handsome, but he thought that if he stood upright and if he kept his mouth shut he looked fine.

He decided to buy a gift for Atl because he'd seen an ad for diamonds near a bus stop once that had informed him that diamonds celebrate the greatest love stories. They're forever.

He wandered around the jewelry department, staring at rings, earrings, necklaces, pins. They looked too frilly, too simple, too elaborate, too cheap. He settled at last on a watch. It was completely black save for the hands, which were white. He asked the lady behind the counter to wrap it.

Domingo walked out nearly broke and feeling very happy even though he had only a few bills in his pocket and he was starting to feel hungry.

It was dark by the time he made it to Atl's apartment building. He stood outside for a while, trying to figure out how he was going to get in, before an old lady with a dog and a bag of groceries opened the front door. He politely held the door for her and was able to gain access to the building this way.

He looked at the mailboxes in the lobby. A few of them were labeled with the occupant's name. Others said simply TENANT. None said Atl. He figured he could remember her door, just as he'd tattooed the way to her building in his mind, and climbed the stairs to her floor.

When he reached her door, he held his breath and knocked. He couldn't hear anything inside. Domingo knocked again. Silence.

He was going to knock a third time when the door swung open suddenly. The dog growled at him. Atl leaned against the doorframe, frowning. Her eyes were a bit red, like she'd been up for a long time.

"Hi. Atl. Um . . . What are you doing tonight?" he asked lamely. He'd practiced his greeting. It had sounded better in his head.

"Go away," she said.

"Wait," he said, holding up his hands in front of him. "I figure you want a steady person. Steady food, no? And . . . the other day, it was, ah . . . it was fun."

"Fun," she repeated.

"I just . . . I have this hunch about you. I think we could be friends. That's what you said, no? That you're looking for a friend."

He was going to add that she seemed kind of lonely and he was kind of lonely too, but she stared at him so hard all he could do was look down at his shoes knowing he'd probably fucked it up. He ought to have given her the gift first.

"You're not getting any more money, all right?" she said. "I don't need food right now. There's no sense in you coming here."

"You only eat young blood, no?" he asked.

"Yeah. I do," she said. "Before you even think about it, that doesn't make me a Lucy Westenra, all right?"

"Like in *Dracula*? I read that one," he said.

He'd also watched a black-and-white movie with that bloke, Germán Robles, which wasn't quite *Dracula* but wasn't far from it either. He should ask her if she'd seen the film.

Her frown deepened. He heard voices coming down the hallway. People were walking their way.

"Get in," she said, pulling him inside quick.

CHAPTER 5

A tl had made a mistake. The kid had found his way back. She was a silly girl. She would die.

She rubbed her wrist, nervous. She could kill him, could stuff his body in the bathtub. It would decompose, and what if he made a ruckus and what if . . . what if . . . Somebody was coming down the hallway and what if those were cops? Surely they were cops.

Cool it, she thought. She had made it all the way from Sinaloa. She had avoided Godoy's agents and fooled everyone in Guadalajara, back-tracking and sneaking into Mexico City. She was young and she was not prepared for this, but she was not foolish. What was he? Nothing but a street kid without common sense. She would make him leave. If he wouldn't go willingly, *then* she'd kill him.

"Yeah, *Dracula,*" she muttered as she locked the door.

Atl stared at Domingo until he lowered his gaze, studying his shoes. Had he . . . bathed? And the clothes looked new. What was this, a bizarre courtship ritual?

"I read the comic book adaptation, actually. It was good. I figure it's the same thing as the book, no? I . . . you know this article it talked about vampires and children and blood and there was a picture of a baby—"

She drank the blood of young people, not babies! Suddenly Atl was more offended that he thought she ate infants than worried because he'd returned to her apartment.

"Be quiet," she ordered.

The voices were drawing closer. She heard laughter, a giggle. Three, four people. They were in front of her door for a moment, but they kept walking. Not cops. Just other tenants.

Atl let out a sigh and looked at Domingo. He had extended his hand as if to pet the dog.

"He'll bite your hand off," she warned him, and Domingo stopped in midair.

Izel had given Atl her first dog. Izel loved animals. She was fond of her axolotls, but she also had a thing for snakes and spiders. When they would drive around and Izel spotted roadkill, she would often stop to look at it. Sometimes she buried the animals in the desert.

"What's it called?" Domingo asked.

Atl crossed her arms, leaning her back against the front door. "I said I'm not paying you."

"I know. I didn't come for money. I have a gift for you."

He took out a white box from his jacket. It was wrapped with a red bow. Atl tore the paper off. Instinct. That innate desire for presents and secrets. A compulsion similar to the one that drove her to count grains of rice and beans in jars.

It was a watch. Atl felt it going *tick-tick-tick* beneath her fingers. Such a pleasant and reassuring sound.

She shook her head, raising an eyebrow at the boy. "Why are you giving me this?"

"I wanted to get you something pretty. Do you like it?"

"Take it back," she said, tossing it to him and slowly circling the living room like a wild cat inspecting its cage.

"It's not a cheap plastic one. It's a nice one."

"Look, you've got to get a few facts straight, all right? I'm not in Mexico City on vacation. You don't want to hang out with me. Trust me, I'm more likely to bite your head off than give you a hug. Understood?"

She spoke more to herself than to him. He was nobody of importance. A speck, a nothing.

"You can really bite someone's head off?" Domingo said, excited. "That's cool!"

"Jesus," Atl said, standing still and staring at him. "Are you some sort of fanboy?"

Domingo shook his head. "No."

"Why are you here?"

"You seem all right. I like your dog," he said. "I didn't have anything to do so I thought I'd say hi."

What an idiot, she thought. He wasn't even there to blackmail her, not that he had the air of a blackmailer. But maybe she was the greater fool because she was starting to think, starting to consider . . . a tlapalēhuiāni. They had different names for them—some called them Renfields or blood lackeys or other nicknames, but she thought that was a disservice— although the rules were constant regardless of names. Human servants, loyal to a vampire. The particulars might vary, but in general it was a type of vassalage, taken rather seriously by vampires. Renfields represented an extension of the value of the vampire's clan, so you would not have a Renfield dressed shabbily or behaving in a dishonorable way. Killing a vampire's Renfield was akin to injuring a family member, and Renfields were protected by whatever treaty was arranged between vampire clans. Vampires tended to keep only one or two Renfields, though they might employ many humans in their service. Or in the case of the Necros, they might *enslave* many humans and still keep a Renfield.

She'd never had one. Not yet. She was still a girl, meant to live with her clan, in the shadow of the older women, for a few decades more. To learn and assist. She was not yet old enough to earn the privilege of tlapalēhuiānis, nor of weapons and warrior's marks, nor the trappings of an adult.

And yet . . . Atl was alone, adrift. She needed food. She needed help.

Atl began to move toward the kitchen. She wanted a cup of tea with lots of sugar. She wanted to open the windows and feel the night air against her skin. She wished he would leave. Or not. She could smell it. His life, his youth.

"I'll give you a cup of tea and you leave afterward, all right?"

"Sure. What were you up to before I got here?"

Atl didn't reply. She put the kettle to boil, observing the steam curl up. She grabbed the cups, the tea bags, and poured the water, adding three sugar cubes to her tea. They sat at the kitchen table. He watched her with interest, a man attempting to solve a puzzle.

"Do you have a sweet tooth?"

She stared at him, frowning. He shook his head.

"Sorry," he muttered. "I didn't mean it as a joke. I only see vampires in the papers."

"Go figure."

Atl lifted her cup. Like a mirror, Domingo raised his own and took a sip. Humans gave many physical clues about their thoughts. Perspiration, heart rate, inflections. He was nervous, but not scared.

"I'm not trying to be obnoxious. I just think you're interesting," Domingo said.

"Oh, you're just trying to get into my pants," she replied.

He looked at her from above the rim of his cup, mortification making his lips tremble.

"Not really," he mumbled.

Cualli curled down by her feet as she finished her tea. There were benefits to humans, of course. Her dog was useful, had saved her life before, but it was not infallible. *A human servant.*

"You should keep the watch," he said, sliding it toward her, across the table. Then he walked out of the kitchen.

Atl blinked in surprise. "Where are you going?"

"You said you wanted me to leave after I drank my tea," he said, shrugging, hands in his pockets. "I'm heading out."

"I'll buy you dinner," she said.

It sounded like it would be the nice thing to do. Not that she really *cared* to eat with him, but she wanted to make a good impression. Atl needed Domingo to feel at ease.

"No, I don't—"

"Please," she said, rolling her eyes. "Like you weren't hoping for that."

He grinned at her. Atl grabbed her vinyl jacket and Cualli's leash.

Atl nursed a glass of water, ignoring the salad in front of her, while Domingo wolfed down a whole plate of huevos rancheros. She watched him as he pushed every last morsel around the plate with a tortilla, gulping his soda and removing bolillos from the basket. He was slim as a bamboo stalk, but she thought just like bamboo he wouldn't break.

"You're not going to eat?" he asked her when he paused to look up at her.

Atl leaned her chin on the back of her hand and shook her head. "I can't eat that," she said. Just seeing him eat was gross. His meal looked utterly greasy. But she thought it best to order at least one thing.

"What do you mean you can't?"

"This junk would make me sick."

"But it's very good," he proclaimed, and held up the bread basket.

Atl looked at the bread with disinterest. He might as well have offered her a plate full of stones.

"It doesn't matter. My body can't process it."

"That sucks," he said.

"On the other hand, I have a much higher tolerance for alcohol than you'll ever have," she replied.

"Do you get hangovers?"

"Not from drinking booze."

"From what, then?"

Atl looked out the window, making sure Cualli was still sitting outside the restaurant, where she'd left him. He wouldn't go anywhere without her order, but she was still nervous when he wasn't right by her side.

"Blood," Atl said. "Drugs."

She thought of home. The parties. They'd hire humans and then they'd drink from them. And then they'd drink tequila, bottles and bottles of tequila, and there was always a pick-me-up, some of the synthetic drugs that vampires loved and that would have fried a human's head. Atl partied with her cousins, drove a convertible but also owned two motorcycles, kissed beautiful vampire women and punched the vampire boys who were too grabby and didn't know how to play nice. The nights never ended and neither did the blood. Izel complained about her high tabs and her fast friends, but Atl gave her the finger. Vampires didn't really live forever, but she felt she might, when there was still home and her clan and her unencumbered youth.

Izel, she thought. *Izel, Mother, my aunts, my cousins.*

Domingo leaned forward and knocked the salt over. The tiny grains rolled across the table. Atl stared at them, counting them. If she didn't count them she was going to scream.

"... mind ..."

"Sorry?" she asked finally, lifting her eyes toward him and brushing the grains of salt away.

"Do you mind if I ask for dessert?"

"Fine."

The restaurant was nearly empty, but their server was busy chatting with the cashier. Domingo raised his arm, trying unsuccessfully to attract their attention. Normally Atl wouldn't have *wanted* to attract their attention, but the sooner she got the boy his dessert, the sooner they might go home. There were certain matters they needed to discuss.

Atl decided to raise her own hand. The waitress looked at them and took out her notepad.

"Yes?" she asked.

"My brother wants dessert," Atl said.

"Umm ... can I have a banana split?" he asked.

The server jotted down the order and walked away.

Domingo looked confused. "Why did you say I'm your brother?"

"It's an easy way to explain why we are hanging out together," she said. Atl doubted anyone could peg her for his elder going by her looks, but her attitude was that of a woman grown, not a timid girl on a date.

"We are the same age."

"I'm twenty-three," Atl said.

"That's the same thing."

She was, essentially, as much of a girl as him and she suspected Domingo might know more of survival than she did, having gotten by as he had in the streets. Pampered as she was Atl had little more than instinct and bluster. But she refused to admit it and she felt it was important to establish a hierarchy.

"It's hardly the same thing," Atl scoffed. "I'm a lot more mature than you."

Domingo seemed to consider that as he wiped his face with a cloth napkin. "Do you have any real siblings? You know, back wherever you come from."

"No," she said, and did not volunteer Izel's name. It lodged there, in her throat, like a thorn.

"I had two brothers," Domingo said. "One of them was sort of nice, but the other was an asshole."

"What happened to them? Did they die?" she asked.

"Nah." The boy shook his head. "I just haven't seen them in months. I don't go home too often."

The server returned, bearing a banana split. She placed it in front of Domingo. He stared at the ice cream for several minutes until Atl had to roll her eyes.

"It's going to melt," she pointed out.

"Yeah . . . I know. It's just it's so pretty. I don't . . . um . . . I only see things like this in magazines."

Domingo lifted a spoon and carefully began to eat. Atl felt funny, looking at him. There was plenty of food to go around back home and Atl never wondered where her next meal would come from. But it came from kids like this. Kids who stared at a cherry like it was a ruby, like a banana in a glass dish was an exciting new discovery.

"You don't want any?" he asked.

"I'd vomit all night long," Atl said.

"Okay," Domingo said. He kept eating merrily.

The bare lightbulb of her apartment created stark planes of light and shadow. It reminded her of a German expressionist movie she'd once seen, a scene in which a murderer runs across the rooftops. Atl peeled off her jacket and looked over her shoulder at Domingo, who was staring at the dog.

"Fine," she said. "Cualli, sit."

The dog sat obediently.

"You can pet him."

Domingo hurried forward, rubbing the dog's head while Cualli endured the caresses with stoic indifference.

"It's a very nice dog," he said.

"I know."

Dobermans were supposed to be smaller than Cualli, but she'd always wanted a big dog, even if Izel said that the tiny Xoloescuincle was the breed the Aztecs owned. In their mythology, it accompanied humans in the journey to the underworld. Atl sulked and kept a Xoloescuincle when she was small, but eventually that dog died and Atl became a teenager.

She asked for a Doberman, a large one. Izel called her dog the Beast for this reason, but Atl called him Cualli, and he really was the best boy ever.

Domingo scratched the dog's ears and Cualli groaned with delight.

"Are you hungry?" Domingo asked her.

"Maybe," she admitted.

"You can have some of my blood. I don't mind."

Atl pressed a hand against her chest, pausing and carefully considering her options. "Domingo, would you like it if we were friends?"

"For real?"

"Yes. But being my friend is a bit different."

"I'll bet it's different," he said, smiling goofily, his crooked teeth showing.

"No, it's not just the blood."

"Then what?"

"It's a bond. You'd be my tlapalēhuiāni." She moved closer to him, brushing his hand. "Bloodletting was very important to the Aztecs, did you know that?"

"No."

He probably didn't know Aztecs from Mayans. None of the gods, none of the mythology, none of the names she'd learned since childhood. There had been vampires in America long before the Aztecs rose to power, and they had interacted with humans, of course. But the Tlahuelpocmimi had blended so seamlessly into Aztec culture it was difficult to determine who had influenced whom, whether the emphasis on blood and sacrifice had come from exposure to the vampires or whether the vampires had gravitated toward this tribe because it meshed with their worldviews.

"The face of all earthly things at one point is sacrifice," Atl continued. "The codices show noblemen and -women piercing their tongues, lips, and genitals. Drawing blood with bits of bone and maguey thorns, because we offer ourselves to the universe and to others. We can only pay our debts with blood. The ultimate gift is always blood."

Domingo looked justifiably intimidated as she spoke, but she noticed the spark in his eyes, the hunger lurking there.

"People aren't very good to you, are they?"

"Not all the time," he muttered.

"The blood rituals are part of a reciprocal relationship. Do you know what 'reciprocal' means?"

He shook his head.

"It's when two people owe each other."

A murky simplification, Izel would have said. The bond with the tlapalēhuiāni was powerful. The transference of blood was symbolic, but it also served to create a mental connection. A Tlāhuihpochtli could not command a human—tales of vampires hypnotizing their victims had their basis in the Necros—but the vampire and the human, after coming in contact with each other's blood, could share memories and even a crude form of telepathy. Atl's kin called this the xiuhtlahtōlli, the precious speech. Since the word "xiuh," precious, was associated with turquoise, the tlapalēhuiāni wore pendants or bracelets made with this stone to indicate their high-ranking status.

And just as the turquoise was precious, so was the human a vampire picked as its tlapalēhuiāni, and picking one was a delicate, painstaking task: it did no good to choose a weak or unsuitable candidate. After all, this would be the human who would protect, represent, and assist the vampire for decades to come.

Which is why Izel would have cautioned Atl against selecting a boy she hardly knew.

But Izel was nothing but ash; she was bits of blackened bones.

"I can take care of you. If you'll take care of me. If you'll be loyal," Atl said, shoving her misgivings away.

"I can be loyal."

"Give me your blood and I'll give you mine."

"And then we'll be friends?"

Atl grabbed his arm, pulling up his jacket to reveal his wrist. To his credit, Domingo barely flinched as she shifted and pressed her mouth against his skin. His blood was very sweet. Clean and fresh, like drinking from a spring.

She drank greedily, enjoying each drop. It might have only been better if she'd had a chance to down a few glasses of tequila. Booze and blood. She'd had them aplenty, before things went to hell. Now . . . now blood and blood alone would have to do. But it wasn't so bad, was it? For a fugitive she was doing quite well. She'd be fine. She'd survive.

Domingo closed his eyes and muttered something. She felt his body collapsing against hers, nothing but an old rag doll. His heart fluttered in his chest, like a scared bird. She let him slide down onto the floor and knelt down next to him. Atl slashed her wrist with one of her nails.

She stared at the line against her wrist, the rich, dark blood. This was more than a pact; it was a true connection. Once she gave him this, she could not take it away. There should have been a selection process, a ceremony, the burning of copal. She was going at it wrong and she was too young to have a tlapalēhuiāni. The Aztecs did not consider a warrior a man until he had captured his first prisoner of war. Her people did not think a warrior was a woman until she had made an honorable kill or pleased the gods with her deeds. Youths had no business with a tlapa-lēhuiāni.

Fuck it.

Atl pressed her wrist against Domingo's mouth.

"Be mine," she said.

He did not swallow the blood at first. But it was easy to force him to do it. She pressed her wrist against his mouth with such vehemence that he'd either swallow or choke. The boy did swallow, slowly.

"Yollo. Tonal. Nahual," she said. "The three principles. The flesh of the body. The spirit of the body. The animal brother."

The boy shivered. She held him as a mother might hold her child, his head pressed against her shoulder, her chin resting on his head. Cualli stared at her and whined.

CHAPTER 6

Nick ignored the gnawing hunger as much as he could, he really did. Vampires had markedly different appetites. Nick's subspecies ate food along with blood. In fact, his kind was quite voracious. He had a predilection for junk food. Twinkies, chips, soda, popcorn. They helped keep him mellow and staved off the hunger. Nick ate a lot during a single day, gobbling tortilla chips, going through three bags of cheese doodles, and downing two bottles of vodka. He put it off for as long as he could, then finally walked to the kitchen, dragging his feet the whole way.

When he opened the refrigerator and pulled out the bags, he knew he would not drink any of the blood Rodrigo had procured. Just the smell of it made him want to vomit. It smelled like the plastic it came in. Rancid blood. Tasteless mush.

He might as well drink his own piss. Not that Rodrigo would care. Rodrigo didn't give a shit what Nick felt, and hadn't wanted Nick to come in the first place. He sensed the older man's disapproval in every quiet look, every movement of his head. But Nick had more of a right to be there than Rodrigo. Atl had killed his kin, and not only did he want payback, but he was also going to prove to his father that he was ready to handle the family's affairs.

Of course, Rodrigo disagreed. Rodrigo knew everything.

Dad should have sent me alone, Nick thought. He squished the bag of blood between his hands. Nick squished so hard that the bag burst open, spilling blood over the floor, which made his stomach grumble. But when he sniffed it, it still smelled disgusting.

Enough. He needed to eat. Real food, not the garbage Rodrigo was stuffing in the fridge. La Bola was on sentinel duty and Rodrigo was in his study, but Nick didn't need to break down doors to get to where he wanted.

He went to the bathroom, locked the door, and opened the small window. It would not have been large enough for a normal man to squeeze through, but Nick was not normal. His bones cracked and he twisted his limbs, dislocating his joints, and out he slid, slipping down the edge of the wall like a lizard.

The Aztec vampires could fly a bit, he'd heard, but Nick was a Necros, so all he could manage was to climb up and down the sides of buildings. Not that it mattered. He didn't envy the powers of the others. Most vampires were so caught up in tradition, in bullshit pomp and ceremony, that they forgot the reality of the world around them. The Necros were pragmatists, willing to seize modernity with both hands while the others cried about the good old days. His kin were creatures of action.

This was why Rodrigo made him so angry. Instead of catching the girl before she reached Mexico City, they had lost her trail and were now trapped in this ridiculous place. Nick was told to simply sit still and wait. Nick wouldn't have to be hungry if it weren't for Rodrigo's ineptitude. After all, how hard was it to find a stupid spoiled chick like that?

Nick reached the alley behind the apartment building, cracked his knuckles, and headed away. The other night, when he'd gone to the Zona Rosa, one of the girls in line at the club had told him about an interesting joint where you could slip in without ID.

He found it without much trouble. The Hyena was an old Porfirian house in the Condesa, painted a bright blue. It was one of the more fashionable establishments in the area, supposedly Bohemian and really a bit snobbish. The interior was just what Nick was looking for: lots of taxidermied animals on the walls and stuffed birds hanging from the ceiling. Coyote heads, horse rears, a whole bull near the bar. The music was Eurotrash, with tiny beats and obscure vocals. It was loud. Loud was good. It pleased him.

Nick ordered a drink. He didn't bother with any food. He wasn't there for overpriced nachos meant for tourists—he wanted blood. He zeroed in on a girl in a tiny neon pink miniskirt. She wore several silver crosses on her chest. The sight of them amused him. But no, not her.

He looked around and saw another. This one wore a black, lacy outfit. Her hair was a matching black and her makeup was excessive, caked too heavily, artlessly applied. He thought she looked a bit like Atl, a vague resemblance that stirred him, made him lick his lips.

He drifted toward her, smiling and asking if she was having a good time. She gave him an answer he did not catch, so he nodded and asked what she was having. She yelled into his ear, a screeching, irritating sound, but he continued smiling and ordered shots of black vodka for her. They danced.

Three songs later Nick told her it was too warm inside and it was too loud, and she agreed eagerly when he said they should step out for a minute.

Humans were so simple, so stupid, so trusting. Like this silly girl, wearing a ring on each finger, one of them a mood ring that sparkled blue and then green.

They ventured into the alley behind the club.

She kissed him and Nick kissed her back with the indifference of a man pressing his lips against a piece of mutton. But she did not care. She did not notice. Her hands drifted toward his belt and he considered his options. Sometimes sex and blood mingled well together. He didn't mind playing with his food.

Nick grinned against her mouth and bit his own tongue, hard, then kissed her again, his blood coating her mouth. It took only a few seconds and the girl went lax in his arms.

"Take off your shirt," he commanded her, and she did, an obedient doll.

"Your name is Atl."

"My name is Atl," she said.

She sounded wrong. Atl had a beautiful voice.

"Kiss me," he said, deciding it was better if she didn't speak.

She did. But then, when he looked at her, he frowned. He liked doing this. He liked using his power to control humans, wrap them around his little finger. But Atl would never, ever yield to him.

Staring at the girl, he realized what a cheap imitation she was.

"Put your top back on," he said.

Her black hair, now that he looked at it more carefully, was a bad dye job. Her eyes, which had seemed as dark as Atl's inside the club, were a honeyed brown. She looked nothing like Atl. The mere sight of her repulsed him.

"Bite your tongue," he said, and she did. Hard.

Blood dribbled down the corner of her mouth.

He threw his head back before crashing down on her, his serrated teeth tearing the skin like it was papier-mâché. Yes, they were also different from the Aztec vampires: his kind had fangs. They had sharp teeth and strong neck muscles to pull and rend the skin. The Tlāhuihpochtli had her nails and a stinger.

A stinger. Nick thought that was ridiculous. Give him strong fangs to eat his meat.

Nick slurped at the blood and took another bite of the woman's flesh, enjoying the taste. She whimpered and in response he bit her harder, bit her right ear and tore a chunk of it. After that she didn't complain and he was able to drink without her annoying noises bothering him.

He could hear the music coming from the club, he could feel its vibrations as he pressed the woman against the wall. Her heart beat erratically and she opened and closed her mouth, like a fish out of water.

It was good to have a proper meal again and he was enjoying himself immensely when the girl had to ruin it, suddenly growing still. She had died quickly, useless in every single way.

He wiped his mouth with the back of his hand, and then looked around. The music was still beating loudly. No one had seen him. He dragged the girl behind a bunch of wooden crates. He discovered a dirty blanket on the ground and covered her with it.

CHAPTER 7

My arm hurts. That was Domingo's first thought.

Cold. That was the second.

"Drink," Atl said.

It was a glass. She was pressing a glass against his lip and it felt cold. Domingo swallowed.

"Open your eyes."

He did. She was sitting beside him, on the floor. Domingo blinked. His head felt like it was about to explode.

"Am I a vampire now?" he asked.

Atl chuckled. "Don't be silly. I told you that wasn't possible. You should stop believing the crap they say about us."

He rubbed his hands together. "It's what they put in books," he said. More like comic books, but what was the big difference?

Atl snorted and pressed the glass against his lips once more. Domingo swallowed obediently.

"The books, right. All that garbage from before 1967 still sticking around," she said. "Can you hold this?"

"I can try."

Domingo clutched the glass with both hands and slowly raised it to his mouth.

"What about 1967?" he asked, because he wasn't sure of the reference.

"Doesn't ring a bell?"

"No. I didn't do well in school, though," he admitted.

It hadn't been Domingo's fault. Most days his mom didn't pack a lunch for him and it was a pain in the ass completing his homework with his stepfather bellowing. His brothers were not much better. He had liked art class and music class and reading, but the teachers were indifferent and many of his classmates unkind. He didn't mind dropping out.

"That's the year humans discovered we existed, that it wasn't just folklore and superstition. There was a huge panic. A bunch of countries tried kicking the vampires out. Spain and Portugal made a big show of it. That's how we ended up with so many European varieties in Mexico."

Yeah, he vaguely remembered hearing about that, but this had happened long ago, before he was born. Besides, Domingo was more interested in the splashy vampire stories—these often involved guns, gangs, and drugs—but since he had a real vampire talking to him now he'd thought he'd ask. It was an educational moment, and his teacher had always chided him for letting such moments go by, too mesmerized by comic books to consider a dusty history fact of any value. But he wanted to know everything about her.

"How come we don't have vampires in Mexico City, then?" Domingo asked.

"'Cause you guys are pussies," Atl said with a shrug. "You'll need iron pills. Anytime we drink from a human we are supposed to give them iron pills, my mother's orders. Finish your juice."

He took another sip.

"So, like, no type of vampire can turn a human into a vampire, ever?" he asked.

"No. Some can make you real sick and kill you if they bite you."

Domingo stared at Atl. She snatched the glass from his hands, chuckling again.

"Not my type," she said as she stood up and walked toward the kitchen. "But vampires *are* a completely different species. *Homo cruentus.*"

Domingo did not try to follow her. He was too tired to get up. He sat there, his back against the wall. He wiggled his fingers and felt like a hundred ants were walking up his arm.

"Homo . . . you're gay?"

Atl's laughter drifted from the kitchen. She came back with the glass of juice refilled and handed it to him.

"My species is *Homo cruentus,* though there are different subspecies. I suppose if you were to be really precise you might say some of us don't qualify as members of a subspecies since you have to be able to interbreed." She stopped, noticing his puzzled expression. "Do you know what a species and a subspecies are?"

"Not really," he said.

"It's like we are different types. Wolves are *Canis lupus.* They are a species. Dogs are *Canis lupus familiaris.* There's also dingoes, which are called *Canis lupus dingo.* They're two different subspecies."

She crouched down next to him as she spoke.

He nodded. "I get it now. I wasn't too good at science in school."

"When did you stop going to school?"

"'Bout four years ago," he said. "I got kicked out of my home."

"How come?"

He took a sip of juice and shrugged.

"I used to stay out a lot. I'd come home real late at night. My stepdad said if I didn't start bringing in money and stopped hanging out with troublemakers he was going to kick me out. One night I came home and he wouldn't let me in. He had dumped my clothes by the door, in a trash bag. That was that."

"What did your mother say?" she asked, looking surprised.

"She didn't really say much and I didn't want to come back, anyway. My stepdad was always hitting me with the belt. One time he hit me with the iron and another with a frying pan."

The belt was small potatoes. Now the iron, that one had hurt. Domingo had to get stitches.

"What about your real dad?"

"He went away a bunch of years ago. I don't know where he is now. I've got two brothers and we've all had different dads."

It sounded a lot worse when he said it than when he thought about it. Things just were the way they were, but judging by the way she was looking at him maybe it had been worse than he'd thought.

"Drink up," she said, helping him tilt the glass.

Domingo downed the rest of the juice in one huge gulp and wiped his mouth with the back of his hand. She took the glass from his hands.

"What's your mom like?" he asked.

"She's dead," Atl said simply, turning the glass in her hands, a finger sliding along its rim.

"I'm sorry. How'd she die?"

"She died. What do you care?" she said, standing up. "The sun will be coming up soon."

She wasn't wearing the watch and there was no clock in the living room. Domingo didn't know how she could tell. Maybe it was one of those vampire powers.

"I need to sleep," Atl said.

He wanted to ask, "Can I look at your coffin?" but stopped himself in time, realizing how stupid that might sound.

"Will you do me a favor?" she asked.

"Um. Sure."

"I need you to go look for someone today. It's a guy. His name is Bernardino. I have his address but I haven't been able to visit him."

"That doesn't sound too hard."

"Wait."

She moved away and returned with a small cloth bag. She reached into it and took out a single jade bead, placing it on the palm of his hand.

"Go see Bernardino and tell him that Atl, Daughter of Centehua, needs his help. I need to find someone, and only he can tell me where she is. Give him this piece of jade."

"Who do you need to find?"

"This person," she said.

He took the folded piece of paper in her hands and looked at it. Her handwriting was very tight and neat, not the sloppy strokes that Domingo managed when he chanced to write something. "Verónica Montealban," said the note. Below it Atl had scribbled "Bernardino" and an address.

"Will you go? Today? This is extremely important. A matter of life or death."

"I'll try to go," Domingo said. "I'm feeling a bit tired right now, but definitely, I—"

"I'm serious. This is important. You can rest for a few hours. There's a mattress in the bedroom."

She looked worried and he did want to help her. Domingo shuffled tentatively into the bedroom. The dog padded behind him. It was very dark.

"I can't see much," he muttered.

She turned on the light. There was not much *to* see. Atl did have a mattress in the center of the room, but no sheets. She slid a closet door open and rummaged inside, tossing him a blanket. Domingo placed it on the bed and lay down.

Atl flicked off the light. He was at the edge of the bed, waiting for her to join him. Instead, he heard the closet door slide shut and then nothing but a deep silence. He counted up to ten in his head before wetting his lips and gathering the courage to speak.

"Atl, you ain't coming to bed?" he asked.

"No," came the muffled reply.

"You don't have to sleep on the floor. It's not like I'd try anything," he said. "If it makes you feel better, I can take the floor, no worries."

She chuckled. "I like small spaces. Just as the animals in the desert have their burrows, I have mine."

"Oh," he said.

He shifted his position and wrapped himself in the blanket. He hoped he hadn't sounded like a creep asking if she'd come to bed. He didn't want to give no wrong impression.

"Do you want to hear something interesting? Tarantulas line their burrows with silk to stabilize the burrow wall. They also use silk trap lines to alert them of potential prey."

"That's neat. How'd you learn that?" he asked.

"My sister told me that," she said, and her voice was faint.

He waited for Atl to say more, but she did not. Domingo wrapped the blanket around himself and slept. When he woke faint traces of light had begun to slip underneath the curtains. The room was still dark, but he could make out the outline of the closet and the shape of Atl's dog resting by it.

There was his answer. Mexican vampires slept in closets. Who would have thought?

Domingo tiptoed outside the bedroom, quietly closing the door behind him. His stomach was rumbling. It was time for a meal. He could use a good bowl of birria. He grabbed the apartment keys that were dangling by a hook next to the door and stepped outside. When he reached the first landing, he slipped on his headphones and pushed play.

CHAPTER 8

People had to get themselves murdered on Saturday. Never Tuesday or Wednesday, when Ana Aguirre was off duty. Always Saturday. She shouldn't be on duty on the weekends. As a matter of fact, Ana should have been working a pleasant desk job supervising junior officers. But Castillo had blocked that move yet again. The twat. If Ana Aguirre had ever held dreams of a real career in law enforcement, they had long been dashed under the persistent hammer of the outdated Mexican police system.

Worst of all, when she arrived at the crime scene, knelt down, and lifted the blanket, she saw it was a kid. A young girl in a tight miniskirt, her top drenched in blood.

Ana looked at the girl and couldn't help thinking of her own daughter, Marisol, who was seventeen. Ana kept working this shit job for her daughter. But she worried. She wasn't home nearly enough and the city had a hungry maw, one ready to swallow the young and the innocent.

Ana aimed her flashlight at the girl's face. The neck had been torn, savaged.

"Hey, you've got anything for me?" she asked, turning toward a policeman who was lounging against the wall, smoking a cigarette.

"What you see's what you've got. It looks strange as fuck. Vampire, no?"

Ana tilted her head. Great. She'd left Zacatecas to avoid the vampire gangs. It seemed they were all over the country. All over except for Mexico City. Not because it was a city-state, autonomous in many respects. That was just a geographical demarcation. No. Mexico City had held tight because it was territory of the human gangs, and the gangs, usually unwilling to cooperate, had managed to come together against the single enemy that mattered to them: the bloodsuckers.

But violence lurked at the edges of the city, in Neza and other areas. There, in the slums, the vampires sometimes made their incursions, trying to expand their fiefdoms. They failed. For now.

"I phoned and they told me you'd know what to do," the policeman said.

Like hell, Ana thought, but she knew why they'd placed her on this case. Because none of the others wanted to touch it. Because she was from

Zacatecas and it didn't matter if you'd lived in Mexico City for six years, you were still an outsider. Because she came from the gang lands. Because Castillo hated her. Because the shit jobs always wound up dripping her way. Because she had put forth a sexual harassment complaint against another officer one time, and everyone had laughed it off, saying no one would want to smack the ass of such an ugly woman.

"When did you find her?"

"I called it in half an hour ago. Took you long enough to get here."

Ana wanted to backhand the punk. He looked shy of twenty. Probably thought he was God's gift to the Secretariat of Public Safety simply because they'd issued him a baton.

"Well, anyone see anything?"

"Nobody saw nothing," he said.

"You sure or you just guessing?"

The young man gave her a blank look. They'd already set the yellow tape across both ends of the alley and onlookers were peering curiously at the cops. A couple were even raising their cell phones and trying to take photos.

For souvenirs, she thought bitterly. She considered lodging a complaint about this cop's performance, then decided the paperwork wasn't worth it. Her note would end up at the bottom of a file, anyway.

"She had the blanket on top of her when you found her?" Ana asked.

"Yeah."

The vampire had covered her. She didn't think it was modesty. Although he'd done a shoddy job of it, he'd probably been trying to delay the finding of the corpse. Had he simply dragged the body to the next alley he would have found a pothole so large it could probably fit half the girl's body. It wouldn't have taken too much effort.

Stupid, she thought.

"Go talk to your friends over there and see if they have any witnesses for me, will you?" she said, pointing toward a couple of cops who were talking animatedly with some of the onlookers.

The young man huffed, but obeyed her. Ana leaned down and took out her camera. In theory, forensics would come over and photograph the crime scene, but that was in theory. Many times they just wouldn't show up, because there was too much shit going on, there weren't enough of them, or they didn't want to get up and drag their sorry asses out of bed. Mexican police work didn't play out like in the movies. There was almost no investigative work. They relied heavily on confessions and wouldn't even blink if they contaminated a crime scene. Physical evidence was used in about 10 percent of convictions and the rest were signed affidavits. Things were changing, supposedly. Ana was one of the shiny new breed of detectives, a real investigator, but that was a bunch of PR mixed with only a little substance.

She was tired of this game.

Ana snapped photos and took notes, wondering if she should even bother but doing it anyway. She was up and about already, so she might as well work. No reason to give Castillo more fuel for his fire.

"There's a chick who says she saw the dead girl with a guy inside the nightclub," the young policeman said as he returned, pointing at a teenager with spiky hair and tremendously tall high heels who was standing nearby.

"All right," Ana said. "Call forensics and see if they'll get their ass here before someone from the morgue hauls the body away, will ya?"

The boy looked terribly annoyed, but he had the good sense to comply. Ana went toward the young girl in the heels, quickly pulling out her notepad and her pen. They were supposed to have standard-issue minitablets, but hers had broken and nobody had bothered to give her a replacement. Ana preferred the feel of a pen between her fingers, anyway. Old school but reliable. Just like a knife. Electric zappers were also good for vampires. But knives had their appeal. She still carried the good old silver knife with her.

Cut off their heads and burn the bodies. No other way.

"They're telling me you saw the girl inside," Ana said, and the teenager gave her a vehement nod of the head.

"Uh-huh. Sure did. She was with this majorly hot guy."

"What did he look like?"

"Platinum blond hair, pale. He was wearing nice clothes," the girl said.

"Age?" she asked, her shorthand neat against the yellow pages of the notepad. She'd taken typing classes in high school. Technical high school. She had been trained to be a secretary and picked an application for the local police department instead.

"About my age. I dunno. Nineteen? Twenty, maybe. Hard to say."

"Anything special about him? Any marks, tattoos, piercings?"

The girl seemed to think it over. She rubbed her arms and finally spoke. "He didn't have piercings. But, yes, I remember a tattoo."

"What did it look like?" Ana asked.

"He took off his shirt to dance," the girl said, mimicking the motion of a man lifting his arms. "He was wearing a wife beater and I could see, kinda, part of the back of his neck. It was a shark."

"Anything else you saw?"

"No. I was inside 'til someone came running in and said the cops were here and someone had killed a girl. I just wanted to see."

I hope it was amusing, Ana thought.

Ana got home around 6 a.m., nearly time for Marisol to wake up for school. She peeked into her daughter's room. The girl was peacefully asleep. Ana recalled the spectacle of the dead girl in the alley and shook her head.

God, a vampire kill. She hadn't looked into one of those since Zacatecas. You took statements, nodded, maybe caught one, and then a couple more bodies popped up in another part of the city, like mushrooms after the rain. It never ended. It was a fact of life. That was what brought her to Mexico City. It was safer, and they were starting the new investigating units. Reforming the police system. She was going to have a chance to be a "real" detective.

Not that I'm anything "realer" now, she thought as she walked into her bedroom and peeled off her uniform. It was a dark blue, form-fitting suit woven with a nano-fiber worn under a standard-issue raincoat in the same color. It itched, and she often found herself scratching her neck.

Ana carefully folded her clothes and lay down on her bed. She lay on top of the covers and wondered if the examiner was going to get to the girl's corpse that evening. Probably not. The girl was nobody of importance and Ana didn't have much pull around the office. If the coroner looked at the girl and if he deigned to produce a report, it might be weeks later.

She didn't think Castillo really expected this crime to be solved and the vampire, in all likelihood, was already out of the city.

She felt bad for the mother of the girl, who was probably hearing about her daughter's murder right about now—she'd told the young, surly officer to see about that.

Ana wondered what she would do if Marisol did not show up one morning.

Don't think that, she scolded herself.

Ana turned and looked at the corner table where she kept a statue of the Virgin of Guadalupe, along with a plastic image of San Judas Tadeo and her mother's rosary.

Mexico was going to hell. It *was* hell. If she'd had any money she'd have left the country. Somewhere nice and quiet, without vampires and drug dealers. But she didn't.

Ana pressed a hand against her forehead and wondered what gang the vampire belonged to. The shark didn't sound familiar. But the bite marks did. She could bet this was the work of a Necros. She'd seen bites like that in Zacatecas and had learned to recognize the telltale signs of several vampire species.

The Necros, with its strong mandibles and big, sharp teeth, was easy to identify. The Tlāhuihpochtli left fewer, smaller marks—smudges blooming on the neck and wrists. Only once had she come upon a Revenant and it had scared the hell out of her. The thing . . . it had . . . it was . . . And the victim. Like a mummy, the flesh shrunken and the body twisted. The devil's work.

She rolled away from the shrine to the Virgin and closed her eyes, hoping for a restful sleep, but the image of the dead girl flickered behind her eyelids, superimposed like a negative.

Ana woke up far too tired. Vampires drained you one way or another. She rose from bed and found Marisol in the kitchen, frying an egg.

"Hey, are you back from school early?" she asked.

"No," Marisol said. "You're up late. You were supposed to cook dinner."

"I'll make dinner now."

Ana extended her arm to open the refrigerator, but Marisol shook her head. Her mouth was doing that thing where she wasn't quite smirking but it was damn close.

"There's no vegetables. There's nothing. You haven't gone to the supermarket."

"No, we went."

Ana opened the refrigerator and stared at a solitary avocado, a bit of parsley, the wedge of cheese with a dab of mold on it.

"Told you," Marisol said. A full smirk now.

Ana grabbed a can of diet soda and did not bother pouring it in a glass. It would only mean one more glass to clean. There was already a pile of dishes waiting in the sink. "I need to buy a new school uniform," Marisol said as she flipped her egg with the plastic spatula.

"What's wrong with your current uniform?" Ana asked.

"It's not the official uniform."

Ana sipped her soda, shaking her head. "It's got green and blue squares on the skirt and a blue sweater. How is that not official?"

"You know very well the nuns want me to wear the one they sell at the school shop. Not a cheap copy," Marisol said, sounding like Ana had sent her to school dressed in a paper bag instead of real clothes.

Ana put the soda can down on the kitchen counter. "Well, the nuns can go piss themselves, Marisol, the school manual doesn't say it's mandatory that we buy it there."

"The other kids can tell it's a knockoff."

Once again Ana regretted having enrolled Marisol in a private Catholic school. The school fees were outrageous. But public school was no good, with the teachers always on strike and the lousy facilities. Marisol needed a private school so she could have the best teachers, a chance to learn a second language, to make something of herself. Employers advertised jobs in Mexico by specifying the age and even the goddamn school a kid had to have graduated from. No students from the UNAM, no one over thirty-four, no married people, no kids, send a photograph, and indicate religion. Under those fucking circumstances you had to try to give your child an edge or they were going to be trampled upon by the richer kids from the Tec or the Anahuac; kids who had lighter skin, heavier wallets, and the right last names. No, Marisol needed this high school. If only Ana could afford it. Money was tight.

"I bet you're not going to let me go on the class trip to Acapulco, either," Marisol said as she tossed the egg on a plate and handed it to Ana. Then the girl cracked another egg and began frying it.

Ana leaned against the refrigerator and held the plate in one hand. "I don't have the money."

"You could ask Dad."

As if that would help. Ana was supposed to receive alimony, but any cash from her ex-husband was sporadic and unpredictable. He had remarried and he had a new family; he didn't trouble himself with the old one. Ana was grateful for this, since it meant he had stopped nagging her about moving back to Zacatecas so he could see his daughter. If she started complaining about the alimony he might start talking about that again, a topic Ana felt no desire to revisit.

"Your father won't be able to help. This is not a field trip. It's a glorified party, and I'm not paying so you can go get drunk on a beach. Plus, it's the state with the highest concentration of vampire cartels. There are half a dozen different families disputing territory there. No damn way you are headed into that Necros nest."

"Really, Mother? It's the same everywhere."

"No." Ana shook her head again. "It's not the same everywhere. There's no vampire cartels chilling in Mexico City."

"You yourself have told me that the gangs—"

"The human gangs are not going to leave you in an alley with your throat torn out," she replied, slamming her plate against the kitchen counter.

Marisol looked at her. Ana recognized the same defiant stare she saw each morning in the mirror, the same hooded eyes and thin mouth. Marisol was a younger version of Ana, and this troubled her. She didn't want her daughter to be like her, to make the same stupid mistakes.

"Look, Marisol, we just can't afford it. All right?"

Marisol nodded. She had finished cooking her egg and turned off the stove. "Eat up. It's getting cold," her daughter muttered.

CHAPTER 9

The house was in the Colonia Roma, where Domingo seldom ventured. The Roma had been a fine area since the time when people rode carriages and ladies wore corsets. It was no longer aristocratic—the super wealthy lived in walled-off complexes or the newer Polanco and Lomas neighborhoods; yet it retained plenty of its grandeur and tradition, showcasing its history in its wide avenues, its parks, its boulevards, and a number of elegant old houses, very European. It was, nowadays, morphing into a hipster haven. The grungy elements of the area paired well with the bookstores, antique shops, art galleries, cafés, and restaurants with far too pricey items on the menu. A latte always went down better when you could pat yourself on the back and declare yourself très chic because you were having a snack at a butcher shop turned trendy eatery, right smack in front of a street where prostitutes lined up in the evenings to engage in their daily trade.

It was a place for sophisticated older people and hip young ones, with magnificent trees and faded mansions, a taco stand here and there to remind you it was not quite the Belle Époque and you were still in Mexico City. It was not a place for Domingo, who preferred the downtown crowds, the pressure of people in the subway, the underpasses and alleys. There were too many private security guards walking around the Roma, who were eager to stop a young man in a cheap yellow jacket. They stared as he walked by, but if Domingo had learned a lesson in his short life it was to keep walking and stare straight ahead. The private security guards couldn't arrest him, anyway. They could beat him if they didn't like the look of him, but that was about it.

Domingo kept his head down and walked with his hands in his pockets as he checked the address again. It took him a while to find the house because the number was half-hidden behind a layer of graffiti. It was one of those old casonas that seemed like it would stand forever, braving earthquakes and pollution. The gate—an iron double-door—was rusty with age. The place looked abandoned. This was not entirely unusual. Yes, the area was now fashionable and gentrified, but there were houses here and there that had gone to hell in the '80s and never recuperated, some of them occupied by upper-class squatters—university students and artists with proletarian leanings—and others by the regular, run-of-the-mill squatters who had never read Marx and did not give a fuck about globalization talk.

He wondered if he was at the wrong address. Domingo gave the gate an experimental push. It swung on its hinges, groaning a welcome. He closed the gate behind him and walked down a small inner courtyard, past a fountain decked with chipped blue tiles and to the door of the house itself.

The door seemed terribly heavy, like the door of a castle. Well, what he imagined a castle door might be like. The closest he'd ever gotten to a castle was the Castle of Chapultepec, and he was pretty sure that didn't count because it was a museum.

He'd never seen a door knocker except in horror movies, but there was one, a heavy iron ring, which he slammed against the wood. He waited, staring at the fountain, which was filled with dirty, murky water and an abundance of leaves. Several pots overflowing with wilted plants sat by the fountain. A couple of them were cracked and earth had oozed out.

An old woman opened the door, her white hair pulled back in a bun. She squinted at Domingo.

"I'm looking for Bernardino," he said, reaching into his pocket and showing the woman the jade bead Atl had given him. "Atl, Daughter of Centehua, sends me."

The woman nodded and let him in.

Domingo had spent nights sleeping in old, abandoned houses or in tenements that had stood for more than a century. Many of these places were humid, dark, and unpleasant. However, as he followed the old woman in, toward a staircase, he thought he had never been in a place this cold.

Not only was it chilly, it was dirty too. Yet in the dirt, he noticed things that looked like the genuine article. Antiques. Pricey shit. Cool-looking furniture. Tea sets in a glass case. But there was also a lot of garbage: hundreds of newspaper pages with solved crossword puzzles, plastic toys that came free with fast-food meals, books stained with mold, broken watches, a very large TV set from another era with a crack running down its screen.

A dozen dolls sat on a wall, lined up in their white dresses, wearing matching lace hats. Their blue and green and brown eyes seemed to follow him as he climbed the steps.

There was the faint smell of mildew and the stronger smell of cat piss.

When they reached the second floor, the darkness of the hallway hit him like a wave. He slowed down, afraid to run into a piece of furniture. The old lady did not say anything. She did not offer to turn on the lights, but merely waited a few paces ahead of him.

Domingo continued walking, careful to keep a hand on the wall just in case he should trip. They reached a door and she opened it. It was very dark inside. A darkness thicker than in the hallway.

Domingo swallowed. He clutched the jade bead, then slipped inside the room.

He saw nothing.

"Who sends you?" asked a voice in the darkness. It was a wonderful voice, rich, strong, like the voice of a radio announcer. A very fine voice that enunciated each word with a slight accent.

There was the kiss of a match being struck and then light bloomed. He saw an oil lamp next to the dim figure of a man sitting on a couch. The man rose and began walking around the room. He lit another oil lamp, lit candles. The darkness began to recede, and Domingo saw more bits and pieces: a rug, two cats—no, three. No, four. A lot of cats in the room. Faded paintings decorated the walls and thick velvet curtains hid the windows.

"Atl," Domingo said. "Daughter of Centehua. She sends me."

"I do not know Atl."

"She gave me something for you."

The man lit two more candles. Domingo saw him properly now. The man was wrapped in a frayed crimson robe, leaning against a cane. He had a great lump on his back. A hunchback. His skin seemed . . . thin, almost translucent. His eyes, when he glanced at Domingo, were a dim, sickly yellow. He looked old, rather ugly.

"Show me."

Domingo stepped forward and opened his hand, the jade bead resting upon his palm. The man stretched out his thin, bony fingers and picked up the bead, holding it up.

"The Iztac clan, the people of the white-feathered hummingbird. Tlāhuihpochtin," the man said. "The first vampires in Mexico, did you know that?"

"Yes," Domingo replied, and then, before he could stop himself he spoke again. "Are you a Revenant?"

Domingo's knowledge of vampires was fragmented; the Necros were the ones who appeared most often in popular culture. But the silhouette of the Revenants was distinctive, with their crooked spines, and though he'd seen only a couple of drawings of them he remembered that telltale detail.

The vampire smiled, pocketing the bead. "Most definitely." He pointed to an overstuffed leather chair. "Please sit."

Domingo did. There was a toy wooden horse in a corner. He noticed a pile of newspapers by the man's chair and these also had crosswords that had been solved. He had the crazy desire to go through the stuff. It was the garbage collector in him, eager to find empty bottles and secret treasures. He stilled himself, resting his hands in his lap, trying to keep himself from repeatedly tapping his foot. He was nervous.

"I thought there weren't any vampires living in Mexico City," Domingo said.

"This house was built during the reign of Santa Anna, more than a hundred and fifty years ago. It was the time when he was imposing great taxes. Taxes for dogs. Even taxes for breathing. He taxed you by the number of windows and doors your home had. People bricked their windows and their doors. But I didn't mind. It was good for me.

"Then came the Revolution. You could hear the cannon in the distance. I remember the smell of charred corpses drifting in under the door. A great quake hit in '85. Half the Roma fell to pieces. But not this house. Not this one."

The vampire placed his hands atop his cane and stared at Domingo.

"This is my home. It will always be my home. There are too many noises outside, too many cars and smells and people, but not here."

"I wouldn't want to move, either. You have cool stuff. What's that thing over there?" Domingo asked.

The vampire looked over his shoulder. "One of my phonographs."

"What does it do?"

"It plays music. It's very old. Would you like to listen to it?"

"Sure."

The vampire shuffled toward the machine. Domingo thought the contraption looked like a box with a gigantic flower or a big trumpet sticking out of the top. It had a delicate handle, which Bernardino pulled. Music began to stream from the phonograph.

Domingo listened with interest as the recording hiccupped and played. The vampire was smiling. His teeth were yellow and very large.

"Have you ever thought of selling it?" he asked.

The vampire's smile disappeared. "No," he said with a finality that made Domingo wince.

The phonograph went quiet and the vampire sat down again. Domingo looked at him, afraid to speak and say the wrong thing. A cat rubbed itself against his legs, purring, almost making him jump out of his seat.

"Here, here," said the vampire, and the cat left Domingo alone and jumped onto the vampire's lap.

The vampire propped his cane against the side of his chair and began petting the cat, his thin fingers carefully stroking its fur.

"Your mistress, what's her name again?"

"My mistress," Domingo repeated.

The vampire smirked, looking mightily amused. Domingo didn't like that. He hated feeling like he was the butt of a joke.

"Yes. What was that name?"

"Atl."

"Beautiful name. Beautiful girl. She must be. Her mother was a beauty. My kindred, well, they are this," the vampire said, pointing to himself. "Kyphosis, the great ugly hump. But I have my advantages."

"She sent me because she needs to find someone. She wrote the name down for me."

Domingo grabbed the crumpled piece of paper and gave it to Bernardino. The vampire looked at it with an easy indifference, nodding.

"Atl has money."

"She does, does she? She also has a serious case of idiocy," the vampire said. "I haven't lived this long to take a bullet for a woman I do not know."

"I don't understand."

"The person she wants will not like being found. And she will know it was me who gave Atl the information. Even worse, Atl wouldn't come to me unless she were in a dire situation, which I will not speculate about. I refuse to get involved. Tell her that."

"But you've got to help her," Domingo said, jumping to his feet. "She said it was life or death."

"Sit down," the vampire said angrily, lifting his left hand. "You have no manners."

Domingo didn't know how it happened. One second he was standing and then the next his knees buckled and the man was pushing him down back into the leather chair, pressing a hand against his neck. Damn. He was fast.

"You don't know the first thing about being an envoy. She was rather silly to send you," the vampire said. "What did she think I'd do, hmm? Invite you in for tea and cookies? This girl must want you dead."

She's my friend, he thought furiously.

The vampire released him and Domingo rubbed his neck.

"A friend," the vampire said with a chuckle. "A snack, maybe."

Bernardino picked up a cat and peered down at Domingo.

Domingo stared at the vampire.

"Did you just read my mind?" he asked, shocked that the vampire could actually do that. It seemed more impossible than the other stuff they said about vampires, like turning into bats or mist. Okay, maybe not mist.

"Yes, I read your mind. Pray that's the only thing I do. I might kill you for coming here, insolent brat. It might teach a lesson to that stupid girl who sends you. What does she think? Who does she think she is? People have begged for my audience, sent gifts and proper letters, there are protocols, and there is tradition, people have . . ." He trailed off, frowning, as if he'd run out of breath.

"Sir, she really needs your help," Domingo whispered.

Bernardino lifted a hand dismissively and stepped away. He stroked the cat's back and shook his head, muttering a couple of words in a language Domingo failed to understand.

"My apologies. Time and isolation do strange things. Of course, the levels of serotonin do not help," the vampire said.

"The what?" Domingo asked.

"Serotonin. A neurotransmitter. The low levels in our brains make us violent, impulsive, self-destructive. It's worse in some types than others. We are not very nice creatures. You are foolish to seek the company of vampires. Have you any idea what I am talking about?"

"Humans are not very nice either," Domingo said. He thought about the Jackal, who beat him. Domingo didn't want to say that everyone was an asshole, but many people are assholes when you're living in the streets.

"Apples and oranges. Most humans would not look at you and wonder what your bone marrow might taste like, would they?"

Okay, yes. Maybe. But it wasn't like you wouldn't get killed in the streets for your wallet, and sometimes simply for the hell of it. Kids disappeared and they weren't snatched by vampires. Maybe vampires were bad, but other things were just as bad. Cops could spend the weekend beating you or pimps could decide they needed a new warm body. Atl wasn't beating him and she wasn't pimping him.

"It doesn't matter what she thinks of me," Domingo said. "What matters is she sent me and she needs an answer, so stop trying to scare me, I ain't gonna scare. So, what's it gonna be?"

Bernardino chuckled. The way he carried the cat it seemed like he was carrying a baby. Domingo wondered if vampires liked animals. He might ask Atl about that. There were a ton of things he didn't know about her.

"You are . . . plucky," the vampire said. "It amuses me."

The vampire's face had the coldness of an autumn moon yet Domingo sensed he had passed muster, even if he didn't know the protocols the old creature was so worried about.

"Whatever you say, as long as you help Atl," he replied with the stubbornness that can only be present in one's youth, when a boy doesn't know any better.

"Ah, Atl. Yes. Very well. I can't give you exact coordinates. I can give you another name, though."

The vampire moved to stand by the curtains, ripping a piece of paper from a pile of notebooks and scribbling on it. He motioned for Domingo to come closer. He rose and walked to the vampire's side.

"Elisa Carrera," Bernardino said in a low voice, handing Domingo the scrap of paper.

The vampire pulled away the curtain, revealing a bricked window. He smiled. Domingo could see the tracery of dark veins upon his skin.

"Run along now," the vampire muttered. "We are done. I'm tired."

Domingo moved toward the door. The vampire began to crank the phonograph, stale notes spilling out. The cat meowed.

CHAPTER 10

I t took a while, but Ana found what she was looking for after combing through the police's image database. It was not well organized, which was what caused the delay, but she didn't want to stamp UNSOLVED on this file without at least giving the investigation some minimal effort.

And there it was, under the gang and symbols category: the shark tattoo. It belonged, just as she'd thought, to a group of Necros. Northern narcos. The Godoy family. She'd heard of them. The discovery did not make her happy.

Most countries had taken measures against vampires since the '70s, measures that grew increasingly hostile. Many vampires, a lot of them from Europe, knowing how these things went, simply underwent a mass migration toward the countries that would take them. Countries with corrupt officials who would issue admission papers for vampires who should have been turned back at the airport. Places where citizenship was easy to purchase or sanitation officials were not too stringent if one could cough up the necessary dough. Mexico, corrupt yet stable, free of wars and political upheavals, was a favorite destination, though Brazil and Argentina also enjoyed a steady influx of vampires.

By the time Ana was in high school in the '80s, all ten vampire species were represented in Mexico, in varying degrees. Most numerous were the Necros.

At first, things remained pretty much the same. This stasis was interrupted in the '90s. More vampires arrived or expanded their power base, rivalries grew, alliances evaporated. In Mexicali, the Chinese vampires that had controlled the city and much of Baja California for decades suddenly faced encroaching rivals. In other states near the border, Tlahuelpocmimi clans that had commanded respect by their sheer age—they could trace their roots to Pre-Hispanic Mexico—saw their authority undermined by well-armed bloodsuckers fresh off the airplane.

Ana remembered speaking to an old, toothless Chinese vampire who said that what had really altered the balance of power had not been ease of movement among vampires itself: the Necros changed the game.

"The Necros, they hold nothing sacred. They threaten the tlacoqualli in monequi," the old vampire said, using a phrase the Aztec vampires employed that meant "the middling," a balanced state.

He had a point. Many of the Necros were shunning the old traditions, discarding concepts like sanctuary or sacred ground. It made sense. The European subspecies was adaptable, perhaps even at a biological rather than just a temperamental level. As with all vampires, it was difficult to trace their origins, mostly because vampires were reluctant to discuss anything to do with themselves, but people suspected the Necros had emerged only recently, perhaps in the Late Middle Ages. Perhaps they were an offshoot of the Nachzehrer. Others, however, said such rapid evolution was implausible and the Necros had most likely existed for thousands of years in an isolated corner of Europe before expanding throughout the Old Continent during the fourteenth century.

Whatever their origins, they had sharp teeth, an aversion to sunlight, superhuman agility, a voracious appetite and a desire to exert control over their territory. None of these traits were necessarily unique to their type. No. Their most notable attribute was their capacity to spread a peculiar disease. A human could be infected via sexual contact or by imbibing the vampire's blood. The disease would kill the human, but first it would turn them into mindless slaves. Although several types of vampires could supposedly influence human thoughts, Necros were notorious for their ability to manipulate and use the humans they came in contact with.

Ana had once read about a protozoan called *Toxoplasma* that made infected mice approach cats, the parasite's ultimate host. It seemed to her that humans who came in contact with Necros suffered a similar fate, their minds and bodies slowly disintegrating until they were nothing but empty husks. A slow, ugly death.

At least you died quickly, she thought, looking at the pictures of the butchered teenager. She rubbed her hands together and decided to have a smoke outside. Vampires, and then the Godoy clan, were no small matter. This discovery was best addressed with nicotine in her system.

Ana took the elevator down, walked a block, and bought a coffee at a cafetería that offered a cheap brew rather than fancy caramel mocha bullshit and ambient music, then sat to have a smoke in a corner. Ana patted her pockets, trying to find her matches. She suddenly remembered that she'd tossed them out. She was trying to quit, though it never took.

"Need a light?"

Ana glanced at the woman sitting at the table next to her. She was wearing a red overcoat and equally red lipstick, her hair pulled back in a ponytail. The woman extended her arm and handed her a heavy black lighter. Ana lit her cigarette, took a puff, and handed the lighter back.

"Thanks," she said.

"You're welcome."

Ana looked down, noticing that the woman was also wearing red high heels.

"I'm Kika," said the woman.

"Hi."

"You're Ana Aguirre."

Ana turned to look at her, frowning. The woman smiled and shifted in her seat, leaning back and taking out a cigarette of her own. Ana stood up.

"Don't get twitchy. Finish your coffee. I'm not here to shoot you," the woman said with a dismissive gesture.

Ana sat down slowly, her eyes fixed upon Kika.

"How do you know me?" Ana asked.

"I've been told you're investigating the death of a girl."

Ana looked to the left, toward the barista, who was checking his cell phone. She could hear the sharp sounds of each notification he received. *Ping. Ping. Ping.*

Still looking at the barista, she replied. "Yeah, what's it to you?"

"They're saying it looks like a vampire did it."

"So?" Ana said with a shrug.

Kika mimicked her, replying with a shrug of her own. "I don't like vampires."

Ana's voice lacked any emotion, it was colorless. "Who does?"

"My dislike of vampires is precisely why I'm here."

"Oh?"

Kika changed seats, pulling a chair and joining Ana at her table. Gang member, very likely, even if she seemed to dabble in unorthodox outfits. Not that Ana wanted that to be the case, but the way this conversation was going there were few other options to consider, though movie extra from a remake of *Gilda* might fit the bill. She had the femme fatale aura down pat.

"Vampires in Mexico City are bad for business."

"Whose business?" Ana asked.

"Several people," Kika replied, looking at her manicured nails. Surprise, they were painted red.

"Vampires sometimes come here," Ana replied.

"Not downtown they don't."

True enough. Maybe they ate people living at the edges of the city, in the more distant quarters. Those were odd excursions, the work of reckless, young creatures. They didn't venture into the heart of the metropolis.

"No, not usually."

"Have you identified the vampire who is on the loose?" Kika asked.

"Not yet," Ana said.

"It's Nick Godoy. He's come down from the border zone. Some major shit went down over there and he's chased a girl here."

"What makes you so sure this Nick Godoy did this?" Ana asked.

"He's got more balls than brains. He told everyone in Guadalajara who'd listen to him that he was going to catch up with a Tlāhuihpochtli in Mexico City. And a little birdie who was listening told us about him. Now there's a dead girl and it looks like a vampire killed her. Can you add one plus one? It's him. If he's here, she's here too."

"Case cracked, then," Ana said. "That still doesn't tell me who you are. Or why you care about a random dead kid."

"It doesn't matter."

"You're with Deep Crimson," Ana said, finally voicing her thoughts. It wasn't like keeping quiet was going to make the woman go away. Might as well call a spade a spade.

Kika smiled brightly, her silver bangles clicking together as she tapped her cigarette against the edge of the ashtray. Deep Crimson, then, one of the five big human gangs who resided in Mexico City. Crime. It drenched the country. Mexico ran red. But Mexico City was spared the worst of it. Mexico City was squarely under human control, and here the gangs, the criminals, the pimps, they were people, not flesh-eating monsters. Heads didn't roll in Mexico City, because Deep Crimson, the Tritons, the Maximiles, hell, even the Exorcists and Apando, patrolled the metropolis as much as the cops did. Back in '92, some vampires had tried to make inroads into Mexico City. The result? Fifteen vampires burned to a crisp, their bound corpses a graphic reminder of what awaited any bloodsucker who wandered into this area.

But that didn't make the human gangs buddies with cops.

"Yeah, I am. I've got friends who want to talk to you."

"Fuck a meeting," Ana said. "Piss off before I smash this mug against your face and ruin your makeup, all right?"

The woman did not seem intimidated. "We want Nick and Atl," she said.

Ana was going to keep true to her promise to smash that coffee mug, but the words caught her interest, making her reconsider.

"Slow down two seconds. Who's Atl?"

Kika took out a tablet and slid it across the table. Ana looked through several photos of a young woman. She stood with a Doberman in one photo, alone, and with a group of older women in another.

"She's a Tlāhuihpochtli. The Godoys and her family are engaged in an all-out war. Rival factions."

"And?"

"When vampires are busy killing themselves in other parts of the country, it's a cause for celebration. When they start killing humans in our streets, it's a problem. If you give these parasites one centimeter, they'll take a whole kilometer. Vampires heading into Mexico City like they own the place? That's bad. That's very bad. It's *disrespectful*."

"I've got the case under control," Ana said, wrapping both hands around her cup of coffee.

"You got shit and you know it," Kika replied. "What are you going to do when you find Nick Godoy? Arrest him and bring him over to police headquarters?"

Ana sighed and touched the bridge of her nose. "That's the procedure."

"We are willing to offer you support."

"If you want to cooperate with the investigation," Ana said, "you can give me whatever information you want and I'll take it from there."

"I'll give you what we've got, but what we want is them. Nick and Atl, and any other asshole from up North who came with them to Mexico City."

"So you can kill them."

"That would be for the best, don't you think?" Kika asked.

"I'm a detective," Ana said, though she couldn't muster any conviction when she spoke.

Kika raised the corners of her lips in amusement. "You can't catch them alone. You'll die if you try. And I sincerely doubt your department is going to send backup."

Ana knew it was true. She had been going through the motions with this case, but she was sure that when push came to shove Castillo wasn't going to give one shit about a vampire who killed nobodies. And if she told him this was part of something bigger, that there were members of two cartels in town, he'd assign it to someone else. Someone else who could claim the glory.

She was screwed, either way. As usual.

"I heard you're a good investigator," Kika said. "But you don't have much to show for it, do you?"

"Who does?"

"You *could* have something to show for it. A couple of vampire corpses for your buddies and maybe even a bit of money."

Ana shook her head, putting out her cigarette. "You mean help out a nice gang like yours?"

"I mean we could assist you and you could assist us. We can probably find these leeches, eventually, but we could use professional help and police resources."

"I thought you had friends in my department. Don't they have better resources?"

"Everyone has a big mouth in your department. But *you* caught several vampires. Even an Imago. It sounds exciting."

Ana raised her cup of coffee to her lips, her hands surprisingly steady as she took a long sip. God, she didn't want to think about it. When she'd killed it, the flesh had melted off its bones and she'd seen its true face. Dear God.

"I killed one of those," Ana said. "But it was a long time ago."

It was practically an accident, she thought. *A fluke. Maybe it wanted to die.*

"I came to Mexico City to get away from vampires," Ana said.

"Exactly. You want them out there, eating more people? First it'll be these two. Next, who knows? Four? Six? A dozen? Thinking they can just walk in, like this is their damn home?"

"Catch them by yourself, then," Ana said, pulling back her chair and standing up.

She took a step before Kika grabbed her wrist.

"My friends want someone who knows what she's dealing with. We've never seen a Tlāhuihpochtli," she said, and for the first time the young woman's face grew stony.

Well, of course not. They were not the most common vampires, especially these days. Humans had the upper hand in terms of numbers, but you could easily find the Necros and Nachzehrers hanging around, partially because disease had decimated a good percentage of the Pre-Hispanic vampire population a few centuries before. There was also the fact that both the Necros and Nachzehrers could reproduce with more ease than other breeds. While a Tlāhuihpochtli might give birth to one or two children during its entire life span, and this life span could be centuries, the Necros could reproduce every few decades, meaning they could potentially have four or even five children. It made a very real difference once you added them up.

"I'm no Van Helsing," Ana said, pulling away.

"You haven't even heard the monetary offer," Kika said, her voice chipper once again, her face relaxed. "Look, why don't you sleep on it? Come on over and pay us a visit. My friends are very rich and they really want to meet you. Let us help you. And . . . let me hold on to these."

Kika grabbed the tablet she had allowed Ana to look at and pulled it away, out of Ana's reach. The woman then took out a pen and scribbled a phone number on a napkin, depositing it on the table, right by Ana's hand.

Ana did not speak. She grabbed the napkin and stuffed it in her pocket.

CHAPTER 11

Rodrigo had a dog that used to piss on his furniture. He tried to train it, he put newspapers down on the kitchen floor, but it would just piss on the couch anyway. Rodrigo was certain the dog knew where to piss, but liked to do it on the couch to vex him.

It was the same with the boy. Nick probably knew better; he just decided to monumentally ignore Rodrigo. Puberty. It turns vampires and humans into major assholes. Though, to be fair, Nick had been an asshole long before he was a teenager. Now, in his twenties, Nick fancied himself a fucking rock star, with his sunglasses and his light brown hair dyed a platinum blond and about a dozen chips too many on his shoulder. Maybe if his father had reined him in . . . but no, for all his smarts Mr. Godoy tended to be far too lenient with his precious boy.

Rodrigo opened the door without knocking. Nick was sprawled on the large bed, bits of chips on the sheets. Candy wrappers littered the floor. Two empty one-liter soda bottles lay in a corner. When Rodrigo took a step forward, he felt the sole of his shoe stick to a piece of bubble gum.

Rodrigo crossed the room and flung the curtains aside, daylight darting in. At first Nick slept peacefully, no change reflected on his features. Suddenly, he twitched. Nick opened his eyes and jumped up, shrieking.

"Close the curtains!"

Photophobia. You had to love it. Sunlight didn't turn vampires like Nick into ash. Short-term exposure was more of a nuisance than a real danger, but it could, at the very least, cause blisters. Long-term exposure might give them third-degree burns, which, while not fatal, healed slowly. Hurting them, frankly, was more fun than having them crumble into ash.

Rodrigo closed the curtains. Nick had tumbled onto the floor and pushed himself against the wall, his eyes wide and spit trailing down his chin.

"Good morning," Rodrigo said nonchalantly.

"What the hell do you think you're doing?!"

"I'm just seeing if you want breakfast. Feeling a bit peckish?"

Nick did not reply; his eyes had narrowed into two dark slits. A red, ugly rash was starting to bloom on his cheeks from his brief exposure to the sun. Good. Rodrigo hoped he developed a few nasty blisters.

"Probably not, seeing as you've already eaten," Rodrigo said, squatting down, forearms resting on his knees. He looked straight at the vampire.

"I don't know what you are talking about."

"This," Rodrigo said, taking out his cell phone and pressing it against the kid's face.

Nick frowned as he looked at the screen and began scrolling through the story. Rodrigo stood up, let him read for a couple of minutes, then spoke.

"Girl dead, found beyond nightclub alley. Throat torn out," Rodrigo said.

"Who cares?" Nick spat back.

"Vampire bites! The cops will be searching for you."

Nick rose, his movements those of a spider, a tad jerky from the exposure to sunlight. A tad uncertain. But his voice was assertive. "They won't find me."

"Because you cover your tracks so well? Might as well have carved your name onto the bitch's chest."

Rodrigo snatched the phone back and stuffed it in his suit jacket's pocket. Nick didn't look the least bit guilty about his actions. Not that he expected anything else from such a pampered bloodsucker.

"Do you want to go back home in pieces?" Rodrigo asked.

"We could be back home now if you knew what you were doing," the boy said dismissively.

Rodrigo glanced at his shoes. They'd been polished recently and he could practically see his own reflection, though the image was distorted, distended, just like he felt in that instant.

"I know what I'm doing. It's trying not to attract attention. Trying to catch a vampire with no one else knowing and without the authorities figuring out I'm with another damn vampire," he said, looking back up at the kid.

"Mexico City is like any other city. The authorities can be bought," Nick replied.

"Sometimes. And sometimes, when the vampire is the son of a narco like your dad, the authorities just want to fry you in hot oil. We are behind enemy lines, idiot."

"Don't you call me that," the boy said.

He noticed that Nick's fangs were showing and that his pupils were dilating. He was ready to attack. Rodrigo had his gun and more than twenty years of experience with bloodsuckers, but vampire bites still hurt.

"If you're thinking of biting me, you better make sure I'm good and dead. Otherwise you are going to be in a lot of trouble."

"You're an old man, Rodrigo. I don't think there's much you could do if I took a chunk out of you."

"Let's see you try," he said. It was best to push against the brat. Vampires delighted in weakness, sniffing out the lame lamb.

Nick growled, but Rodrigo could see that his impulse to attack was evaporating. The kid was stupid but not *that* stupid. Rodrigo hadn't spent so many years in the employment of a vampire by being gentle. Goons working for vampires are not sweet and loving. Mind you, Rodrigo didn't like getting his hands dirty, never had, but when push came to shove he wasn't above cutting an asshole's head with a machete.

The kid knew this, and if he'd forgotten he was suddenly reminded of it.

"Fuck you," Nick muttered. The boy sat down on his bed and began rummaging by it, probably looking for candy. "What have you done so far, anyway? You don't know where she is."

"I don't have Atl's coordinates *yet*." Rodrigo stressed this last word, feeling the point needed to be underlined. "She's sneaky. But I do have a team of people assembled. They'll be able to bring her in once we find her."

"I still say we don't need no stupid team. We should be able to nab a girl."

"We made that mistake before, didn't we?"

He smiled, recalling the look on Nick's face when the "girl" landed a good kick on him. Nick was young and he healed fast, but there was no denying Atl had inflicted a nice amount of damage on this cocky boy. Atl was not as strong as Nick, but what she lacked in brute force she seemed to make up for in agility.

Rodrigo pushed away a bottle of soda with the tip of his shoe and walked around the bed, toward the door. "No matter. We should be able to catch her and kill her quickly enough, if you don't fuck it up by eating random girls."

"Whatever," Nick said, stuffing a chocolate bar in his mouth.

Rodrigo took out a cigarette and lit it, feeling the weight of it upon his fingers. He smoked and did not say anything for a couple of minutes, letting his silence settle upon the room. Nick looked at him, waiting. Rodrigo removed the cigarette from his mouth. A red-hot poker is always cooler than a white-hot poker. When Rodrigo spoke he did not allow the rough anger that had invaded him minutes before to color his voice, instead branding each sentence with a white-hot anger that burned even deeper.

"Your father thinks you are ready for this. I disagree. Nevertheless, he's entrusted you to a task. But he's also entrusted you to me. From now on,

I will have total obedience or you will find yourself with more than a sun-rash around your mouth. Go back to sleep."

Nick stared at him and bowed his head, a snake momentarily tamed.

Rodrigo slammed the door shut and stood there, savoring his cigarette.

CHAPTER 12

When Domingo returned she had not woken up yet. Her dog was sitting in front of the closet. It raised its head and growled at him.

"Easy, Cualli," he said. "I just need to—"

But the dog wouldn't have any of it. It growled again. It was a mighty big dog, and Domingo didn't want to end up with a chunk of his leg torn off. He sat at the edge of the bed for about half an hour, trying to muster the courage to knock on the closet door, before giving up and retreating to the kitchen. He set the kettle to boil, made himself tea, and went back to sit in the living room. He was tired and dozed off after a while. He had a dream that he was running. He reached a chain-link fence topped with razor wire, climbed it—or leapt up, he wasn't sure—his hands holding on to the wire. The long barbs dug into his skin, blood trickling down his palms. The pain, however, did not seem to matter.

He opened his eyes and it was night. Atl was standing on the other side of the room, staring at him. Domingo stood up and palmed around for the light switch.

"How long have you been back?" she asked. He couldn't see her proper, she was draped in shadows.

"A while. I didn't know if I should try and wake you. Your dog, it growled at me."

"Did you speak to him?"

"Yeah. I can't find the light—"

She walked over, effortlessly touching the switch. She wore the black jacket and jeans, not black, but a dark shade of gray. Monochromatic, like the panels of graphic novels. His yellow jacket provided the one note of color to the room.

Domingo squinted, his eyes adjusting to the brightness, and began searching his clothes. He took out the piece of paper the vampire had handed him and held it up. She took it.

"This is all he gave you?"

"That's all."

Atl frowned. Her disappointment was easy to read and Domingo found himself wincing, quickly trying to make things better.

"I can go back," he offered.

"No, it should do. It should lead somewhere," she muttered.

"Do you want tea? I made some for myself. I can make you a cup."

"No."

Her dog padded into the room and Atl bent down to scratch its ear, the Doberman staring at Domingo with its small black eyes.

"Atl, who are you running away from?"

The way she looked at him, the way she lifted her chin and her eyes narrowed, told him real quick that he shouldn't have asked.

"Why do you think I'm running?"

"I just know. It's a—I dunno."

He thought he ought to mention the dream, but he kept quiet for now. It might only make it worse. She already looked half-spooked.

"I'm not going to tell no one," he said quietly.

Atl stood up and pushed her hair back behind her ears with both hands. She shook her head. She seemed . . . kinda offended. He thought she wasn't going to tell him anything and then she leaned back against the wall, arms crossed.

"I'm trying to get away from some drug dealers."

"Can't you call the police?" he asked, sliding his hands in his pockets. He had a pack of bubble gum somewhere.

She laughed. For all her talk of being his elder and apparently so much more mature, it was girlish laughter.

"What do you think they'll do first? Throw me in a cage because I'm a vampire or because I'm a narco?"

"Like, what, *you* sell those synthetic pills and shit?"

He thought of the parties he'd attended and the stuff that was up for grabs there. Not much, to be honest. Street kids were more likely to be sniffing glue, paint thinner, and rubber cement than doing blow. But once in a while, he would go to a rave in a rugged warehouse. There, the upper-middle-class kids who spray-painted themselves with glow-in-the-dark paint mixed with the street kids and the poor from the lost cities—the poorest of the poor neighborhoods, where people lived in shacks made of tin and whatever they could find. There, too, sometimes you'd find a rich kid from high up the slopes of Santa Fe. And there Domingo had met guys and girls passing pills with funky names. Crimson Dreams. The Snail. Four Times Three. He'd tried one and didn't like it. It had dulled him too much and had made his head spongy. Domingo didn't have much more than his wits, so in his view, he couldn't be messing with them. Even if he thought he could, he didn't have the cash for it.

Try as he might, though, he just couldn't picture Atl at a rave, carrying a plastic baggie full of pills, selling them and counting the money before putting it in the change purse at her waist. It seemed way too . . . ordinary for her.

"*I* don't sell anything."

"I don't get it."

"My family is in the drug trade. They run—well, they ran—a tidy operation for years and years up North, supplying drugs for the vampire and human markets. Very lucrative. Then a few years back other groups started moving into our area. It's gotten . . . rough."

He remembered the headlines flashing in the newspapers, the ticker going round the screens in the subway. Narco vampires were always killing each other up North. That's all you heard about them. Rough. Sure.

"Anyway, we've been having problems with this one guy. Godoy. One of those new Euro vampire lords who have been messing with our operations and stirring the pot. My mother thought she had it under control . . . and then they killed her."

"Jesus. So you ran off?"

"My sister said I should be ready. I looked through the window. . . ."

Atl's voice trailed off. She looked down at her hands, as if she were concentrating, inspecting them very carefully. Suddenly she snapped her head back up and stared at him.

"They killed my sister, my family. That's when I ran. Now they're going to make an example out of me."

"I'm sorry," he said. "Won't the cops arrest them, anyway?"

"You don't get it."

Atl unzipped her jacket and tossed it on the floor. Then she turned her back toward him and lifted her shirt. She had a tattoo between her shoulder blades. It looked like a bird with a long beak, stylized and odd. Sort of like the pictures he'd seen in his history book when they talked about the Aztecs. Like the picture from one of them codices.

"What is it?" he asked.

"My family's crest. The hummingbird. We're not a small-time gang. I'm not a small-time thug. The police won't do shit. Well, except maybe kill me or jail me. Or jail me, then kill me."

Domingo extended his left hand, reaching toward, but not touching, the intricate drawing. Atl tugged her T-shirt down and threw him an irritated look. He pulled his hand back.

"I need to find a place with an internet connection," she said.

"I know a café where they don't ask for ID," he said. "That's . . . umm . . . that's what you want, right?"

Atl scooped up her jacket from the floor and nodded.

* * *

He took her to the café near the basilica. The person at the door waved them in, taking their money without bothering to check their papers. Even if someone had said something, Domingo knew it would take no more than a few words to convince the employees to let them use a computer.

"That was easy," Atl said as they navigated a narrow hallway, looking for an empty booth. "I thought you needed an ID for everything."

"It's no big deal. There's this talk about how biometric IDs are super necessary and cops can stop you to look at your papers for no reason, but it's not a problem. Most of the time no one asks me for papers. I know the places where they never even bother thinking about asking, anyway."

"Why don't they?"

"'Cause I'm not important," he said with a shrug. "If I was a superhero my power would be invisibility."

"What about sanitation?"

"Sanitation is looking for Cronengs. They don't care about me."

Domingo didn't even know why they bothered harassing the Cronengs. It's not like they were going to get proper medical treatment; all they did was ship them to that old convent in Coyoacán they had turned into a crappy sanatorium, and if that was full they were off to Iztapalapa. The Cronengs died quick, anyway. They shuffled around the city, with their sores and their tired faces, begging for coins, and nobody really gave a shit as long as they weren't loitering in the nice areas.

"They do care about vampires," Atl said.

He found a booth and opened the door. It was narrow and it smelled of cheap air freshener, but they squeezed in. Atl pulled out the keyboard and began typing.

"What are you looking for?" he asked.

"The telephone directory. Shit."

"What?"

"There's like a hundred Elisa Carreras."

Atl brushed away the screen. She began typing again.

"That's better," she muttered. "There's only one Elisa Carrera who does translation work."

Domingo leaned down next to her, mouthing the address.

"How'd you know she's a translator?" he asked.

"Verónica Montealban was a translator."

The monitor flickered, cheap thing that it was. Atl gave it a whack with the palm of her hand and the image steadied itself.

"You think she changed her name?"

"Yes. You have a pen?"

Domingo looked in his many pockets and handed her a pencil and a scrap of paper. Atl noted the address on-screen, then flicked the terminal off. She pushed away the keyboard and opened the door, motioning for Domingo to follow her. She walked ahead of him. They were about to reach the exit when someone tapped him on the shoulder. Domingo turned around.

"What's up, man?" Quinto asked. "You missed my party."

He was an okay dude, Quinto. A few years older than Domingo, but still cool. He even had a cool haircut, tapered sides and longer at the top, and wore a neat gold earring.

"Hey. Yeah, I know," Domingo said. "I was short on cash. And I've been busy."

"Too bad. Belén was there."

Which meant the Jackal had been there. Which in turn meant it was probably a good thing he had missed the whole thing, since the Jackal had it in for him. Nevertheless, it might have been nice to see Belén.

Eh. He wasn't sure.

"Domingo."

Domingo turned around. Atl was standing near the exit, in the shadows. She stepped forward with that liquid way of moving she possessed, terribly elegant, her face coming into the light.

"I'm leaving," she said, hands in her pockets.

"This is my friend Quinto," Domingo said. "This is . . . um . . . my cousin."

"Hey," Quinto said, smiling broadly, showing his teeth. "How you doing? Quinto Navarro. And you are?"

"His cousin," Atl replied, her face serious.

Quinto chuckled. "You're funny! I dig that. Totally dig that."

Quinto grinned at her. Domingo recognized that smile. Quinto never missed an opportunity to pick up girls. He worked at a pharmacy and could easily score a variety of pills, which meant he was popular around his neighborhood. He'd also gone to veterinary school for two years and operated on the Jackal's dogs when they got injured, which gave an extra luster. The Jackal made most of his money by collecting "fees" from the street kids who washed windows at certain intersections. You worked for him and you paid your dues. If you didn't pay your fee, the Jackal would beat you to a bloody pulp—and since he was a big gorilla of a guy, often with three or four gorillas on the side, it could get real bloody. So you paid. But the Jackal, priding himself on his business sense and his ability to diversify, had happily expanded into the world of dog fighting, 'cause he was such a big fan of that crap.

"You've got some eyes," Quinto told Atl, and Domingo felt as though he were slowly blending into the shadows, disappearing as Quinto focused utterly and completely on Atl.

"Why, thanks," she said, but her voice was indifferent.

Atl leaned against the wall and Quinto leaned a bit toward her. He was trying to look suave, making eyes at her, the stuff that worked with the girls they knew. Domingo had asked Quinto how he did it and Quinto had told him it was natural charm, at which point Domingo gave up on the idea of hotties pining for him.

Atl shifted away, her expression turning from cool to flat-out frosty.

"Domingo, are we heading out?" she asked.

"Yeah," Domingo said.

"Just let me borrow him for two seconds," Quinto said, winking at Atl and pulling Domingo away before he could protest.

"We're in a bit of a hurry," Domingo explained.

"You didn't say you were busy *busy*. Who's the chick? Don't try to give me that bullshit about a cousin. I know she ain't related to you."

"She's a friend, all right?" Domingo said, pulling his hands into his pockets and finding a piece of bubble gum, which he unwrapped.

"She's a babe."

Domingo grumbled a soft sound that was entirely noncommittal and wished Quinto would stop staring at Atl like she was a cut of choice meat. It made him feel very embarrassed. She was going to think humans in Mexico City were members of a race of troglodytes—which was a really fancy way of saying "caveman" that he'd picked up from a graphic novel. Domingo didn't want to be a troglodyte. It just sounded nasty.

"How'd you meet her?"

"Just . . . walking around downtown," Domingo said, popping the gum into his mouth and chewing loudly.

"Well, you should most definitely go to my next party, okay? Bring her along. I'm dying to get into her pants."

"I don't think you're her type," Domingo muttered. "See ya around."

He walked toward Atl and they exited the café together. Outside an organillero was playing his musical instrument, turning a crank and making a metal cylinder spew an old melody.

"Sorry about that," Domingo said. "I wasn't planning on bumping into him."

"He's annoying," Atl said.

Domingo chewed his bubble gum and gave her a sideways glance. "He's all right. Most of the time. He's lent me money when I needed it once, before I moved into the garbage business."

She made a face, as though she'd just stepped on something nasty. He'd never felt ashamed of his work. Things were what they were and that was it. But the look on Atl's face made him feel . . . small.

Domingo found an empty soda can and began kicking it down the street.

"How'd your family get into dealing drugs?" he asked.

"They started in the '40s, cultivating opium. The Americans wanted it and Sinaloans harvested it. Then in the '60s it was pot. Everyone in the hills was harvesting it. It was small stuff, though. It was the '70s when it got real. Cocaine was hot. People were making a lot of money. In the beginning it was mostly humans dealing cocaine, but families like mine got into it. Vampires control the drug trade now. I think the government tried to clean up Sinaloa in the '70s, but then we figured out a way to survive, as we always do."

Atl smirked, brushing a strand of hair behind her ear with her gloved hands.

"Of course, then just a few years later we had these European vampires inching into our territory. Motherfuckers in snakeskin boots and stupid cowboy hats. Guys like Godoy. Fucking Necros. Colonizers! Nothing is ever enough for them, nothing!"

Necros. Big fangs. Pale and skinny. Hair on their palms. They sounded cool, since—if you believed TV and shit—they also tended to have fancy clothes and some type of sports car, which was awesome.

"They're supposed to be hot, no?"

"They're also filthy," Atl said. "They'll make you sick if you come in contact with their blood. If they fuck you, same deal, meet the worst STD ever. You get a literal mind fuck."

"Like, gonorrhea or what?"

"No. They make you do anything they want. Eventually you die, but not until you've done the bidding of a pasty asshole for a good long while. It doesn't work on other vampires, but humans should really stay the hell away from them."

"Oh," Domingo said. That didn't sound so cool. "Well, at least you can't get it. Though what happens if you eat someone who was infected by a Necros?"

"I would reject the blood. It's a very simple rule of thumb: tainted blood, vomit. It's like trying to chug down expired milk."

"Gross."

They were now right behind the old Basilica of Our Lady of Guadalupe, where unauthorized street vendors gathered to offer candles, images of the Virgin, and pieces of tin in the shape of an arm, heart, or foot that were supposed to heal the sick. In December the place was simply impossible to navigate, hundreds of people swarming it to pay their respects to the Virgin. That evening it was not so busy and the vendors would be packing up soon.

"There was some writing on the internet," Domingo said, "something about disease among vampires. It means you get sick, don't you? Sick from stuff other than dirty blood, no?"

"Human diseases can't kill us, but then the Necros aren't human. In the times of the Aztecs, when the first Necros arrived upon our shores, they quickly spread disease among the local vampire populations. Many members of my family died simply due to coming in contact with the Necros, greatly reducing our capacity to fight against the invaders. Germs can be much more effective than swords. And then there is the issue of tainted human blood and the illnesses the European humans carried. What could we eat if the humans were sick and dying too?"

He kicked the can in her direction and she kicked it back.

"The Necros probably ate too many rats in the Middle Ages and that's why they're so filthy," Atl said. "*We* were warriors."

"What kind of warriors?"

"We guarded Huitzilopochtli's temple. It was more of a warrior-priestess kind of deal," Atl said.

"Ain't that, like . . . Aztec?"

"Yes, Aztec," Atl said, laughing. She spread her arms. "Mexico City used to be a city of canals. People would go down in canoes instead of streets and there were great temples downtown. And that's where my people used to live."

"That's cool. Being a warrior. Must be cool."

Domingo kicked the can too hard. It rattled, spinning away from them and under a vendor's table. Atl stared at it.

"Must be," Atl muttered.

She was standing in front of a stand selling T-shirts with the image of the Virgin on them, and the irony wasn't lost on him that this was a vampire, right by the basilica, right by a bunch of rosaries and crucifixes and cheap plastic saints. She looked sad, and he had no idea if it was because of the talk of her people or maybe because vampires don't deal well with Catholicism, but he wanted to make it right.

"Do you want to see my place?" Domingo asked, and he knew it sounded dumb, but he wasn't smooth like Quinto and other guys. He never knew the right words or the right stuff.

Atl didn't answer. She was still staring at the can.

"It's real close. That's the only reason I'm saying. 'Cause it's nearby."

A few stops on the subway and they'd be there, it was really nothing at all. Atl finally raised her head to look at him.

"A quick stop," she said.

Domingo guided her into the tunnel, carefully illuminating the way with his flashlight. It was an easy walk, but you had to watch the bends of the narrow tunnel and sometimes the ceilings dipped and if you didn't hunch down a bit you'd end with a big bump on the forehead. During his first weeks underground, that's exactly what had happened. Now he had mapped the tunnels and he could walk them in complete darkness. Still, it never hurt to flash a bit of light in there, especially with the rats around. And, who knew, maybe a hobo could have snuck in. Domingo was sure no one else knew about these tunnels, but he had learned to be careful.

"What is this place?" Atl asked, and he could tell she was a bit in awe. He congratulated himself on deciding to change the scenery.

"There are a few tunnels around downtown. Someone told me they were used by priests and nuns or guerrilla fighters, I'm not sure."

"When?"

"A long time ago, I dunno," he said. His grasp of these things, like of so many others, was incomplete.

She looked up at the tunnel's ceiling. Water dripped around them, slipping through tiny cracks. It was cold and humid below, but Domingo didn't mind, he peeled layers on or off as necessary.

"How did you find it?" she asked.

"I was looking for a ghost station."

Atl chuckled, her voice echoing around them.

"Not like scary ghosts. Seriously. There are supposed to be abandoned stations down here. There's one that is used by soldiers, like a secret one. And one is near a subterranean lake. I've never found the lake, though."

He jumped over a puddle and turned around to offer Atl his hand, but she needed no assistance and evaded it with the ease of a dancer, landing next to him and giving him a smirk.

"It probably doesn't exist," she said.

"Well, I'm not sure. There are all kinds of weird things beneath the city. I know a guy who said they once found an abandoned bag on one of the trains and there was a human fetus inside. And there are rats. There's this huge rat that hangs around near La Merced. It's bigger than a dog."

"Maybe it's a dog."

"It has yellow glowy eyes."

"Well, then, that's scientific proof," Atl said, sounding amused.

"You sound really skeptical for a vampire."

She smirked once more. "It's probably because I am a vampire."

They reached Domingo's chamber and he hurried in, quickly illuminating the room with several of his lanterns. He had a lot of stuff, but he tried to keep it in order. There was his pile of clothes, a pile of plastic, a pile of old electric parts. Atl drifted toward the wall covered with illustrations from books and magazines. It was random clippings. Pretty girls mixed with funny drawings. Panels of Tarzan hovered next to a postcard of a painted ocean, which was the closest he'd been to a beach.

Atl leaned down to look at the image of the vampire woman in the white dress, and he felt himself blushing, feeling foolish.

"*Dracula's Mistress*," she said, reading the title out loud. "How Gothic."

"I . . . I've read comics about vampires of that sort," he said, rubbing the back of his neck with his left hand. "The ones that turn to mist. Of course, you don't turn to mist."

"No one turns to mist. That's just stuff they tell kids to sell shit."

"It sounds cool," Domingo said. "Plus the whole harem."

Vampires in the stories were hyper rich. They got to live in castles and had lots of servants. They were mesmerizing. And there had to be an element of truth to the stories because Atl did have money and she wasn't nowhere near ugly.

Atl sat down on a plastic chair and leaned back, stretching her legs, her lips curving into a dismissive smile. "A harem?"

"Vampire guys have lots of babes with them. Dracula has three, four, probably more than that. Lavud also has a few. Your vampire men, the ones like you, they must be good with the ladies."

"There's no vampire men like *me*. Men of my subspecies don't shift form, they're weaker, and they live shorter life spans than the women. I guess you could call it a sex-linked disorder."

"Oh. But still, I mean, do you have a guy back home?"

"No," Atl said, picking up a graphic novel and thumbing through it. "No vampire women, either."

Domingo felt better hearing that. For a moment he had been afraid there was a big vampire dude waiting for her, in a cape. Okay, maybe not a cape. A leather jacket. Though he found it hard to believe that vampire men or, you know, women, were not all over her.

"Yeah. I know how it goes. I used to have a girlfriend but that's not the case anymore," he told her because he figured it sounded like the mature thing to say. He was attempting to go for "aloof" and "sophisticated," like they said in the magazines.

Atl stretched her arms up, as if reaching for the ceiling, and yawned, tilting her head. "Hey, just so we are clear: I'm not looking for a boyfriend. Especially not a human one."

"I didn't mean it like that," Domingo stammered.

Though maybe he did mean it a *little* like that.

"Just in case," she said, staring at him.

An uncomfortable silence descended upon them. Just when he thought they had a rhythm to their conversation going. Domingo chewed on his lower lip, racking his brains for something to say. Something to pull Atl back, something that would be interesting.

Domingo wanted to be interesting but he didn't have much to say. He could tell her about the garbage, how the business of being a binner works, how you find stuff and sell it for scrap. It was the only thing he really knew a lot about. That, and comic books. 'Cause his stories, about the ghost station and the big rat, sure as hell didn't seem to interest her.

He wanted to tell her something that didn't make him seem like such a kid. But all the stuff he shared with folks like Quinto were dirty jokes, comments about this or that hot chick from whatever show; useless chatter she'd surely dismiss.

"Have you killed anyone?" he blurted.

"Enough," Atl said, pushing herself up. "Well, I did your tour. I should head back to my apartment."

"Or you could stay here," Domingo said. "You can have my bed."

Technically it was a mattress on the floor, but he thought it counted as a bed. He even had covers that matched, dark green.

"I'm heading to my place."

"Okay," Domingo said. "I just want to grab a few comic books and—"

"Stay here for now."

"What for? I thought you needed my help, my blood."

"And some fucking space to breathe," Atl said, irritated. "Come look for me four hours before sundown, all right?"

He walked her back to the entrance they'd used, which led back to an abandoned building. Atl slipped out without a word or a look at him. He watched her walk away, hands in her pockets.

CHAPTER 13

When she was a kid, Ana had liked watching cowboy movies with her grandma. There was a simplicity about them that appealed to her: good guys win. She always wanted to be a good guy. Or gal. That's why she got into law enforcement. Unfortunately, real life is not like in the movies. All that Hollywood junk where they have super-advanced tech and clean, heroic cops? Not true. Of course, back when she first donned the uniform she thought she was going to magically clean the force from within. Those hopes had been dashed in Zacatecas, but the faint glimmer of heroism still remained.

Mexico City, they had told her, was different. The police force there was being reformed. Before, women could only aspire to be traffic cops or belong to the incredibly sexist Ladies Auxiliary, which was mainly dedicated to visiting public schools and telling kids how fun it was to be a cop. But not the *new* Mexico City police, this was going to be a state-of-the-art, modern force. Women would be required. Especially women like Ana Aguirre, a police officer with solid experience in Zacatecas and a letter of recommendation. *Detective* Aguirre had a nice ring to it. At bare minimum there were no vampires in Mexico City. It was safer, less violent, and with the drug dealers she'd busted Ana hadn't made many friends in the narco world.

It turned out to be a crock of shit. They had printed manuals with gender-appropriate terminology and the like, but detectives still called gay men "faggots," women were "bitches," and if a "lady" was raped the first question to ask was what she'd done to incite the crime. The worst part was that nobody wanted Ana there. Castillo plain detested her. In Zacatecas, Ana had been tolerated, if not fully accepted, because she proved useful. Most of the other police officers had no idea how to deal with vampires, and they didn't want to learn how to. Ana was willing to go into the neighborhoods with a high concentration of vampires, she was willing to question suspects who made her colleagues wet their pants, and she could handle herself if some sick fuck decided he wanted to take a bite out of her.

It had been her grandma who taught her that. The old woman had lived through the Mexican Revolution and even in her old age she was an excellent shot. A country girl, Ana Aguirre's grandmother had been exposed to much folklore and superstition. Some of it concerned vampires, and, it turned out, her stories were accurate. The result was that while other humans around the world had grown insulated from these tales, forgotten most of them, and entrusted themselves to modernity, Ana Aguirre's grandmother had not, and she had been able to lavish her knowledge upon her granddaughter.

But in Mexico City vampire knowledge was not valued. Here she was just an annoying broad, her hair streaked silver as she inched toward fifty, someone to push around rather than respect.

Still. She was trying to do right. When she walked past her desk she tossed her raincoat on her chair and hurried toward Castillo's office, skipping her customary smoke. He waved her in, looking none too happy to see her.

"All right, Aguirre, what do you want today?" he asked.

"That case, the girl attacked by a vampire behind the club," she said, not bothering to sit down. She knew this was going to be a brief conversation.

"Yes, yes. What about it? Luna says it's probably a junkie vampire who went bananas. Didn't we have a couple of those biting an idiot in San Ángel or some place like that?"

Luna? What did Luna know, he couldn't tell his dick from his thumb. A junkie vampire might have been a prime candidate at the outskirts of the city, not smack in the middle of the Condesa. If human junkies were bad, then vampire junkies were three times worse. They just couldn't control themselves. A vampire high on Medusa's Tears or whatever the drug du jour was wouldn't have passed without notice.

"I think it's a narco vampire from the North. Actually, two vampires. Necros versus Tlahuelpocmimi."

"And they're in Mexico City to do what, go walk around the Alameda and get an ice cream?" Castillo asked, leaning back in his chair and knitting his hands together.

"I don't know."

"Well, what do you know?"

"I know there's a vampire called Nick Godoy and he has a tattoo just like the one the kid who was dancing with the dead girl had. If you told Mecía to give me a hand so I'm not at this alone and maybe if forensics actually processed evidence this century, maybe—"

"Aguirre, Mecía is busy. There's more than dead hookers from Santa Julia to deal with, you realize that?"

"What does it matter what colonia she was from?" Ana asked.

But of course Ana already knew the answer. A dead girl from a bad neighborhood who had saved her pennies so she could spend a night out on the town—who maybe was hooking, not just partying, as Castillo said—couldn't get expediency or much attention.

"Aguirre, we both know this junkie is likely long gone from here. Do the paperwork and close it, all right?"

Castillo grabbed his mini-tablet, which was resting atop a pile of file folders, and began swiping his index finger across it, their meeting apparently concluded. Ana paused by the door and looked at him, skinny fucker with his cheap tie and his monumental indifference. She slammed the door shut, which gave her some small satisfaction.

At the Tacuba subway station Ana saw two dozen police officers—called "Robocops" because they were wearing superheavy uniforms, gear more appropriate for an old Schwarzenegger or Stallone flick than anything else—take out their clubs and start beating the living shit out of a bunch of illegal street vendors who were peddling their wares near the stairs. The local city government was cracking down on street vendors and vagoneros, and this in turn meant cracking skulls. Sure, they called it "relocating," but it did not amount to that and the vendors always came back, anyway. She assumed that the Robocops whacking people left and right were there to settle a score or impart a personal lesson, and not on official business, because normally the method they employed to scare off the vendors was throwing tear gas at them.

Ana kept walking. Outside there were more established vendors in stalls occupying most of the sidewalk. Since they didn't have access to proper power outlets and carried no generators, they stole power from the public electric poles. As a result poles at the street corners were tilting precariously to the side, under the weight of a myriad of cables, though they never quite plummeted to the ground.

The competition at Tacuba was fierce, and at night each stall blinked with Christmas lights, lightbulbs, tiny neon signs, the music blaring and voices rising. There were vendors offering nuts and dried fruits, headphones, pencils and pens and markers, bubble gum, oatmeal bars. Illegal DVDs and video games for kids were located next to a stand dedicated to hardcore pornography. It was hard to walk around Tacuba with the swell of people and stalls, but Ana was tall and strong and she imposed herself even without her uniform so that most people wisely moved a bit to the side.

She cut to the left, took a side street, then wandered down an alley until she left the bustle of the street vendors behind and continued down quieter streets. She passed a shop selling piñatas and a barbershop until she reached a small green building, its paint peeling, a large neon pyramid indicating she had reached the Center of the Unified Faith. Mexico was still resolutely Catholic, and most of the faithful in Tacuba worshipped at the old-fashioned Parroquia San Gabriel Arcángel, a great stone building that had once served as a monastery. The Center of the Unified Faith, however, was one of many New Age churches sprouting up around the country. Apocalyptic churches and the cult of the Santisima Muerte drew substantial crowds, but these New Age joints also had their devotees.

Ana considered smoking a cigarette, but again she was missing a lighter. The front door said PUZH TO OPEN, and Ana did with a sigh. The inside of the temple was as unimpressive as the outside. Plastic flowers and strings of lights constituted the main décor, with a large golden tapestry showing a pyramid hanging behind an empty podium. The faithful sat on plastic chairs and bowed their heads, music with a faint, decidedly inauthentic Middle Eastern whiff piping in through a couple of speakers.

There weren't very many people in attendance. Ana followed the instructions, finding a side door and heading up to the second floor. There she was greeted by a couple of surly-looking young men in red jackets who led her down a hallway and to a large room that was wallpapered in gold and red, with an elaborate Persian rug on the floor and billowy red fabric hanging from the ceiling. In a corner, an old fan moaned as it spun its blades, tired and discontent.

An overstuffed couch had been placed in the middle of the room, and a woman, attired in a red velvet robe, lay there, staring at the ceiling. A young man sat on the floor attempting to deseed a pomegranate. Behind the couch stood Kika, incongruous in a cocktail dress and heels. There were others, of course: men standing in a corner, the boys who had escorted her, a fellow pacing by the windows.

"Welcome, Detective Aguirre, it's nice of you to drop by on such short notice. Would you be wanting a drink?" the woman asked.

"I won't be staying long," Ana replied.

The woman shifted on her couch and sat up, glancing at Ana. She looked maybe close to sixty but Ana knew she was younger than her. Valentina Saade had headed Deep Crimson for nearly twenty years. She had been the girlfriend of the previous bastard who ran the criminal organization, back when it wasn't really that much of anything. One day she must have been tired of being someone's personal punching bag and she cut off his dick. She'd been running Deep Crimson since then, possibly because nobody wants to mess with a lady who is willing to slice off your dick with a rusty knife and possibly because she had a great deal of common sense. It was probably a bit of both.

"But you must at least have a drink." Valentina snapped her fingers and motioned to the young man at her feet. "Get a couple of glasses and the red."

"No, really—"

"Calm down, darling, you're not on duty."

Valentina smiled, showing Ana a gold tooth.

"Funny front you've got yourself here," Ana said, glancing at a large glass pyramid that sat by an open window, next to a couple of potted plants.

"I have many spiritual concerns. Everybody does. I'm sure you've noticed the state of the world. All the diseases afflicting us: drug-resistant strains of gonorrhea and tuberculosis, that horrible Croneng's disease, increasing cases of sterility, rampant violence in the streets."

"Yeah, a pity."

"I find refuge in my faith, in this holy abode. Except recently I've felt my sanctuary might be violated: vampires, Detective Aguirre. Vampires in our midst. It is an affront. The Condesa is mine."

Tacuba, Condesa, Popotla, Verónica Anzúres. Deep Crimson territory, the lot of them. With vampires controlling drugs outside the metropolis, someone had to provide the goods inside the city. Deep Crimson dealt in a lot of marijuana courtesy of fine hydroponics systems, but the big-ticket items were the synthetic drugs. A lot of their income also derived from robberies, kidnappings, and run-of-the-mill extortion. Smaller, subway gangs, composed of teenagers, generally affixed themselves under the patronage of these larger criminal groups, though there were those with entrepreneurial spirit going at it solo.

"As I told your friend here," Ana said, fixing her eyes on Kika, "I would be happy to look at whatever information you may have that might help me solve my case."

"Come now, you don't have a case. You didn't have one yesterday and you won't have one tomorrow, not without us. We need to work together."

The young man had returned with two glasses for Valentina and Ana. Ana shook her head, rejecting the drink. Valentina had no such qualms; she gingerly grabbed the glass and drank deeply. The young man settled by her feet once more.

"I'm a cop," Ana told her.

"And a good one. Kika is impressed with your record in Zacatecas."

"Eight dead vampires," Kika said, smiling at Ana.

"I didn't go around hunting vampires. Those vampires died because they didn't know the meaning of the words 'handcuffs' and 'arrest.'"

Ana had always prided herself in being more John Wayne than Clint Eastwood. She didn't love shooting random people, giddy to star in her very own spaghetti Western. Some bastards did. They became cops because they could give free rein to their desire to shoot strangers, but Ana's grandmother had been very clear: you don't waste your bullets needlessly.

"The point is that they died, Detective. That's exactly what I want: dead vampires. Kika must have communicated this point. We have resources. We have weapons."

Valentina motioned to Kika.

"We could offer some form of compensation for your trouble," Kika said, casually walking around the couch and handing Ana a small card.

Ana grabbed it and stared at the numbers. The word "bonus" was underlined. Christ.

"You don't even have to kill them. You can be a consultant," Kika said. "Easiest cash you ever made."

Both women smiled at her. The boy at Valentina's feet continued working on the pomegranate. Ana looked away, her gaze fixing on the wallpaper with its pattern of fruits and vines.

"We both want the same thing, Detective. We want safer streets," Valentina said. "Mexico City is an oasis."

"You are suggesting I help you murder two people."

"Two criminals. Kika, do you have the information?"

The younger woman grabbed a tablet and presented it to Ana. A photo of a corpse. Ana slid through them. Corpses and more corpses. Several were charred, unrecognizable. A woman. Blood splatters and viscera.

"What am I looking at?" Ana asked.

"The future," Valentina said. "They did this."

"The Godoy boy and the Iztac girl did this?"

"Godoy killed Atl Iztac's mother. Her clan retaliated. These are the results. You've seen the girl that vampire killed behind the nightclub. That is the beginning. How many more corpses do you want to drag to your morgue?"

Ana looked down at the screen again. Under the pressure of her fingers a portion of the photo she was looking at seemed to distort. Her mouth felt dry.

"How about that drink now, Detective?"

Valentina was toying with the stem of her glass while Kika had taken out a cigarette and was blowing out smoke rings. She wondered how this girl had gotten involved with Deep Crimson; she looked a bit too bubble gum to Ana, like a kid playing gangster.

Then she thought of Marisol and frowned.

Ana wanted a better life for the both of them. She certainly wanted those two vampire narcos off the streets. She was not interested in more random murders. Deep Crimson members were no saints, but who was she kidding, it wasn't like the cops were any better. Castillo didn't give a shit.

Fuck it.

"'Consultant' is the right word," Ana said, speaking quickly. "I'm not bringing those two in for you. I'll watch, you provide the muscle. And I need half up front, tonight."

"Give me the account number and I can initiate the transferal," Valentina said. "Or would you rather have a plain, old-fashioned suitcase?"

"A bank transfer is fine. From a discreet account, I hope."

"Wouldn't dream of it any other way. Kika, darling," Valentina said, raising a hand and making a languid motion.

The young woman smiled and took the tablet from Ana's hands, fiddling with the screen and presenting it back to her. Ana entered the necessary numbers. Then the young woman pressed a button. Just like that it was done. Ana had never wanted a smoke more badly in her life, yet at the same time she felt almost relieved.

"Weapons, you've considered that?" Ana asked.

"Whatever you need," Valentina said.

"You can't kill a vampire with bullets. Your best bet is a cattle prod," Ana said.

"That works?" Kika asked, sounding interested.

"It stuns them, sure. Vampires are stronger and more agile than us, but they are wildly susceptible to certain stimuli. A number of chemicals induce something akin to anaphylactic shock. Some get it from coming in contact with stuff as innocent as garlic. This girl's type, it's silver nitrate. I'm sure you can get darts with it. We had them in Zacatecas."

"And the boy?"

"I'm not sure there's anything that can truly knock a Necros off his feet hard, except sunlight. You can smoke him a bit with UV light, but it won't kill him. Silver blades will screw him. Bullets can also pound some damage into him, but you shouldn't believe the lies they spew on the internet. A gunshot, blessed bullet or not, will not kill a vampire by itself."

"You know your stuff."

Ana thought about her years spent trying to keep order in Zacatecas, and the numerous vampires she'd encountered. Yeah, she knew her stuff. She had a morbid fascination with the bloodsuckers, to be sure.

"Don't make the mistake of asking for actual silver bullets," Ana added. "Lead, coated with silver, will do. Pure silver is terrible, the bullets are less accurate. And if you can't get silver-coated bullets don't worry about it too much. The darts are the thing to aim for."

"We'll need a few days," Valentina said.

"Good. I'll look for your vampires in the meantime," Ana replied.

"We should have a toast, to—"

"Some other time, thanks," Ana replied.

She walked down the stairs without bidding Valentina a formal good-bye. When she reached the street she paused by the building's main door, listening to the buzzing of the neon sign. The clatter of heels alerted her to Kika's presence before she turned her head.

"Why the hurry, Detective?" the woman asked, sliding next to her.

"I've got work to do, don't I?"

"Then you'll need this."

Kika handed her a large envelope. Ana opened it and saw that there were photos inside. Pictures of Atl and Nick. Also copies of the images she had looked at on the tablet, the parade of corpses.

"If we have anything else we'll let you know," Kika said. "Right now that's it, just pretty pictures and a bit of background on them both."

"Thanks."

"I can call a car for you. It's going to rain."

She could hear the faint, ugly music from inside the temple, seeping out into the street. Ana shook her head.

"I'll take my chances," she replied.

CHAPTER 14

Cualli was at the door, waiting for her. She rubbed the dog's head and tossed food in his bowl before stepping into the shower.

Atl looked at the bathroom tiles with disgust. There were traces of dark mildew between them. She supposed she shouldn't complain. The building had running water, after all. Nonetheless, it was one more thing to despise about this damn city.

She stood for a long time under the hot water spray. It reminded her a bit of the sweat lodge, of home, and this made her lips curl into a smile.

Atl toweled her hair, rubbed her palm against the mirror's surface. Nobody could accuse Mexican vampires of being pale, but there were other common signs identifying them. The redness of the eyes was the most noticeable. It crept up slowly, from lack of nourishment. A redness at first, and then their eyes grew more bloodshot until they were completely red. Mouse eyes. Mickey eyes, as they joked.

It was far from that right now. But the dark circles had returned. She moved her head slowly, trying to figure out if she seemed too thin. But no. It was okay.

She needed to feed more often. Vampires couldn't live off nibbles. But if she got too greedy she'd drain Domingo dry and then her blood supply would vanish. She wasn't a fucking Necros who couldn't control her appetite. It was just . . . she was used to overindulgence.

She thought of Domingo's goofy smile and his dark hair over his eyes, his bony body and long limbs. That silly question about a boyfriend . . .

It was laughable—almost painful—to see Domingo trip over himself trying to please her. God, he was so damn . . . sappy. If she put a gun in his hand, he'd probably go right ahead and kill someone for her. Which is exactly what she needed. Still, it made Atl shake her head. It made her want to yell at him, demand that he get a clue. He was too naïve, a trait she did not much appreciate, though she must admit there was a certain charm to his lack of guile.

Plus, he's not bad looking, she thought.

Her sister would have laughed if she'd heard that. Izel said humans were the equivalent of Neanderthals compared to their own kind.

It would be like Miranda bedding Caliban, she mused, and immediately regretted the thought. Some Necros slept with humans, but it was not a polite thing to do. The equivalent of the country bumpkin, who, lacking taste, chews with his mouth open and loudly yells to the server.

Atl fixed herself a cup of tea and sat in the kitchen, sucking on sugar cubes. She was lonely. She didn't want a boyfriend, just as she'd told him, because that sounded stupid and she'd never had one before. When she slept with someone it was quick and easy and she didn't need them hanging around her afterwards. Besides, any long-term interest would be seen as favoritism, as a way to fight for power within the clan. She didn't give people that chance. Yet Atl was used to belonging to something, to that large clan. She was never by herself. There was a gaping hole inside of her and she wished to dearly clutch something, someone, close. Even if it was a human. As long as the someone was kind and would make her forget. Domingo would be kind, she thought. Kind and soft and the world was too damn hard.

She imagined Izel whispering in her ear. *Got a crush, have you? It would be one step above fucking sheep, that's for sure.*

Really, she thought, rolling her eyes. *You die and you're still giving me advice in my head.*

'Cause you need it.

What she needed was sleep. A bit more and she was going to start hallucinating that Izel was sitting next to her. Uncomfortable conversations with your deceased relatives should be saved for the Day of the Dead or a night of binge drinking.

Atl felt cold, another side effect of the lack of blood. She headed to the bedroom, put on her jacket, and grabbed the blanket from the floor. She slipped into the closet, curling on the floor and wrapping herself in the blanket. Domingo's watch lay in a corner. Its soft tick was pleasant. She counted in her head as the little hand went around.

The knock on the closet door woke her up. She slid the door open and glanced at Domingo, who gave her a nervous smile in the darkness of the room. His face was half-hidden by his mop of brown hair.

"I'm here."

"Good," Atl said, reaching for and grabbing the watch before she stepped out of the closet. She stuffed it into one of her jacket's pockets.

The room seemed colder. Atl bit her lip, wondering if she'd get the shivers soon. She didn't want to get them on the street. People might think she was a Croneng, they'd assume she was sick with that stupid disease.

Atl stood by the window, trying to see how much sunlight there was. What if she postponed the visit?

"I'm sorry about what I said."

"What?"

"You were offended. I only asked if you'd killed anyone because . . . I dunno. It's . . . um . . . the kind of thing they say about vampires."

Atl glanced at Domingo. He was nervous. She didn't want him nervous. She didn't want him thinking she was dangerous. There was no room for doubt.

"I've never killed anyone. I don't hurt people," she said.

It was so easy to lie. He wanted to believe her and smiled brightly when she said this. She figured he lied to himself quite often. He couldn't be as good-natured and content if he didn't. He glued pictures of beautiful models, postcards with palm trees and vampire comic books by his bed and sank into fantasy.

In a way, she envied him. "We should head out," she said.

"I was wondering about that. Can we go out? It's still daytime."

"I was hoping it would be raining and I could take the umbrella," Atl said. "I like cloudy days better. I can walk around in the daylight. It's just harder on me."

And it takes too much damn energy, which I don't have, she thought ruefully. She wished she could avoid this trip, but she needed to see Verónica in person. It wasn't like Bernardino, where it was a good idea to send Domingo. Having an intermediary smoothed things over with vampires. Not the case with the human woman.

Atl took out her sunglasses and put them on. She tried not to wear them, but it might be best that afternoon. She had a feeling her eyes were going to be completely bloodshot by nightfall.

"Let's take Cualli for a walk."

The subway was giving her a migraine. She could smell the dirt and accumulated sweat rolling off people's bodies. It was a miasma of disgusting proportions, which was not the least lessened by cheap colognes and perfumes. The stench of cigarette smoke clung to their clothes, wafting through the subway car.

Domingo didn't smell that bad, but she wished he would take a bath every morning, though she supposed it to be in bad form to point this out.

"You know, I really think this is, like, the coolest dog ever. Its coat is so shiny," Domingo said, chatty as always. She was getting used to that. "How'd you get the Doberman?"

"Cualli takes care of me. I've always had a dog, since I was a child."

When she'd fled south, she thought about leaving the dog behind. But she couldn't part with it. Cualli was part of her life, her constant companion for many years.

"You know, I've never figured how that works."

Atl clutched the dog's leash. "What?"

"You know . . ." Domingo leaned next to her ear, whispering. "Vampire children."

She thought about her childhood, her family home. Mexican families tended to be extended, several generations clustering together, but Atl's family had been massive. The women lived in one house, a complex, really, and the men in another located just across from them. Boys were raised in the women's complex, but at the age of ten they were sent to the male quarters to learn the way of men: agriculture, medicine, scribing in the traditional codices, and soothsaying. Women were schooled in combat, commerce, and politics.

Atl's father was a talented soothsayer, could predict events none of the other men glimpsed, or so they told her. He'd left when she was very small. There had been an altercation, the discovery he'd been embezzling money. So he took off. "What about it?" she asked.

"Well . . . what'd you eat?"

"Milk. Fruits."

"Not blood?"

She thought about pulling his leg and telling him yes, blood, but then he might actually believe it.

"My diet changed when I hit puberty," she said instead.

"Was it scary?"

"Were you scared when you started growing hair in your armpits?"

The subway seats were rock hard and this with the scents around her aggravated the ride. Atl leaned forward, so her back wasn't flat against the plastic seat, and looked at Domingo.

"Not really."

"Same for me. It was what I expected," Atl said.

Domingo sat quietly for a couple of minutes before turning to her again and whispering in her ear.

"Are you going to get old? Or will you look like this forever?"

A man walked the length of their subway car, selling potato chips and peanuts. The peddlers always worked in pairs: one sold the product, the other was the lookout who, whistling and making hand signals, would alert his partner if a cop was approaching. There was also a small-time Mafia at work. Certain lines were controlled by a specific group, and you couldn't just show up and try to sell shit if you didn't pay an initiation fee to the local boss.

The man with the peanuts glanced at Atl and Domingo, but seeing their Doberman, kept walking by.

"I'll age, but I'll look young for a very long time," she told Domingo.

"How long?"

"I can easily remain young for decades and decades. It's quite similar for most of us. When I'm eighty I'll seem forty. There's a point where our bodies just remain still, seem to stop aging."

"That guy I went to see, Bernardino, I think there was something wrong with his bones."

"Yeah, that's an issue with his kind. Their bodies . . . age more quickly, grow deformed, though I'm not exactly sure how it happens."

Atl was given to understand Revenants could absorb the life force of humans or vampires, and rejuvenate their bodies—even transfer that energy *to* others, like a walking battery—but her mother offered few details on their biology. She also offered few details on Bernardino. He was a rather obscure figure, someone her mother had had a feud with, one of the members of her old entourage. If she hadn't been so afraid to meet him, so afraid of breaking protocol, she might have liked to ask him a few questions about her mother.

"If I live long enough I'll have health issues of my own, eventually," Atl said, and chuckled.

"What?" Domingo asked.

"Nothing, it's just not something I think about too often. Life expectancy is not very long for us right now. The drug wars are taking their toll."

Atl had always known what her life would be like. Mostly it would consist of supporting her older sister. At one point she'd marry, likely one of her second cousins, to preserve the family line and fortify their alliances. Izel had spoken about Javier, who was a few years her senior. But that milestone was still far off; their mother had said any planning in this regard was premature. Her sister had been pushing it, though. She had been worried about the stability of their position in Sinaloa, and she said maybe Atl could wed and head to Encinas, home to the Tlauhyo branch, their sister clan in Baja California.

At the time Atl had felt it was a way for Izel to punish her. She had viewed it as an affront. Who got married at her age? You needed to be fifty or sixty. Their mother hadn't had Atl until she was well into her nineties. If she went to Encinas she wouldn't be able to do what she pleased. She already felt confined, having to listen to her sister. God, how she had hated Izel for suggesting it! Atl realized now the proposed match was an attempt to protect her.

She'd never see Encinas, or what remained of her family. If some remained. If they were still there she couldn't risk getting in touch with them, ever.

A dog and a human companion, that's what Atl had. Not much.

"Sorry," Domingo said.

"No, it is what it is. It's life. It's a better life than many other people have," Atl said as she looked to the train doors and shook her head because there was no point in crying over these things.

The doors of the subway car opened. The peanut vendor got off and more people climbed on. The car was getting fuller now, but it wasn't rush hour yet. A man with a guitar boarded last and began strumming the instrument, singing a popular corrido. She stared at a girl wearing a bracelet made of yellow beads, counting the beads in her head. This compulsion to count things was common of several vampire subspecies, an anxiety-reducing behavior that could assist the vampire in coping with the loud noises, sounds, or smells around them. It got worse when she was tired, the need to count. It wasn't a good sign.

"... Atl?"

"Yes," she whispered, trying to pull herself back and focus on him.

"It's two more stops. Hey, are you okay? You seem a bit weird," Domingo said, frowning.

"I'm fine," she muttered.

"Your hands are trembling."

So they were. Atl clutched one hand with the other. The emptiness in her stomach was increasing, the ache of the hunger building. She should have brought sugar cubes. They helped take her mind off the hunger. The lack of blood lowered her glucose levels, driving her close to what humans called hypoglycemia.

She was starting to lose her shit. Just like in Guadalajara. She'd faced off with Godoy's men, managing to escape, though suffering a few scrapes. She ran. She jumped a barbed-wire fence to land on an abandoned property where a hobo was sleeping under a few newspapers. He wasn't young. He was an old guy, his face wrinkled. But she had been hungry ... and she'd attacked him. Ripping his throat open with her talons. A few minutes later she had puked the blood out, a sticky, dark, smelly mess that had splattered over the ground.

She had barely managed to drag herself back to her hiding place, back to Cualli. And then she'd gotten lucky. Because a girl was walking back home from a party as the sun edged the sky, dawn announcing itself.

And she'd fed. She'd fed well.

She couldn't do that shit in Mexico City. It had been sloppy. Stupid killings, the bodies like markers pointing to her location in neon. No honor in it, either. Just fury and hunger.

"You don't have gum, do you?" Atl asked.

Domingo patted his clothes and handed her a pink strip of bubble gum.

"Do you want something else? Do you need us to step down and go to a bathroom?"

"No," Atl said. "I just need this."

Focus. It wasn't really that bad. It's just that she was a pussy who had never worked for a meal, never spent a day—never mind several—eating but her fill, never mind hungry. At a biological level, though, she could take it. Her body could take it. Psychologically? It was getting weird.

Though that was perhaps not that uncommon. Atl had never expected to be in this position, half-starving, hiding in Mexico City. And lost and so lonely it frightened her because she had never learned how to be alone.

The subway car moved jerkily and she clasped his shoulder, steadying herself, glad he was with her.

Aw, come on, her sister said. *Are you going to faint in his arms?*

"How'd you end up collecting garbage?" she asked him. There were *definitely* some psychological issues at this point and she didn't want to dwell on them.

"I just fell into it. When I left home I wandered around the city and met a group of kids living on the street. They washed car windows at the stoplights or sold candy to people on the street."

It sounded familiar. Her family often recruited kids like Domingo for their operations. They'd offer them a hundred pesos to stand at a street corner and keep watch for them, in case the cops were in the mood for busting one of their joints. There was always a young fool willing to do anything for cash.

"Then I had enough of that, of them. It was harsh for a while. Quinto lent me money and that helped me. I started collecting bottles 'cause some-one told me they gave you money for those at the recycling center. And when I was taking bottles there I met this rag-and-bone man who does a lot of business. He's constantly looking for people to bring him stuff. So I started bringing him things. He likes the stuff I collect. He says I've got a good eye for it."

"No offense, but it sounds like a shitty business," she said.

"Nah. Garbage is good. Trash pickers work hard. We sift through the crap and find treasures. It doesn't pay too much and there are people who get a lot more than you do. But there's no one beating you at the end of the day."

You'd be better off dealing drugs up North, she thought. *You'd make more. Die faster, and that's not too bad sometimes. Not that I intend to die fast.*

"Plus the Jackal never let me take a bath. Now I can go to the baths whenever I want. He ain't there to tell me if I can bathe or if I can read my comic books. It's honorable work. And I don't get to hear him say I'm vain and stupid and ugly."

"You're not stupid," she said, but not with any degree of kindness. It was a simple fact.

"You don't have to tell me that. It's all right. I don't mind."

"You can't go around believing that you're shit, all right? I said it was a shitty job, not that you were shitty. That dude who said you were stupid and ugly? I'd bet he's jealous," she said, and this time she did attempt a small amount of kindness, probably because she was tired or, you know, going crazy.

"That'd be something."

Domingo scratched his head and smiled at her, showing her his goofy teeth. His teeth were bad, but his hair and eyes were dark and attractive, both a pleasing, rich shade of brown. She liked pretty things and he had his charm. She had to admit that one reason why she'd zeroed in on him was because he'd looked nice enough when she spotted him. That was a stupid, shallow reason to pick a food source and Izel would have mocked her for it, but then what did she know about picking food? She hadn't ever thought about it so naturally she defaulted to assuming if a human looked good and smelled good he would taste good. Humans chose fruit like that, didn't they? They wanted red apples without bruises or scratches.

Their stop was coming up. She drummed her fingers against her leg, chewed the bubble gum slowly.

"Just . . . um . . . so you know. I think you're really cool," Domingo said. "I think you're the coolest person I've ever met."

"It's bound to be a small social circle, huh?" she replied.

Domingo just smiled even more, in earnest appreciation.

"You're a cool kid too. All right?"

He was. Sort of.

Atl grabbed the dog's leash and stood up just as the subway came to a halt and the doors opened. Domingo followed Atl, stumbling behind her.

Elisa Carrera's building was in a nice spot of town. Not super swanky, but nice enough that they had installed security cameras and there was a guard at the front. Two things Atl didn't like, but there wasn't anything that could be done about them.

The woman who opened the door to Elisa Carrera's office didn't look very much like the photograph Atl had studied. Her hair had gone gray and there were deep wrinkles under her eyes.

"Yes?" asked the woman, eyeing their dog. "It's a bit late. I was about to close."

"It's an urgent matter. We have a referral," Atl said.

"Who referred you?"

"Bernardino."

Elisa's face changed. It softened, wax drifting close to a flame, before hardening in a few quick seconds. Atl thought she might slam the door in their faces and then Atl would have to pull the stupid thing off its hinges, cause a scene, which she really didn't want to do.

"We aren't here to do you harm," Atl said. "We just want to talk."

"Who are you?" Elisa asked, her eyes narrowing.

"I'm Atl, Centehua's daughter," she said, though the resemblance should have been obvious. She took after her mother.

"If that's true you're very far from home."

"It is true. May we come in?" Atl asked.

"Yes," Elisa said.

The office was small. Elisa's desk took up much of the space. It seemed large enough to sit three people, a grand monstrosity of carved wood with a chair to match. There were bland photos of boats and landscapes with the words RELAXATION and MEDITATION printed beneath them. There was also a poster about Jesus and footsteps in the sand, as if banality could be exponentially increased.

Atl and Domingo sat across from Elisa. The dog curled at Atl's feet and Atl patted its head.

"What do you want?" Elisa asked, and regarded them wearily.

"I need your help," Atl said. No sense beating around the bush and it wasn't like she was interested in a long conversation.

"I'm done helping your kind," Elisa said. Her certainty struck Atl as inappropriate.

"My mother is dead," she replied.

To Elisa's credit, the only reaction to that announcement was a slight tremble of her hands.

"I'm very sorry," Elisa said.

"I'll be dead too, if you don't help me. I need to get out of Mexico."

"I knew your mother. But if she's gone then she's gone, and so are my ties to your clan." Elisa spoke crisply, the tone the one a strict schoolmistress might employ with the children.

"There are people looking for me. They'll kill me if they find me," Atl said, spelling it out, because maybe it needed to be spelled in very large, very crimson letters.

"That's very sad, but there's nothing I can do."

Elisa pushed her chair back, as if she were about to rise. Atl spoke quickly, knowing she was losing the woman's interest.

"You can falsify documents. Passports, ID papers. Stuff that could get me to South America. I have money," she said, grabbing the envelope she was carrying in her jacket and dumping it on her desk. The woman looked at it as though she'd just skinned a live animal in front of her. Cualli, sensing turmoil, raised his head, alert.

"My sister left secret accounts for me to access, too. But not here. I need to get to South America and you do this stuff. You help people create new identities. I can pay you very well, a lot more than this, if you'll help me."

"I haven't done that in years. I run a clean business now. Clean life."

"Really," Atl said flatly.

Atl fixed her eyes on Elisa's hands. Her nails were painted pink. It wasn't a cheap manicure, she'd spent money on it. But it was starting to chip away. She saw the tiny spots with missing flecks of paint. One spot, two spots, three. Millimeters.

Atl raised her eyes and stared at Elisa. "I'm running out of time."

Elisa stood up with her back to them, looking out the window. She wasn't giving in, not yet, but she was wavering. Atl licked her lips. They felt chapped.

"I can't stay here much longer. Mexico is too dangerous."

"What are you doing here, anyway?" Elisa muttered.

"I didn't have anywhere else to go. I thought you and Bernardino might help me."

"You have cash. You can probably fly abroad." Elisa made a motion with her right hand, pointing up.

"Yeah, and the airport has too much security and too many scanners. I'd be dead before I get to my seat. It has to be by ground."

"Then I don't understand why you simply didn't try to cross the northern border. It would have been easier to take your chances with the coyotes, no?"

Yeah, like Atl hadn't thought about that.

"The Necros dominate the North, so that's a no go. They don't own Guatemala. Not yet. There will be checkpoints, but with the right papers I can make it down into South America and make a home there. It's easier this way."

"Nothing is *easier*," Elisa said. "It's just another way to get killed."

"Well, I can't exactly head back north right now so the only option is south. You used to be a runner for my mother. Surely you can make one more run."

"Have a good journey. You can walk yourselves out, I trust?"

She ought to have more respect for me, Atl thought. *For my family.* Though there was precious little left of her family to respect.

Elisa placed her manicured hands on the desk, lacing them together. She returned Atl's stare.

"My mother was your protector," Atl said in a low voice. "She pulled you out of the gutter. She housed you, fed you, clothed you. If things were the other way around, if it were your daughter asking her for help, she would offer assistance."

"I paid my debt to your mother. I paid it in blood and I don't owe you anything. Why don't you go bother Bernardino? Maybe he can do something."

Atl scrutinized the woman's face. She analyzed the stern line of her mouth, the gray of her hair. Elisa said the words but she didn't *mean* them. Elisa was pretending, and Atl knew the deck was stacked in her favor, that she need only find the right words.

"I've come for your help. My mother would have . . . well, if she were alive, she might have come to you herself," Atl said. "I didn't know where else to go and she told me that you were the only person she trusted in the whole world. She absolutely trusted you."

That was not exactly what Atl's mother had said. No. She'd said that Elisa was like all other humans: a weak fool, predictable and simple. A useful fool, at times. And that if things should worsen Atl would do good to find her because she was not crafty enough to betray anyone and sufficiently nostalgic to remember her years as a vampire's assistant fondly.

Elisa was leaning forward. Her mouth opening a little, almost as if she was hesitating to ask a question.

Atl lowered her gaze, focusing on her hands.

"She said you were like a sister to her. That's why I came." Atl listened to the tick of a clock upon the wall, waiting patiently. Elisa shifted in her seat and sighed. She had her.

"Crossing the border is one thing, but you want to go all the way to South America and you're talking about identity papers. What you ask is not achieved quickly," Elisa said. "Fake passports, fake ID papers, bio-IDs . . . And the car, of course. I suppose I'll have to drive you across. It might take me a few days. I can't produce this stuff out of thin air."

"I can manage to survive for a few days."

"I said it *might*," Elisa cautioned her. "I'm not sure if I'll be able to do it. Security gets tighter each day. No one wants more vampires in their territory anymore. Most governments consider you a plague, you know? Have you heard how they're dealing with your lot in the U.K.? They've now got a police force dedicated to handling your kind."

"Yeah, the Van Helsings. I heard that. They're only in the large cities, though. Never fancied seeing London anyway."

"They've had their powers extended, just a few weeks ago."

"We've been around for a long time," Atl said. "We'll be around for a while longer."

"You've also been hunted for a long time. For a reason."

Mother had told her that in the old days, before the Europeans washed up on the coast of Veracruz, when her kind were priestesses, the Great Temple ran red with rivulets of blood, offerings of hearts and heads to the gods. The bodies of sacrificial victims tumbled down the steps of the temple. The people below stabbed, pierced, and bled themselves in sacrifice. They were not a plague, nor vermin, nor common killers that hid in the shadows. Not the Tlahuelpocmimi. Not her family.

"So we have been hunted," Atl replied coolly. "Yet despite your greater numbers, you humans haven't quite figured out how to get rid of us."

"One of these days, maybe."

Atl decided she did not want to get into this conversation. It would lead nowhere and she was tired.

"I'll need two sets of IDs," Atl said instead. "And all the other bits, so we can start over again."

"He'll be going with you?" Elisa pointed at Domingo, who was sitting very still and quiet in his chair.

Atl glanced at the young man. "Yes. He's human, though."

"I can tell. Do you have a passport? A current ID?" Elisa asked. "If you're in a database I'll need to scrub you out of there."

"No, I don't, miss," Domingo said politely.

"He has no fixed address," Atl said.

"What's your name?"

"I'm Domingo, miss."

"Domingo, if you go south with this girl you might get into a lot of trouble."

Elisa again sounded like a schoolteacher when she spoke, warning a kid about the dangers of doing drugs. Atl scoffed.

"I'd like to see Guatemala. If it's okay with you," Domingo replied.

Elisa nodded. Her expression was skeptical. She let out a bitter sigh. "Stand against the wall; I need to take your photo."

Atl went first, her eyes wide open as the flash went off. Then it was

Domingo's turn. Elisa muttered to herself and sat behind her desk again, shaking her head.

"I need to get in touch with someone," Elisa said. "Will you two be all right until next Thursday?"

"Yes," Atl replied. "What time should we come back?"

"Not here. There's a bar in Plaza Garibaldi, the Tenampa. Meet me at ten."

"We will."

Elisa tapped her fingers against the desk. Their meeting had clearly concluded and Atl pushed her chair back.

"Who killed her?" Elisa asked, just as Atl opened the door.

"Godoy," she said.

Elisa nodded gravely. She didn't ask anything else and Atl walked toward the elevator, one hand in her pocket, the other on the dog's leash.

On the subway she thought of axolotls and her mother's head, delivered in a cooler.

Hide, Atl. Hide, Izel whispered in her ear.

CHAPTER 15

The ride back was quiet. Atl kept her head down in the subway. Sometimes she would close her eyes and Domingo would think she was asleep, but then a sudden movement would jolt her and she'd snap her eyes open. When they reached her apartment she walked straight toward the bedroom, flopping upon the bed and pressing her hands against her face. Her dog padded in behind her, lying down at the foot of the bed. Domingo hovered at the door, not knowing if he was allowed inside.

"Are you okay?" he asked. "Do you want some of that tea?"

She did not reply. Domingo put the kettle on to boil. He found the sugar, the tea, and picked two mugs. One of them was chipped, a hairline crack running down a side of it. He dragged his thumb over the crack. When the tea was ready, he walked back to her room.

He knelt by the bed, a cup in his hands, and looked at her. With her eyes closed, Atl's features seemed to soften, like a switchblade that has yet to snap out. He guessed he *should* have been afraid of Atl, but he wasn't. The terror wasn't there. It was as simple as that. He supposed he was foolish, but couldn't be bothered to worry. Not yet, at least.

Domingo bit his lower lip, wondering if he should wake her up. He extended his right hand, his fingertips resting upon her shoulder.

He felt an immediate jolt, like an electric current, running through his veins and something like a spark lighting him inside. All of a sudden the apartment was gone, melting beneath his feet. He saw a barren desert landscape with a sky of the most unbelievable blue; a blue he'd never seen before. A tortoise walked before him, slowly following a highway that was a black ribbon, twisting, turning, melting into the distance, and he sank into the highway, into the melting blackness of the pavement. Then he was running through a city. Past warehouses and shacks, past a circle of homeless people sipping booze in the darkness, until he reached a chain-link fence and scrambled up it. The fence was gone and he was holding a gun in his hands, and then it wasn't a gun, it was a decapitated human head. He dropped the head and it rolled onto the floor, spreading a coat of red upon the white tiles. Red the walls and red the ceiling and red every single speck of everything until—

Atl's hand wrapped around his wrist, steadying him, and he stared at her.

"You're going to drop your cup," she said in a hushed voice.

Domingo blinked.

The cup, he thought, and looking down he realized yes, he was holding a cup.

He took a deep breath.

"I got you a drink," he said.

Atl sat up on the bed and took the cup from his hands. She sipped her tea. Domingo stayed by the side of the bed, still too rattled to attempt to stand up.

"They're just memories," Atl said.

"Huh?"

"Memories," Atl said. "My memories. It happens, when you've shared your blood with someone. There are echoes, bits and pieces that stay in your head. When you touched me . . . I'm tired, I wasn't prepared for it, and you saw."

That's almost like a superpower, he thought.

"I saw a highway," he said, frowning, and now he did move, by her side, sitting on the bed. "And there was a human head. What was that? Was that real?"

"They sent the head in the cooler," she said, speaking as if she'd informed him about the weather or the time of day.

Domingo blinked.

"My mother's head," Atl said. "They chopped her head off and delivered it to our house in a cooler. The funny thing about a decapitated head is that it looks completely fake. You stand there and think, 'This isn't real,' because it's simply so rubbery. And my sister, they killed her too, burned her." Her eyes fixed on him, cold, unpleasant. Her gaze was hard, black enamel.

Domingo didn't know what to reply. He swallowed.

"They killed her. But I got back at them. I got them where it hurts. There is a phrase, ātl tlachinolli, 'the water that scorches the earth.' My name means 'water' but it is also war."

She laughed, a brief burst of derision.

"What did you do?" he asked.

She shoved the cup back into his hands, shaking her head. "I shouldn't be talking to you. I'm too tired and hungry and it's not making any sense and you shouldn't know this. You shouldn't listen to me."

Atl covered her eyes with both hands. He thought she might cry by the way her voice cracked, and it might have been better if she did because he was befuddled, watching her sudden distress and not knowing what to do. She teetered at the edge of panic but did not quite fall.

"Do you want blood?" he asked. His body, after all, was the only thing he could offer.

She snapped her head up and stared at him. "Blood volume is replaced within twenty-four hours. Red cells need about a month for complete replacement. Did you know that?"

"No."

"I can't be drinking too frequently, no matter how much I want it."

"Um . . . you don't look too hot."

"It's my fault," Atl said. "I'm soft. Pampered. My sister was right. She should be alive. She'd know what to do, how to do it right. I just keep messing up."

"It's all right," he said, resting a hand upon her shoulder.

Atl smirked. He saw the white of her teeth. Normal teeth. Not fangs like in the comic books. But her eyes were odd, red, like she'd been weeping.

"Your eyes," he said. "They're—"

"I can feel it," she said. Atl walked to the bathroom; the dog followed her, quiet as a shadow. She leaned against the sink, opened the faucet, and splashed water on her face with both hands. She placed her lips against the faucet and drank directly from it. When she was done, she looked into the mirror with a sigh. She peeled off her jacket, tossing it to the floor. She followed it with her blouse and stood in her undershirt.

"Are you going to shower? Should I turn around?" Domingo asked, and he immediately wondered if he was a total perv for asking that.

"No."

"No, I shouldn't turn around?"

"No, I'm not showering," Atl replied, stepping out of the bathroom and sitting in the middle of the living room, her hands resting against her knees. "I'm . . ."

The dog headed toward her, sat next to its mistress, and her hands fell upon its head, an automatic gesture. Her lips moved, but she made no sound. The silence seemed to stretch for minutes and minutes.

"You know, I used to have a swimming pool as big as this apartment," she said, the words slurred, as though she'd been drinking. "And now here I am. My kingdom for a fan. Or an ice tray. I feel warm and cold at the same time. Damn it."

"If you really want a fan I can get you one," he said.

"You don't need to get me anything. You don't . . ." She sighed. Her hands twitched and she clasped them together, as if in prayer. "Talk to me for a bit, will you?"

"What do you want to talk about?" he asked.

"A movie you saw. Your favorite color. Anything," she said, shrugging.

"I saw *Dracula* on the TV one time. Black and white," he said, sitting down in front of her.

Atl rolled her eyes at him. "Good God, it's always Dracula."

"I saw Germán Robles one time, for real. Well, I was walking down Florencia and he was having a coffee at a coffee shop, just like everyone else."

"Who?"

He scooted closer to Atl, infected with the glee of sharing something new with her. "You know, Germán Robles! He was in movies. He didn't look like he did in the movies, he was old, ancient, but I recognized him. He's got the same eyes, used to play a vampire. He played Karol de Lavud."

"You talked to him?"

"No," Domingo said. "I was pushing my shopping cart and I didn't think they'd let me in. You know, it wouldn't look none too good to pull a shopping cart into a coffee shop to tell him hi."

"I suppose not."

"I've always thought vampires should be like Karol de Lavud," he said, remembering the small TV set, the black-and-white images late at night.

"How's that?"

"Well . . . uh . . . ," Domingo said. "With a cape."

Atl cocked her head a little, smirking at him. "A cape?"

"It looks cool."

"No, it doesn't."

Domingo shrugged. He thought the old vampire images were awesome, with the mist and stars and moonlight and the cape flapping in the wind, but he supposed Atl might have a point. After all, there was no mist in Mexico City, just smog, and you couldn't see any stars thanks to it. It was a lot less romantic, though Atl still cut an impressive figure. Even in her undershirt and jeans, no cape in sight, there was something almost magical about her. Like she didn't *need* no mist and moonlight, her sharp features and the blackness of her hair enough to freeze any mere mortal in his tracks.

He'd moved closer, but she moved closer still, her knee bumping his own.

"You like music?" he asked, glancing down, fearing he was about to blush, pretending to fiddle with his music player.

"What have you got?"

"Everything," he said. "Concrete Blonde. Bosé. Depeche Mode. It's mostly old stuff, but, here," he said, handing her the headphones.

Atl carefully took the headphones, as though she wasn't quite sure what to do with them, and put them on. Domingo pressed play. She frowned, but her frown soon relaxed.

"You like?" he asked.

"It's alright. How'd you get this stuff?"

"Here and there. You've heard it before?"

"Not really. When I go dancing they don't have this type of music."

"It helps to listen to something when I'm working. You know, to keep the rhythm. Takes me places, too."

"You're funny, Domingo."

"In a good or bad way?" he dared to ask, but she just laughed and brushed his leg with her fingers for a fleeting second before she began tapping her fingers against her knee, softly, following a rhythm.

"I should go to sleep," she said after a while, taking off the headphones and returning them to him.

"I'm going to head back to my place," he said, pointing toward the front door. "You know, to give you your space, like you like."

"No," she said, surprising him with the casualness of her tone. "You can stay. If you want. There's the bed and there might be food. I'm not sure." Atl headed to the bedroom, opened the closet door, and slipped in. She closed it from the inside and the dog sat outside it, giving Domingo a menacing stare.

"No, worries, Cualli," he said in a placating tone, standing at the doorway. "I'm not going to hurt her."

Domingo walked slowly into the bedroom and lay on the middle of the bed. He placed his hands against his chest, as though he were dead, as he'd seen vampires do in the movies when they slept. It was an uncomfortable position. He rolled on his side, put on the headphones. The music was loud and cheery, music to dance to.

He wondered if Atl might have danced with him. Not right now, not here, but maybe in another place. Maybe if she weren't being chased by bad guys they could have gone to Quinto's party.

CHAPTER 16

Nick switched the blood pack from one hand to the other, still unable to bring himself to open it. He'd been drinking alcohol all afternoon to keep his stomach at bay, but there was no denying it now. He needed blood and the only thing around the apartment was the blood packs in the freezer. Rodrigo and La Bola were keeping their eyes on him like hawks. There was no chance to slip out again.

God, Rodrigo. He thought himself so high and mighty, when he was nothing but a servant like all the others. One day Nick was going to be the boss. He'd show the old human . . . the lofty peacock who looked down at him like he was scum. It was Rodrigo who came from nowhere, had been a nothing until his dad plucked him from the shithole where he lived.

He might even bite Rodrigo, force him to drink his blood, turn him into a mindless puppet.

They said the other vampires couldn't make slaves like that, that their blood didn't work in this way. Atl's kind, he'd heard, treated the whole blood-sharing thing like some sort of reverential, sacred process. Aztec bullshit about life, sacrifice, renewal.

Nick just thought it was fun to make himself a few slaves.

He grabbed the bottle of tequila and took a sip, sliding back on his bed and contemplating the ceiling.

Atl Iztac. If it weren't for her he'd be enjoying himself back home, no need to open blood packs and feed from them like a ninny. When he got his hands on her . . . well. He was looking forward to a bit of torture. If they hacked and sliced her, then she'd heal, and they could hack and slice again. It might even be fun to turn her into one of his whores. Well, that was probably not the right word. Atl was a category above the stupid bar girls he picked up. Concubine? Was that the right word for this? He'd have to ask Rodrigo. On second thought, he didn't want to ask the old man a single thing.

Concubine, then. Whatever. The word didn't matter. What mattered was that Atl was just like Rodrigo: thinking herself so high, so above them. The Tlahuelpocmimi went on and on about their ancient heritage, their noble lineage, their days of pyramids and empires, without bothering to realize that it was in the past and they, *we*, are now in the same damn business. This was a new empire. And it belonged to Nick and his brothers.

He'd met Atl one time before this whole mess began, back when the situation between their clans was cold but not icy. He'd been at Hive, a neutral-zone joint, which meant you couldn't bite the humans or spray bullets at other vampires. Nice place, good booze, safe and cozy, run by a Nachzehrer who had a love for the '70s so the décor was vintage disco.

He'd been in a booth with Justiniano, a couple of his cousins, and assorted hangers-on when in walked a group of girls who seemed to attract a great deal of attention from the people around him, eliciting whispers. He asked Justiniano what the fuss was about and he said they were youngsters from the Iztac clan, which normally didn't hang out around Hive, preferring other clubs.

"And who's that one?" he'd asked, pointing at one girl who distinguished herself from her friends by her outfit and attitude, dressed in white, arms crossed as she stood by the bar surveying the scene.

"Atl Iztac, she's Centehua's youngest daughter," Justiniano said.

It was that part of the night when Nick picked up a chick. He liked them blond and big-breasted, but this lithe brunette had an utterly delicious mouth. He thought he'd spice it up.

"Fuck me," Nick said. "All right, let's say hi to her."

Justiniano had whispered that wasn't a good idea but Nick shushed him. He traced a direct line to the girl and took off his sunglasses when he got to her, flashing her his trademark smile.

"Hey there, princess," he said. "How you doing? I'm Nick."

She turned her head and stared at him, her lips pursed together. "Let me guess," she said. "Necros, aren't you?"

"Got me there, princess."

"It wasn't difficult."

The bartender dropped a shot next to her and she picked it up with one gloved hand but did not drink it, pressing it against the hollow of her throat instead as she looked away. What a neck, eh? And the breasts might be small but he could tell they'd be worth it. She'd be worth it.

"I have a private booth here, you know. We could go sit down."

"I don't think I'm going to stay long enough to sit down," she said.

"Music is not to your taste?"

"The clientele," she said. She drank the shot and slammed the empty glass on the bar.

All right, he liked a tad of attitude, but not that much of it. He'd tried to be nice and she was not reciprocating, and that pissed him off. Girls didn't dare pull that bitchy act with him, he was Nick Godoy. "Hey, baby, you've got a case of lousy manners," he told her, clutching her arm.

She leaned forward with the grace of an uncoiling snake.

"I'm not your baby. Fuck off," she said, shoving him away and motioning to her friends.

"Whore."

"Touch me again, I'll cut your dick."

Nick watched her in amazement, tipping her chin up like she was some fucking princess. That's probably what she thought she was. A damn Aztec princess, and she looked at him like he was garbage.

Justiniano hurried to his side.

"That . . . that stuckup bitch," Nick said, emitting half a laugh. "Did you see that? Who does she think she is?"

"Forget about it," Justiniano told him.

Only he hadn't forgotten about it. How could he? Whenever he chanced to hear her name he recalled that scalding humiliation. And when his dad had told him Atl Iztac was on the run Nick had been delighted and eager to assist with her capture. Payback was a bitch.

He tossed the tequila away, fed up with it, and opened the vodka instead.

After gulping nearly half that bottle he remembered that they were under instructions from his father to kill the girl. He frowned. That wouldn't do. He'd taken a real liking to this idea of keeping her for a while. Nick set aside the vodka, sat up, and looked around the bed, pulling the dirty sheets and the pillows. An empty soda can rolled onto the floor. He found the phone.

It only rang once before his father answered.

"Yes?"

"Father, it's me."

"What is it?" The voice was flat, stony.

"Nothing much. Rodrigo is being an idiot and we lost Justiniano," Nick said, grabbing the soda can and spinning it in his hands. He lay back on the bed.

"Where are you?"

"Mexico City."

His father's voice was the same, a neutral tone, though Nick could feel the tension beneath it, the suppressed anger.

"Why?"

"You should ask Rodrigo," Nick said. "Atl got away and we're trying to find her."

His father was quiet. Nick stretched an arm behind his back, scratching his nape. "I wasn't calling you about that, though. I want you to tell Rodrigo that we should capture her, not kill her."

"Why?"

"It would be more fun," Nick said, crumpling the soda can and tossing it against the wall.

"This is not about *fun*."

It is for me, Nick thought. He rolled his eyes. "Well, I don't think she should die quickly. It's too simple. We should make a real good example of her," he replied.

"I'll think about it."

He hung up with that. Nick frowned, staring at the receiver. He wished he'd gotten something more solid than *I'll think about it.* He really did want the damn girl.

Nick made an incision in the blood pack he'd been avoiding and began drinking. He did his best to pretend he was drinking her blood, going as far as to close his eyes and sketch a clear mental picture of Atl. The darkness of her hair, blue black it was. The face that was so proud, with an avian quality, more the raven than the swan. That face, reduced to a ruin under the onslaught of a blade.

He threw his head back and ripped the blood pack apart, letting the contents rain upon his tongue.

CHAPTER 17

In the morning, Domingo considered waking Atl up, but then he remembered it was daylight and maybe that wasn't a great idea. Instead, he hung out around the apartment, listening to music, until his belly grumbled. In the kitchen he found two cans of beans but no can opener. There was also a big bag of dog food in a corner and a bowl next to it that served as the dog's feeding dish. He refilled the dog's dish, then grabbed Atl's keys and decided to have a meal outside. He discovered a tortería just a few blocks from the apartment. He ordered a cheese and ham torta and while he ate it, he started thinking about money, 'cause he hadn't gone to work in several days and he didn't have much cash left after buying new clothes and the watch. He didn't want to be a bum, having Atl pay for everything, but he also couldn't go picking plastic bottles off the streets if she needed him around.

It was nice being needed; it made you feel special.

Domingo wrapped half the torta in a napkin and put it in one of his large jacket pockets for later. He did not waste food. He never knew when his next meal was coming.

He went to hang out in front of a newsstand, looking over the newspaper headlines and staring at the magazines. The guy selling newspapers shooed him away after a while, telling him he couldn't be reading everything if he wasn't going to pay, so Domingo walked a few more blocks and stood in front of a different newsstand.

When he got back to the building, it was late and the whole place was swarming with activity. The front door was open and there were lots of people in green-and-blue sanitation suits at the entrance.

"You know what's up?" he asked an old lady who was standing outside.

"Sanitation sweep, what do you think?" the woman grumbled. "They're looking for Cronengs, as usual."

Domingo panicked, thinking of Atl. He managed to walk up the stairs without running, simply staring down at the ground and praying none of the sanitation officers stopped him. They didn't, and he managed to fit the key in the lock and open the door, immediately closing it behind him.

"Atl!" he yelled, and rushed to the bedroom.

He was relieved to see Cualli was still sitting in front of the closet. The dog stared at him when he approached, but didn't growl, and Domingo knocked on the closet door. When Atl didn't reply, he slid the door open.

She was on the floor, in a sleeping bag, her eyes closed tight. Domingo hesitated for a second, remembering what had happened last time, and touched her hand.

"Wake up," he said.

She turned toward him, eyes open wide. "What?"

"There's a sanitation crew in the building. We gotta get out."

"Damn it," she muttered. She jumped to her feet and hurried to the living room.

She picked up the blouse and vinyl jacket she'd taken off, put them on, and suddenly stood, very still.

"Atl?"

"Hush, I can hear them," she whispered. "They're on this floor, walking down the hallway." She quickly moved toward the large living room window, opening it and looking up.

"What are you doing?" Domingo asked.

"Going to the roof. When they come, open the door and pretend everything's normal. Okay?" she said.

"How are you going to—"

"Just look normal."

She jumped out the window. Domingo panicked and poked his head out, and saw her climbing up the side of the old structure, her shoulders hunched. Once again, he had the impression that she was a great bird of prey, although her shape was still human. He thought of those old gods with animal heads he'd once seen in a book, and she reminded him a bit of one of them. She disappeared onto the roof so quickly Domingo thought he might have imagined the whole thing. He held his breath for a moment and swallowed.

Sanitation. Right. He could deal with those guys. He'd tangoed with them before. Sometimes they bugged him when he was walking in the street. No biggie.

Domingo went back to the bedroom and took out the sleeping bag and the blanket in the closet, tossing them on the bed. Then he rushed to the kitchen and placed his torta in the refrigerator. He left a cup in the sink. That was the closest the apartment was going to get to normal without any furniture. Domingo glanced at the Doberman, which had been following him around, and hoped to God it didn't attack anyone.

The knock on the door came and he opened it.

The woman standing before him was holding a tablet and didn't look at him as she spoke. "Sanitation sweep. We'd appreciate your cooperation. Please hand over your ID and state your name."

"I'm Domingo Molina but I don't have no ID," he said.

"You are required to carry your ID."

"It's just I never have had one, miss," he replied, sticking his hands in his pockets. "I'm seventeen, if that makes any difference."

The woman now raised her head, sighed, and gave him an irritated look. "Do you live here alone?"

"Just me and my dog," he said, feeling the Doberman drifting closer to his side.

The woman glanced at the dog, scribbled on her tablet. "Carlos, can you check the rooms?" she asked, speaking to a man who was standing behind her. "The super gave us his notes and it says here a girl lives in this apartment. Where's she?"

Domingo stepped aside to let the man in. "I don't know. The guy that's renting me the place didn't say nothing about a girl."

The woman let out a deep sigh, made an annotation. "It figures the paperwork would be wrong. Okay, so you live here?"

"Yeah. For now. I move around. Been working for a rag-and-bone man lately. I help him carry the stuff, sell it. Thermoplastic clothing is his specialization. Me? I like gathering electronics. It's good wo—"

"Give me your hand."

Domingo obeyed. The woman pressed a thin, white plastic stick against his palm. It beeped.

"Temperature is normal."

"That's good, right?"

The woman nodded. Domingo took out a piece of gum and started chewing it. The dog was sitting still, eyeing the sanitation worker.

"It's empty," said the other sanitation worker, returning from his short trip.

The woman was looking at her tablet again. Apparently it was much more interesting than Domingo.

"You realize that you have to register with the health station in your borough, right? It's the law."

"I know, ma'am, but I don't have no ID."

"Yes, well, even if you're a minor you need to fill out the form and register. If more people followed that simple procedure we wouldn't have to be knocking on so many doors, trying to find Cronengs, would we?"

"No, ma'am."

"Your dog, it's enhanced?"

"Yes, ma'am," Domingo said, because there was no point in denying it. The bioluminescent tattoo was a dead giveaway.

"It should also be registered at the health unit. All modified pets should."

"Okay. I didn't know. Got it off a shelter. Idiot rich wig threw it away, couldn't quite believe it 'cause normally I wouldn't be able to afford such a nice—"

Both sanitation workers looked bored as hell. The woman interrupted him again and Domingo took that as a good sign. It meant she was about to move on. He was right.

"I'm going to put a green seal on your door, which means you're not sick with anything and you're not harboring drugs, but you have to visit the health station within ten days, all right? Also, bring your dog so they can enter his info into the computer. There's going to be a note in the system and if you don't do it, we'll come back and take you there, along with the animal. It's a lot easier if you just go."

"Sure."

The woman handed him a pamphlet with an address and information printed on it, then bade him goodbye. Domingo locked the door, sat on the floor, and waited. He could have sworn it took forever, and he was about to run to the roof when Atl simply flew back into the apartment. Okay, she didn't *technically* fly, but she jumped inside with a certain grace and flexibility that was definitely birdlike.

Atl looked at him, and her face was not really human; it was a bird's face, though it lacked a beak. Instead of hair she had lustrous feathers. She shook her head and the feathers disappeared, leaving only pitch-black hair behind and a face that was so thin and sunken it seemed positively emaciated.

"Thanks."

"You're welcome."

"Sugar," she said, hurrying toward the kitchen.

"Do you wa—"

He had no time to ask more because she had grabbed the whole box with the sugar cubes, which had been left on a kitchen counter, and was eating like a wild animal, stuffing cubes into her mouth. When she was done, she rested her back against the refrigerator and chuckled.

"It's not good," she said.

"What's not good?"

"The hunger."

"You can bite me. It's cool."

"Conservation, Domingo," she said. "I can't squander . . . damn it."

"You should just take . . . um . . . a bite," he said.

Atl looked amused. She patted his arm. "You're too generous."

"I know what it's like to be hungry."

She looked at him in this strange way, like he'd said something really nasty, only Domingo didn't think he'd said nothing bad. He hoped not. He didn't want to be mean. And then her face twisted and changed, like she was hurt, and she glanced away.

"Hey, it's cool," he said. "Look, it's fine." He showed her his wrist, holding it up for her.

Atl looked at him again, at his wrist, and slowly pressed her lips against it. He felt her tongue flick against his skin, and then the sensation, like a needle had gone through his body. When she pushed herself away from him, only a couple of minutes later, he caught a flicker of something in her mouth. A long tube that coiled away.

"What do you call that?" he said, rubbing his wrist. "In your mouth."

"It's a proboscis. Some people call it the stinger. It's similar to the feeding mechanism of butterflies."

"That's how vampires eat, as if they were butterflies?"

"My subspecies does."

"Can you show the stinger to me?"

"Can you show me your penis?" she shot back.

Domingo flushed and dipped his head. "Sorry. I'm just curious. I don't mean to be an ass," he mumbled.

"It's an idiotic thing to ask."

"I won't ask anymore." Domingo stared at his shoelaces. He shifted his position and ran his hand over the old kitchen counter. His fingers brushed against a single sugar cube that had been left behind, and he handed it to Atl. She took it with a sigh.

"I know you're curious," she said. "It's not . . . it's weird hearing those questions. Look, you can ask stuff, sometimes I'm just not going to like it, all right? And I won't answer everything you ask."

"Okay," he said. "It's just you're very interesting." She smiled; her expression was one of amusement, perhaps approval, though he could not tell for sure.

"Drink some water," she said, suddenly grabbing a glass and opening the tap. "I don't want you fainting."

Domingo drank the water in a few gulps, then held on to the glass with both hands. "You're looking better," he said.

Her face did not seem so hollow, her eyes were not so red, and there was a vivacity about her.

"I feel better," she said, flexing her fingers.

Talons, he thought. *She has talons.* Dark and sharp and deadly looking, and yet, her hands were beautiful.

"Can I ask something?" he said.

She inclined her head, raising an eyebrow at him. "What?"

"How'd you do that? The bird thing. Changing."

"It's natural to me. It's like walking. You just learn to do it one day."

"Does it hurt?"

"No."

He tried to picture what it might be to have feathers growing from his head, to have talons instead of fingers. He could not, and remained puzzled.

"It's not *that* odd. Not for us," Atl said with a shrug. "There are some who can turn into . . . Hmm. 'Wolves,' I guess, would be the right word."

"Have you seen a vampire become a wolf?"

"That I've seen, yes."

"It sounds neat. Though I still think turning into mist would be cooler. Sucks nobody does that."

"You can't have everything," she said.

Domingo wondered if she could fly. He'd ask her another time. He didn't want her to get mad again.

"You did well, by the way," she said.

"Yeah?"

She smiled at him. "Yeah."

"They'll come back in ten days if I don't go to the health unit, but I figure that doesn't matter, right? We should be gone by then," he said.

They walked back to the living room. Atl stood by the window, glancing at the sky, then tugged at the curtain, blocking off the light. "We'll go out when it's dark."

"Where to?" he asked.

"We need a gun."

CHAPTER 18

The bars in the downtown core were coming alive by the time they got off at the station in El Zócalo, that great plaza that had existed since the time of the Aztecs. Old houses, built in the nineteenth and eighteenth centuries, spread around them, transformed into restaurants, shops, and entertainment joints. She kept Cualli on a short leash as they drifted among the crowds of revelers ready for a late night, and even when they moved to side streets and alleys that were empty, she kept the dog close. She felt safer with the Doberman by her side.

"I think it's around here," Domingo said, squinting. "It's hard to tell."

"You said that two blocks back," she reminded him.

"No, I'm sure this time."

Atl gave him a noncommittal look and snorted. Guns were difficult to come by legally in Mexico City; there were only a couple of authorized stores in the whole city and you required a letter from the local police department attesting you didn't have a criminal record. Plus, you needed your ID papers. Atl had neither, so she must find an illegal supplier. Easy, if you knew someone, and Domingo said he did. Harder, when Domingo couldn't remember where the supplier lived.

Atl had never had a burning desire to own guns. Her sister had given her a switchblade knife, which Atl kept tucked in her jacket, and a gun, which she'd left behind. But she hadn't had much of a chance to use either. The gun had been gold-plated and custom engraved, with flourishes and hummingbirds. She remembered the weight of the weapon and how it felt the first time she raised it, pointing at a pile of bottles they'd arranged for this purpose. Atl's aim was terrible and Izel had a good laugh at her expense, but after the first few appalling misses, she started to get the hang of it. Although Atl could never handle a firearm as well as Izel, she had managed to become a fairly decent shot. That didn't mean she liked it, though.

"Ah, here," Domingo said, and crossed the street. "This is the place."

They stood before the entrance to a vecindad. The heavy wooden door was not locked, and Domingo pushed it and they walked into a narrow hallway.

It was not a nice vecindad, not one of those places that had been repurposed and repainted, made to look like a palatable pad for yuppies and artsy types after the rental freeze ended in the '90s. The walls of the vecindad were bare, old stone, cracked here and there. There were cables running above their heads and along the walls.

Stealing electricity, she guessed.

The hallway soon opened onto a large patio with many stone sinks and lines set for drying clothes. There were doors leading into apartments every few meters and a big staircase at the other end of the patio. A group of girls walked by them when they reached the foot of the staircase, dressed in their nightclub finery, their skirts short and the perfume heady. They giggled when they saw Domingo, whispering a few words, but when their eyes settled on Atl they did not laugh, apparently intimidated by the sight of her dog. The girls scattered away. Domingo and Atl went up.

Mid-staircase they came face-to-face with a large shrine to the Virgin of Guadalupe. Domingo paused to pay his respects, making the sign of the cross. Atl merely stared at the face of the religious icon. Her family had been priests of the God of War and though they no longer worshipped in the same fashion, she had no desire to follow the customs imported by the Europeans. Saints and virgins and angels.

They veered on the second floor to the left and stood before a door. Domingo bit his lip.

"What?" Atl asked.

"It's just I don't like being here. This guy is friends with the Jackal."

"Can he get me a gun?"

"Yes, I'm sure he can."

"I don't care if he's friends with the devil. Let's do this, unless you have another weapons dealer."

"Can't say I do," Domingo mumbled.

Domingo knocked on the door, creating an echo that bounced down the hallway.

The door opened and a woman, her hair dyed an absurd shade of cherry red, which was almost a requirement for young women, stood in the doorway in a fluffy bathrobe, frowning. "It's late," she said. "What do you want?"

"I'm here to see Mario," Domingo said. "I'm Quinto's friend. He brought me here one time, with Belén and other people."

"Mario! It's one of the street kids that hangs out with Quinto!" the woman yelled.

"Let him in," came the reply.

The woman stepped aside and let Domingo in, but then she made a face at Atl and pointed at Cualli. "You can't come in here with your animal."

"My animal goes where I go," Atl said.

"Your animal—"

"What's the deal?" asked a male voice, and Atl saw a burly, pale man standing behind the woman.

"She's got a dog. I don't want it in here," the woman explained.

"Let her and the damn dog in; they're here for business."

The woman rolled her eyes and flicked her hair behind her shoulders. Atl walked into the small apartment, the man motioned toward a table, and they sat down. The man sat across from them. Behind him she saw a poster of *Rambo II* on the wall. A large TV and a couch occupied a good portion of the living room/dining room area. The rest of the space was taken up with boxes.

"You've got to forgive the girl; she ain't got no manners. I'm Mario. What can I help you with?"

"Guns," Atl said.

The man gave a snort of laughter. "That's a different one. Kids like you, they usually want drugs."

He probably thought them a couple of fools who were headed out to dance to cumbias and ruidosón. In the North the hot thing was to gather and dance at a slaughterhouse, the décor the carcasses of cows.

"You have them?" she asked.

"I have them," the man said. "Something lightweight?"

"No. The most powerful one you've got; .454 Casull would be nice."

The man whistled at her. "Damn. What you gonna shoot?" he asked.

"Polar bears."

"An ittiy-bitty little girl like you and a big bear?"

"I'm not a girl," she replied tersely.

The man chuckled. "Bring me the howdah and a box of bullets," he told the woman.

The woman made a face, but returned with a box of bullets and a wooden box and placed them on the table between them. The man stood up and walked next to Atl, lifting the lid and handing her the weapon. It was a double-barrel pistol in glossy black.

"Inspired by British hunters who used weapons like this to hunt elephants and tigers. A modern take on it, but still very nice. I was going to sell it to one of my regulars, but seeing as you need to hunt polar bears"— the man gave her a smile—"I could be persuaded to change my mind. For the right price."

"I'm very persuasive," Atl said.

"Are you?"

"Sure," Atl said, placing a wad of bills on the table.

"That don't look too persuasive."

Atl added two more bills to the pile of money.

"Well, what do you know. You were right. Can I also interest you in some pot?"

"We're busy. But it was great meeting you," Atl said, grabbing the weapon and the box of bullets. She had no desire for chitchat. Judging by the face of the red-haired woman, neither did she.

"Yeah," Domingo said. "It was super great."

It started to rain when they reached the street, a drizzle that could hardly be called rain, but Domingo still pulled up his hood. She was grateful for the drops splashing on her head. She took off her jacket, wrapped the gun and the box of bullets with it.

"Do you know how to shoot it?" Domingo asked.

"Sure I do."

"You've owned many guns?"

She thought of Izel, her arm firm as iron as she aimed. First-born. Stronger, better than Atl at everything. "Not really. My sister did."

"If you shoot a vampire, can the vampire die?"

They jaywalked their way across the street, moving fast.

"With regular bullets? No. But if they find me, it'll be humans who come after me. Rodrigo can't afford to bring vampires into the city."

Unless Nick is with him, she thought. *He probably is.*

She'd asked for a powerful gun for this reason, just in case. It needed to have a kick in order to do real damage or it would be like throwing marbles at him. Last time they'd met she'd been lucky. She didn't know if her luck would hold.

Atl frowned. She did not want to think about that now. They'd successfully contacted Bernardino and Elisa, procured a way out of the city, and evaded sanitation. So far, so good. It was not worth spooking herself over Nick and Rodrigo when they might never find her.

"Tell me more about the Jackal?" she asked, because Domingo had brought up the guy before and she was curious.

"He's a dude that organizes dog fights and stuff."

"Yeah, all right. How do you know him?"

Domingo took out a piece of gum and chewed it noisily. "He was a guy with the street kids I lived with, older. They call him the Jackal 'cause of the way he laughs. You had to do what he said. He'd give you candy to sell and take a cut. Or he'd send you to wash car windows at an intersection. When he wasn't telling me to wash cars, he'd have me go to the place where he kept the dogs he used for fighting. I helped clean the cages."

Domingo glanced at her from the corner of his eye. His voice had grown more hushed and now it was a whisper, though Atl could hear him well enough and see him also in the semidarkness of the streets.

"There was a girl, a street kid, Belén. The young girls, the pretty ones . . . he was always after them. Always trying to sleep with them. Belén, though, she was going out with me. She wasn't . . . I mean, I dunno, she wasn't a girlfriend *girlfriend,* but it was close enough. He gave her presents and he was real sweet to her."

"What happened?"

"I told Belén she shouldn't go with the Jackal, that he was nasty. The Jackal figured I was the one putting ideas into her head, you know, that she wasn't shacking up with him because of me. So he decided to teach me a lesson."

Domingo took a deep breath, as though he were about to dive underwater. "He told me my meddling was costing him some fun times with Belén and that I'd have to pay him for causing him grief. He said I was such a damn talker, talking Belén's ear off, that maybe I should put my mouth to good use. He told me I should get on my knees and kiss his shoes. He made a big show of it, told everyone to watch as I did it. Said he'd have his friends beat me if I didn't.

"So I did. And then, he tells me to lick his boots. And then he takes off his shoes and tells me to lick his damn feet clean. So I did it. I couldn't look at anyone in the eye and I felt Belén staring at me all day long. I thought of running to the subway and throwing myself on the tracks."

He raised his head and looked at Atl, his eyes very large and honest. "That's when I left the street kids. I went away and started collecting garbage. Everything was better. Only she wouldn't leave with me. She stayed and she's with the Jackal."

"I'm sorry," she said.

"It's fine," he said with a cool firmness that made him sound beyond his age. "Things change. I'm glad they've changed. Besides, I've met you and you're nice."

His words were devoid of malice or deceit; they made her grimace, slicing through her composure. She wanted to touch him and so she extended her hand, meaning to lace her fingers with his, snatching it back at the last minute.

"You have too high an opinion of me," she said. "One day, I think you'll realize that."

CHAPTER 19

It was late in the afternoon by the time Ana found the needle in the haystack. She'd combed through recent police reports and moved to sanitation reports. A fresh one had just come in, courtesy of an eager, anal worker who filed it darn quick.

Domingo Molina. Male, 17, no ID papers, no health issues, required to visit nearest health unit to register himself. Has pet, biomodified Doberman. Also not registered, also required to visit health unit for registration.

Ana pulled out the envelope Kika had given her and found the photo she was looking for. It was the girl, Atl, with her dog. She had a large Doberman with a tessellation of light running down its neck. The report talked about a boy, but Ana felt sure she'd hit the jackpot.

She raised her head and looked at the desks around her, glanced at Castillo's office. The door was closed. Quickly she gathered her things and headed out.

The cab dropped her around the corner from the apartment she was looking for. There were a couple of kids standing in front of the entrance. She showed them Atl's photo, but neither one recognized her. Ana went around the block, showing the picture to other people, but they shrugged.

She was dying for a smoke. A few blocks up the street there was a busy avenue and she found a convenience store. Once inside she hesitated, and in addition to the cigarettes grabbed a soda and a Gansito. She doubted it contained a single natural component, but sometimes synthetic is what you are after. The cashier rang the items.

"Hey, have you seen this girl by any chance?" she asked, holding the photo up.

The cashier stared at the photo, frowning. "Yeah, I've seen her a couple of times. What she do?"

"Runaway," Ana said. "When was the last time you saw her?"

"A few days ago, I think. She didn't take her change. It was a big bill."

"Thanks."

Ana stepped outside and lit her cigarette. She enjoyed the smoke for a few minutes before she took out her cell phone and sent a text message.

She grabbed a cab and waited at a twenty-four-hour automat, which was baby blue throughout, from the tables to the chairs and the machines dispensing the food. The whole retro vibe was very much in these days. It was too early for the late-night club hoppers to stream inside, so Ana had the place pretty much to herself, unless she counted the homeless guy asleep near the entrance.

Ana slid her credit card into a slot and pressed the touch screen. A sandwich came tumbling down. She moved to the drinks area, placed a cup under a spigot, and pressed the right code for coffee.

She sat in the back and glanced at the ornate carved ceilings, remnants of the 1910s. They were playing 1950s music, "Aquellos Ojos Verdes" by the Trío Los Panchos. A clash of styles and eras.

Kika walked in briskly, sporting a long red coat and matching lipstick. She sat across from Ana, resting her elbows against the plastic table. She looked terribly perky, as if she'd just had two coffees and an energy drink mixed with a bit of coke to top it off.

"This is a bit casual," Kika said, looking around. "You could afford a better dinner now that we are partners."

"I like sandwiches," Ana replied dryly. "I also have a lead, *partner*. I think I found where she's staying."

"You think or are you sure?"

"It would take more time for me to be sure, and I assume you'd like me to be quick." Ana took out her notebook, scribbled the address, and showed it to Kika.

Kika nodded and took out a cigarette. "Smoke?" she asked.

"I'm fine."

Kika shrugged. She lit her cigarette. Kika wasn't very old. Mid-twenties perhaps. Atl and Nick were pretty young too. She recalled the savage pictures she'd seen and wondered what, if anything, separated her own daughter from kids like these.

I am what makes a difference, she thought. *And I'll make sure she never deals with any of this.*

"Do you have any leads on Nick?" Kika asked. She slipped out her phone, her fingers flying as she texted.

Ana frowned. "I'm not God. You're lucky I found her in the first place. It's a huge city."

"That it is," Kika said, sliding her phone back into her coat's pocket. "We'll be picking her up in a few hours. Don't tell your boss, but be there for the takedown. I'll let you know exactly what time to meet us."

"I'm a consultant, remember?"

"You won't have to lift a finger. I just want to feel reassured. None of my people have ever dealt with a bloodsucker. We'll have the equipment, but nothing beats experience."

"I don't think it's a good idea for me to be hanging out with you in public," Ana said.

"Come, come. You already took the paycheck."

Ana felt herself blushing as she remembered that. Yeah, she'd taken the money. It was a good amount of money and she needed it if she was going to get herself and her kid out of Mexico City. She dearly wanted out. Out of her life, out of her uniform, and out of this bitch of a country.

"I took half," Ana said, wanting to be precise.

"If you want the other half you should show up," Kika said. "Don't look so glum. Have a cigarette." Kika took out her cigarette case and opened it, offering it to Ana.

Ana stared at the cigarettes, but shook her head. "I'm trying to quit."

"I'd think you'd be jumping over another chance to kill a couple of vampires," Kika said, snapping the case shut and tossing it back in her purse. "It sounds like the stuff to get the blood running."

"You've never been near them, have you?"

"Can't say I have. But it sounds fun."

"You have no idea what you are talking about," Ana muttered.

"Tell me then." The woman scooted forward, smiling.

"Tell you what?"

"What it's like to kill them."

"I don't know. What's it like killing people?" Ana shot back.

"What makes you think I kill people?" Kika asked.

"What's your line of work, then?"

Kika shrugged. "I'm more of a personal assistant. Keep tabs on the money. Recruiting security. Asset collection. Mostly."

"What did you do before this?"

"How come we are talking about me and not you?" Kika asked, chuckling. "You're trying to turn the tables on me, Detective, but you're the one with an interesting story."

"I'm curious about who I'm working with."

"You mean you haven't looked me up in your police databases?"

Ana had looked for the woman in red, but she'd gotten no hits. Could be she was new or could be she was simply smart. The girl held her cigarette in midair and blew a ring of smoke.

"You have a Rita Hayworth vibe," Ana said. "I know your name's not Kika, so who are you modeling yourself after?"

"It's a diminutive of Francisca. It means 'free woman.'"

"You weren't free before."

"Not quite."

Ana sipped her coffee and nodded. She carefully unwrapped her sandwich and began eating it. "Killing vampires is hard. They're tough, they're resistant, and they won't hesitate to bite off your head. But that doesn't make it fun," she said. "I joined an operative. It was not supposed to be big, we were serving as backup for the folks in the Secretariat of National Defense. That's where most of my kills come from. It wasn't glamorous. We had twenty-two dead people, total, including nine of our own. I killed three vampires that night. I joined a second operative as backup a few months later. Killed another two vampires. And then I was done with that."

"Why?"

"I don't know. I thought Mexico City would be better." Ana wrapped the remains of her sandwich and placed her hands on top of it.

Kika was still smoking, the ash falling upon the table. "I'd still like to kill one," Kika said, dropping the cigarette to the floor and smashing it under the heel of a red shoe. "Get some sleep. We'll be seeing each other in a little while."

The younger woman rose but paused for a moment, frowning. "Who's Rita Hayworth?" she asked.

"She was an actress. Used to dance," Ana said.

"All right," Kika said. "See you around."

Ana looked down. The cigarette on the floor bore the imprint of Kika's lipstick. She grabbed her sandwich and exited the eatery.

She was up early and made an effort to cook eggs and quesadillas for Marisol. Her daughter seemed startled by the sight of Ana in the kitchen.

"Marisol, sit down, have a bite," Ana said, setting a plate on the narrow plastic table where they had all their meals. They had no proper dining room.

"Something wrong?"

"No, nothing's wrong," Ana said. "I make breakfast and something's got to be wrong?"

Marisol shrugged. Ana supposed that she had been skimping on the cooking lately, although she did work a lot of nights. It was a hectic schedule. They sat down and ate quietly. Her daughter checked her phone constantly.

"I've thought about the Acapulco thing and I don't think it's a good idea, but we should go see your aunt soon. You know, a trip to Zacatecas. And I was thinking maybe, after that, Cuba."

"Cuba?" Marisol said, raising her head. "Like a real vacation?"

There were no vampires there. And there were other places. Hawaii. New Zealand. But they could speak Spanish in Cuba, the culture shock wouldn't be so bad, and the money would stretch, very, very far. And almost any place would be better than Mexico, wouldn't it?

"Can we afford that?"

"I've got a bonus," Ana said. "I put the bulk of the money into the savings account and I have cash, in the cigar box under the bed, for emergencies. So yes, we can afford it."

"Cool." Marisol went back to checking her phone, but she paused to give her mother a smile before running off to school.

Ana sat for a few more minutes at the table before making her way to her bedroom. The Virgin shot her an accusing glance from her shrine, but Ana could not allow herself to feel any remorse. She was going to capture a pair of vampires with the assistance of a known criminal group and she was going to do it for money, but fuck it, sometimes you have to sin in order to earn your way to paradise. Or in her case, a couple of tickets to Cuba and the promise of a comfortable life.

CHAPTER 20

Mexico City was an apocalyptically dysfunctional place at the best of times, what with the pollution, the flooding, the teetering concrete slums, and the city sinking into the lake bed upon which it was built. However, that day, with the sun hiding behind thick clouds and the rain coming down so heavily, it was damn hellish. Rodrigo wished he could head home, back to the sunny, arid North. But there was too much work to be done.

Rodrigo closed the blinds and circled his desk, standing before a bookcase and staring at a picture of himself when he'd been much younger, sitting behind the wheel of a convertible. When he'd started working this business, Rodrigo hadn't intended to get himself so involved with vampire narcos. He just liked cars. Vintage cars, custom cars. His brother had a garage and a gentleman had come in one day to get some work done on his vehicle. He'd struck up a conversation with Rodrigo and they'd talked cars, and the man wondered if he was a good driver. It turned out the old man was a Renfield who'd come from Europe with a few bloodsuckers two years before, right after vampires started immigrating to Mexico in big numbers.

The U.K. had major restrictions against vampires, but it wasn't the only country with a hard attitude when it came to bloodsuckers. Spain and Portugal had plain expelled them in 1970. France, Germany, and Italy didn't like them much either, though they had not kicked them out. There had been major clashes in the late '70s and a clusterfuck in Paris in 1981. By 1985 Mexico City was a no-vampire zone. Also by 1985 Rodrigo was a Renfield.

Rodrigo tore his eyes from the photo and glanced at the phone number on the notepad.

Rodrigo didn't have as many contacts in Mexico City or as much pull as he would have liked, but he did have people he could rely on. So far, they'd produced nothing. Atl had vanished into thin air, slipping into Mexico City with an ease he thought was beyond her capacity. But a nice juicy tidbit had just rolled in.

An employee with the Secretariat of Public Safety informed him that the person assigned to the case of the girl Nick had killed was called Ana Aguirre. Lately Aguirre had been accessing the databases and pulling information about both Nick *and* Atl. That the investigator could have tied the killing to Nick did not sound so far-fetched, but Atl . . . that could not be a mere coincidence. This woman knew *something*.

Rodrigo dialed the number and waited.

"Hello?" a woman said.

"Is this Detective Aguirre?" he asked.

"Yeah."

"I'm calling about a mutual friend. His name is Nick Godoy." He could hear her adjusting the telephone, moving the mouthpiece closer.

"Who are you?"

"Look, I'm really terribly sorry for disturbing you, but I'm interested in knowing how your investigation is going. I'm especially interested in hearing why you are looking into Atl Iztac."

"Who are you?" she asked again.

"Why are you linking Nick to Atl?" Rodrigo countered.

"Who have you been talking with?"

"That doesn't matter." She hung up on him. Rodrigo smirked.

He thought about calling her back, but decided he had bigger fish to fry. Nick's dad had sent a text message, wanted to know how things were going. Although Rodrigo had very little interest in talking to his boss, he decided he might as well do it now. It was better to get these things out of the way.

"Hello, Mr. Godoy, it's Rodrigo," he said.

Rodrigo was very polite to Godoy. He never called him by his first name, even after all these years. He'd been twenty, driving merchandise across the border for small-time gangs, when he met Godoy. Rodrigo was smart, bookish, spoke English without an accent, didn't look the part of a gang member. Godoy, an ambitious vampire who had made it through both world wars, took notice of Rodrigo. Godoy's Renfield was getting creaky, and this young chap was brighter than your average goon for hire. Godoy saw potential. Rodrigo saw money.

"My boy, I've been expecting your call."

Yes, and Godoy always called him "my boy," even though Rodrigo was hardly a boy anymore. To be fair, he supposed everyone was a "boy" to the vampire. Godoy was inching toward a hundred and looked forty-ish. Sometimes Rodrigo's back ached and he envied the vampire's youth. Other times he was glad to get old and one day, very soon, slip out the back and into retirement.

"I'm sorry I took so long. We've been busy," Rodrigo explained.

"So I heard. Nick phoned."

"Oh?" Rodrigo said. He was supposed to be the only one contacting Sinaloa.

"He said you're in Mexico City and have lost the girl."

Damn it. That was not the way he wanted the conversation to begin. Rodrigo sat down behind his desk and modulated his voice so he sounded perfectly calm. "That's not exactly accurate," Rodrigo said.

"She was not supposed to get that far."

"We had trouble in Guadalajara."

"You did not mention that when we last spoke. You also did not say anything about visiting Mexico City."

Rodrigo did not want to say anything because he knew exactly how it would sound: like he'd fucked up. The truth of the matter was, yes, it had all gone south, but it had been in great part thanks to Nick. Godoy thought a great deal of his son, but the boy was raw, impulsive, and stupid, an explosive combination. "We know she's here."

"Where?" Godoy asked.

"I'm working on finding her."

"Nick said you lost Justiniano."

"Yes," Rodrigo said. Justiniano had been the kid's personal escort, not a fellow Rodrigo had especially liked, but at least he was able to keep Nick under control. Well, so much for that.

There was an unpleasant silence. "I almost feel like pulling you out, Rodrigo. Let someone else clean up this mess."

Rodrigo recalled the vampire's idea of cleaning. It involved chopped bodies dumped in a vat of acid. Rodrigo was not about to let his career end in shame with his tail between his legs, or worse, as an unidentified corpse dumped next to a highway.

"I can do it. It's been a bit more complicated than I'd anticipated," he said, thinking about Nick's murder feast the other day. He hoped Nick hadn't told his dad about that, though the boy probably had enough common sense to keep those details to himself.

"Complicated, yes," Godoy said. "Overly. She's a *girl*."

Well, she's got some balls, Rodrigo thought.

"She's Centehua's daughter. She's got money and enough contacts to hide for a bit. But not forever. Sooner or later someone's going to turn her in. I'm working old contacts as best I can. Street level, even cops. I've put the word out and her photograph. Someone will spot her."

Before she leaves the country, he thought. If Atl had any brains she was already trying to find a ticket out of Mexico, though it was going to be tough. He had spread her image wide and far. Every Necros remotely near the northern border was expecting her. She couldn't fly out of Mexico City, and if she stepped foot in the outskirts of the city, she'd be toast. No, Atl was still in Mexico City because it was the only place left to hide. For now.

"Solve this. Do it quick."

"Yes, sir. She'll be dead in a week's time."

"No."

"I'm sorry?" Rodrigo said.

"Nick feels like playing with her. I agree. A quick death is too good for the girl. Let's make a memorable example of her."

Rodrigo mouthed an angry "motherfucker" to the phone but he kept his voice level. "It's going to be difficult to abduct her and drag her out of Mexico City and back home," Rodrigo said.

"I don't care if you have to break her limbs in order to do it, make sure she's alive."

This was his punishment. There was no point in rejecting it.

"Yes, sir," he said. Rodrigo hung up, moving back toward the bookcase and running a hand through his thinning hair. He glanced at the photo of himself and thought of the days when his only concern had been getting his hands on nice cars and racing them.

CHAPTER 21

She dreamt of her sister, and when they were little. Izel was holding her hand and they were running down the stairs to hide from her cousins. Atl must have been four and Izel nine. Giggling, happy girls. Then the dream changed and Izel was a charred corpse, unrecognizable, a dark lump left upon the ground. The corpse writhed, opened its mouth. "Our hearts want nothing but a war death," it said, the same line Atl had once recited.

When Atl woke up, there was one thought ringing through her head: *I should have been with her.* She'd always been such a petulant child, too busy picking fights with Izel to help the family. She had not wanted to help out with anything because that would spoil her easy life, would burden her with responsibilities. Moody, resentful, she figured she'd grow up later.

There's trouble brewing, her mother had said, but Atl dismissed it. And when trouble came Atl was stupid and afraid.

Her head still foggy with sleep, Atl stumbled into the kitchen, managing to fill herself a glass of water.

"Hey," Domingo said. "How you doing?"

"Fine," she muttered.

Cualli walked into the kitchen as well. Domingo patted the dog's head.

"He must like you," she said, looking at them and trying to remember if there had been any time when Cualli liked anyone but her.

"He's awesome. I never had any pets, you know? I would have loved a dog. Cats are just so—"

"Aloof?" Atl ventured.

"I was going to say smelly. Bernardino's house reeks of cat piss, you wouldn't believe it. If Dracula's castle had smelled of cat piss I swear he wouldn't be in that many films."

Domingo grinned at her and Atl chuckled. He was too honest, by far, and too silly, and still she enjoyed his company. For a moment things felt okay. Like the unbalanced mess of her life was now tipping in the other direction, balancing itself out. "Let's go get a bite. For you, I mean," she said.

"Sure."

She grabbed her jacket, put the leash on Cualli, and out they went. It was raining, and Atl paused next to the building's entrance to open her umbrella.

Cualli growled. A few split seconds was all the warning Atl had, but it was enough. She saw them from the corner of her eye. She held her breath, pretended to fiddle with the dog's leash and the umbrella, as she counted nine of them. They wore no uniforms. Not cops, not sanitation. They were human. Rodrigo and Nick seemed to be nowhere in sight. Were these their goons? Or someone else's? It didn't matter. They were waiting for her.

Atl released her grip on the leash, dropped the umbrella, and let her breath out.

She shoved Domingo behind a car and pulled out the gun, shooting two of them dead before they had a chance to blink. The others raised their weapons and shot back at her, but the loud bangs of pistols firing did not thunder along the street. Instead, there was a low, whooshing sound. Something silvery flew past her. Atl jumped behind the car next to Domingo, evading the projectiles.

Silver nitrate darts. Shit. She would have preferred regular bullets. This could get nasty.

"What's happening?" Domingo babbled.

"Bad guys," she said. "Sit tight. Cualli!" She saw the dog leap in the direction of one of the men, knocking him down with its weight. There were startled cries and Atl stood again, shooting a couple of them while they were trying to drag the dog off their friend. She missed her third shot, hit a car instead, glass shattering upon the pavement. Darts whooshed by and she sat down again.

"Behind! They're also behind!" Domingo yelled.

Atl turned and saw three men coming from the other end of the street. They aimed at her. She blew off the head of one of them and ran across the street, ducking and pressing her back against another car. Domingo followed her. He was too slow. The two men who had been aiming at her now ran in his direction, pinning him to the ground and wrapping a plastic tie around his wrists. She heard Domingo scream, but ignored the cry and glanced at the building closest to her. If she was fast enough, she could climb up its side and escape through the roofs.

She looked across the street and noticed two corpses, their necks torn by her dog. That still left six attackers, although two were currently busy with Domingo.

Cualli was barking and Domingo was being dragged away, kicking and screaming. She watched as they tried to place him into the trunk of a black car. Domingo attempted to hold on to something and they punched him, once, twice, thrice, until he fell to his knees.

Damn it.

She stood up, shot one of them, but the other, he was quick. She felt the dart sink into her leg, and it let out a loud hiss. Like an idiot she'd stepped out into the street with a gun and no ammo. Her bullets were now gone and there were still five bastards against her.

Fuck it. She'd do this with her hands.

Atl took a mighty leap, landing on top of the guy who had been punching Domingo and knocked him down, slamming his head against the ground. He cried and flapped his arms, and she broke his neck so he'd stop screaming.

She turned toward Domingo, who lay sprawled on the ground, and pulled him up. "Anything broken?" she asked. "Because we may have to run."

"No," he replied.

Another dart. This one hit her on the shoulder and it hurt much worse than the first, causing a stabbing pain that led her to trip and fall. They were coming, the four remaining ones, and she could already feel the effects of the silver nitrate in her body.

She looked down, at the blood dripping down her leg, staining her socks, and there, next to her shoe . . . keys. Not her keys. Car keys. Keys to the car they were trying to stuff Domingo in. She grabbed them and rushed toward the passenger seat, opening the door and sliding inside.

"Get in!" she yelled.

They shot a third dart. It shattered the front window of the car, bits of glass raining upon her lap. Domingo shuffled onto the backseat and Cualli jumped in behind him.

She tossed her empty, useless gun onto the passenger's seat and pressed on the accelerator. She sped away, her hands stiff against the wheel. A light turned green, turned red, and she did not care. Amber, red, green, she kept going until she felt a deep, shivering pain and had to stop. She vomited over herself. A sticky, black mess.

She slammed on the brakes, opened the car door, and stepped out, teetering and stumbling, and suddenly there was the barking of the dog and a body next to her.

"Hey," Domingo said. "You need to drive. I can't drive."

"I need to sleep," she croaked. Her legs buckled, but he was there. He helped her stand, asked her if she could take a step, and surprisingly she could. She dragged herself forward or he dragged her with him, but somehow she walked.

CHAPTER 22

I t would have been easier if Domingo had his shopping cart with him. He could have tossed Atl in it and wheeled her away. Instead, he was stuck half-dragging her into the subway station. This was his territory, and he felt a lot safer once they caught a train. Atl slumped onto one of the seats, her head resting on his shoulder.

Most people didn't even glance at them. Atl's clothes were dark and the blood didn't show. Even if it showed, maybe they wouldn't have cared. He imagined they looked like two dirty street kids with their dog. They probably thought that Atl was drunk or high. Either way, nobody spoke to them.

They got off the subway car and things went well until Atl had to climb the stairs leading outside the station. She lost her footing, causing two bums who were sitting by the stairs to stare at them while he whispered to her, begging her to walk with him. Domingo had to put her arm around his shoulders, pulling her up. Soon they were in the tunnels and had reached his home.

He lowered her onto the mattress and lit several lanterns, then grabbed one and placed it on a hook above the bed.

"You need to take out the darts," she said. "My leg. My shoulder. They're . . . that's . . . silver nitrate. It's . . . anaphylactic shock."

"Okay."

He rolled her pants up and found the dart she was talking about. It was burrowed deep into her flesh. When he pulled, it seemed to sink deeper and Atl let out a gasp.

"Sorry," he said. "It's messed up. It's embedded into your skin."

"Yank it out," she ordered.

"I can't . . . I . . . wait." Domingo took the lantern away and dashed to the other side of the chamber, opening and closing boxes until he found what he was looking for: a pair of old pliers. He had rubbing alcohol, but no bandages. He tore a T-shirt into long strips and hurried back to her side. When he set the lantern down, the shadows on the wall seemed to tilt and bob up and down.

He pressed one hand against her leg and held the pliers with the other, pulling a small, metallic needle out. Blood seeped out and he grabbed the rubbing alcohol, cleaning the wound.

"The other," she said. Atl yanked off her jacket and rolled onto her side, her back to him.

Again he pulled out a needle, this time from her shoulder. Another had embedded itself right above her heart, and when he took it away blood sputtered like a river and though he kept pressing the T-shirt against it, it didn't seem to stop.

"Atl, what do I do now? Do I get Elisa? Do I take you to Bernardino?"

"No. I can't have Elisa panicking. Bernardino . . . *never* him. Okay? Too . . . unpredictable . . . dangerous."

"Who, then?"

"Nobody. I'll get better. I need to sleep," she said, clutching the shirt against her chest. "Let me sleep."

Domingo pulled a blanket over her. He boiled himself a bit of coffee over his portable stove and sat in a corner, biting his nails, thinking about what had happened and taking sips of coffee. It had been so fast. He'd barely been able to string two coherent thoughts together before chaos had exploded and some guys had been trying to pummel him.

It had been scary. He'd known Atl was in a shitty situation, but it had been an abstract thought. This was real. It wasn't something he'd read or seen on the TV. Those men had tried to put him in the trunk of a car and God knew what would have happened if they'd succeeded.

The dog came to sit next to him and they both stared at Atl for a good, long time. His coffee cooled down and Domingo crouched close to the bed. He pressed a hand against her forehead.

She was burning with fever.

He thought of the vampire comic books he'd read and the news stories he'd watched, but none of them had talked about sick vampires. Dead vampires, yeah. Dead by a stake to the heart, or decapitated, or a bunch of other things. But sick vampires . . . he had no idea what was happening to Atl and he thought she was getting worse. Her skin was sticky with sweat and her breath was very fast, as though she'd just been running.

She needed to go to the emergency room. She needed a doctor. But if Domingo took her to a doctor they'd call sanitation, the cops.

He knelt down next to the bed, touching her arm. He noticed she was wearing the fancy watch he'd given her and he ran his hands over it.

Domingo swallowed and unbuckled the watch, stuffing it into his pocket.

He ran a hand through his hair.

"Stay with her," he ordered the dog.

*   *   *

It was only ten o'clock, early for a party, but Quinto's parties started as early as possible and ended late the next morning, so by the time Domingo slipped into the apartment a good-sized crowd had already gathered. All the windows were open to let in the night air. The music was loud and lively. He pushed his way through the living room and noticed that Belén was sitting with the Jackal. He pulled his hood up, hoping neither one noticed him, and managed to stumble into the kitchen, where Quinto was leaning against the sink, drinking a beer.

"Hey, you came!" Quinto said, clasping his shoulder. "Do you have a drink? Is your friend here too?"

"Quinto, I need a favor, all right man? I need you to come and help me with an injured dog," Domingo said.

"A dog? Right now? Man, you're crazy. I'll check it out tomorrow."

"Look, I can pay you," he said, tossing him the watch. "It's worth a lot of money."

Quinto inspected the watch carefully. He frowned, giving Domingo a suspicious look. "How'd you get something like that?"

Domingo bit his lip and shook his head. "Doesn't matter how. Come on, man. Please."

"I don't know."

"We can take your car. It'll be quick. It's over at my place."

"Maybe later."

"*Now*, man," he said, glaring down at Quinto, who was on the tiny side and generally reluctant to confront anyone.

"Shit, dude. Okay, fine. I'll look at your damn dog," Quinto said, gulping his beer and tossing the bottle in the sink.

They had to cross the living room to reach the door. Domingo saw that Belén and the Jackal had caught sight of him this time, and were staring in his direction.

"Hurry up, before the Jackal decides to talk to us," Domingo said. Nothing good could ever come when the Jackal took an interest in you and Domingo didn't need no shit that night.

Domingo shoved Quinto out the door and they rushed down the stairs.

Quinto's car was an old, white Volkswagen beetle from the '60s. A damn classic, Quinto said. As soon as they slid into the vehicle, Quinto blasted the tired radio with heavy metal songs in German. The music was so loud it didn't allow for any conversation, and Domingo was grateful for that. Once they reached the tunnels, though, Quinto started humming, as was his custom.

The humming stopped as soon as they stepped into the room and Quinto took a look at his bed, which was stained with many strokes of red.

"Shit, man! What you do? Kidnap and kill a chick?"

The Doberman, which was sleeping by his mistress's feet, raised his head when Quinto screamed.

"We had an accident. I need you to help her out."

"What damn accident? Jesus," Quinto said.

"Just . . . will you look at her? She's running a fever."

Quinto grimaced, but sat next to Atl and rolled her onto her back. He jumped to his feet as soon as he saw her face and frankly Domingo couldn't blame him, 'cause she looked pretty bad. She'd coughed more blood and her chin was streaked black. Her features were not wholly human. There was something of that bird of prey look about her; she seemed deformed, alien. It reminded him of a picture he'd seen of an animal called a harpy and also of someone named Medusa, and still there was a bit of beauty in the strangeness, though, just like there's always a certain beauty about a wild animal.

"What the hell?!" Quinto screeched. "She's not—she's, she's—"

"She's a vampire and she's hurt," Domingo said, cutting him off. "I need you to help her."

"Help her? No way, man! No way!" Quinto said, waving his hands wildly.

"Yes way! Right now."

"What do I know about vampires?"

"Well, you patch up them dogs."

"Two years of veterinary school, dude!" Quinto said, holding up two fingers for emphasis. "That's not the same as a vampire. No. Take your damn watch back." Quinto tossed the watch at him.

Domingo caught it and held it tight. He took a deep breath. "If you don't help me out, that dog's gonna kill you," Domingo said. He was a bit surprised to notice how calm he sounded.

"What?"

"That's an attack dog," Domingo said. "It's a modified dog and it's meant to kill people and I can make it eat your face."

"Dude, come on," Quinto said, attempting a laugh and only managing a pathetic, frightened half chuckle. "That's not right."

"Cualli," Domingo said, and the dog growled, eyes fixed on Quinto.

"You're serious? You'd kill me over a vampire bitch?"

Quinto had been okay to Domingo and Domingo didn't want to be an asshole, but he forced himself to nod. 'Cause she needed him. She was depending on him. "Take a look at her."

"All right! Keep the dog away."

Domingo stepped back and sat on the floor. He called to the dog and it went toward him, though it gave Quinto a wary look.

Quinto took Atl's pulse and hovered over her, pulling away the T-shirt she was clutching. "What happened to her?"

"She was shot with these darts, silver nitrate. Said she was going into shock. Ana-something shock."

"Anaphylactic shock?"

Domingo thought that was the word. "What's that?"

"It's an allergic reaction."

"What do we do?"

"I'm not sure. Look, normally I'd say give her an epinephrine shot, but she's not human and she should be dead by now by the way she's looking. Her heart's racing like crazy."

"I took the darts out but it seems to have done no good."

"I need more light."

Domingo grabbed one of the lanterns and held it up while Quinto stared at her legs and arms.

Quinto shook his head. "I think there are fragments of the dart in the shoulder. The arm's swollen, too. Look, I don't have no equipment to treat her here, not even a stethoscope. I'm not sure what you want me to do."

"Where would you have the equipment?"

"Over at the kennels. But that's the stuff I use on the dogs, dude. No guarantees it would help."

"Then let's take her there."

"You crazy? The Jackal would have a shit fit if I took her there. He's paranoid about the dogs. You want him breaking your arms?"

"I'll worry about that later."

"She's covered in blood. My car—"

"Then we'll wrap her in a blanket and her jacket. Let's go."

Quinto looked like he wasn't going to move an inch, but the dog growled and he grabbed a blanket.

The city seemed strange as they drove to the kennels, quiet and gloomy, the only noise in the car the back and forth of the windshield wipers and the patter of the rain. Quinto wasn't too thrilled that, on top of a vampire, he'd asked him to bring the dog along, but they'd all crammed into the Volkswagen in the end, with Atl in the backseat.

Quinto parked the car behind the old factory that had been retrofit-ted to serve as kennel and fighting arena for the dogs, and together they carried Atl inside. The place was a major disaster zone, a jumble of crates littering the main entrance. They walked down a narrow hallway that led to a large room filled with cages, most of them occupied by sad-looking dogs, and kept going. Their destination was the "hospital"—that's what Quinto called it—a room that was fitted with several tables and special instruments so Quinto could patch up the dogs. Quinto turned on the lights and the room lit up.

"Over here," Quinto said, and they lowered Atl onto a wheeled veter-inary surgery table. "Christ. Okay, let me wash my hands and find my things."

Quinto rushed around the room, pulling bottles off shelves and grab-bing scissors, knives, and pliers. He dumped them onto a smaller table and dragged it next to Atl, muttering to himself.

"Okay, I see this asshole. The projectile, whatever the hell it was, broke into shards and is embedded in her arm and leg. I can clean it up and stitch her up, but I have no damn idea if I should administer epinephrine."

"What do you mean?" Domingo asked, watching Quinto as he made a small cut on Atl's arm.

"It could give her a heart attack for all I know. Okay, here's one shard. Pass me that dish."

Domingo stretched out his hand and held out a white ceramic dish. Quinto dropped a metallic sliver into it.

"I guess you shouldn't give it to her, then."

"Well, I don't know. Her face is swelling. She's lost a shitload of blood. Do I give her a transfusion? Where the hell do I get blood? I have no idea what I'm doing here. Here's another shard."

Quinto dropped the shard into the dish and Domingo watched him as he pulled several more bits of metal out and then stitched and bandaged Atl's arm and leg.

Quinto kept muttering to himself. He grabbed a syringe and looked at Domingo. "I'm going to try and give her an intramuscular injection. I don't know if this is going to help or not." Quinto pushed the plunger down.

He took Atl's pulse and shook his head. "Let's try again."

Quinto kept checking Atl's pulse, watching her and shaking his head. "I think it's working," he said at length. "Shit. It's like trying to treat an elephant. She's got a ton of adrenaline pumping through her body and she barely twitches."

"Is she going to be okay?"

"I don't know. There's nothing I can do about the blood she lost."

Domingo smoothed Atl's hair away from her face. It was starting to change, slowly morphing into a more human shape. "And now? What do we do now?" Domingo asked.

"I think you ought to let her sleep. This is so wrong. Damn, what is it with you and girls? First you get your ass beat because of Belén and now you're hooking up with a monster?"

"She's not a monster."

"Vampires . . . they suck people's blood, man. Come on, you know that."

"She's not going to hurt me."

Quinto gave him a skeptical sigh and crossed his arms. The light in the room was harsh, drawing stark lines upon Atl's face so that he felt he could almost see every bone underneath her skin.

"I'm off," Quinto said.

"What? Where? You can't leave her alone. What if she needs help in a couple of hours?" Domingo protested.

"Yeah, *I* need to shower and go straight to bed."

"Quinto—"

"Look, I'm just going to pull out the old cot you slept on a few times and nap. If she needs me, come and look for me in the back, all right?"

"All right. Thanks, by the way."

Quinto didn't reply. He moved toward the door, but paused to give Domingo one last look. "She's a vampire. You need to get rid of her before it's too late."

Domingo did not reply. He bent down to pick up Atl's jacket, which Quinto had tossed to the floor, and placed it on top of her, also drawing up the blanket they'd wrapped her in. He guessed he ought to find her clean clothes and a clean blanket, but there wasn't much in terms of that around the room and he was afraid of looking outside and Atl suddenly having a relapse while he was gone. She was looking better now, but there were no guarantees she wouldn't need more medical attention.

He patted her hand and pulled up a chair, sitting by her head.

He supposed he was dreaming, because he was standing in the middle of the desert and there was a tortoise crawling next to him. Domingo looked at it. The sun bleached the desert white, the animal looked like it was made of porcelain. He turned and saw a fire burning in the distance. Smoke billowed up, black, staining the sky, but when he approached the fire had stopped burning and there were only ashes left. A pile of ashes blanketing the desert, which was now gray.

And that's when he saw them, under the shadow of a dead tree: three bodies. Two teenage boys. Someone had inflicted tiny cuts on their faces and bodies, then cut off their heads, and the severed heads stared at him, their eyes bulging out. The third was a pregnant woman. A shot had blown off half her head. Her belly was a bloody mess.

He knew, in a corner of his heart, that this was a true memory and no nightmare. It was Atl's memory.

Domingo opened his eyes and lifted his hand, glancing down at Atl. She was breathing slowly, eyes closed, and her face now was that of a normal young woman. Just a girl, asleep, but for the first time he felt apprehension, the trickle of fear upon his shoulders.

And then he heard it. Footsteps. Several people.

He whirled around to find himself face-to-face with Quinto. He wasn't alone. The Jackal and two of his buddies were with him.

"Hey, asshole," the Jackal said. "I came to meet your new girlfriend."

"Fuck," Domingo whispered.

CHAPTER 23

A tl waited for Izel to scream. She waited for her to wail. She waited for anything except the calm, restrained look on her sister's face, as though someone had dragged an eraser across a blackboard, cleaning the slate.

"Aren't we doing something?" Atl asked.

"I am making arrangements for the funeral," her sister said.

"I'm not talking about the funeral. I mean *something*."

Izel was standing beside the large axolotl tank, observing the white and black salamanders as they swam up and down.

"You know, people tend to focus on the neoteny of the axolotl. It reaches sexual maturity without ever undergoing metamorphosis. But its more interesting aspect, the reason why we've always kept a few as pets, is their healing ability. They are capable of regenerating whole limbs, even vital parts of their brains. We are able to do that too, of course. In that sense we are like cousins."

"What the hell are you talking about?" Atl said.

"We will grow anew. We have been damaged, but we will heal."

Atl circled the axolotl tank. "Yeah, and that's fine, but what are we doing about them? What are we doing with Godoy? What are we doing with the assholes—"

"We do nothing," Izel said.

Atl did not speak, could not find the words, any words, for the span of a good couple of minutes. "Mother has been murdered. They delivered her *head* to us," Atl said.

"I know. The elders spoke yesterday, I am the cihuātlahtoāni now. And I say there shall be no retaliation."

"No retaliation?" Atl repeated. "They sent us her damn head!"

They hadn't even bothered returning the remains of their two cousins who had been with their mother. Rumor had it they'd fed the corpses to their dogs.

They did write a note to go with the head: GODOY CONTROLS THIS TOWN, BITCHES.

Izel's nails were pressed against the glass; she tapped them once, twice, thrice and raised her head to look at her sister. Her eyes were two pieces of onyx. "They'll send us more heads if we attack them. Our cousins, our aunts—"

"Our cousins, our aunts, they want revenge."

"Revenge is too costly."

Atl scoffed and stared at her sister. She acted so strong, so sure of herself, and now here she was, unable to make what should have been a simple decision.

"You think if we stay here, with our arms crossed, they'll magically leave us alone? They took out Wu last year and they've kicked out two of the Nachzehrer clans. If we don't make a stand now we'll be next."

"I can probably negotiate a solution," Izel said.

"You'd speak to them? You'd barter with the men who killed our mother?" Atl asked, aghast. "They broke the rules."

Atl inched closer to her sister. The rage she felt could have filled the stupid tank, the whole damn room, while Izel looked indifferent, as if their mother were on vacation and everything was fine.

"We are in a vulnerable position. My resources are limited."

"To hell with your resources. What about the family?" Atl asked. "Our hearts want nothing but a war death."

It was a line from a poem they had both learned as children. But Izel, rather than looking uplifted by the words, seemed disgusted.

"You don't give one shit about this family," Izel said. "You never have."

"And you're probably glad Mother's dead so you can boss us around like you've always wanted," Atl said, her voice rising, shrill and strange, like she'd never heard it before. She was at the edge of panic.

Izel slapped her hard, her ring cutting Atl's mouth. Atl tasted her own blood and glared at her sister. Izel turned back to the axolotl tank, while Atl grabbed her jacket and barged right out of the room, hurrying downstairs.

Three days later, Atl killed two of Godoy's nephews and his favorite concubine. It was easy. They had a couple of bodyguards with them in the apartment, but the guards were human and there were old codes against slaying enemies' wives or concubines. They were not expecting Atl, safe in their expensive nest. Godoy had violated those same codes when he killed Atl's mother on neutral ground, but apparently he feared no retaliation.

She pounced on the guards from above, dispatched them in a minute, and then dosed the vampires with UV light. They shrieked and shrieked, but she bound them tight and injected them with allicin. They quieted down after that, and she continued cutting them with ease. She chopped off the boys' heads. It was messy work, although the boys were small—just teenagers—and that helped. The concubine was considerably older and pregnant. Atl stabbed her in the womb twelve times. The woman pleaded for mercy, but Atl grabbed one of the guns that the guards had been carrying and blew off most of the vampire's head.

She convulsed for a long time before dying. Atl watched the whole performance, impassive. She'd never killed a vampire before and had only harmed a couple of humans one other time, at a club, but it had felt natural and she knew she'd behaved the way she was supposed to. She believed she'd regained what she'd lost. Dishonor. Honor.

She told Izel what she'd done right away.

"They'll come for us," her sister said. "They'll come for both of us. How could you?"

"The family wanted it. Mazatl and Nahui and the others, they told me so," Atl said.

It was true. She hadn't lied when she said her cousins and aunts desired revenge. They had expressed deep reservations toward Izel. Cousin Nahui had even told Atl, point-blank, that leading required certain skills and Izel might not have them. Mazatl had brought up their parentage, reminding everyone that Izel and Atl were the offspring of a weak man who had let the family down.

Atl ought to have spoken in her sister's favor, assuaging any fears, but instead the cries stoked her anger. *Someone*, they said, had to take decisive action for this terrible crime, which had not only left them in shame, but marked them as vulnerable and incapable of controlling their territory as well.

Your name is Atl, her cousin Nahui had told hser. *Why are you not the ātl tlachinolli, the water that scorches the earth? Instead you behave like a gentle stream that laps the ankles, licking Izel's feet.*

If Atl didn't push back the family was going to fall apart at the seams: the cihuātlahtoāni could be repudiated. Atl was not going to be branded with such a seal, her lineage shamed and shamed again. She did what she thought was right. She supposed, afterwards, that perhaps Godoy had wanted her to do this. That he'd arranged it so someone from her clan could manage the killings—that was why the guards had been so easy to dispatch. But then, so what? Blood was in their future, one way or another.

"Let them come," Atl told her sister.

They did. They rammed their trucks through the doors of their home and walked through the property with flamethrowers in hand. She watched from her window, saw the tongues of fire sweep across the patio and heard the shrieks of her cousins, her people.

"Hide," her sister ordered. "Hide, Atl! Hide!"

And then, when she ought to have grabbed a knife or a rifle or anything she damn could, when she ought to have been the warrior her bloodline dictated, she ran. She rushed down the back stairs, toward the kitchen, opened the lid of one of the flat-top refrigerators where they stored food supplies for their human servants, and slid in, closing the door behind her.

The sounds were muffled by the metal and plastic walls of the refrigerator, like when one swims underwater.

Small spaces.

Atl lay there, waiting. When she finally dared to push the lid open she chuckled, thinking that if anyone was watching her it would be a great parody of a vampire film. Instead of pushing open the door of a coffin, she was pushing the lid of a refrigerator.

But no one was there to watch her.

The house was quiet. She walked slowly through the hallways, stepping over broken glass, coming upon mutilated corpses. Several had been partially burned. She recognized Izel by the bracelet on her arm. The rest was a black lump with a vaguely human shape, mouth open in an eternal scream.

Atl slid down against a wall, resting her hands upon her knees. While she lay there, Cualli came bounding out of the house. She thought she was imagining it, but no. It was her dog. She hugged it, burying her face against the Doberman's neck.

She stepped out of the compound into the cool desert night, Cualli at her heels. She walked around and stumbled over a tortoise. She looked down at it. The sight greatly amused her and she thought Izel would have known what species this was.

She watched it walk away from her, slowly tracing its steps across the desert, though the desert was strange that night. The sand was red beneath her feet, and the moon had disappeared. She coughed, and this black, disgusting substance oozed from her mouth and she knelt upon the sand, a river of black bile and blood streaming out, and she tried to stop it but it would not stop. It. Just. Did not. Stop.

Someone touched her shoulder and she stood up, opening her eyes . . .

. . . and she was no longer in the desert. She was crouching on the floor.

Atl tried to slow down her breathing.

Gray cement walls and there was a metal door . . . no, a mesh wall with a door. Across from her she saw a dog. Not Cualli, but a mutt. She was in a cell, just like the dog across from her was in a cell.

"You're awake. My God, I'm so glad you're awake."

Atl blinked and turned her head. It was Domingo touching her shoulder, Domingo crouching next to her. He smiled.

"I'm . . . yeah . . . where am I?" she asked. "I was hurt."

"My friend, Quinto, he patched you up."

Atl glanced at her arm and saw the bandage. She remembered the darts. If she was awake it meant they'd taken them out, though much of the damage had already been done. She'd had a noxious substance pumping through her system and her body was still struggling to come to grips with it.

"But then . . . ah . . . we are in the Jackal's place. It's the kennels where he keeps his dogs."

"Why?"

"He thinks he can make money off you."

Atl looked around, at the small space they were sitting in. They'd dragged a mattress in, stained and lumpy. Atl's balled-up jacket lay on it. Also a blanket.

"He's not great on hospitality, is he?" Atl muttered, wiping her mouth with the back of her hand and sitting on the mattress. She flexed her fingers with some effort. She felt slow, tired; pain radiated from every muscle in her body. "How's he making money off me?"

"He says people are looking for a vampire. After that fight in the street . . . they, um . . . I guess there's a price for your head."

"Gee, a price," Atl chuckled. "I'm becoming very popular."

Domingo did not seem amused by her comment. He licked his lips and stared at her.

"Where's my dog?" Atl asked.

"I heard it barking a while back. It's nearby, but I can't see it from this cage," Domingo said.

"They better not have hurt him. I'll cut their balls if they have."

"I imagine the Jackal wants to keep your dog for the fights. I think it's safe."

"So are we. If he thinks we are worth something alive." She touched the bandage on her shoulder, slipping it off and glancing at the wound. The arm was stained black from the silver nitrate, with wild streaks radiating from the place where the dart had pierced the flesh. When she touched the skin, it hurt, and she winced. She slipped the bandage back in its place.

"Damn it, they had to go with silver nitrate," she said. "We need to get out of here. I can kick that door down and we can make a run for it," she said.

"That's probably not a good idea."

"Do you have a better one?"

"No. I don't think you're supposed to move a lot."

"Bullshit." She stood up and took a step forward. One step was all it took and she felt the bile gathering in her throat and started coughing again. She almost lost her balance and fell down, but Domingo hurried to her side, steadying her.

Atl croaked and black bile spilled down her shirt. He helped her back to the mattress and they sat down side by side.

She was filthy. She smelled of blood and vomit. She could barely keep her eyes open. She began to cough again.

Domingo took out a rag from his pocket and handed it to her. Atl pressed the rag against her mouth and frowned. Finally, the coughing subsided.

"Yeah, I get your point," Atl whispered, tossing the rag on the floor. The coughing fit had robbed her of her energy and she let herself sink against the mattress.

Her only weapon was her switchblade knife, and she wasn't sure if she still had that. It should be in her jacket, but maybe they'd looked for weapons. Or maybe they hadn't cared, with her so weak.

She had, perhaps, a knife. She had Domingo, too. Though he might be willing to protect her, she doubted he could smash the door down, carry her in his arms outside, and evade the people keeping them in the kennels.

"Are you hungry?" Domingo asked. "Do you need to—?"

Food. She did not want to think about that. The pain was so bright right now that she could not even consider eating. The pain erased any other concern. But once the pain died down, once her body began to heal in earnest, the hunger would arrive in full force. She was not sure what she'd do at that point. She remembered the old man she'd killed in Guadalajara. She wasn't even able to keep his blood down, and yet she'd killed him because she'd been in too much of a frenzy to care, or notice, what she was doing. If that happened again, she didn't know if she could keep herself from harming Domingo. Or if she would even want to.

If it came to it. She didn't want to die.

He can be replaced, she told herself.

But she wouldn't think about that now. *Later. I'll consider it, later.*

"I need to feed, yes. But right now, I'd probably barf it out again," she said.

"What do we do, then?" he asked.

What do we do. She was a girl. A girl who had played at murder and only succeeded in getting her sister killed in the process. A girl who could not be relied on to provide good counsel. A girl who ran off into the night, launched herself into a wild escape. A girl who was sick and tired. A girl who couldn't pretend she was a tough cookie who could get through this intact.

She looked at him and he seemed really interested in her answer, with that open, eager look on his face he seemed to get quite often. Domingo was such a *boy*. She might be a girl, but she'd never been what he was. She'd never be that.

"We wait," she told him.

"All right," he said. "It'll be all right, you know? I got a hunch about it."

A sweet boy with a goofy smile and hair in his face and such *faith* in Atl, or the universe, or something. She wondered how he managed to keep believing in anything.

"Yeah," she said, and her mouth had an acidic, unpleasant taste to it. "It'll be all right."

I'll kill him. Later. If necessary, she thought. But no. She didn't want him dead. She looked away from him. *Dear God, don't be stupid.*

CHAPTER 24

The dogs barked, announcing the arrival of people. Domingo stood up and approached the door, nervous. Atl had heard the noise too and she was sitting up, reaching for her jacket.

Quinto appeared and gave him a sheepish smile. He was carrying a backpack, which he set down on the floor. "Hey, Domingo," he said, lifting his right hand in greeting.

"Hey?" Domingo asked, pressing his hands against the mesh door. "You lock me in this cage and you 'hey' me?"

"Look, dude, I didn't have a choice. The Jackal was mighty curious about you after you went to find me at the party. He phoned me and I had to tell him."

"Awesome."

"Your girlfriend is still alive, ain't she?" Quinto said. "Besides, you told me you were going to kill me with your damn dog. Fair is fair."

Domingo curled his fingers around the mesh, staring at Quinto. Quinto bent down to unzip the backpack and rummaged in it; he found clean bandages, opened the little panel they used to feed the dogs, and handed them to Domingo.

"You need to change her dressing."

Domingo scowled, but went to Atl's side and began bandaging the wounds anew. The old dressings were completely soiled and useless, so he tossed them aside. When Domingo was done Quinto spoke again.

"You thirsty?" Quinto asked, holding up a flask. "I also have a sandwich for you, Domingo."

"What if you poisoned them?" Domingo asked.

"Don't be an idiot."

Domingo grabbed the flask and the sandwich, and went back to Atl. Her hands were not steady enough to hold the flask, so he had to press it against her lips. When she was done drinking, he drank and took small bites from the sandwich.

"Who is the Jackal trading with?" Atl asked. She sat with her back against the wall and did not look at Quinto.

"I don't know for sure. Rumors have been spreading that there was a vampire on the loose and some northern guy was willing to pay for her. And the dog."

"Nick," Atl whispered, and glanced up at Quinto. "When are the buyers coming?"

"I don't know. They should be here soon enough. I'm just supposed to keep an eye on you and make sure you don't die on us before they arrive."

"How thoughtful. You know, if you let me go now, I won't have to kill you," Atl said.

"But I'd kill him," the Jackal told her, stepping forward. He was wearing the flashy metallic jacket he loved and gray sweatpants.

Next to him stood Belén. She appeared utterly shocked. Two other men rounded out the party. These were the Jackal's usual thugs and did not seem to find the scene before them particularly surprising.

"You're the Jackal?" Atl asked.

"You got that right," the Jackal said, looking smug. "Seems I'm famous. Did he tell you about that time I made him lick my boots?"

"Fuck you," Domingo said.

"It was very fun. Maybe we can have some fun with you, too, sweetheart, although I have to say you're not looking too hot." The Jackal frowned. "Quinto, what the fuck is this? They said they want her in one piece and she looks like shit. You sure she ain't going to keel over and die? If she dies I'm cutting your balls."

"No, don't be thinking that. She should be able to make it."

"I need blood," Atl informed them. "I need it now."

The Jackal gave Quinto a questioning look. "That true?"

"I don't know! I'm not an expert in vampire medicine. What am I supposed to do, stop by the Red Cross for plasma?" Quinto said, looking at Domingo. "If she is really hungry there's Do . . ."

Quinto trailed off, but Domingo understood well enough. The Jackal chuckled and his men smiled.

"What's Nick paying for me?" Atl asked.

The Jackal shrugged and took out a toothpick, picking at his teeth. "Something or the other. Doesn't matter."

"I have money too."

"Doesn't look like it, sweetheart. I'll stick with the guy who owns the Mercedes."

"I'm Atl of the Iztac clan. You should let me go now. *Immediately.*"

The Jackal moved closer to the mesh door of their makeshift cell and wagged a finger at Atl. "Bitch, you ain't going nowhere and if you know what's good for you, you better shut your mouth before you harsh my mellow."

There was a loud buzzing sound and the Jackal took out his phone while biting down on his toothpick. He pressed his ear against the phone and barked a loud yes, twice, then hung up.

"You guys keep an eye on her. I gotta go greet our friends."

The Jackal walked away. Domingo sat on the mattress and placed an arm around Atl's shoulders. Her breathing had suddenly sped up, as though she were running. She began to cough again. Domingo had to let go of her because her body was contorting in such a violent fashion. He watched as she coughed again, spewing bile, and then she fell on her back. Her mouth was overflowing with blood.

"She's choking," he told Quinto. "She's choking on her own blood."

Quinto, Belén, and the two men looked at him with mute incomprehension. Domingo tossed himself against the mesh door, shaking it hard.

"She's going to die! Quinto, help her!"

Quinto took out his keys and with shaking fingers opened the door. Belén and the two men just stared at the unfolding scene, watching as Quinto dragged his backpack inside the cell and began rummaging in it.

"Do something!"

"I'm trying to find the damn epinephrine!"

Quinto managed to pull out a syringe and drove it into Atl's chest. She immediately yanked it out and rammed it into Quinto's eye. Domingo stepped back and lost his footing.

Atl pulled out a knife from between the folds of her jacket and threw it at one of the men, hitting him square in the middle of his forehead. The other man reacted quickly enough, grabbing a gun and shooting at her, but the bullet did not hit her and she landed on the man's chest, breaking his neck with one clean movement.

Then she was up and standing with such speed Domingo did not understand what was happening at first. Belén gasped as Atl grabbed her by the neck, her long fingers squeezing.

"What are you doing?" Domingo asked.

"I need blood," Atl said.

"Don't hurt her!"

Atl turned her head and stared at him; her voice was hard. "I won't. Get my dog," she said.

Domingo scrambled toward Quinto and pulled the keys out of his pocket. Quinto was moaning in pain, but Domingo had no time to help him. He hurried down the hallway, looking at each of the meshed doors. Cualli was way down the hallway, and when he came back with the dog, he found that Atl had Belén pinned against a wall, her mouth pressed against the girl's neck. Belén gave him a panicked look.

"I told you not to hurt her!" he cried.

Domingo pulled Atl back. She looked at him with her other face, her bird's face, her eyes narrowed into two angry slits.

"Atl, let her go," he said.

She hissed at him and continued feeding. Belén was weeping, tears streaming down her cheeks.

Domingo swallowed. He bent down and grabbed the gun one of the men had dropped. His hands trembled. He had no idea how to use the weapon and he didn't want to do this but he knew he had to. Atl just wasn't herself right that instant.

"Let her go," he said. "You're going to kill her."

"Don't interfere."

He pressed the gun against her back. "Atl, stop. I mean it."

Atl spun around and clutched his face with one hand, tilting it a little and tilting her own head in turn, staring at him. Her eyes were dark and hard as obsidian.

"You mean it? Have you ever pulled a trigger, hmm?"

"Atl," he muttered. "You said you wouldn't hurt her."

"This won't kill her."

"Fine. Let her go now," he said, and somehow he managed to speak calmly.

She seemed to respond to his tone, her hand sliding down his face and pulling away.

"Very well," Atl said, and she shoved the girl aside like she was a wet rag, then walked into the cell where Quinto lay whimpering.

Domingo caught Belén in his arms and held her as she sobbed. For a moment he thought Atl was going to kill Quinto, but all she did was grab her jacket from the place where it lay on the mattress and put it on with the greatest care, as if it weren't stained and filthy. Then she walked out, pulled her knife from the corpse where it was lodged, and hid it between the folds of her jacket. When she raised her head to look at Domingo her face had shifted and seemed human again.

"You should run now, girl," Atl said.

Belén disentangled herself from Domingo's arms and, obeying Atl, rushed down the hallway, away from them. She knew the building, and Domingo was confident she'd find her way out safely. Or she'd hide until it was safe enough to exit.

"Do you want to follow her?" Atl asked him, her voice a challenge.

No, he thought, and another part of him cried a definitive *Yes, I want out of this.* And he wondered why he was doing this, why he was sticking to her. The answer was not a coherent thought, merely the thump of his heartbeat.

He shook his head and offered her the gun he was holding. She snatched it from his hands.

"You know a way out?"

"There's a loading area," Domingo said. "We can get out from there."

Atl raised her head, as though she were listening for something. "They're here. We need to hurry."

CHAPTER 25

Rodrigo said he had a team of people ready, but in Nick's opinion the seven goons that comprised the team looked damn shitty. Nick didn't know what sewer the new recruits had crawled out of, but they certainly didn't seem very skilled. Hell, none of them had even met a vampire before. They were Mexico City lads, cocooned in their shit city for far too long. Nick looked at their weapons, scattered over the living room, and smirked.

Regular guns. As if that could kill one of his kind. Nick grabbed a rifle that had been left on a large dining room table and held it up, pointing at one of Rodrigo's paintings. He quickly turned his attention toward the knives, which were more interesting, and the stun batons. Now that was real vampire-hunting gear.

"I told you not to touch anything," La Bola said.

"I'm not breaking it."

"You have to stay in your room."

Nick rolled his eyes and snorted. La Bola was pathetic, stammering whatever words were put in his mouth. This was what his bodyguard amounted to: a fidgeting moron. Nick wished Justiniano had not died in Guadalajara. He'd been a smart cookie. The girl's stupid dog killed him. When they found Atl, he was going to skin the dog before her very eyes.

"Look, Bola, either I get out of this apartment or you get out in a body bag."

"Don't be so melodramatic," Rodrigo said from behind him.

Nick turned around and stared at the old man, scowling.

"If you want to go out, we are making a business trip and could use your company. I might have found our lady friend."

"You found Atl?"

"Maybe. I imagine you want to come along for the ride? Unless you'd like to stay here and watch a few cartoons. The team is ready to go."

Nick gave Rodrigo the finger, but followed him down to the car anyway. Bola and the shitty team were just behind them.

"When were you thinking of briefing me?" Nick asked once they were inside the car. No one ever told him anything.

"I got the news only a little while ago. I've been sharing Atl's photo and description with every lowlife in Mexico City I've ever had dealings with, and apparently we hit the jackpot."

Rodrigo handed Nick his phone and Nick looked at the picture on the screen. It wasn't a terribly good image, but it looked like Atl, her eyes closed.

"Who's got her?" Nick asked.

"A nobody who got lucky. She's alive and badly injured."

"It should be a piece of cake, then."

"Don't get cocky," Rodrigo warned him.

They drove for a while and when the lights turned red at an intersection, a young kid sprang forward with a rag in his hand, ready to wash their windows. Nick was going to shoo the kid away but Rodrigo spoke up.

"I'm looking for the Jackal," Rodrigo told the boy.

"Sure, mister," the boy said. "Keep driving. Turn right after five blocks and ask for him again."

Rodrigo did as the kid said and at the next intersection there was a girl who was also washing windows. She approached the car and the game was repeated again. In total, they had to speak with three kids in order to reach their final destination: an old factory with the windows on the first floor shuttered. The outside had been painted and repainted with graffiti. They parked their cars, and the seven goons, along with Rodrigo, Nick, and La Bola, assembled before the factory's doors. Nacho and Colima were told to remain in the cars, just in case a quick getaway was necessary.

Only a couple of minutes after they had parked two teenagers opened the doors of the building and let them in, guiding them to a room with nothing but peeling walls and a few chairs. Half a dozen young men, including a kid who could not have been older than thirteen, were sitting on the chairs, smoking cigarettes and chatting with each other. When they walked in, one of them stood up, tall and strong, his head shaved. Up close Nick saw he was noticeably older than the rest.

The man shook their hands.

"I'm the Jackal," he announced.

"I'm Rodrigo and this is Nick. We have the reward."

Rodrigo took out a briefcase and opened it, showing its contents to the Jackal. The Jackal seemed very pleased, chuckling. He had an unpleasant voice, a bit high-pitched.

"Good. I have your girl and your dog."

"I'm eager to see them both," Rodrigo said.

"She's over here," the Jackal said, and started walking.

They followed him. The Jackal's men were chatty, while Rodrigo and Nick remained quiet. They rounded a corner, and even before he could see anything Nick knew something was wrong. He smelled the blood. The Jackal was going to open a door, but Nick shoved him away.

The Jackal protested loudly, but Nick slammed the door open and walked into a hallway lined with cages. Just as he thought. He spotted two men on the ground. Nick spun around, glaring at the Jackal.

"What the fuck is this?" Nick asked.

"Well, I'll be damned. I didn't think your lady friend could manage this. No worries. They'll be trying to head out through the loading bay or the side entrance," the Jackal said. "We can cut them off if we split up."

"Well, let's cut them the hell off!"

The Jackal barked orders at two of his men. Rodrigo ordered four of their own goons to go with the Jackal's boys; the other three remained with them.

"All right, let's nab them," the Jackal said, chuckling some more.

They rushed back the way they had come. Rodrigo's goons had their guns and stun batons out, but Nick hadn't bothered bringing anything. He cursed himself for this basic mistake.

"This way, this way," the Jackal urged them. They stumbled into what must have once been a large loading area, now littered with broken crates and garbage and perfumed with the scent of blood. And there she was, killing a man, one of the Jackal's boys who'd obviously tried to bar her escape. He also spotted a young man and Atl's dog, though they were both of little importance and seemed to be cowering in a corner. His focus was the girl.

Nick stepped forward, ready to smash her to shreds, but Rodrigo grabbed Nick's arm.

"Get her! Hurry up!" cried the old man. He looked at the Jackal. "You too, you morons. There's no payment if she gets out of here."

The Jackal yelled a few orders and the three young men—teenagers; "men" was not the right term—escorting him quickly rushed to surround Atl, no questions asked. She kicked one away, sending him slamming against a bunch of old crates. Rodrigo, meanwhile, was still holding Nick by the arm.

"Let go," Nick muttered.

"They can handle it. No need for you to get your hands dirty."

"I'm not a child."

"This is their job."

The Jackal was yelling into his phone, telling someone to hurry to the loading bay, and Rodrigo turned to speak to the goons.

Nick watched as Atl pulled out a gun and shot two of the teenagers who were trying to seize her. Her gun emptied, she tossed it away, then turned around and evaded one of Rodrigo's goons. As a Tlāhuihpochtli Atl simply did not possess the greater strength of a Necros. But what Atl might not pack in strength, she made up for in speed. It was not impossible for a human to take her down in her current state, but it wasn't that easy, either. And the man trying to get a good shot at her now was woefully unprepared.

She yanked his rifle out of his hands and blew his head off with a single shot.

Nick's nostrils flared, the whiff of blood making him salivate. They were doing it wrong, bunch of amateurs.

"I don't care," Nick said, shoving Rodrigo away. "You want something done right you do it yourself."

"Nick, you asshole!"

He gave Rodrigo the finger and headed straight toward Atl, snatching a stun baton from the nervous hands of one of Rodrigo's goons.

Man, he was going to have fun. She saw him approaching and her eyes narrowed in recognition.

Yeah, bitch. It's me again.

"Hey," he told her. "How've you been? Long time no see, you cocksucking whore."

CHAPTER 26

The moment Nick stepped forward, Atl knew things were about to get very messy. Humans were one thing. A vampire was quite another. She was really in no state to fight anybody, with just a bit of that girl's blood coursing through her body. Atl was running on adrenaline and bravado, and both of these were evaporating, fast.

"Hey," he told her. "How've you been? Long time no see, you cocksucking whore."

"Fuck yourself with your glow stick," she shot back.

Nick leapt toward her, slamming the stun baton in the direction of her head. Atl barely had time to raise the rifle and repel the blow with the weapon. Nick was strong, damn strong, and she felt the strength of his blow as it hit the rifle's barrel.

She spotted a young man creeping behind her and shot him smack in the chest, jumping back as Nick lowered the baton a second time, missing her by a couple of inches.

She kept backing away, realizing she was getting dangerously close to a wall, while Nick tried to make contact with the baton. She darted to the left and took quick aim at Nick, shooting him in the chest, but he kept coming toward her as though she hadn't shot him at all.

The vampire growled, opening his mouth and showing her multiple rows of razor-sharp teeth, like a shark's. He flipped the baton from one hand to the other.

"Tired yet?" he asked.

"Not yet," she whispered, and jumped up into the air. She slammed her foot on Nick's head and landed behind him with a grunt.

Nick turned and took a swipe at her, but Atl evaded him and hit him with the butt of the rifle, giving it all she had. The blow was enough to send Nick staggering back. Atl charged forward, ready to smash his head into a pulp.

A shot rang, then another, and she felt the bullets bite into her flesh. Atl hissed, flipping around to see the Jackal standing behind her. She kicked him and he flew against the crates, his gun spilling from his hands and rattling against the floor. When she turned around to face Nick, he was inches from her and the baton made contact with her neck.

The electric shock was excruciating. Her whole body vibrated and her hands opened spasmodically. She let go of the rifle, the weapon tumbling to the floor.

Nick raised the baton. Someone shot at her, just to make it even worse, and she gurgled, saliva and blood mingling in her mouth. She spat it out, felt the blood dribble down her chin.

"Who told you I needed help, you twat?!" Nick yelled angrily, turning toward whoever had shot. "Hold your fire, I'm enjoying myself!"

Atl raised her clawed hand and took a swipe at Nick's leg. He yelped and she jumped up, pulling the stun baton from his hands. Before she could hit him with it, he roared, tackling her so hard she thought he'd broken her spine.

Breathless, she lay on the floor beneath him. He grabbed her head with both hands, slamming it against the floor. She forced herself to raise her hands and clawed him in the face, trying to go for the eyes. He snarled and bit one of her hands, his serrated fangs digging into her flesh. It felt like having her fingers caught in a bear trap. Atl tried to shove him off, but the teeth seemed to sink deeper in, until she finally managed to hit him in the head, at which point he let go.

Her chest was burning from the exertion and she panicked, thinking she might pass out. He probably had the same thought, because he smiled down at her, his white, sharp teeth making for a terrifying grin.

"Ready to give up?" he asked. "Should I hit you again?"

"Go to hell," she said, the taste of her own blood filling her mouth, and she had to spit again.

"And I thought we were starting to get along." Nick stood up, grabbed the stun baton, and promptly tumbled to his knees as Cualli began savaging his legs. Nick shrieked, trying to kick the dog away.

Atl reached for the rifle she'd dropped and pressed the trigger, blowing a good chunk of his jaw off with the shot. The vampire blinked and opened what remained of his mouth, massive amounts of blood dripping down his face. He began to shriek so loudly she pressed her hands against her ears.

"Atl!"

She spun around and realized that Domingo had managed to open one of the dock doors, pulling the steel curtain up. Atl ran past Domingo, who was staring at the mangled bodies strewn over the floor. She yanked him behind her and they stumbled out into the street, rain pelting them as they rushed down an alley, the dog chasing after them.

"No, no, no," Domingo said when she turned right. "Over here."

She followed him as they ran through a web of alleys, reaching a mesh wire fence. Behind it was a large vacant lot strewn high with garbage.

"Here," Domingo said, lifting a corner of the fence. "I know where this leads."

"I can't walk anymore," she said. Hell, she could hardly breathe. Every mouthful of air burned her lungs.

"You can. You are. Come on," he said, and his voice was hard, not the way he normally spoke, unsure and half-afraid. He knew what he was doing.

She wanted to lie down but he was insistent, pulling her with him. She thought they'd never reach the street. Rain sluiced down her back. Empty milk containers, glass, plastic, crunched beneath her feet, singing a discordant melody. Domingo's sweaty hands remained steady against her own, forcing her to follow him.

Kill him. The thought made her blink and stumble, the rain sliding under her jacket, under her clothes, chilling her.

It was a good idea. She was hurt. She was hungry. She needed the strength. The blood.

She looked at him, at his face, which showed no fear. Only concern. She thought about slicing his neck open with her sharp nails.

"It's okay," he whispered, touching her cheek. "Stay close to me."

She shivered and found that she was able to keep following him, though there was also that nagging thought, the desire for blood pooling in her belly until she finally gave up, decided to hell with it, with him. She gripped his arm and pulled him close to her and . . .

. . . and realized they were there, in a street, the glare of the streetlamps shining down on them.

She chuckled, her hand slipping down, away from him.

There was a taxi stand with a withered, lone driver reading a magazine, waiting for a fare. Atl leaned down next to his window and squeezed the man's neck with one hand. The man dropped his magazine and opened his mouth. She did not give him a chance to speak.

"You're going to drive us wherever we say or I'll break your neck," she told him.

The taxi driver blurted a weak yes. Atl opened the back door and Domingo and the dog jumped in. She followed them, resting a hand right by the driver's shoulder, to make sure he didn't get any funny ideas.

"Take us to the Roma," Atl said.

"Wait, are you going to see Bernardino? You said not to go to him," Domingo said.

"I'm not okay. I need help and a place to hide. There's no safer place than Bernardino's house."

"How do you know?"

"If he's survived this long in this city, then he's not a delicate flower."

"Why didn't you let me take you to him in the first place?"

Atl turned toward Domingo and she had no time to explain about the ways vampires didn't get along with other clans, about their territorial impulses and the fact that Bernardino was either an ace up her sleeve or the worst hand she'd been dealt yet.

"He's dangerous. But everything is dangerous now. Everything," she said instead.

She flexed her injured hand, looking at the bite marks on it.

Atl leaned against the wall as Domingo knocked. The heavy door opened, revealing an old woman. She did not seem too pleased to see them, though she stepped aside and let them in without a word. Domingo helped her up the stairs, and it was a minor miracle that Atl did not take a tumble, considering that her legs had the consistency of jelly.

"Bernardino!" Domingo yelled.

"You've come back."

The hallway was very dark, but Atl saw a silhouette at the far end of it, a silhouette that quickly acquired a recognizable outline. The vampire, hunched down with age, leaning on a cane, gazed at her, his face devoid of any emotion.

"I'm curious to know what you think you are doing here," the vampire said.

"We were attacked," Domingo said. "There was a big fight."

"I can see that. I still don't understand what could have compelled you to visit me."

"I'll owe you a great debt if you offer us sanctuary," Atl said.

"I'd rather not."

"My mother—"

"Is dead," Bernardino replied dryly. "You better leave. It is against the rules for you to be here."

What rules! There were no rules anymore. The Necros had seen to that. Atl squeezed her eyes shut. She might weep, otherwise. She thrust a hand forward, clutching Bernardino's arm.

"Please, don't make me beg."

Bernardino was hunched down, his spine crushed by the weight of time, but he still managed to be substantially taller than Atl. He looked down at her, the way one might examine a spider before crushing it.

"She told me about you," Atl mumbled. "She said you were her friend."

"Isn't that the same lie you told Elisa?" Bernardino asked.

"You know it's not a lie."

He tilted her chin up, as if to get a better look at her. His eyes narrowed and he released her with a huff. "You look like her," he muttered, his voice tinged with irritation.

"These old ties that bind us . . ." He trailed away, lost in thought for a moment, then seemed to refocus sharply, his voice unpleasant. "You smell sick. Come in here."

Atl shuffled after him, into a room lit with numerous candles. It was a study, the walls lined with bookcases, a desk against a wall. She found a chair, currently occupied by a cat. She shooed the cat away and slid onto it. Her hand was throbbing and she had to bite her tongue not to start whimpering.

Bernardino lit a lantern and held it up as he approached her.

"What happened to you?" the vampire asked.

"Silver nitrate darts. They removed the darts, but I'm not well."

"You have a stench about you. The stench of rotting flesh. Take off the jacket."

Atl obeyed him, wincing and tossing the jacket on the floor. Bernardino motioned for Domingo to hold the lantern up and he did. The vampire took away the bandage on her arm, a finger sliding upon the wound. He grabbed her hand, which she had squeezed into a fist, and made her open it, causing a new wave of pain to hit her. He stared at her palm.

"You were bitten."

"Yes."

"By a Necros."

"Yes."

He released her hand.

"The wound is infected. You can't heal properly with this and it can quickly spread, killing you," Bernardino said in a matter-of-fact voice.

"Infected?" Atl mumbled. It seemed she could not manage more than staccato answers.

"A Necros bite, in your debilitated state, is a sure recipe for death. Do you understand?"

"What do we do?"

"Amputate the hand and hope the infection does not spread."

"Wait, what? Cut her hand?" Domingo said, putting the lantern down and turning to Bernardino. "You can't do that!"

"She'll heal. It won't be a permanent loss."

"Like what, she can grow a new one?"

"Like the axolotls," Atl whispered.

Domingo did not hear her or did not care for her words. He spoke loudly and placed himself between Atl and Bernardino.

"I don't think you can cut anything. She's lost a lot of blood. She's barely able to stand up," Domingo said. "You can't."

"She'll die, then."

"I won't let you hurt her."

"Amputate it," Atl said.

Domingo and Bernardino both turned their heads to look at her. She gritted her teeth, her hand throbbing, her body twisting with pain.

"Amputate," she repeated.

Bernardino opened a large mahogany case, pulled out a black leather bag, and placed it on the floor, by the desk. Next, he cleared the desk, shoving his papers aside. He dragged a small table closer and opened the bag, taking out knives, a saw, suture needles, and other surgical instruments. He placed them neatly next to each other. Atl swallowed.

"Don't worry. I've done this hundreds of times," Bernardino said, catching her worried gaze. "I attended patients during the Revolution."

"Wasn't that a hundred *years* ago?" she asked.

"I will return. Wait here, I won't be long," Bernardino said and took a couple of the instruments, exiting the room. He did come back quickly, with a few bottles in hand, too, then went out and this time returned with towels, and continued speaking casually, placing everything on the desk. "The tools are sharp and you should be able to cope with the pain. That is all that matters. Come, you'll have to lie down."

Atl stood and stumbled as she walked toward the desk. She sat on it, then lay down, pressing her lips together.

"Hold up the lantern," Bernardino told Domingo.

Atl supposed it would be better to close her eyes, but she found that she was unable to perform even this simple gesture. Instead, she lay looking at Bernardino. First he scrubbed her arm and hand with what she thought was turpentine, then brushed another substance on the skin, pressing a moist cotton compress for a few minutes over the area before removing it. She assumed he was trying to sterilize the hand, but he wore no gloves and she really didn't want to look at his instruments closely.

He applied a tourniquet to stem the blood flow. It was a curious contraption, consisting of two metal plates, something that looked like a buckle and a screw.

"Ready?" he asked.

She nodded.

He clamped his hand around her arm and, with a sharp knife, made a few quick incisions, lifting the skin as though it were the cuff of a coat. He cut her muscles down to the bone, cut nerves, and though she could withstand pain much more efficiently than a human she was terrified.

Bernardino grabbed the saw and she did not want to see this, she did not, yet she watched as her bone was exposed and then came the firm and slow saw. She did close her eyes when it sliced through, she closed her eyes tight and tried hard not to flinch.

The scent of chemicals, of clean linen and gauze, of her own blood, the pain, made her eyes water and she wanted to cry out. She bit her tongue, instead. Somehow she remained stiff as a board, terror cleaving her, as Bernardino's fingers fluttered against her skin.

Mother, sister, she thought. *Save me.* But they were both dead and with her good hand she could feel the hard surface of the desk beneath her and dug her nails into it.

The soft caress of thread dragged through her flesh was almost soothing after the saw. He threaded quick, methodical stitches. *Sister,* she thought and wanted to weep, but she swallowed her sob.

Bernardino touched her mouth and she opened her eyes. She had no idea how long the operation had taken. It seemed to her it had been forever.

"Don't be scared," he said. "You are weak and need sustenance. I will feed you. It will hurt."

"No other way?" she asked, understanding what he meant and feeling she would not be able to withstand any more pain. *Like a battery,* her mother said. *Like a charge. Tonalli, the life force.*

"You've lost too much blood," Bernardino said. He glanced at Domingo. "You might want to look away."

Atl nodded and Bernardino leaned down, his face coming close to her own until his mouth was almost touching hers. And then he exhaled, pressing a hand against her neck. Atl had kept still during the operation, but she jerked wildly as Bernardino touched her. She felt she was being burned alive, it was like pouring hot coals into her mouth. The fire spread, invaded every pore and every single muscle in her body, and she trembled, half in fright and half in agony until he stepped away and the touch was severed.

Atl took a deep breath and closed her eyes.

"What did you do to her?!" Domingo yelled.

"Gave her a fraction of my life. Saved her."

"Atl?"

She felt like she was sinking into icy waters, the murmur of the sea invading her ears and blotting the voices. The cold snuffed out the light and she breathed slowly and then, just as quickly, she was thrust up, up through the surface. She opened her eyes wide, bolting up from the table.

Both men stared at her and Atl returned their stare, swallowing, trying to remember how to speak.

"I'm okay," she said.

"I have a room for each of you. There's a change of clothes and hot water," Bernardino said. "I'll have your soiled items cleaned at once."

"We'll leave tomorrow, I promise," she said, wishing her voice didn't waver so much when she spoke. "Elisa is getting me out of the city."

Bernardino did not reply. He pointed at a door, then motioned to Domingo to follow him.

Her room was sad and had an air of neglect. It was crammed with knickknacks and ancient oil paintings. There were tiny china dolls arranged upon a shelf. Their heads and dresses were covered in dust. Wasn't the main ingredient of dust human skin? Who had told her that? Had it been Izel?

The clothes lay upon the four-poster bed. The outfit was old and must have been fashionable in the '50s, a skirt, a blouse, gloves, and heels. But then the whole house was old, trapped in time.

Atl peeled off her dirty clothes and slipped into the bathtub, the warm water relaxing her body. She was careful to keep her injured arm outside the tub, so the bandage wouldn't get wet. It was a small feat to wash her hair and body, and when she was done she sat in the tub staring at her arm, the place where there had been a hand. Finally she snatched a towel, rubbing her body vigorously. She drank from the tap and she swished water around her mouth until she had washed away the taste of bile.

She slipped into the blouse first. The skirt, which had a gaudy pattern of palm trees, proved to be more problematic. She could not zip it up with only one hand. She looked at her wrist, at the bandaged stump.

There was a knock.

"What?" she said, and turned around.

"Sorry. Bernardino said you might need help," Domingo explained.

"Yes," she said. "Come in. Zip me up."

Domingo darted in and quickly zipped up the skirt. She stood before a full-length mirror, staring at her reflection.

"Atl, what did he do to you?" Domingo asked. "You were shaking. I thought he'd hurt you."

"He feeds differently than I do. Bernardino absorbs life. I guess that is the best way of putting it," she said. "He feeds from human or vampires, it doesn't make a difference to him. He's also capable of giving life. It took away the hunger. And it gave me strength. My clan . . . we call it tonalli."

In the days of the Aztec Empire, warriors cut off their enemies' heads because they thought they could steal their tonalli, that life essence that resided in the head. And this reminded her of her mother, dead, decapitated, and Atl had to sit down on the bed.

"Are you all right? You sure he didn't hurt you?" Domingo asked.

"It was unusual and uncomfortable for me, but it's fine even if blood is what I crave."

If she were to sit in complete silence she was sure she might be able to feel her muscles knitting themselves, each tired cell weaving itself anew.

"He wasn't lying, was he? It'll grow back, right?"

"If you cut off a part of the axolotl's brain, it'll grow back," she said. "It's not that hard."

"How long will it take?"

"I don't know. I haven't lost a limb before. It's not like we had been removing arms and legs in my family, just for laughs," she said, turning toward him and giving him a venomous look. "Izel would know. She's dead, though. They're all dead by now. It's damn pathetic when you think about it: I'm the one who's still ticking and I shouldn't be. I am the worst of them all."

"I'm so—"

"God, stop apologizing!" she shouted.

He was quiet, but he extended his hand, touching her arm, squeezing her good hand.

She cried. Stupidly, like a child. Izel would not have cried, but she was not Izel. The tears rolled down her cheeks and she had not cried when they killed her mother or when they killed Izel, but somehow she was able to drown in her self-pity and cry over her stupid hand.

Domingo tugged at her, pressing her against him, embracing her. A hug. A ridiculous hug, as though that could offer her any comfort. But she let her head rest against his chest, reclined against his skinny frame.

"It'll be okay," he said. "They're not going to catch us."

"How do you know?"

"It's a hunch. I'm really good at hunches, you know?"

"Ha," she said.

Atl tilted her head slightly. He was very close to her. He was so silly. And sweet. She couldn't think of anyone sweeter.

I'm looking for a friend, she'd told him, and she hadn't mean it like *this* but maybe she had. She was lost and looking for someone to hold on to.

She shifted, moving closer still, her lips against his neck. He clutched her good hand.

That voice, that sensible voice that sounded like Izel, spoke to her. *Don't.*

It was as if she suddenly realized she was drinking salt water. She pushed him away. Not gently. Hard.

Domingo's eyes flew open wide. His face was pained, confused. He blushed and looked down at his feet.

Atl was equally confused, because as soon as she'd shoved him away she wished he'd touch her again.

"You should clean up too," she muttered.

"Yes," he said. "I will. I'll come back."

omingo wandered out of Atl's room and almost bumped into the old servant, who looked ripe for a starring role in a Frankenstein movie. She handed him a bundle of clothes and Domingo went to his room, which Bernardino had shown him before.

The bathroom was huge, intimidating. The tub was made of porcelain, although time had eroded its shell, revealing the cast-iron interior along different patches. He spotted silverfish scuttling inside it, but when he opened the tap the water was nice and warm. He appreciated the soak and he liked even better the clothes that Bernardino had picked for him. The shirt had mother-of-pearl buttons and the trousers were of a nice black material. He put a vest on top and thought that he looked very polished and the sizing wasn't too bad.

She'd like me like this. Of course she wouldn't like me dirty and smelly. No wonder she pushed me away.

In the kitchen he found bread and cheese, and ate quietly by the sink. But then, glancing at his reflection in a pot, he felt doubt.

It doesn't mean she's going to like me.

He reached the living room, which was gloomy, lit by a number of candles, and sat down on an overstuffed couch. Cualli followed him in, lying at his feet. Domingo patted the dog's head, letting out a sigh. A cat sat high upon a bookcase, eyeing the dog with an irritated stare.

A big clock stood against the wall next to him, ticking loudly. He'd never quite seen a clock like that in real life. It had a wooden case and everything. Domingo listened to it, following its ticking.

The *tick-tick* went on for a long while and its rhythm gave him enough courage to stand up and seek her out.

"Bad idea. You and Atl," Bernardino said. "Your attempt at a romance."

Domingo raised his head and looked at the vampire, who was standing by the door, holding an oil lamp between his hands. He looked the part of a vampire who had ventured forth from Dracula's castle.

"I'm sorry?" Domingo replied.

"Don't bother denying it."

Domingo shrugged, unwilling to commit any words. Bernardino set his lantern upon a table and smiled at Domingo, though the smile was hollow and held no mirth. It was a copy of a smile. A fake.

"She seems to enjoy your company, she may even like you, and yet. Don't deceive yourself, my boy, this is not a love story."

Even in this dim light he knew the vampire could probably see the silly expression on his face, his open mouth, the surprise that made his cheeks burn and then quickly turn his face away. Too late, though.

Bernardino rested a hand against the lantern, and this time when he smiled it was different. It was a cutting gesture. Real and full of mockery. "Vampires, we are a diverse lot. So many differences. Yet we are united by one simple unavoidable fact: we are our hunger. It is no surprise, when you consider it. We have been surviving for a very long time against a rather cunning and adaptable foe. Humans are nothing if not adaptable. I can't claim the same of us, though we are persistent. Yet we make it through, despite being outnumbered by your folk, despite times that change too quickly, because of that undeniable truth. In the end, we are always our hunger."

Bernardino's hand, splayed against the glass of the lantern, generated strange shadows that darted across the walls.

"I don't understand what you mean," Domingo said.

"Hunger. It is the primal instinct, the vector that guides our actions. Do you know, boy, what Atl would do, if faced with a choice between saving her life or preserving yours? She'd kill you. Love is a strange thing to us. We do not revel in it. We only know hunger."

"That's a load of crap," Domingo said.

"Because she has not killed you yet?"

Domingo knit his hands together and stared at them. He remembered what Bernardino had said just a little while before, about ties that bind. "Your kind loves. You, for example," Domingo said. "You must have cared about Atl's mother. She must have been your friend. Why would you help Atl if not for love? Love for her mom, maybe, but love. You felt something for her."

"You are confusing friendship with duty. Vampires have been governed by codes for ages and ages. The young ones, they've forgotten this. They forget the old rules, dismiss our ways. But I still live by my code."

"Why do you care how I feel about Atl?"

"I don't. Moths. Flames. It's an old story. I'm merely making an observation. Something to pass the time, you might say," Bernardino said.

Domingo slumped forward. Bernardino lifted his hand from the lantern and the odd shadows vanished. The vampire tilted his head slowly, as though he were trying to get a better look at him. Domingo could see the veins running across Bernardino's face. His skin seemed as thin as the wing of a dragonfly. Bernardino was alien, completely different from

Atl. When Domingo looked at Bernardino he saw the vampires of movies and legends. When he saw Atl all he could see was a girl.

"Of course, you see wrong," Bernardino said. "We are both exactly the same."

It didn't surprise Domingo that the vampire had read his thoughts again. He wondered what the whole point of talking was if the vampire could simply know what he was thinking, but maybe it wasn't as precise as words. Maybe it was just fun. Something to pass the time, as Bernardino said.

"Ask me the question you want to ask me," Bernardino said.

Domingo frowned. He was wondering if there were ever any exceptions. If maybe once in a while vampires *could* love. If that love might extend to a human or if it was restricted to members of their own kind.

The question sat on the tip of his tongue and then, all of a sudden, Domingo decided he wasn't going to ask it. He needed to talk to her, not this man. He stood up, walking past Bernardino.

"She is my responsibility now, at least for a little while," Bernardino said. "That pesky code I told you is at work."

Domingo paused at the entrance. "Meaning?"

"It's stakes and sunlight in the stories, isn't it? The vulnerabilities, the things that can get one of us killed. Stakes, sunlight, garlic, those old, trusted weapons. But those are just *things*. The trouble comes if you make the mistake of forgetting the hunger. Forgetting what you are."

Bernardino moved to occupy the couch where Domingo had been sitting, tangling his long fingers together.

"She's young. It's easy to forget if you are young. Easy to become confused. Be careful, Domingo. She'll consume you, if you let her, but you could also end up costing Atl her life. We wouldn't want that, would we? Stay down here. Keep your distance. Let her be."

The clock began to chime, marking the hour. Domingo grabbed the lantern. "I can't."

Her door was open, but now that Domingo had climbed the stairs, he couldn't make up his mind about whether he should walk in or step away. He elected to lean against the doorframe, looking at the bed where she slept. He understood what Bernardino had said, and yet he also had understood nothing. All he knew was that he liked this girl and maybe she liked him . . . and yet, Bernardino said . . . and she . . .

"It's really weird when you stare at me like that," she said, eyes closed.

"Huh?" Domingo said. "I'm . . . I'm a—"

"Come in."

"That's a bit of a reverse, you know."

Atl shifted in bed, turning to look at him. "Reverse what?"

"Of vampire stories. Humans are supposed to invite vampires into their home, otherwise they can't walk in. It's like that, but the other way around."

"I wonder exactly how much nonsense you read about vampires before you met me," she said.

He loved the sound of her voice, like incense. It belonged in vast, elegant rooms lit with candles and strewn with fragrant, pale flowers.

"Quite a bit," Domingo said. He placed the lantern on a side table and approached the bed, although he stopped short of sitting on it. He simply hovered next to her, biting his lip. "Most of it was probably wrong, but you never know."

"Sit down. You're making me nervous," Atl muttered.

He sat down and tried to recall exactly what he was going to tell her before he walked into the room, only to find he'd forgotten. If he'd known poetry he might have attempted to recite Neruda or at least express, in some small fraction of a way, how she moved him, how he wished he could rescue her, kiss the ground beneath her feet, anything, anything, he'd do anything for this woman. But he was a kid from the slums who didn't understand much of poetry.

"I took a bath," he said instead, lamely. God, he was so lame.

"Good," Atl said. "Do you have a room or are you going to take the bed? I plan to sleep there."

She pointed at a large chest sitting at the foot of the bed. Domingo supposed that Atl could fit inside it, although it wouldn't be too comfortable.

"'Cause it's a small space?"

"Yes," she said.

"I guess it's better than a coffin. Less morbid."

She smiled, went toward the edge of the bed, and lifted the chest's lid.

"Atl, wait," he said, raising a hand, as if to signal her to remain still.

"What is it?"

He thought about what Bernardino had said about hunger and he also thought about the pretty shape of her mouth, and although he didn't quite remember what he was going to ask, he realized he had a different question entirely.

"When we met, you said you hadn't killed people. But you've killed a bunch of people in the past couple of days. Did you lie to me?"

"I thought you'd be scared if I told you," she replied.

"It's scary, all right. But you could have explained."

"No, I couldn't."

"Why not?"

"Because of the way you are looking at me."

"I'm just looking at you, that's all. It's nothing weird. It doesn't change stuff. We're still friends."

Atl gave him an angry huff and crossed her arms.

"Who'd you kill?"

"What do you care? It doesn't *change* stuff," she replied, mocking him.

"I've seen things. From your memories. It's ugly. I know it's ugly, I'm just asking."

"What do you really want to know?" she said, her voice harsh and unpleasant. She had not asked a question. It was a challenge.

He realized he should keep his mouth shut and just let her be. He realized Bernardino was probably right. Domingo walked toward her, brushed her arm, gently seeking her attention.

"Atl, just tell me," he said. "Please?"

"You'll see me as a monster."

"No."

"Of course you will. You'll be repulsed and I'll deserve it. I am a dishonorable coward and an idiot."

He reached out his hand and touched her cheek, and, thankfully, there was a confidence to the movement of his hand that he had not thought he possessed. Atl held his gaze, but made no attempt to move away or closer to him. He tilted his head slightly and planted a kiss on the corner of her mouth, very brief, like the question mark at the end of a sentence.

It was probably unfair of him to do a thing like that when she was tired and injured, but he had no idea what was going to happen the next day. Things were crazy, with people trying to kidnap them and kill them. God knew if he'd ever get a chance later. Maybe she wouldn't like it and she would get mad at him, and he wouldn't blame her if she did.

Atl didn't seem angry, though. She looked lost, like she'd been running through a winding labyrinth and couldn't find the exit. She made fun of him in his naivety, but she didn't know anything either.

"I killed two vampire boys and a pregnant vampire. And then, later, I killed an old man and a young woman. Humans, those two," she said, her voice soft, like he hadn't heard it before. "I've killed many people and I'll continue to do it if I must."

Domingo looked down at her. Atl's eyes were very dark, filled with something that seemed grim, close to resignation.

"But you're a good vampire," he blurted out.

Of course, there was no such thing and he knew it even before he said it. But he liked to believe it. He liked to think that there were heroes and villains, he liked picturing Atl as a damsel in distress. He liked the black and white of the comic book panels, the simple speech bubbles above characters. Good vampires. Bad vampires. And she had to be good because she was attractive and young and his friend. Right?

"I needed to kill them. No. I *wanted* to. I thought about killing you, too. More than once. You understand now?" she asked, the softness of her voice turning to iron. "No, of course you don't. I can't expect you to."

Atl pulled away from him and crossed the room, to stand by a window, though she could see nothing outside since the curtains were drawn.

Words failed him. Not that he'd ever been particularly good with them. He stood in the middle of the room trying to make sense of everything, and though his brain had arranged the pieces very neatly, his heart was in a complicated knot.

"I understand."

She gave him an exasperated sigh. "You could leave, you know?" she said, looking at him over her shoulder. "I wouldn't blame you if you did."

"I've known that all along."

"Maybe you should go."

There is a point when a man may swim back to shore, but he was past it. There was nothing left than to be swallowed by the enormity of the sea. *Anything.* He wanted her to know he didn't care and he'd give her anything. "Not now."

"Why not?" she asked, sounding exasperated.

"I wouldn't expect you to understand."

She held his gaze for a beat and then she smiled, just a tiny bit of a smile, and he thought he'd never seen anything as glorious as that smile, ever, and who cared about the rest if he could look at it a little longer. It was madness. Having successfully kept himself from all vices he had managed to intoxicate himself with her.

CHAPTER 28

Rodrigo waited awhile, but he spoke when Nick started gnawing at a boy's face.

"I think that's quite enough. We need to get going before the cops come poking their heads in here," he said, looking at his watch.

"Do you have her?"

"No, I don't," Rodrigo said, knowing that he might have caught Atl if he hadn't had to pause next to Nick, to make sure the bastard didn't suddenly die in the middle of a damn factory. But pause he did, and by the time he ran outside, the girl, the boy, and the dog had vanished. He walked around the factory, hoping to find a trace of them. When he went back to where he'd left Nick, the place was littered with bodies and the floor was sticky with blood. He'd almost slipped, and now stood regarding Nick as he continued to feast on the fools who had been holding Atl.

"We're down three men," he said. "It's time we left."

"Look at me! I need to feed!" Nick yelled, raising his head.

She'd blown off half his jaw and a part of a cheek. The flesh was starting to knit itself but it looked raw, like a damn hamburger patty. Nick started spitting teeth onto the floor. Teeth and blood.

"It's not a corpse buffet," Rodrigo said. "We need to head back to the apartment."

The boy Nick had bitten wasn't dead yet, despite missing a good deal of his face. He moaned pitifully. In response, Nick bent down and savaged him further, tearing chunks of flesh with whatever teeth he had left. At this point he wasn't really feeding, just giving shape to his rage.

"Nick."

Nick sprang up and grabbed Rodrigo by the neck, holding him up. His nostrils flared and he growled. Rodrigo couldn't feel the ground beneath his feet. He hated the thought of dying in the middle of this filthy place, strangled by this boy vampire, so he steeled himself, pushing down his fear and instead glaring at the kid with as much venom as he could possibly muster.

Nick snorted and let go of him. Rodrigo rubbed his neck, wishing he could cattle-prod this twat while knowing it was impossible.

"Done with your tantrums? Then let's move it."

"Fine," Nick said.

* * *

Vampire anatomy. One of those things you never expect to take an interest in when you join a gang, when you become their lackey. Though, to be fair, Rodrigo had always been interested in how cars worked, so it wasn't that surprising he'd discovered how vampires worked too. It had come in handy a few times. This was one of them.

Nick hissed and complained, but Rodrigo was able to disinfect the wound, apply an ointment, and apply a dressing with ease. Then he had to pull several of Nick's teeth. It was better this way. New teeth would come in quickly. If he left the banged-up ones in their places it would only slow down the process. When Rodrigo prepared a shot, Nick frowned.

"What's that?"

"The painkiller. Do you want to feel the skin and muscles growing?"

"It'll make me sleepy," Nick complained.

God, what a whiner he was. "You need to sleep."

"I don't *want* to. I want to find her. You let her get away."

Rodrigo didn't bother to inform Nick that *he* was the fool who had lost a fight against the girl. He simply held the syringe up. "Would you prefer if I kissed it better?"

"Fuck you."

They stared at each other.

"Do it," Nick muttered. His voice sounded funny due to the damage to his face and Rodrigo almost wanted to smirk.

He injected Nick three times. The boy began lolling his head after the third shot and Rodrigo called for La Bola. Together, they carried Nick to his bedroom.

Rodrigo had a tremendous headache. He was exhausted. He poured himself a glass of whiskey, dragged himself to his bed, and fell asleep almost instantly.

When he woke up it was near dark. Rodrigo walked to the kitchen to check on their blood supplies. They were down to three bags. It wasn't going to be enough, not with Nick in this state. He grabbed the phone and dialed a contact of his.

"I need more of the last delivery," he said.

There was an uncomfortable pause. "You watched the news yet?"

"No."

"Turn the TV on."

Rodrigo grabbed the remote and flicked through the channels, stopping at a news station. They were showing footage of the outside of the factory where they'd been. The TV was on mute, but the words VAMPIRE ATTACK were superimposed upon the bottom of the screen.

"What does that matter?" Rodrigo asked.

"It's gnarly, bro. The cops are looking for you."

"What else is new?"

"Deep Crimson's also looking for you. I don't want no problems."

"Price is not an issue."

"Sorry, bro."

His contact hung up. Damn it. Procuring blood would become a lot more difficult now. Nick was going to wake up with an appetite and all he had were three measly bags of blood. Of course, he only had three bags because the damn kid went through them like they were candy.

Shit.

He wanted to get into his car and drive away. Drive until he reached a solitary beach down the Pacific coast. Trade his suits for T-shirts and shorts. Rent a house. Adopt the anonymous, boring life of a retired old man.

He couldn't.

Rodrigo took a deep breath.

He was used to solving problems. All that was required was a little creative thinking.

The woman called herself Dulce. He found her next to a bike repair shop, wearing a plastic, transparent poncho that allowed customers to see her underwear. She looked like she was in her midtwenties. Bubbly, though not pretty. She might have been attractive once, but time and drug use had left her with a weary, hardened look. Dulce told Rodrigo she really liked his car and suggested they go to a nearby motel—or they could do it right there in the car. He said he wanted her to go back to his place. She balked at that, but then he offered her a bit more money and told her he was doing this as a surprise birthday present for his friend, who was feeling a bit down. Her accent was northern and he added he was originally from Monterrey.

That seemed to calm her down. On the ride back, she expressed her love of cumbias and Rodrigo replied at the appropriate intervals. Once inside the apartment, he quickly guided her to Nick's room. Nick was sprawled over the bed, his face buried in the pillows, and Dulce stood by the door, smiling.

"Let me wake him up," Rodrigo told her. "Boy, is he going to be surprised."

Rodrigo crouched next to the side of the bed and whispered. "I have a girl for you," he told him.

Nick turned his head and stared at Rodrigo. His eyes were bloodshot.

"Come here," Rodrigo told Dulce, motioning to her. "Come here and meet my friend."

Dulce stepped forward, moving to Rodrigo's side. Her pleasant, sweet smile faded as soon as she caught sight of Nick. She took a step back. Nick caught her. He was fast and she was unable to scream. All Rodrigo heard was a whimper.

He left the room, not bothering to watch as Nick fed. He went to his studio and put on Silvio Rodríguez, listening to the soothing melodies. He ran his fingers over his books, pausing over a particularly pleasing first edition. He allowed his eyes to wander to the photo of him sitting in a convertible. Young. Optimistic. Foolish.

He sat behind his desk and poured himself another whiskey but didn't drink it, instead holding the glass between his hands.

Three or four songs later there came the footsteps. The door opened and Nick walked in, his face smeared in crimson; his clothes drenched in blood. He smelled of carrion. That deep, uncomfortable stench that Rodrigo had gotten used to, working for a vampire for so long.

"Her blood was thin," Nick complained. "Give me a drink."

Nick snatched the glass of whiskey from Rodrigo's hands and downed it.

Of course. No gratitude from this younger generation, these children with their mouths like sharks and their vicious appetites. None whatsoever.

"I want Atl. I want Atl's blood and Atl's flesh. I want her alive for a hundred days and a hundred nights, skinned and bleeding."

"Someone else has the same idea," Rodrigo said.

"What do you mean?"

"The Jackal said she was suffering from silver nitrate poisoning and that one of his guys pulled several darts out of her arms. How do you think she got those? Not from us."

"Cops," Nick said, rubbing the back of his hand against his mouth.

"Not exactly standard equipment."

"Then who? Does it matter?"

"There's a detective who might know. Ana Aguirre."

He'd been thinking about Aguirre as the boy fed. From what his contact had told him and from Rodrigo's own quiet inquiries, Ana Aguirre hailed from Zacatecas, where she'd developed a reputation as a vampire killer, and one who seemed to know what she was doing. While most cops thought the best way to deal with vampires was to spray them with as much lead as possible—and that did help, but wasted ammunition and manpower—Rodrigo looked at her file and saw cases of vampires who had bitten the dust thanks to anaphylactic shock, electrical shock, UV burns, and the like. It was possible, he thought, that Ana Aguirre had found Atl before Rodrigo and Nick did. It was also possible she had knowledge that would prove useful. Nothing like a vampire hunter to help them hunt a vampire.

"You said it wasn't the cops."

"I know what I said. Do you still feel hungry? I'm thinking you could use a snack."

Nick smiled, a ghastly, painted smile. A child's grin set upon a horrid mask. He handed Rodrigo the empty glass.

"I'm always up for takeout."

CHAPTER 29

M usic. Atl knew she should rest, conserve her energy. Sit and heal. The music, however, made it hard to keep her eyes closed. That, and the burning headache that threatened to split her skull in two. She opened the lid of the trunk and followed the music straight into a room that seemed colder and more humid than the rest of the house, if that was possible.

A phonograph was playing, the needle running across the worn surface of a record. She'd never seen a real vinyl record before and stood mesmerized, watching the disc spin and spin.

"It's called 'Stardust,'" Bernardino said. "Most music is like nails on chalkboard to my ears, it drives me mad. This isn't like most music, though."

He was sitting on a couch upholstered in brocade, a tabby on his lap. His clothes, just like the couch, were from another era. It was as if he were keeping the current century at bay.

"It's nice," she said.

Bernardino nodded, his hands resting against his cane. His fingers were long, his eyebrows joined in the middle, and he was terribly pale, his skin reminding her of a deep sea–dwelling creature. She'd never had a chance to meet one of his kind. Not that she'd wanted to.

"How did your mother die?" he asked.

"Decapitated. The Necros did it. Godoy, he killed her."

"Your sister, she is also dead?"

Atl nodded.

"I imagined as much."

"I think everyone else is dead too," she muttered.

"Probably not. Your lot is hardy."

He gently put the cat on the floor and stood up, shuffling to her side. There were stacks of records by the table and he grabbed one, switching it. The singer was a woman this time, talking about a man she loved.

"How is the arm feeling?" he asked.

"Fine, I suppose."

"Let me see."

Atl raised her arm and he removed the bandage, running his fingers along the stump. Atl glanced away. She didn't want to look at it.

"It heals well and fast," he said, slowly placing the bandage back in its place.

"Not fast enough for me. I need my hand."

"There's nothing I can do about that."

She didn't want to seem ungrateful, so she gave him a small smile. "Thank you, by the way. For helping us."

He returned the smile with a stiff nod and hunched over his records, as if looking for something else, though he made no effort to go through them.

"My mother said you were a surgeon," she said. She really had no idea why she had said that, since she did not want to start much of a conversation with him. Bernardino had helped them, but he still scared her. Yet there was also something fascinating about him, he was uncanny. Not only a different organism, but a relic from a whole different era. Like watching a dinosaur walking the Earth.

"For a while. When I was younger." His mouth moved slowly, the words were sluggish.

Bernardino stared at the phonograph, lost in thought. She didn't think he'd say anything else, but he spoke again, his voice more animated.

"It was interesting work."

In the late nineteenth century, during the Porfiriato. That was as much as she knew. Mother liked to talk about the past, but not her own past. The family's past, the clan's. Everything was narrated in a collective manner.

"Did your mother tell you how we met?" he asked.

"No."

"It was during the Revolution. She was only a few years older than you, I'd think. Or younger? Perhaps she was younger. The city was going mad. It was when the soldiers rose in arms and Madero was killed. The city was ringing with the sound of bullets; corpses were burned in the middle of the streets. I was afraid I'd be killed, and had gone into hiding."

"What happened?" she asked.

"I was found out and managed to run away, though they were catching up with me. I can't recall who they were by now," he said, waving his hand dismissively. "I ran into a street, thinking they'd catch me and burn me. And then there came a rider on a galloping horse. 'Come, come on,' she yelled. She gave me her hand, and I jumped behind her, though for a good full minute I didn't realize she was a girl, with that hat upon her head and the gun at her hip.

"When we were safe, she introduced herself. At first I was suspicious, thinking maybe she'd saved my life only to rob me and toss me on the side of the road, but she had not. Like I said, she was young, she was naïve, she thought it was important to do the right thing, even if that meant saving a vampire she owed no allegiance to."

Atl had a hard time picturing her mother as young or naïve. She'd been the leader of their clan for nearly three decades. A determined, stern woman, but not one she could see socializing with this man, or spending any time in this cold house. Her mother loved the desert, its warm days and the nights when they could count the stars.

"The last time I saw her it was 1979. Yes. She'd come to Mexico City for a visit, but the country was changing. The vampires were leaving. It was not good for us anymore. She came here, to see me, and told me I ought to head north, where things were much better. Of course I told her I'd never leave my house. It's been my house for a very long time, I said. She told me I'd get myself killed, like I almost did during the Revolution, but I wasn't afraid.

"I knew I'd probably never see her again, so I gave her a gift. She liked to collect Aztec artifacts, your mother, didn't she?"

Atl remembered the house back north with its ancient pots and figurines, her mother's fascination with archeological digs, the talk of the old clans, the old ways. It was gone now. Shattered, burned.

"I'd found this old jade necklace. Very beautiful. An authentic relic. I gave it to her, as a parting gift. But she was angry at me and simply broke it. The beads spilled over the floor."

Ah. So that's where the bead came from. Her mother had explained nothing about its provenance, simply telling Atl and Izel that it would get them a meeting with Bernardino, if they ever needed to meet with him.

"Perhaps she might have mentioned that time, with the soldaderas," he said, bobbing his head up and down. Atl had no idea what he was talking about.

"She did not tell me about what happened during the Revolution."

"What did she tell you?"

"Only that you'd been her friend," Atl said. "I could not understand how she could say you'd been a friend to her when you were of a different clan, a Revenant of all things. It sounded crazy."

"Most of the time we were not friends. Allies, perhaps, when circumstances demanded it. The last time she visited me, it was duty that compelled her. A favor, you might say. It doesn't mean we'd forgiven each other, for our respective sins, but I suppose she thought she owed this to me."

"What sins?" Atl asked.

"That's a long story and much blood was spilled. But it was a long time ago. Long, long ago. I forget bits and pieces of it, but I remember her."

The record had stopped spinning. Silence settled into the room. Bernardino stared at her.

"Your friend is here," Bernardino said, his eyes still fixed on her.

True enough, she could recognize Domingo's footsteps. Domingo peeped into the room. He shuffled his feet, giving Atl a shy glance.

"Are you busy?" the boy asked.

"No," Atl said.

She was acutely aware of herself, of him. Having Bernardino around did not help, his eyes darting between Domingo and her with the expression someone might have when solving a crossword puzzle.

"It's nearly ten o'clock. We need to talk to Elisa," Atl said.

"You want to go to Garibaldi?" Domingo asked.

"Yes, of course I do. We have a meeting with her."

"I can go by myself," Domingo said. "You should stay here and rest."

"I need to speak to her. I can't just send you out, as if you were going on an errand."

"But you've sent me on an errand before. You should—"

"I am not going to discuss this with you," she said, cutting him off. She already had a headache and her arm was throbbing. She wanted very much to yell at him and tell him he had not been appointed her knight in shining armor. *She* decided what they did. He was hers to command. Not the other way around.

"You look like shit. I bet you feel like it. You're not strong enough to be running around the city," he told her.

"I can take this. I don't know if you've reali—" she began, unable to believe he was contradicting her.

"I'll be going with you," Bernardino said, interrupting her.

Atl stared at him.

"You will?" Domingo asked.

"You do have a point. Atl is not quite herself yet. She might need my strength."

Domingo gave Atl a questioning look and she nodded stiffly. Despite her protestations she could feel her energy ebbing away and she had no desire to fight *both* of them on this point, damn them. But she'd have a chat with Domingo, later.

CHAPTER 30

It rained like a motherfucker. Ana stared out the window while the other detectives typed on their computers. Several of them were probably playing online poker or watching porn. She doubted any one of them did any real work. Ana certainly couldn't work, not today.

Castillo had screwed her over again. Now that the case had grown bigger, she wasn't the main detective handling it. It had gone to Luna, and the fool was spending his time giving interviews, happy to be getting his name out there. Typical attention whore.

Ana smoked her cigarette and watched the rain fall, turning everything gray. They weren't supposed to smoke inside the building, but it didn't matter. Nobody enforced it.

Her phone rang.

"I'm feeling like we could use a talk," Kika said. She sounded way too chipper considering the circumstances.

"I'm working," Ana muttered.

"Take a break. There's a Chinese café a few blocks from you, the Blue Lotus. You know it?"

"I've walked by it."

"See you soon, doll."

Ana opened the window and flicked the cigarette butt outside. She grabbed her umbrella and walked six blocks until she reached the ratty, narrow café that Kika had mentioned. Maybe it had once been a "Chinese café," back in the '40s, when such establishments—a cross between a bakery and a restaurant—proliferated and popped up through downtown Mexico City, but little remained of its heritage except for its name, written on a flickering neon sign. Inside, sad, sparse paper lanterns hung from the ceiling and a calendar proclaimed it was the Year of the Snake. She had the impression the calendar was wrong but she didn't quite remember the Chinese zodiac.

Kika sat near the back. She smiled at her and handed her a menu that was bent and stained. Chop suey sat next to enchiladas, a cacophony of dishes with no rhyme or reason.

"How's your day going?" Kika asked.

"Shitty. Did you see the news this morning?"

"How could I miss it? The words 'psychopath vampire' were splashed over *El Universal*," Kika said, moving her hands as if she were holding an invisible newspaper.

Yep. That's exactly what it had said. The reason why Castillo had dragged Ana into his office and yelled at her, quickly blaming her for the mess. If she'd only caught the rogue vampire quickly, none of this would have happened. He told her she obviously did not know her asshole from a good lead and would now be "assisting" another detective. He'd also accused her of tipping off the reporters about the story, when she knew without a doubt it had to have been one of the photographers, trying to make an extra buck by selling crime scene pictures, or a prick like Luna. Maybe both, in conjunction.

"I imagine it was as bad as the papers made it seem," Kika said, glancing down at her own menu, running a finger down each item.

"Worse. A bloodbath. There'd been a fight, so you had the people who died during it and the people the vampire killed after. He was hungry and very pissed. He ate one guy's face."

"You have any witnesses? Anything?"

"I have a witness, a person who survived the mess. Apparently a bunch of entrepreneurial folks found Atl and, since she was injured, managed to lock her in a cell. They were making a deal with Nick. He was coming to collect her. She broke out, there was a big fight, and the result is I'm not sure whether she's dead, he's dead, or they're both dead somewhere."

Kids. They'd found a bunch of dead kids. And they were also chasing kids. Two deadly children, not much older than her own daughter.

A waitress arrived and gave them a tired glance as she pulled out her notepad.

"Coffee," Ana said. "Cream, too."

"Beer and pork chops. And bolillos."

The waitress looked rather skeptical about their choices.

"I don't think our collaboration is working as planned," Ana said. "That thing with Atl? It was a mistake. She got away and all we had was a bunch of dead people in the street. I'm lucky I'm here."

"Life's unexpected detours take us to our destination in the end," Kika declared, as though she were a walking, talking greeting card.

"Well, what's unexpected is that after the massacre at that factory my boss has sidelined me. I gave him Atl and Nick's pictures. Luna is doing some shit with checkpoints and distribution of the images. I'm not leading the investigation anymore. I'm probably of no use to you now."

"I wouldn't say that. You got us very close to her. I have faith in you. You want the other half of the money, right?"

"I want a decent night's sleep, is what I want," Ana said.

The waitress returned with the coffee and the beer. She forgot to bring any cream and Ana stared at her drink, irritated.

"You're the closest thing to a vampire hunter in this town, Ana. We don't have anyone else to go to."

"Why don't you just let them kill each other?" Ana asked, utterly exhausted by the conversation. "They'll manage it, eventually."

Ana grabbed a napkin and folded it in half, then in another half, while Kika drank her beer, looking cool and chill. If the young woman ever had a bad day, she didn't let it show.

"I told you why already. It's disrespectful. Vampires start getting the idea they can just waltz into Mexico City, how soon before they're snacking on us and messing it up like they do in the rest of the country? It's a question of pride."

"Yeah, I don't give a fuck. I'm worried someone thinks I'm working with you, or at least suspects something's up."

"You're imagining things."

"I'm not imagining shit. I got a phone call the other day, very unsettling, asking why I was researching Nick and Atl."

Ana had not breathed a word to Marisol about what she was doing in her spare time, but she had checked the locks on the door and made sure the electronic peephole was in good working order. Marisol was under strict instructions to never open the door when Ana was away anyway, but it didn't hurt. As an extra precaution Ana had arranged for Marisol to ride the daily school shuttle back and forth from school, which she normally didn't do because it cost an extra fee. Since it was a private school the shuttle carried an armed guard.

"Come on, you *do* give a fuck," Kika said, brushing away Ana's concerns like they were useless garbage.

"My boss is going to fire me if he figures out I'm working with you," Ana countered.

"Who cares?" Kika took another swig of beer and smiled at Ana. "Don't start with the lame excuses. You won't need your stupid job soon enough. Are you scared?"

"It's scary when you're going against vampires. Maybe you don't care, because you think this is a staff barbecue, but I know what they can do."

"If the pictures in the papers are correct, I also know what they can do. Disgusting."

"The reporters are enjoying it," Ana said. "Naked girls on page three and a guy that was gutted on the cover."

"When I was a kid, I remember reading those old romantic books. The Gothic paperbacks. Remember those?"

Ana stared at the calendar and what, she supposed, was the Chinese character for Year of the Snake printed below the Western letters. She remembered the Chinese vampires she had bumped into, their atrophied muscles giving the sensation that they were always shuffling around. The Revenants had similar problems: kyphosis, arthritis. Not like in the books, no. Not romantic, either.

"No," Ana said. "But then again, I have never been a big reader of romance books."

"Well, they had castles in those books and they vampirized young virgins, offering them eternal love. The truth, though, well, the truth is more interesting. Corpses on parade. It'll be a blast putting a bullet through their skulls. Stake. Something."

"I'm not interested in discussing vampires in cheap novels," Ana said. "I'm heading out."

"You can't let me eat by myself."

Ana considered staying for a bit longer. She decided against it. The coffee looked terrible, anyway. "I got work," she said. "I'll phone you if anything comes up."

"You're not scared, Detective Aguirre," Kika said, raising her bottle in a salute. "You're eager."

Ana took out a bill and left it on the table. The walk back to the office had her thinking more about types of vampires. She bounced between reciting their characteristics in her head and remembering the faces of the two young ones who were responsible for the bloodbath she had been staring at on her screen.

Deny it as she wanted to, Ana knew Kika had a point. Ana was good at one thing and that thing was dealing with vampires. They fascinated, repulsed, and obsessed her. She was disgusted by this whole business but she also needed to see this case to the end. Try as she might, she couldn't turn her head away.

And yet by the time she reached her desk, she was ready to go home. The office zapped her life, it was the real vampire. Tops five minutes after she sat down, another officer came walking by.

"Hey, Aguirre, I've got a guy who says he saw something in connection to your case."

"Tell Luna about it. He's the lead on it," Ana muttered.

"Like I wouldn't have tried that. Luna's not here."

He was probably banging his mistress in a cheap motel that charged by the hour.

"Will you talk to the damn guy?"

"Yeah, sure. Send him over," Ana said.

She pulled out the voice recorder and her notepad. A man in a striped shirt sat down across the desk from her, looking nervous.

"I'm Detective Aguirre. They tell me you want to speak with me?" she said, and did not even bother sounding like she was interested. She should have had the damn coffee and a bit of food.

"It was a terrible stench, just awful. Like rotting meat," he blurted. "It was that psychopath vampire from the papers."

She could smell the booze even from across the desk. Ana looked into the old guy's face and hoped this wasn't an alcoholic who'd had a vivid hallucination. The crazies came out in force anytime a big crime took place.

"Sir. Let's slow down. You say you saw a vampire?"

"They were riding in my car."

"Okay. How did they get into your car?"

"How do you think they got in?" the man spluttered. "I drive a taxi. They just got in. I had no idea until she grabbed me by the neck and threatened me and she smelled bad, terrible, like meat that's gone bad. There was a boy, too. And a damn dog."

Ana held her pen up, pausing. "A dog?"

"Yes, a big dog. They made me drive them around."

She leaned forward. "Do you remember where you took them?"

"To the Roma."

"Where in the Roma?"

"I don't know. A house." He shook his head. "I was too spooked to pay attention to it. But my friend, he told me today that you guys give rewards for this stuff. How much are you giving?"

"Sir, does your taxi have a geolocator? Taxi companies use it nowadays to track where the vehicles are."

"No. What do you think I'm rich to be having this fancy geolocator shit?"

She bet he was driving an illegal taxi. "I don't think anything. *You* think hard. Can you remember anything about the street you dropped them off at?" Ana asked.

"It was in the Roma. It's what I know."

The Roma. It had been a big vampire quarter, once upon a time. They'd all left. Except she remembered hearing a rumor from Archibaldo Ramos, who'd been in hot water—well, more than usual—a couple of years before when they busted him trying to run a prostitution ring near Coyoacán. Cops weren't very nice when people weren't paying their bribes, and Ramos thought he could just pull the wool over everyone's eyes and not have to pay anyone off. Ramos, whom she'd met several times before, was aware she had an interest in vampires and tried to gain brownie points by regaling her with vampire stories. He'd mentioned the vampires of the Roma and hinted one remained there. At the time she thought he was just bullshitting her. She wasn't so sure anymore.

"All right, that's good. I'll file your statement," Ana said.

"What about my money?"

"There's no reward money."

"That's bullshit, lady! Plain bullshit!"

Several officers turned their heads to look at them. Ana could have the guy arrested, but it would mess up her plan. She reached into her wallet and found a bill. "Here's a hundred and get out," she said.

The guy took the bill and crumpled it, but he didn't say anything else and walked out. Ana logged in to one of the databases and scanned it for info. She then grabbed a few papers and went over to the officer who had sent the taxi driver over to her.

"I'm heading out again. If Castillo asks I was sick, all right?"

The officer, who was busy browsing ties on the internet—she could see the site on the monitor behind him—sneered at Ana. "Suddenly got your period, Aguirre?"

"I think you're the one who's PMSing, asshole," she said.

She was sure that was going to go in her file, under "lack of team spirit and cooperative skill building," but she didn't give one fine fuck.

CHAPTER 31

At night, Plaza Garibaldi was overrun with mariachi bands and drunkards. Adventurous tourists walked around, trying to ignore the indigents gathering at the fringes of the plaza. It was a seedy place and no amount of rehabilitation could possibly bring the area under the blanket of respectability, though the city planners had given it a half-hearted attempt, stringing numerous green and red lights on buildings in a futile attempt at festivity.

There were a lot of bars near the plaza. The Tenampa stood out due to its yellow façade and its history: it harked back to the '20s and the story went that Frida Kahlo used to hang out there. It was, like anything else in the area, a little tacky. The Tenampa was also crowded, though Domingo imagined it had been crowded for decades. Three mariachi groups and a jarocho band played in the joint, while roaming mariachis walked around the tables, looking for customers willing to pay for a song.

There were men walking around selling electric shocks, holding up their boxes with jumper cables. It was an attraction imported from up north, from Tijuana and Juárez, but it had caught on with the drunk patrons. A variant was called the Mexican roulette, which had four people passing the contraption around until one of them was zapped.

A mariachi asked them if they wanted a song for what must have been the third time and Bernardino waved him away. The vampire looked miserable, hunched over a glass of mezcal, a hat shadowing his face and a thick scarf around his neck, but not bothering to take a sip. Domingo was nursing his first beer, too nervous to do much drinking. Atl, on the other hand, had downed three glasses of tequila.

Domingo thought they painted quite the picture: a surly old hunchback in black; a young, bright-eyed woman with her arm in a sling; a teenager in a fancy vest. Though, to be fair, everyone was too drunk to pay them much attention.

"I don't quite believe it," Elisa said as she approached their table, a backpack slung over her shoulder and a dainty purse dangling from her right arm. "Bernardino. Here. Aren't you averse to people and noise . . . and, well, everything?"

"I would have preferred that we met at a different place, but yes, here," he replied.

Elisa took off her coat. "I didn't think you'd get involved in this."

"Well, I am."

"What happened to your arm?" Elisa asked, looking at Atl.

"An accident," she replied.

Elisa pulled up a chair and sat down. She placed the backpack on the table. Atl unzipped it and found a large envelope.

"ID cards. Health cards. Passports," Atl said, taking each item out. Atl grabbed one of the ID cards and looked at it, then opened the passport. "They look legit."

"They'll work," Elisa said.

"What about the ride? When can you drive us out?" Atl asked, holding up one of the cards, examining it more closely.

Elisa hesitated, sliding her hand across her wrist. "There's a problem with that."

"Meaning?"

"I'm not driving you anywhere."

"That's not possible," Atl said, placing the documents on the table.

"I'm not sure if you know this, but the city is going wild," Elisa told them. "Cops found an abandoned factory filled with corpses and they're talking vampires. They've got checkpoints set up; they're checking buses and cargo trucks. I won't do it."

"So you can't take us to Guatemala," Atl said.

"It is too dangerous. You can have your money back." Elisa tossed Atl's envelope in front of her.

"I don't want the damn money," Atl exclaimed, slamming her hand on the table. "I need your help to make the border crossing. You said you'd get me out."

"I said it was complicated," Elisa replied.

"Can't we just take a bus?" Domingo asked.

"Sure. When we get to the terminal, we'll ask security to let us on nicely. I'm sure they won't question us when they notice I'm missing a hand or anything. Good God." Atl grabbed her glass and downed it in one quick gulp, wiping her mouth with her sleeve.

"Sorry," Domingo muttered, rubbing the back of his neck.

"She could stay with you," Elisa said, speaking to Bernardino. "Things will cool down in a while and it'll be easier to leave the city. The roads should be better."

"They can't be with me," Bernardino said. "It's too dangerous. I've already had to send my Renfield away, out of caution. I can't be their bodyguard."

"What other option is there?" Elisa asked.

"If you think—"

"Don't worry about it," Atl said, clumsily stuffing the papers back in the envelope. She was trying to keep herself in check but it wasn't working, her hand was shaky, barely able to grip her documents. "I got into Mexico City and I can get out by myself and—"

"Cross at Ciudad Hidalgo," Bernardino said nonchalantly, reading her mind by the looks of it. "It will be controlled by Necros," the vampire informed her.

"The South is still in dispute," Atl protested. "It's not controlled by them."

"After what has recently happened I'm sure Godoy has shared your picture with as many associates as he can. I'm sure it's even been shared with people who are not his associates at all. One way or the other there are going to be too many people interested in you. You can't manage on your own. Not if Elisa is right and this has exploded the way it has. You fucked up and the situation has changed."

"What do you suggest?" Atl asked.

"There are old trails in the jungle. Stuff only villagers use." Bernardino said, "You can get far if you know the right person. I do. I can help you get into Guatemala, but I can't get you out of Mexico City. Not that I wish to. But I see no other option at this point."

"I hopped on a truck to get in," Atl said. "I could hop on another."

A group of mariachis had begun to play at a nearby table. They were singing the corrido of "El Caballo Blanco." People started to sing with them. Atl had poured herself another glass of tequila spilling much of it.

"I've seen what the checkpoints are like," Elisa said. "They're not going to let the truck through without a search."

"So? We keep quiet," Atl said in a clipped voice.

"And if they have thermal scanners? Every bus, every car, anything with wheels is going to be searched. This stuff's too hot right now."

Atl did not reply. She leaned back on her chair and raised a hand, covering her face for a minute before she downed her drink. A thought popped into Domingo's head.

"You don't need no wheels to get out of Mexico City," Domingo said. "You can walk out."

The three of them stared at him.

"Walk out?" Atl said, sounding incredulous.

"They're not going to have people at the landfills."

Atl straightened up in her chair, raising her chin.

"Go on," Bernardino said.

Domingo licked his lips. "Bordo Blanco overflows into the State of Mexico, okay? It's not supposed to, but that's the way it is. In theory there's the containment wall and the canal running by to divide it neatly, but that doesn't happen. Once you get across the drainage canal you're outside Mexico City pretty fast. You can keep going from there. All we have to do is walk through the landfill and cross the canal. And there's a way to do that. There's a path."

"And there'll be no security?" Atl asked.

"No. Look, the landfills are not ruled by cops, they're ruled by the people there. Zamora is the boss at Bordo Blanco and I've bought garbage there for the rag-and-bone man. I've hauled stuff and I've been across the entire landfill. I can take you."

Bernardino raised his eyebrows and glanced at Domingo, giving him a smirk. "You've managed to surprise me, boy," he said.

Domingo smiled. He drank his beer.

"Well, it seems you are in good hands and you have the papers you need. There's nothing else *I* can do," Elisa said, pushing her chair back abruptly, like she'd left a cake in the oven and her house was about to burn down. "I trust I won't be meeting with you again."

"No," Atl said. "Thank you."

Elisa grabbed her purse and her coat. "Lovely seeing you," she told Bernardino.

"Likewise," Bernardino said, showing his yellowing teeth, a note of derision punctuating his words.

Elisa paused to incline her head toward Atl, in what Domingo thought was a microscopic salute. Then she walked out of the joint without another word.

A waitress came around to ask if they wanted more drinks. Three mariachis were headed to their table, eager for business. Bernardino tossed several bills on the table and grabbed his cane.

"Let's go. I can't stand this infernal place. My head feels as though it might burst," Bernardino said.

Domingo took a final sip of his beer and stood up. Despite the cane, Bernardino moved surprisingly fast, evading drunkards and servers, leaving them behind in a heartbeat. Once outside, Atl and Domingo were able to catch up with him.

"Who's the right person?" Atl asked. She sounded anxious, and the way she walked next to Bernardino only seemed to reinforce this impression, something about her reminding Domingo of the incessant fluttering of a hummingbird. "You said you knew the right person."

"Manuel Tejera."

"Can he get me into Guatemala?"

"If he wants to. He'll want to after I've spoken to him," Bernardino said firmly.

"Do we go see him now?"

"Yes."

Atl slowed down for a second, then lost her balance and stumbled. Domingo grabbed her, steadying her. Her eyes seemed glassy and she winced.

"Bernardino, she's not looking too good. Maybe we should do this tomorrow. Or we can come back together, you and me, while Atl rests."

"I'm fine," Atl said.

"No, you're not," Domingo said. "You shouldn't even be here."

They evaded a puddle of barf smack in the middle of the sidewalk and Domingo leaned down, closer to her.

"Atl—"

"You can't send me home for a warm glass of milk," she said, irritated.

"I'm not trying to be a dick, it's just I don't like seeing you in pain," he said, a hand resting against her shoulder. "Atl, you can trust us. We can do this for you."

"Make up your mind and tell me if you're coming or not," Bernardino warned them.

"I said I'm fine."

Atl elbowed Domingo away and walked next to Bernardino. He followed them with a sigh.

The symbol of the subway station at La Merced was a basket filled with apples, clear commemoration of one of the most famous—or infamous—markets in Mexico City. In the time of the Aztecs it had been home to the House of the Birds and after the Spanish conquest it was the place where authorities determined the prices of grain. The displays in the subway station had informed Domingo of this fact.

During the day the market sprawled across dozens of blocks where merchants, sex workers, and buyers spent their days haggling. At night the street sellers of La Merced had packed their wares away. The stores were closed. But it was still a lively place, with the prostitutes working the streets. Rows and rows of women in miniskirts, high heels, and pounds of makeup stood texting their friends. When they walked by they looked up for a second at them or flashed them a crimson smile.

Bernardino led them to the doors of a vecindad, which, like most other buildings in this quarter, hailed from the previous century or two. There was no buzzer and Bernardino did not even pull out a key. He simply pushed the door open, and open it did.

The interior patio smelled heavily of dry shrimp, and Domingo realized, looking at crates piled high, that it was because there *was* quite a lot of shrimp there. La Merced belonged to merchants, and Domingo wasn't surprised to see someone had decided to store goods in the patio, forcing people to walk around the crates.

The shrimp made him think of the sea, which he'd never seen. He guessed he might see it now, with Atl.

Bernardino led them to a door that had been decorated by attaching dozens of plushies and plastic toys to it. There were naked dolls, plastic figurines without their limbs, and a one-eyed teddy bear. It was creepy as hell, and made Domingo give Atl a worried look. But she stood stoically as Bernardino rapped on the door.

There was a faint movement of the curtains in the window to the left of the door and then an old man opened the door for them. He was gray, this man, as though he'd been placed in the washing machine too many times. Even his lips seemed gray. His T-shirt, of a color that only approximated white, was stained yellow at the neck.

"I didn't think you left your home anymore," the old man said. "I thought you'd turned into a regular old hermit."

"Invite us in," Bernardino replied.

"I like that about your kind, Bernardino. You are polite. You don't break windows and storm into a house. Come in, then. Come."

The apartment was tiny. The living room, kitchen, and dining room were in one spot. A curtain with a pattern of daisies, dangling over a piece of rope, divided the small space. Domingo figured behind the curtain was both the man's bed and the bathroom.

"You look good."

"I don't think I can say the same," Bernardino said smoothly.

"My liver," the old man replied, patting his swollen belly. "I'll be dead next year. It doesn't matter. High time, I say. Sit down."

They sat around the table. Its surface was covered with a yellow-and-white piece of plastic instead of a tablecloth. A statue of San Judas Tadeo sat next to the salt and pepper. On the wall, dirty with age and spotted with humidity, there was a green cross, Jesus resting on it. Several dolls had been nailed to the wall, like butterflies in glass cases.

"You got yourself new Renfields?"

"No. They are friends. Of a sort. Manuel, meet Atl and Domingo."

"Hello, young folks," Manuel said. "Do you want coffee? I drink it with a smidgen of mezcal, myself."

Domingo looked at the man's dirty shirt, his greasy hair, and shook his head, though it was not his hygiene that held him back. He'd already had booze and did not want to attempt more, never having been the best at alcohol.

"No, thank you," Atl said.

"Suit yourself." Manuel dabbled in the kitchen, opening a cupboard and pulling out a cup, a box with sugar, a spoon.

"I need you to do something for me. A delivery."

"Didn't think you were still in that business," Manuel said, setting down his cup and sitting down. "What do you need to get across?"

"The kids."

"People? That's a bit of a pickle, isn't it?"

"As if you never trafficked people," Bernardino scoffed.

"Usually I was trying to get them into Mexico. You're talking the other way around. There's a difference."

"Not impossible."

"No," Manuel said. "I'm a bit out of the loop, you know?"

"I've noticed."

Manuel took out a pair of round-rimmed glasses from his back trouser pocket and put them on, examining Domingo and Atl. "Can I look at your hands, dear?" he asked.

Atl complied, pressing her one good, gloved hand on the table.

Manuel chuckled. "I know what that means. She's a vampire, ain't she? You're from the Aztec tribe."

Manuel took off his glasses, using them to point at Bernardino. "Shit ain't like it used to be. They're real paranoid down at the border nowadays. Next thing you know, they'll be having thermal scanners there, too."

"I doubt it."

"Doubt it all you want."

"It doesn't matter. I want you to employ the trails, like you used to. Elisa wouldn't take the gig. I thought you had more balls," Bernardino said.

"Elisa," Manuel said. "That chit. Good for nothing. She never could make a run across without messing something up. I'm not surprised."

"And then?"

"I told you, my liver is killing me," the old man said, rubbing his belly for emphasis. "I want to stay here and watch TV, not run around a dusty road into Guatemala. What would that get me? Me? Money? A bit pointless, now."

"You owe me a favor."

"I know." Manuel sipped his coffee.

Domingo noticed that there were more toys on the refrigerator. They were everywhere, sad and broken, much like the old man. Was this a former Renfield? He didn't seem like much. Domingo had a hard time picturing him next to Bernardino; the old vampire was aristocratic looking, not the type who would associate with a bum. Domingo realized that he himself didn't look like much either. Was he like this guy, only younger? That was a nasty thought.

"We can't have the pickup in Mexico City. They're looking for her. Outside, not far from a landfill," Bernardino said.

"Bordo Blanco," Domingo said. "We'll be at Tenayuca and Catedra."

"How soon?" Manuel asked.

"Tomorrow," Bernardino said. "One a.m."

"Tomorrow's no good, buddy. I got to make sure the car's working right and pack supplies."

"Then the night after that."

"I'll need a bit of money, Bernardino. For business expenses."

Bernardino placed several bills on the table. Manuel grabbed them quickly, crumpling and placing them in his pockets.

"We should celebrate. You sure you don't want a drink?"

"Where's your bathroom?" Atl asked.

"Right there," Manuel said, pointing at the curtain.

Atl stood up. Domingo rose at once, to offer his assistance, but Atl placed her hand on Bernardino's shoulder instead. The vampire stood up and they walked side by side, pulling the curtain away. They stepped into the bathroom together. Domingo heard the click of a lock. He stared at the bathroom door, nervously tapping his fingers against the table.

"Relax. He won't hurt her," Manuel said.

"I know."

"He ain't having sex with her either, in case that's what you're worried about."

"I'm not worried about *that*," Domingo said.

What perverted comment was that? Despite his impressive voice Bernardino was a hunched man of possibly seventy? Eighty? At least, judging by his face. Probably much older. Domingo very much doubted Atl would ever want anything to do with him.

"Well, he might have, once upon a time. Had lovers of all sorts, had a thing for black hair. Not humans, though. They," Manuel said, making a sweeping gesture, "well, they're the same species. They like to fuck each other more than us. We're not that fun."

"Look, I don't really—"

"Haven't had her yet? The young vampires, they have less taboos than the old farts. And I see that look in your eyes. You want the girl. I can tell." The old man laughed, showing him a gap-toothed grin.

Domingo felt himself flushing, mortified by the very thought of admitting such a thing to the old man. "What's with the dolls and toys?" Domingo asked, wishing to change the subject as quickly as possible.

"They guard me, help me keep the ghosts away," Manuel said. "They got their eyes wide open, so nothing will dare sneak into this house."

"You really think there are ghosts?"

"There are ghosts. I killed a lot of people. That's a lot of ghosts. Lots of ghosts. It's the price of hanging out with their kind. Yeah, it's the price," the man said. "Killed for her yet?"

"No."

"You will," Manuel said. "What? You don't want to? Sure you want to. Kill and fuck, kill and fuck. All the same for them. The same for us all, eventually."

Domingo grabbed the plastic San Judas Tadeo, gently tracing the contours of its robe, trying hard to ignore the man's laughter.

CHAPTER 32

Atl rested her back against the cool bathroom tiles and sighed. Bernardino looked down at her, frowning.

"The boy was right. You are weak."

She hated the way he said it, as an indictment. "I'm okay," Atl muttered, uncomfortable.

"No, you're not," Bernardino replied. "I will assist you."

He pressed a hand against her neck and hovered close. His breath was scalding and again she had the distinct sensation that a noxious substance was burning through her body, as though he'd injected acid into her veins.

The sensation died away and Atl shook her head, flexed her hand. She was restored, filled to the brim. For his part, Bernardino seemed suddenly older, with more wrinkles gouging his face.

"It'll be the last time you can expect that," he said very seriously.

"I understand." She could feel the very fibers of her body trembling and rearranging themselves, healing faster. But it wasn't quite right. She *wanted* blood just as a smoker might crave a cigarette instead of a nicotine patch. Even if Bernardino nourished Atl, the blood called for her. It was inevitable.

Atl opened the bathroom door and they stepped out.

The cool air was very welcome, as was the soft drizzle that fell upon them. They were walking fast and Domingo had a bit of trouble keeping up with them, but Atl didn't slow down.

When they reached the house, she went quickly up the stairs, ignoring Cualli, who was waiting by the front door. Domingo followed her, intent on becoming her shadow. Once they reached her room, she slammed the door shut and glared at him, lighting the lantern. For his use. She wouldn't have bothered with it.

"Atl?"

"What was that?" she asked.

"What was what?" Domingo said, giving her a blank look.

"You telling Bernardino I was too damn weak to go to La Merced. Interfering."

"I wasn't . . . you *are* weak," he protested. "Bernardino can do his hocus-pocus life energy thing, but that doesn't mean you've healed."

"I'm not interested in broadcasting my current state to the entire world."

"It's not that hard to see."

"Of course not. Not if you yell it."

Domingo bit his lip, looking stung. Not angry. Just deflated. It was irritating watching him fold onto himself, like a piece of origami.

"He's not my kin," Atl said. "You can only trust your kin."

"I thought you could trust me. I wouldn't let you down. And aren't you trusting Bernardino right now?"

She turned away from him. It was too difficult to explain to Domingo the intricacies of family and clans, of blood ties that bind, and she did not feel she had enough patience to begin to map it out for him.

"I'm trying to help you," he said, all youthful vehemence.

"Yes. I know. You're always trying to help me," she replied, wishing her voice were not so brittle.

"Why is that so bad?"

"You have no idea what it feels like to suddenly be completely dependent, completely helpless," she whispered. She grabbed the change of clothes that was waiting for her on the bed and held it up for him to see.

"I can't even change out of my clothes without your help," she said unkindly, though he was guilty of nothing but kindness.

Atl tossed the clothes on the floor, wanting very much to tear them to pieces. She kicked them away instead. "I hate needing you," she said. "That's what it is. I fucking hate it."

And the loneliness. She hated that too. That feeling that she no longer belonged to anything greater than herself, the lack of kin and company.

"I need you, too," he said.

Atl slowly raised her head and scoffed at him, at the earnest quality of his voice. The way he cringed at her anger, the wounded look washing over him, they were almost infectious.

"It's not the same thing," she replied.

"Yeah. I *know*," he said, and for once his voice held a different note, hurt, yes, but also something decisive.

His eyes cut her, got under her skin, sharper than glass.

Atl whirled away and Domingo summoned enough courage to pull her toward him. She rested her good hand against his chest, frowning.

"I don't want you getting hurt," he said. "That's all. I'm sorry."

She nodded, found the buttons of his shirt, toying with the top one, undoing it and doing it again, her finger sliding to touch the hollow of his throat. His blood, she could almost hear it cresting up to meet her caress.

"Atl," he whispered.

"What?"

"Can I kiss you again?"

"You didn't kiss me the first time," she replied, remembering the piti-ful peck he'd given her the previous night.

He attempted a second kiss, this one a proper one, though truth be told he wasn't terribly good at kissing. All he could manage was to part his lips and stand stiff as a board. She pushed back against his kiss, challeng-ing him, until he seemed to relax, placing an arm around her waist and she reciprocated by resting a hand on his nape, her fingers tangling in his hair.

When the kiss ended she did not distance herself, her body flush against him. Her irritation had faded. There was comfort to be had in his near-ness.

"You're shaking," she said, realizing it sounded like an accusation and not bothering to sweeten her voice.

"Yeah, well, you're very pretty," he mumbled.

They were quiet. She didn't really want him to speak and just stood there, next to him, the lantern draping them in a vague halo of light, il-luminating his features, though she could have seen him well enough without its assistance.

Domingo took a deep breath. "I wasn't sure whether you liked me," he said.

She brushed his arm, giving him a sideways look. "I like you," she said simply.

It was no lie, but she didn't enjoy saying it. It sounded childish. The kind of thing girls might write on a piece of paper and pass around a class-room, giggling. Something she'd never done, nor would she have wanted to, had she had the chance. But now . . . she wanted to wash the pain away, cauterize wounds with touch alone. She wanted to be remade, to go back and undo sins, even to be loved.

For all those reasons she could tell him something true and almost sweet. She could like him, he could like her, and then the world would hurt a little less.

Atl took off her jacket, attempted to take off the blouse and found her fingers fumbling the job. Thankfully, he didn't ask if he could help her. Instead, he wordlessly pulled the blouse from her shoulders, undid the zipper of her skirt. The shoes should have been no problem, but he had her sit on the bed and pulled them off anyway. He managed to avoid looking at her the whole time, his eyes darting to the far corners of the room.

It made her grin.

"Maybe I should turn the lantern off," he offered.

"No, you shouldn't."

Domingo removed his vest, shirt, and belt, though he hesitated at the trousers and shoes and Atl wondered if he was going to get in bed with them on. Finally, he kicked the shoes away, undressed entirely, and sat next to her. Atl looked at him, first a clinical examination of his neck, shoulders, arms. He was a rangy thing, nothing but bones, though she didn't find this displeasing. She discovered a scar upon his collarbone and touched it.

"I liked you since I first saw you in the subway," he whispered. "I'd have done anything to meet you. Never thought you'd speak to me."

She tilted her head. She'd liked him too, the moment she'd seen him sitting in the subway car, wrapped in his yellow jacket. She liked how he looked terribly unsure of himself. She liked the way his hair fell over his face and she liked his smile, which seemed so honest. And he was beautiful, didn't even know it. It was charming.

"Atl, I—"

She silenced him with a kiss, weary that he was going to say something dumb, and pushed him down on the bed, pressing her lips against his neck, not for a kiss, but to feed. When she raised her head she did kiss him on the mouth, the sweet taste of copper on her lips. He let his breath out in one long, shaky exhalation.

CHAPTER 33

A look at the computer's database had shown Ana that Archibaldo had stayed out of trouble for the past year. When she phoned his number on file, she got his ex-girlfriend, who, upon learning a cop was looking for him, gladly told Ana that Archibaldo had opened a tea shop on Darwin Street, at the edge of ritzy Polanco. It was his newest front.

The tea shop was called Safari and the outside was painted a deep purple. The inside was pretentious, with a zebra skin—no doubt synthetic—hanging from a wall. Long, glistening metal tables stretched from one side of the joint to the other. The attendant told her there were "private" drinking cubicles in the back and asked if she was interested in renting one.

"Yes," she said. "And please tell Archibaldo that Ana Aguirre is here to see him. I'll be in the back."

The girl looked at her skeptically. "The owner is not around."

Ana sighed, taking out her badge and showing it to the girl. "Tell him and give me a cubicle."

The girl quickly handed her a plastic chip with a peacock painted on it. Ana went to the back and found a bunch of doors set along a narrow hallway, each one with a different animal on it: lion, panda, monkey. The peacock was at the far end of the hallway.

The room had a divan and an assortment of blue and green cushions on the floor. The head of a peacock had been mounted on a wall. Archibaldo had wallpapered the room with peacocks, as though the theme were not clear enough to even the most clueless spectator.

"Ana Aguirre! You beautiful woman, you," Archibaldo said cheerily as he walked into the room. "You look younger than ever."

"I don't feel young," Ana said, giving him a dismissive look. Archibaldo was a diminutive fellow, balding, and sporting the same mustache—mug shots testified to this—he'd worn since the '70s. He had no charm, though he considered himself a smooth Don Juan.

"You should have told me you were coming over. What tea do you want to drink?"

"How many girls do you have working here?" she asked, extending a hand and touching the peacock's beak. It felt real.

"What?"

"We both know you're fronting."

"I don't know what you mean."

"Come on, Archibaldo. Do I have to remind you what happened last time you tried this?"

The little man took out a handkerchief and wiped his forehead with it, his eyes darting around the room. "You need money?" he asked. "I have—"

"You're in luck. Today it's just information."

"What type?"

"Last time I saw you, you told me stories about vampires. I'm interested in hearing the one about the vampire in La Roma. Where does he live?"

"Wait," Archibaldo said. "I only told you because you like to hear about those things. It was just talking, passing the time, you know?"

"You said there was a vampire left in La Roma."

"Are you sure you don't want tea? I can tell the girl to bring tea."

"Sit down."

Archibaldo obeyed her, sitting at the edge of the divan. Ana leaned against the wall, lit a cigarette, and crossed her arms. "Tell me."

"I told you there *might* be a vampire still in the Roma. God knows I haven't tried to verify it."

"What's his name?"

Archibaldo toyed with his handkerchief. "Now that I pause to organize my thoughts, I don't even remember what I told you. It was long ago and my memory is not so good."

"Are you going to try that one on me?"

"Ana, please, let's have tea."

"You want me to drag you back to headquarters with me?" Ana asked. "Force mineral water up your nose so you can't breathe? Add chili pepper to make it tastier? Huh? Do we have to do the whole song and dance number like we're fucking amateurs?"

Ana had never liked to liven up an interrogation with tehuacanazos and beatings, but she damn well knew others did. And she wasn't above reminding Archibaldo about the techniques her coworkers liked to indulge in. Between the jerks at work and these fucking vampires going around eating people, she'd had it.

"No," Archibaldo mumbled. "I'll tell you."

He was quiet, as if gathering his courage, and Ana held on to her cigarette.

"I met him in the '70s. He was a Revenant. His name was Bernardino."

A Revenant. Well, that wasn't exactly what she wanted to hear. Vampires who can suck your life with a single touch? No, thanks.

"Go on."

"He lived in La Roma. A lot of them had left, were leaving, the area by then. Things were getting hairy with the police. He didn't seem concerned, though. I think he'd been living in his place for a very long time, that he'd been a rich twat since the Porfiriato. You know how vampires can be. Old-fashioned, especially the elderly ones. He was old-fashioned. Didn't see the benefit in moving."

"How did you meet him?"

"He wanted people. You know, to feed. I had girls who were willing to do the work."

"Did you ever see where he lived?"

Archibaldo nodded. "On Parras. Number 25. A big, old house."

"What makes you think he is still living in Mexico City? We haven't had any reports of vampires for years and years."

"When I met him, I heard he was some big shot. He could still pull a lot of strings. He knew many secrets, from a bunch of people. I don't think people dared touch him because of that. He had plenty of money. I don't know, he was the type who could stay and just keep his head down, you know? Make no fuss, keep things going for himself." Archibaldo licked his lips. "Plus, I know he was still around as late as the '90s."

"Did you see him?" Ana asked.

"No, I didn't see him. I stopped sending him girls over after a couple of mishaps. And the guy scared me, all right? He could read someone's thoughts, and that was just too damn disturbing for me. Too much."

"Then?"

"I've got to keep an ear to the ground and know what the competition is doing, you know? I was paying off one of his girls to tell me what my biggest competitor back then was up to. If he was importing Russian babes or if he'd been getting girls from Tlaxcala. Whether he was trying to run a massage parlor or—"

"I get the drift. What about the vampire?" she asked.

"The girl I was paying off told me he was their client now. This was in '98. I don't see why he wouldn't still be around."

No, she didn't see why he couldn't be around either. Safe in the Roma. And for some reason the vampire girl was with him.

Ana stopped at a convenience store and bought a pack of cigarettes, feeling guilty about the purchase. She'd told Marisol she'd quit, again, but that hadn't lasted. Two blocks from her building, her phone rang. She thought it might be Kika.

"Yes?" she said.

"You hung up on me," a man said.

Godoy's people. Perfect. She thought about hanging up again, but spoke instead.

"What do you want?" she asked.

"Go upstairs and we'll kill your daughter. Head to the alley behind your building, now."

Ana felt a tightness in her gut. She found it hard to even think properly, much less reply. "Yes."

She saw them when she reached the mouth of the alley, an older man and a young one. She recognized Nick Godoy from his photo, though half his head was bandaged. He looked more like a monster than a ladies' man now even if he was wearing sunglasses and a hoodie to try to hide the damage.

"Ana Aguirre," the older man said. He was leaning against the wall of the alley, arms crossed. "I've been wanting to meet you. I'm Rodrigo. This is Nick."

"What do you want?" she asked.

"Information. You're investigating the so-called vampire murders."

"Luna is the lead on that. You should talk to him," she said, her voice leaden. She gave him nothing. You couldn't show emotion near these pricks.

"How'd you find the girl?"

"I have no idea what you are talking about."

"Wrong answer," Rodrigo said, brushing a hand against the lapel of his suit. "Nick."

He pounced on her, but Ana had years of dealing with his kind and she pulled out her silver knife just as quickly, slicing at his arm. The kid growled, showing her a multitude of teeth. Ana sliced again, aiming for the chest. She thought the odds were in her favor, but then Rodrigo spoke, slow and measured.

"Drop it or a friend of mine is going to break the door to your apartment down and beat your daughter so badly you'll need dental records to ID her," he said.

"You wouldn't—"

"Didn't you see the news? The factory? We would. We are past being discreet."

She believed him. The fear she'd pushed down bubbled up, knitting in her gut. Ana dropped the knife.

"She cut me!" Nick said, sounding outraged, and then, without pre-amble, he bit her neck.

This is it. Killed by a vampire kid, she thought. However, the bite wasn't terribly deep and it was the restraint that alarmed her. And then the boy bit into his own wrist and she panicked, trying to punch him. He held her tight, pressing the bloody wrist against her mouth. When the blood hit her, everything seemed to slow down.

The boy stepped away and Ana felt this itch inside her head, inside her brain. Damn it, not this. Years in Zacatecas, dealing with bloodsuckers, and now *this*.

"Ask her how she found Atl," Rodrigo said.

"How did you find Atl?" Nick repeated.

Ana spoke, compelled by the alien blood that was now coursing through her body. "A sanitation report. It mentioned a dog that resembled the one she owns."

"How did you know to also look for Nick?"

"Deep Crimson, an important gang. They came to me, told me they wanted help in finding Atl and Nick. I agreed."

"Do you know where she is now?"

"Most likely in the Roma. She is with a vampire called Bernardino. He's a Revenant," she said, her mouth opening and makings sounds on its own accord.

"We should go there right now," the young vampire said.

The old man didn't look so convinced. He shook his head. "A Reve-nant."

"Who cares if it's ten of them?!" the young vampire screeched.

"You don't just step into a vampire's lair if you can avoid it. Does Deep Crimson know the current location of the girl?"

She tried to suppress the urge to speak, knowing it was futile and yet attempting to fight him.

"You heard him," Nick said, taking a step closer to her. She could see herself reflected in his sunglasses.

"No," Ana said. "I was going to phone Kika after I had a smoke."

"I think she should phone Deep Crimson and let them know about this new development."

"Are you crazy?" the vampire said, turning toward the old man, his hands balled into fists. "They'll grab her before we do!"

"I'm indeed hoping they'll get in there before we go, kill that Revenant, and injure her, making it all that easier for us to swoop in and take her. You have a lot to learn, boy."

The vampire chuckled. He took off his sunglasses and stared at her.

"Phone your contact and tell them where they can find Atl," he told her.

Ana's hands trembled as she grabbed her phone and pressed the right numbers.

CHAPTER 34

Sex always looked damn impressive in the movies. Domingo wondered how the actors managed to make it seem so effortless—pretty, even—when it was terribly chaotic in real life, and he fumbled it when he had the fleeting chance to sleep with a girl. Though he supposed he hadn't fumbled it too badly this time around. Well, he hoped he hadn't or that at the very least he wasn't as clumsy as usual.

Atl lay curled on her side, naked, her back to him. She looked rather spectacular and he realized that he'd probably told her she was beautiful far too many times—maybe she figured those were the only words he knew, *God, you're gorgeous*—but he felt like saying it again.

Atl was touching the bandage on her arm. He pressed his face against her nape. He felt terribly alive and needed her as close to him as possible.

"Are you scared?" Domingo asked. "About tomorrow, I mean."

"No," Atl said. "Not more than I've been during this whole trip."

"Where are we going to go after we reach Guatemala?"

"Brazil."

"I don't think they speak Spanish there," he said, suddenly worried.

"You run away with a vampire and the thing that concerns you the most is that you won't be able to speak the language?"

"I guess."

She chuckled. "It's one of the benefits of having money. And I'll have quite a bit of money once I'm abroad and can access all of my accounts. If these IDs hold up, it should all be fine."

Domingo sat up and looked at the tattoo on her back. Now that he had a better chance to examine it, it seemed to him that the hummingbird had a definite, defiant expression that matched Atl's own proud scowls. He touched the drawing, his fingers resting on the wings. "Can you fly?" he asked.

"Yeah. In a way. It's more like . . . I can glide, I suppose. I can beat my wings a bit in the air, though if you were comparing me to a bird I'd be flying more like a turkey than a sparrow. It's not that impressive."

"That means you have wings."

"Yes."

"Bat wings or bird wings? Not butterfly, right? I saw a picture of a lady that had butterfly wings once, but I think that was a fairy in some children's book."

"Bird."

"How come I haven't seen your wings?"

"No need for it. It's private," she said, sounding shy, which surprised him.

"You've seen me naked," he said.

"That's different."

"How come?"

She looked at him and raised an eyebrow. "You ask a lot of questions. You've also seen *me* naked. I'd say that equation is well balanced."

"I wouldn't mind seeing your wings."

"You're not *that* cute," she replied.

Cute. That sounded really good to him, although now that he thought about it, she'd probably been with very handsome gentlemen. Vampires, rather. Vampires that didn't have awful teeth like him. They probably had really good teeth. If they went to South America, or even farther, would they be hanging out with other vampires? Would Atl be whisked away by a billionaire bloodsucker with a Transylvanian accent?

He traced the head of the hummingbird with his hands and kissed her shoulder blade.

"Do you know why it's a hummingbird, and not a raven or a swan or something else?" she told him.

"Why?"

"Huitzilopochtli, the Aztec god of war, was called the left-handed hummingbird. His father was a ball of feathers."

"For real?"

"Yes. His mother swallowed a ball of feathers and he sprang from her womb, fully formed, dressed in his feathered armor. There was a temple dedicated to him, right here in Mexico City, and my ancestors were warrior-priestesses in that temple. The priestesses were very brave. They fought in great battles. My family was heroic. Not like me."

Atl undid the bandage to look at her arm. It was still a stump, though the flesh had healed completely and looking at it one might have imagined she hadn't had a hand for years and years.

"I feel like it's still there," she told him. "I try to move my fingers, but I can't."

"If it makes you feel any better, that guy who attacked you is probably hurting more than you are. And looks a lot crappier."

She smiled, though soon enough she was frowning, her face draining of its mirth. "I suppose you don't really want to see this," she muttered, clumsily winding the bandage.

"Here, let me," he said. He recalled how upset she'd been before, angry at needing his help, and he bit his lip thinking she'd protest. But Atl did not seem upset. When he finished bandaging her arm again, she mussed his hair. He turned his head and kissed her.

His previous attempts at kissing had been rather embarrassing, the excitement making him tremble and flounder, but now he did it right, his fingers buried in her hair, mouth angled over her own.

He wanted to have her again and he thought she wanted him too, but he was afraid to put it too bluntly and look greedy.

"Are the vampires in Brazil like you?" he asked, for the sake of making conversation and perhaps finding a way to casually indicate his desire. Plus, he was genuinely curious.

"No, it's mainly Obayifo there, they came from Africa in the seventeenth century. They glow in the dark. The glow hypnotizes their prey, or so I've heard."

"No way. You're making that up."

"What's so strange about that? There's fish and mushrooms that glow in the dark," she said.

"Fish and mushrooms are not the same as vampires."

She sat next to him, running her nails along his arm. He thought that one day, when he had the chance, he'd have to find the painting of the girl who looked like Atl, the one he'd seen in a catalogue. Madonna of something. He'd show it to her.

"I have wings. Isn't that stranger?" she asked, a hint of mockery on that clever tongue of hers. But also a hint of warmth there too.

"Which I still haven't seen," he reminded her.

"Suddenly you are an unbeliever?" Atl asked, leaning down to look at him.

"Kiss me again and I'll believe you."

She grabbed his hand and planted a kiss on his palm. The gesture was endearing; it filled him with delight. "How come vampires are so different?" he asked her.

"We are all supposed to have a common ancestor and diverged in the distant past, with the Necros probably being the youngest subspecies. However, if you listened to my mother's stories, she said we were created by Huitzilopochtli and when we die, we become stars."

She spread the fingers of her good hand, tracing a line in the air, above her head, as if marking a constellation. She smiled for a moment, but then her expression grew serious and she dropped her hand, pressing it against her mouth. Just as quickly she smiled again, her voice sounding a bit strained, but aiming for levity.

"The first thing we'll do when we get to Brazil is visit a tailor and buy you a suit. A nice gray pinstripe will do," she told him.

"I'm not a suit guy."

"You'll look handsome."

"Let me guess. You have a thing for guys in suits. I bet you lied about not having a boyfriend and you've had a dozen, in pinstripe suits," he said, winking at her, matching her cheery tone. He wanted her to be happy. He didn't want shadows or fear or anything to taint this moment.

"You've found me out."

"I'll keep your secret, hope to die," he said, pressing a hand against his chest.

She watched him, her mouth curving into a grin. Something new there, sweetness dancing at the corners of her lips, a detail he couldn't have known existed before.

"I'll show you a real secret," she whispered.

Atl sat up and turned around. He watched in amazement as wings started sprouting from her back, unfolding, *forming*. Bone and tissue and feathers opened like a fan. They weren't small wings, no little white, fluffy Cupid wings. The wings were massive, and seeing them like that he realized why she'd never shown them to him before: they would have been impossible to hide under her clothes. Feathers of a shimmering black that was almost blue also sprouted along her spine, ending at her tailbone.

"Wow," he said.

"Definitely not a butterfly," she said, looking at him over her shoulder.

He wondered how she did it. He was going to launch into a dozen questions, one after the other.

Atl wrapped her arms around him and then her wings also wrapped around him. He figured he'd ask some other time. Right that second his breath had caught in his chest, burning fast, and he couldn't have uttered a single word even if he wanted to. He was mouthing her name against her skin and begging for something he couldn't even put into words.

Atl lay on the bed. Her wings had disappeared, folded back into her flesh. He caressed her back and was struck with sharp, quick images of the desert, a turtle, dead bodies. More dead bodies. A young woman, dragged into the darkness.

He withdrew his hand, as if he'd been shocked by an electrical socket.

He remembered what the old man said, that he'd kill for her soon enough.

God, he hoped not.

God, it didn't matter.

After a couple of minutes, gently, he pressed himself against her body, nestled against the curve of her back, and closed his eyes.

CHAPTER 35

They were sitting together in the kitchen, Domingo's hand resting on her knee. He was eating a sandwich, she was drinking tea. Domingo looked at her and gave her a smile and a peck on the cheek. Atl thought that if anyone should walk in, they might think this was a regular, happy couple. Bernardino did walk in, throwing them a guarded look. He was carrying a black case.

"I'm coming to check on you," he said. "To see how the flesh is healing today."

He walked out without another word. Atl followed him. Domingo stood up, as if intending to go with them, but she motioned for him to sit down.

Atl and Bernardino went to the study, where he unrolled the bandage and looked at the hand. Bones and muscle were starting to grow and she had a palm and the beginnings of two fingers. Bernardino observed them carefully, bending the fingers, even pricking the skin with a tiny needle. He applied a salve to her skin.

"Sometimes the flesh twists and the scarring is poor. It's not the case. You are doing fine."

"That's a relief."

"There's been a development, hasn't there?" he asked.

Atl frowned as he changed the bandage, but did not reply.

"What would your mother say if she knew you were sleeping with a human?"

"She's dead, so her opinion doesn't matter."

Atl thought about Izel and what she'd told her about humans: Neanderthals. In Bernardino's eyes she'd let a monster rut between her legs. She would have agreed with him just a few days before.

"Even if he's a Renfield?"

"Like you've never—"

"No," Bernardino said, his voice clipped. "I don't play with my food. That is for the Necros. I thought you had more pride."

They burned, his words, and she felt herself branded by them. Atl might have given him a good kick in the gut if they didn't still need his sanctuary. She took a deep breath, composing herself, though she couldn't help the defiance in her voice. "It doesn't make a difference," she said.

"You should be thinking with your head."

"I have yet to lose my head over a boy."

It was only a fancy, the alchemy of danger and exhaustion that some-how had kindled desire.

"I expect a certain degree of naïveté from him, but not from you, my dear. As I explained to our mutual friend, ultimately we are entirely self-ish creatures."

"What did you tell him?" she asked, her voice almost a hiss.

"I told him we are our hunger. I don't think you'd deny that."

It was the kind of thing Izel might have told her, and Izel had always been right.

"Have you thought about killing him?"

"No," she said.

"You have. In the—"

"No," she cut him off, knowing that he was reading her mind and that he was very much right. After they escaped Nick and his men, just a few days ago, she'd wanted to hurt him. She hadn't cared, her head too foggy with pain.

Bernardino looked almost bemused, his lips curling into a smile. "So much for young love," he said.

She opened her mouth and then shut it, uncertain how to respond. Or if she should even attempt a response. Bernardino finished fiddling with the bandage and let go of her hand.

"Don't complicate things for yourself," he said.

Why not? she wanted to shriek, but of course, he was being completely reasonable. She was the hormonal girl who couldn't keep her hands to herself.

"Well, you are healing and I've had a word with you already," Bernardino said. "I suppose you want to return to him for a few more hours of idiotic, useless comfort before our departure. Go ahead."

Go to hell. She dearly hoped he was able to read that thought.

"Did you know Brazil is the world's fifth-largest country?" Domingo asked. "It has a coastline of 7,491 kilometers."

Domingo had found an encyclopedia lying around the house and promptly pulled out the letter *B*. He proceeded to recite factoids to Atl while they sat on the bed. He'd taken off his shirt and was only in his trousers while she wore an old-fashioned white nightgown she found in a drawer. It reached her ankles and the irony did not escape her that it re-sembled the outfit the woman wore in the vampire book she'd seen at

Domingo's place. *Dracula's Mistress.* Only the roles were reversed, since she was the vampire, not the girl fleeing a dark castle.

"It also has major shipping lanes, in case we need to get out of the country," she said.

"You don't think anyone would follow us there, do you?" he asked, lowering his book.

She opened drawers and found a blouse and trousers. The trousers looked too large for her, but there was a belt. She did not want the nightgown anymore. Did not want to look like a joke.

"Probably not," she said.

"It'll be strange being so far from Mexico."

"Having second thoughts?" She peeled off the nightgown and put on the trousers. He was looking at her.

"No," he said simply. "I don't have no one here."

I don't have anyone either, she thought. That was why she'd let herself be swept into this. He hadn't seduced her, not by far, but she'd been seduced anyway by the thoughts of comfort and companionship. Her family was gone, her home razed. She must scrub herself of her name, her identity, her very self. She had a need for an anchor, a friendly face.

Weak, she thought. *You are no warrior, never will be.*

"Are you all right?" he asked, brushing her hand as she drifted by, tucking the blouse into her trousers.

"Fine," she muttered.

"I always wanted to travel places," Domingo said, his hands tracing the contours of Brazil. "Faraway places. Not that I ever could do anything like that. And never with a girl like you."

"A girl like me," she repeated dryly.

She looked at Domingo and remembered what Bernardino had said. Despite his sweet smile he was human, made of fragile flesh and bones. He was meant to snap like a twig. He was meat. Nothing but meat. And she was lifting him and crowning him her companion in a twisted parody of the princess and the frog.

"What's wrong?" he asked, noticing her unkind stare.

"Nothing."

"Did Bernardino say something to you?"

She shook her head. "No."

"He said something."

Atl walked across the room, her arms crossed. A china doll on the shelf stared at her, golden curls and a mocking crimson smile.

"He's wrong. Whatever he told you, he's wrong."

"Shut up," she said, turning her back to him.

Domingo moved from the bed to stand behind her, whispering urgently in her ear. "He doesn't know us. He doesn't know who we are, so he's wrong."

"You don't know me either," Atl replied.

"Then tell me every single thing and I'll learn it."

She moved back to the bed, sitting at the foot of it and staring at the sheets. On his wrists, his neck, she'd left the faint marks of her feeding, as all vampires do. She thought he was going to leave a mark on her, as idiotic as that sounded since he had no fangs or stinger. Yet she was sure of it, that it'd be on her skin.

He was quiet, but the silence hurt more than any recrimination.

Atl sighed. She no longer had any idea what she was doing. She was drifting. It was easy to be pulled by the current, it was pleasant.

"Come here," she said.

He stretched next to her on the bed and held her with his quiet, easy affection. This is what she wanted, for everything to be simple, quiet, gentle, like she'd never thought anything could be. To have something *good* even if she didn't deserve it.

She traced the bones of his arms, his rib cage. She knew the names for each of them. She listed them in her head. Bones that couldn't heal like her own, flesh that wouldn't knit itself back together. Had Nick maimed him, had they shot him, he'd be gone in a second.

And then, there came that other nagging thought: bruises heal, marks fade from purple to blue to yellow, but what about the damn mark he was making right now? How do you get rid of that? Fingerprints that cannot be wiped and incisions that don't cut muscles or tissues. How? She had no idea.

Bernardino was correct. She was losing her head over a boy. But it'd be him who'd lose his life. Or them both, depending on how things went.

The thought made her feel cold.

Domingo had lain perfectly still so far, but when she dragged her knuckles against his clavicle he pushed himself up on his elbows, kissing her, dragging her down. The coldness melted away and she kissed him back. He embraced her again and they lay like that, quietly, until she fell asleep.

Somewhere inside the house, the dog barked. Only once. *Once. Intruder.* It made her jump up in bed. Her sudden movement awoke Domingo, who stirred and raised his head.

"What?"

"Quiet," she whispered. "Put your shirt on."

She now had two fingers and the beginning of a third. When she put on the jacket she pressed her hand against the pocket where the switchblade was nestled and took it out, handing it to Domingo.

"Grab it," she said.

"What's going on?" he asked.

"Someone's in the house," she said, putting on the backpack.

Domingo reluctantly took the weapon and she stepped out of the room, observing the darkened hallway. Bernardino's room was past the staircase, but she didn't think he was there. She could hear music playing downstairs, an old record spinning.

When they reached the ground floor, she saw them coming down the hallway. She jumped up, reaching the ceiling and dangling from it like a lizard and scuttling forward.

She looked down to see two men looking up at her in turn with puzzled expressions right before she let go and pounced on them, slashing their necks with her good arm and swiping their guns.

"They better not have hurt my dog," she muttered.

They advanced down the hallway and some moron stepped in front of Atl, trying to pin her with more of those damn darts, but she wasn't having any of that. She shot him smack in the chest, and then a second time, this time in the head, because she wasn't allowing any accidents.

They were wearing infrared goggles, but she could see in the darkness, no need for fancy gadgets. She dispatched another two before one of them actually managed something smart. She was blinded by a sudden burst of UV light, the brightness making her close her eyes and roll on the ground, her skin itching all over.

"Inject her with that silver nitrate, Kika!" someone yelled.

Shit, Atl thought, and raised her hands in what was surely a futile attempt to ward them off.

"Leave her alone!" yelled Domingo.

There were two shots, the scent of blood, and she opened her eyes.

CHAPTER 36

Kika was near Atl, ready and eager to drive a massive dose of silver nitrate into the girl's chest. Ana felt the tugging inside her head. It was a searing pain that made her groan and through the pain came the unmistakable command.

I don't want her dead.

Nick. Inside her. Inside her mind. Like a parasite. She'd felt him during the drive here and she'd stared at Kika, unable to warn her about what had happened. Unable to tell her that Nick and his friends had decided to make cannon fodder out of them.

For a few seconds she was able to discern his thoughts, vague and deformed, like watching an old TV tuned to the wrong channel, lines running up and down the screen. She had the impression of a strong, sickening hatred and then images of blood and mayhem and the girl . . . the girl he was after. Atl. Cut, mangled, violated, tortured . . . these were Nick's desires, his plans for the woman. Sickening ideas.

Another idea darted through his head. Ana caught a glimpse of herself, throat slit, bleeding to death. Then another vague thought: Marisol, also dead. No loose ends. Kill the cop and the bitch daughter.

And Atl, Atl, Atl, darling Atl. Like a mantra, the name dancing in his head, making Ana want to vomit, the psychotic fuck's thoughts mingling with her own.

She wanted to open her mouth. She wanted to yell and instead her mouth was clamped shut.

I don't want her dead. Give her to me now.

Compelled by Nick, Ana raised her gun and shot Kika and her companion in the back, the sound of the shots echoing down the hallway. The young man who was standing behind Atl stared at her, as though she were an apparition, while Atl lay on her knees, squinting, still blinded by the light.

Grab her.

Ana prepared to obey the order, but then came a hard blow to the head and she dropped to the floor with a loud thud, the gun slipping from her grasp. She heard them as she lay just inches from Kika's corpse, her ears ringing with the violence of the blow. The pain seemed to snap her connection from Nick. She felt like a sudden weight had slid from her body, and she was now mercifully alone inside her head. In pain, but alone.

"Are you hurt?" asked an older male voice.

Ana blinked tears away, trying to focus her eyes. She saw the older man scooping Atl up onto her feet. He was very tall, hunched.

"UV blindness. I'm seeing all fuzzy right now. You?" said the girl.

"Two silver bullets to the leg. Very unpleasant," the man replied.

The young man was now touching Atl, one hand on her arm, the other on her cheek. His mouth was moving but he was speaking so low Ana didn't catch what he said.

"You've seen my dog?" she heard the vampire girl ask.

"Safe and sound in the kitchen," the older man said.

"We need to get him and get going."

"How are we going to reach Bordo Blanco?" said the young man. "We can't just call a cab."

"We'll steal a car," Atl said.

Ana closed her eyes. She heard them walk away. When the house was quiet she stood up, holding on to the wall for good measure. Blood was leaking from one of her ears. She thought it was busted. She took a deep breath.

There came footsteps again. Different ones.

Nick stopped in front of her. "We got cut off back there. Where's the girl?"

She tried to swat his hand away, but he had already cut his wrist again and was pressing it against her mouth. The blood rushed through her veins, the pain was dulled, and she could hear him inside her once more, scratching, scratching, *scratching* until she had to speak.

"They escaped. Both vampires are still alive. He's injured. She sustained some UV damage. There's a young human man with them and they said something about a dog."

"So much for your plan, Rodrigo," Nick said, sneering. "Do you know where they're going?"

"They're heading to Bordo Blanco," Ana muttered.

"Where's that?"

"I don't know."

"It's a landfill," said Rodrigo.

Ana looked down at Kika's corpse, her blood staining the floor. Kika. Who'd thought this was exciting, who was so eager. But life is no adventure and there are no heroes, only survivors.

CHAPTER 37

They ran for five blocks before a car came rolling down the street. Atl jumped onto its hood and the driver pressed hard on the brakes. She quickly jumped down, opened the door, pulled the driver out, tossing him onto the ground and taking the driver's place.

Bernardino took the front seat, while Domingo sat in the back with the dog.

"You tell me where to go," Atl said, taking off the backpack and tossing it to Domingo.

Bordo Blanco was a great valley of darkness. No streets here, no lampposts, just a vast swath of gray and black interrupted only by the faint light emanating from the shacks of the trash pickers who lived there, rummaging through the mountains of garbage and selecting items suitable for recycling. Broken computers, diapers, soda cans, plastic bags, orange peels, the corpses of dead dogs, they formed hills of different sizes, some tiny and others monumental. One day, maybe, they'd turn this landfill into a luxury suburb like Santa Fe, "American-style," and everyone would be kicked out and everything would change. It was hard to imagine such a thing now. A foul smell permeated the land, and flies, terrifying in their size, buzzed around during the day. Also during the day came the trucks, and there was the rumble of the tractors with their great rubber wheels, maneuvering through the garbage, squashing it.

At night, there was only the full moon leaning down, caressing the bitter earth. The people who made their home there, out of the same garbage they collected, were asleep or preparing for bed. Bordo Blanco was quiet, eerie, and Domingo wished he could listen to his music, he was so nervous.

"Come," Domingo said.

He led them into the landfill, through what amounted to a semidecent path, but they had barely walked more than a few meters when a shot rang in the dark. The bullet hit Bernardino and he grunted, pausing in his steps. Laughter, behind them.

"Shit," whispered Atl.

"Come on, hurry. Over there," said Domingo, pointing at the separation plant, a vast shed where workers could sift through the garbage. It had been a gift from a charitable foundation, supposed to ease the life of the garbage collectors, though Domingo could see no rhyme or reason for it. Perhaps it was nicer to go through the garbage under a shed during the rainy season, but it was faster to simply drag the big collection bags through the landfill. He'd heard that they had a real separation plant at another landfill, one that had a conveyor belt fed by the hands of hundreds of garbage workers, but Bordo Blanco was smaller, more modest in its intent.

At least now it had a practical use: they could shield themselves, because Domingo doubted they'd last very long out in the open with people shooting at them.

As they approached the shed Domingo saw the shacks that were set near it, tiny abodes of cardboard and tin.

"We need to go into the shed," he told Atl, pointing at it.

"You go," she said.

"What?"

"Go and hide," she told him. "Take the dog with you. Bernardino and I can fight them. You can't."

Domingo glanced at Bernardino, who was moving swiftly for a man who had been shot twice. The older vampire nodded at him.

"Better get in there," Bernardino told him, and when Domingo did not move he added, "I can't protect two people at the same time."

He didn't want to leave their side, but recognized the wisdom of the suggestion. Domingo rushed past the shacks and into the gloom of the shed, Cualli right behind him. He veered away from a collection of rusty shopping carts, entangled together. He almost stumbled into a large container full of plastic dolls that had their faces sliced off, limbs and torsos missing. More containers, with similar bounties, were arranged against the walls. He crouched behind one of them. The dog hid next to him.

He heard gunfire outside.

Domingo clutched the knife Atl had given him in his sweaty hands. He was trembling and doubted very much he'd be able to use it, but he didn't know what else to do.

"Hey, I know you're in here!" yelled someone.

Domingo did not move. He could hear someone walking into the shed. A flashlight bounced around the walls. He pressed himself closer to the wall.

The flashlight passed by and he sighed with relief.

. . . And then the flashlight returned, aimed straight at his face.

"I see you, kid. Stand up slowly," said a voice.

Domingo did as he was told, but as he rose the dog growled and jumped onto the man. The man let out a loud scream and tried to pry the dog off his leg. He was a huge meaty guy, towering above Domingo, but he seemed unable to deal with the dog, which was firmly biting into his flesh. The man pulled out a gun.

The dog.

Domingo did not think. He simply pressed forward, plunging the knife into the man's back with all his strength. The man didn't collapse, he didn't even seem to be badly hurt, he just spun around, gun in hand. The dog jumped up and bit his hand. The man screamed again, stepped back, lost his footing, and fell heavily. The dog now went for his throat, tearing it with powerful jaws.

The man gurgled, unable to yell a third time.

Domingo stood there, staring at the spectacle, watching as the man twitched, then went suddenly still. The dog kept biting him and he could hear it chewing.

"Cualli, enough," he said.

The dog stopped and withdrew from the dead man. Domingo knelt down, looking at the man's face. He didn't panic, but there was a knot inside him, weighing him down. Domingo closed his eyes but it didn't help, so he snapped them open again.

He swallowed and rolled the corpse over. Domingo pulled out the knife and slipped it back in his pocket. A sudden wave of disgust hit him. He thought about the old man in La Merced and his dolls, which he kept to ward off the ghosts of the people he'd killed. But there was no time for disgust or stupid thoughts.

He looked again at the corpse at his feet and Cualli raised his head and growled.

A bullet hit the dog. Cualli whimpered and moved away before collapsing on the dirty ground.

Domingo hardly had a chance to take a breath before he felt the barrel of a gun nestled against his back.

"You're needed outside," said a woman. "Let's go."

CHAPTER 38

Nick ripped the bandage from his cheek, irritated by the way it itched, and scratched the new skin as he walked around the shacks. Scared humans peered through makeshift doors and windows, and hid quickly as he passed by.

He saw a figure running with a dog. Atl's human friend. No one was getting out of this place, not the dog and not that boy and not Atl.

"Get him back here. Alive," he told La Bola, and La Bola nodded, running clumsily toward a shed. He looked at Ana. "Go with him."

He had never trusted the efficacy of Rodrigo's friends, and he wasn't going to start now. Ana was only a meat puppet, but she was his meat puppet, under his control.

"All four of you, I want that girl alive, too," he told the others.

"Might be easier to finish her off here," Rodrigo replied dryly.

"That's not what my father wants, is it? It's definitely not what *I* want."

No. He wanted her dead real slow. He wanted Atl to enjoy the same pain that afflicted him as his muscles stretched and tried to achieve their proper form.

"As you wish," Rodrigo said.

He snorted. They split up, Nick and two of the men heading in one direction, Rodrigo taking the others.

They stomped through the landfill, the men raising their flashlights while Nick scanned the darkness for the girl. Broken glass crunched under his shoes. The overwhelming scent of rotten food filled his nostrils and Nick wished he had a damn handkerchief. And his clothes . . . his clothes and shoes would no doubt be ruined. He could never wear this again, not after walking through such a shithole.

That was another item to add to Atl's list of sins. She'd dragged him from his home, across the country, all the way to Mexico City and into a fucking landfill. She had insulted him, she had kicked him, she had tried to blow his head off. That bitch had a tab a mile long and Nick was going to collect.

Suddenly he heard three shots in rapid succession, followed by Rodrigo's piercing scream.

Nick spun around and ran to the place where the screams and shots had come from, the two men rushing after him. They arrived in time to see a vampire draped over what had once been Rodrigo and was now a sack of flaccid flesh and bones.

It was feeding.

Nick recoiled in horror and then stood still. He had a stun baton with him but he had forgotten how to wield the weapon, too disgusted to process what was happening. His men seemed equally shocked, their hands trembling.

He took a deep breath. "Kill him," he told the men.

They stared at him, utterly horrified.

Nick bared his fangs at them. "Go, now, or I'll gouge your eyes out," Nick ordered.

The men still looked terrified, but they obeyed. They carried short-barreled, pump-action shotguns and the bullets were silver-coated, but even though they peppered him with bullets, the Revenant didn't seem too concerned, darting forward and pressing his hand against the face of one of them. The man began to convulse and Nick watched with sick fascination as the victim's whole body quickly shrank, the skin turning yellow and wrinkled as life was drained out of him.

The other man had lost his composure and now began shooting without any finesse, shooting both his twitching friend and the vampire. The vampire let go of the man he was clutching and jumped onto the fool with the shotgun, ripping it from his hands, then shoving him against the ground and squatting over him.

Nick, who had been holding back, pressed against the wall of a sad shack, crouched on the ground, and grasped a long, rusty piece of metal—perhaps once part of a fence—that was being used to support a clothesline. He pulled it out and walked behind the vampire. The creature was too busy feeding to notice him coming. He jammed the piece of metal down, into the vampire's back, pinning him down as though he were a butterfly, on top of the dead goon.

"Stake through your damn heart," Nick said, feeling terribly accomplished as he did this.

A muffled groan made Nick turn around. Rodrigo, now closer to a mummy from Guanajuato than a real person, was still alive. He opened and closed his mouth, his hands scrabbled the dirt.

"Ha," Nick said, glancing down at the old man who had pestered him for years and years. "Look at you."

Rodrigo moaned. Nick raised his foot and brought it crashing down into Rodrigo's head. The skull cracked like a porcelain teacup, bits of bone spilling and jumping through the air.

"Idiot," he whispered.

The night air felt good against Nick's face and he grinned.

Ana came then. She was not alone. The teenage boy was with her, his eyes wide with fear.

"Good work," Nick said, clapping his hands. "Bola?"

"Dead."

"So much for that," Nick said. His father might regret the loss of Rodrigo and La Bola, but Nick considered this a great victory for himself. Father would look at him with a newfound respect after this. After he brought him the girl.

"You're her Renfield or what?" he asked the boy.

The boy did not answer, but the way his eyes darted away told him he was right. Why else would Atl be dragging a human around with her?

He threw his head back and yelled. "Atl! Come out, you bitch. I have your buddy!"

Nick squeezed the young man's face between his hands and tilted it, looking at it thoughtfully.

"Say something to the lady," Nick ordered.

When the boy did not reply, Nick sighed, grabbed the electric prod that was strapped to his back, and pulled it out, lowering the voltage and pressing it against the human's chest. The kid squealed, like a pig.

"Oink, oink! I'm going to fry him and squeeze his brains out if you don't show yourself, Atl! You've got three!"

CHAPTER 39

Atl had no idea where she was headed, only that she had to run. *Hide, Atl. Hide.* This mantra, which she'd been following for weeks, comforted her. She was good at running.

And then she heard the loud voice, clear across the field of garbage.

"Atl! Come out, you bitch. I have your buddy!"

She paused, looking back. A ruse? Domingo had the dog and there was Bernardino back there.

Then she heard Domingo scream, a shriek that ripped through the darkness.

"Oink, oink! I'm going to fry him and squeeze his brains out if you don't show yourself, Atl! You've got three!"

"You moron," she whispered.

She couldn't head back. She remembered the night Izel had died, the wait inside the refrigerator, her desperate efforts to evade Godoy's men after that. She'd come too far to let herself be captured.

"One."

She hadn't saved Izel. Domingo was nothing. A child from the slums with only the most tenuous connection to her. He could be easily replaced.

"Two."

She was not a warrior. She was not brave. She was none of the things they said about her ancestors. She wasn't even anything like the fantasies of vampires Domingo spouted, picturing powerful creatures who roamed the night.

"Three."

She was not . . .

"I'm here!" she yelled. "Wait!"

. . . leaving him behind.

She walked back the way she'd come, back toward the shacks. Fear made her stumble but fuck it, fuck it.

Don't be stupid, Izel said in her head.

You're dead, she replied.

You too. Soon. Let him die, better him than you.

We are warriors, remember? Let's fight for something worth a damn for once, she told Izel.

And the murmur of Izel, of doubt, cleared from her head just as she stepped behind the shacks.

Nick had a hand on Domingo's shoulder, locking him in place. In his other hand he was holding an electric prod. A woman accompanied them.

A couple of meters behind the trio were corpses, splayed on the ground. Humans but also Bernardino, impaled on a long metal pipe.

"Thank you," Nick said. "I was thinking I'd have to chase you. It's getting very boring."

"No need for that."

"I'm glad to hear it."

"You can let him go," she told Nick.

"I can?" Nick asked. His face was a parody of a human face and his smile was full of savage mirth. "Maybe it would be more fun to torture you both."

"Let him go."

"I think not," the vampire said.

There was a flash of metal and Domingo rammed the switchblade knife into Nick's stomach. Nick's grip on Domingo relaxed and he looked down, more shocked than angry. He didn't seem able to process the thought that a human boy had just plunged a knife into his belly. Atl didn't quite believe it either, but then Nick roared and there was no time to think and she pounced on him, pulling the knife out and plunging it into Nick's left eye.

She was hauled back by the woman. Atl felt the pressure of the gun at her side and then she heard the shot, felt the pain as the bullet—silver, damn it—lodged in her body. She slammed her elbow against the woman's rib cage with such force she was sure she had broken a couple of bones.

Good, she thought. She brushed her fingers against her side, jamming them into the wound, her nails tearing and enlarging the hole until she was able to pull out the bullet and toss it away, heaving, staring at the ground.

She raised her head just in time to receive a full, swift kick in the face courtesy of Nick.

"You bitch!" he yelled. He stood above her, blood pouring down his face. He kicked her again and she fell back, pushing herself up on her elbows.

He struck her with the electric prod. The charge made her convulse, her legs flailing in the air. He hit her again, this time in her stomach, and she spat out blood.

"Bet you didn't like that, huh?" he said. "Hey, how about we try this with you."

He pulled the knife out of his eye, twisting his head as he did, his teeth showing. When he dislodged the knife he slammed it down, into her stomach, then pulled it out again.

"Bet you wish it was over, little girl," he snarled. "That is not happening."

She rolled over herself, scrambling up, her hand pressed against her stomach. It felt warm, where the knife had cut it.

"Are you giving up?"

Atl squinted as he spoke. She thought of Izel, the turtle, the scent of corpses burning, and raised her head. Nick was coming toward her and she could not summon the strength to fight back.

"No," she said.

Nick tried to hit her with the electric prod. Atl managed to dodge the blow more by instinct than actual thought, but the exertion caused her to gasp. The pain in her stomach was very bad. She couldn't stand straight. Nick tried to hit her again and when she stepped back she lost her footing.

And then she saw Domingo hurrying toward them, carrying the long rusty piece of metal that had been impaling Bernardino. Domingo swung it with all his strength, like a bat. It hit Nick in the head. The crunch of bone made her blink.

Domingo let go of the metal bar and stared at her.

Nick rose. There was so much blood pouring from his head. He opened his mouth, showing her his teeth, and turned toward Domingo with a shriek that left no doubt of his intention.

He was going to kill Domingo.

She jumped up in the air, unfurling her wings, tearing her jacket in the process. She pounced on Nick, landing on his back. He tried to shake her off but she dug her nails into his face and flapped her wings, pulling him up into the air. Just a few meters—a few meters was all she *could* manage—but it bought Domingo enough time to scuttle away.

Nick tried to bite her, his mouth chomping at the air. She released him and he fell down, sprawled upon the floor like a marionette. Atl landed next to him, resting a hand against the ground and wincing, the pain in her body a blinding hot coal.

She really shouldn't have done that.

Nick stood up on shaky feet. His face was even more butchered than before, a mess of unsettling crimson. But the teeth were still sharp and eager, his maw opening, ready to take a bite of her. Nick shuffled forward.

"I was going to take you back alive, but I changed my mind," he said.

Atl retracted her wings.

* * *

Ana groaned. The pain was excruciating. She couldn't breathe properly. She was dizzy. And yet, she was grateful. The pain was so strong, it suddenly made everything clear. The weight that had been stifling her—the young vampire's mind control—had broken. A temporary reprieve, she knew.

But enough, she thought.

She watched Nick as he walked toward the girl. He had taken a lot of damage, but he would not stop.

Bastard, she thought. Her hands were shaking.

From the corner of her eye she noticed movement, a shadow unfolding. She didn't pay it attention, instead focusing on Nick.

She thought about her grandmother's lessons. The way to hold the gun, how to align the target, how to press the trigger. Breathe, Ana, breathe. She thought of herself younger, glued to the TV set, watching the thrilling conclusion to the midnight movie. The good guy always had time to fire one last, crucial shot.

But Ana was hurting. Ana wasn't in a movie and she couldn't keep her hands steady, the weapon seemed to slide from her grasp. For a moment she considered lying there and letting this end without her intervention, without bothering about what happened to that fucking vampire bastard. But she couldn't. Not when she'd seen what he was planning.

She breathed in.

Ana did what she could, took aim and managed to hit Nick in the chest. The vampire hissed and looked over his shoulder at her.

"Stupid woman," he growled, and she felt his control over her again.

She pressed the gun against her own chest, her finger slowly finding the trigger even though she didn't want to. The gun went off and she rolled onto her side.

As she lay dying, the connection from the vampire now forever severed, she smiled.

Because now she could see the shadow. It had contours, a face, and in the shape of that face and the contours of that gaunt body she recognized a vampire, shuffling forward.

Revenant, she thought.

Nick was staring at Atl again, his eyes as red as the blood covering him. Behind him she noticed a figure slowly rising, slowly moving toward them.

Bernardino. But Nick had been too busy looking at the human woman to notice him, and now he was too busy looking at Atl.

Atl licked her lips, standing still. "You look pretty banged up," she said. "I thought your kind was strong."

"Shut up," Nick said.

"Of course, you're not really a full-grown Necros, are you? You're just a kid playing at being a narco."

"Look who's talking," Nick said.

"I'm better than you."

"I'll show you—"

"Try me, fucker," she said, and his focus was solely on her and she, in turn, stared straight at him.

He pounced on her, weighing her down. Atl tore at his neck with her nails while he opened his mouth, ready to bite a chunk of her cheek. She gathered her remaining strength and dug her nails in deeper, skewering him in place, inches above her. He was snapping his mouth open and closed, trying to bite her face, and she was holding him; it was like pushing away an armored tank. Her arms trembled and he drove down harder.

She was beginning to feel dizzy and didn't think she could keep him at bay anymore.

Then Bernardino leaned down and placed both hands around Nick's head. The young vampire opened his mouth, possibly to yell or try to bite the person holding him, but he didn't manage either thing as Atl dug her nails into his jaw, stopping him from turning his head.

Nick then tried to push himself up, away from her, but she grabbed him by the shoulders and held him tight, in a mockery of an embrace to prevent him from escaping the touch of the Revenant. Nick trembled, his mouth grew slack, and she watched as his eyes dimmed and sank into his head, his hair fell out, even his teeth started popping out of his mouth, the nails sliding from his fingers.

Finally, Atl scuttled away from under the vampire, an arm pressed against her belly. He slid onto the ground, slid as though his bones had melted away, and Bernardino bent over him, covering him completely, like a shadow.

When Bernardino was done feeding, Nick was nothing more than an empty carcass while Bernardino's face appeared less wrinkled, his hair almost devoid of any gray, returned to its lustrous black. He was still hunched over, disturbing in his appearance, though. Certain things would not change.

Bernardino approached her and Atl recognized the dangerous glint in his eyes.

We are our hunger, she thought. Bernardino was still weakened. He needed more life. What better life than a vampire's? This was exactly why they feared his kind, why she'd hesitated to meet him that first time, why she'd sent Domingo instead, thinking that if he was displeased, Bernardino would eat her messenger instead of herself.

Ironic.

"I won't fight you," she said, and stood up, her head held high. "Don't hurt Domingo, though."

"That's very considerate of you," he said. "Stupid, but considerate."

Bernardino advanced on her, placing a hand against her neck, leaning over her. She did not flinch.

"I thought you didn't lose your head over boys," Bernardino told her.

"I don't." Atl closed her eyes and welcomed her death with two words.

Instead of the drawing of life she had expected, she felt the familiar thrum of energy as he stabilized her, breathed life into her. The cut upon her stomach began stitching itself together and she let out a low hiss, snapping her eyes back open.

Bernardino staggered back, older again, his hair gone gray, and smirked at her.

"Atl? Are you okay?" she heard Domingo say.

Domingo rushed toward Atl. She felt a kiss upon her brow, then his arms around her. She looked at Bernardino.

You did lose your head, Bernardino's eyes told her. She could not deny it. He'd warned her about this.

She could smell the blood from the dead humans, Nick's blood, her own blood.

"I'm fine," she said, staring back at Bernardino.

She looked at Domingo. He seemed tired, but he was still like a freshly minted coin, and she knew all she'd ever be able to give him was this. The scent of blood and death. Nothing new or clean. And he wouldn't mind.

Sacrifice. The face of all earthly things at one point is sacrifice. She'd never known what that really meant, parroting the words of others, and now she understood.

"And you, Bernardino? Are you all right?" Domingo asked.

"I'm fine."

"I owe you," Atl said, looking at the vampire. "I won't forget that."

"You have an appointment," Bernardino told them.

She wished to thank him more, but he was already trailing back to the entrance of the landfill, walking by the shacks, sinking into the night.

They began to walk in the opposite direction.

"Where's Cualli?"

"The woman shot him," he said. "I think . . . I'm sorry, he must be dead."

She wanted, for a second, to look at the poor animal's corpse, and then she knew she couldn't.

"Let's go," she said.

They were walking past the woman, her eyes open and her head at an odd angle. Dead too. Like the dog. She derived no pleasure from it and looked away, forward into the darkness.

"It's just the two of us now," Domingo muttered as he picked up her backpack, which she'd dropped during the fight.

CHAPTER 40

They stumbled onto the road, the sea of garbage behind them. They moved slowly. The sluggish canal they'd crossed over, full of filth, ran parallel to them. There were still no lights, just the moon, steady, illuminating their path until they reached a bridge and there finally, streetlights.

It was a long walk, eternal. They spotted a solitary convenience store among a sea of gray, square buildings. And stationed in front of the store a battered car, the windows rolled up, with Manuel at the wheel.

Atl grabbed the backpack hanging from Domingo's shoulder and zipped it open, fiddling with the documents inside. She took out an envelope and tucked it into her jacket, then zipped the backpack closed.

"I've left cash in there," she said. "There's also a new ID for you. In a couple of months pay a visit to Elisa and ask her for access to an account. She'll have one for you. It'll be my parting gift. You'll have a good life."

Domingo heard the words, but they were like an echo, faint, distant. The words could not be real.

"Wait, what are you saying?" he asked.

"I'm leaving you here. I go onward by myself."

"You're kidding."

She shook her head.

"You can't. Why'd you say such a thing?" he babbled. "Why'd you joke like that?"

"I'm serious. You are going to be fine. There's money in there and there will be more in the account."

Domingo let the backpack fall to his feet. He did not know if he could speak, his breath seemed to burn his lungs, and he could hardly remember how to utter a coherent sentence.

"No," he said, and gripped her arms. "No, you promised. You have to take me with you. We talked about South America. First thing we do when we get to Brazil is you're going to buy me a suit and we're going to have a dinner in Rio. You can't leave me!"

"Who do you think you are to demand anything of me?" she sputtered. "Let go of me or I'll break your arm."

"Then break it," he replied, holding on tighter to her.

She pushed him away and he lost his balance, falling down. He lay sprawled in the middle of the road, watching her. A cricket chirped nearby. The night seemed terribly vast, like the inked panel in a comic book, threatening to swallow him whole.

"Why are you doing this?" he asked her. His mouth had gone dry.

"You'd slow me down."

"I wouldn't!"

"I don't need you anymore."

Her words cut into him, through muscle and bone. Domingo felt his eyes stinging with tears but he didn't cry. He pulled himself up, scanning her face feverishly.

Atl promptly looked away and closed her eyes.

"Look at me," he said, and his voice sounded harsh and alien. "Don't be such a coward and look at me."

Atl opened her eyes and stared at Domingo. He stared back. He wanted to touch her. He wanted to kiss her and kiss away any doubts, but when he moved toward her she took three steps back.

"You're a liability. I've made mistakes because of you and I can't afford them anymore. You'll get me killed or I'll get you killed. I'm doing you a favor. You're too young to die, especially for me."

"Maybe I don't care if I die. You said you'd take me with you," he told her again, caught in a loop.

She turned her head, looking at the path they had followed, and then she looked in the opposite direction at the car waiting for her.

"I'll tell you one vampire fact, Domingo. One final one for your scrapbook," she said, her voice languid. "We always lie."

She kicked the backpack in his direction and straightened her jacket. Her face was impassive.

"I love you," he whispered. Like the fool he was, the fool he'd been from the get-go, madly dashing after this girl.

A long silence stretched between them. She cupped his face with one hand and kissed him, so briefly Domingo hardly felt her lips upon his, the ghost of a kiss. He leaned down, pressed his forehead against hers.

Atl stepped back. He desperately wanted to follow her, yet managed to remain rooted to his spot as she walked in the direction of the car, hands in her pockets.

"Atl, do—"

She turned her head a fraction of an inch, her eyes very dark, pools of ink, silencing him. She did not say a word. In her eyes he read the answer to the question she had not allowed him to ask.

No one had ever looked at him like that. Like he was every star shining down on them that night and the ground beneath her feet, and every other ridiculous phrase found in books that he'd never believed could possibly be true. And he knew she hated herself in that moment and he knew she loved him precisely because she did not speak a single word.

The car sped away and her gaze stayed with him as he slowly walked back through the landfill.

When he passed by the shed he heard a soft whine. Domingo paused at the doorway of the building and went inside.

The dog was alive! It lay behind a bunch of plastic bags. Domingo kicked the bags away and Cualli stared at him. Domingo walked back toward the entrance, pulled at one of the shopping carts until it came free from the others, and rolled it back next to the dog. He placed the dog inside the cart.

It looked confused. Domingo patted its head.

"It's all right," he said gently. "You're in luck today."

His player still worked, so he switched it on and dug out his headphones. He began rolling his cart away.

omingo dreamt of her a few days later, in the long, long hours before the dawn, the dog curled up next to him. He dreamt she'd stepped out of a car, at the end of a dusty road. She took out a compass from her pocket and held a machete in her other hand. Her hand. It was fine and whole. She was fine.

Atl stepped forward, into the jungle, the trees rising very high above her head. There were many noises: the faint chirping of birds, the roars of howling monkeys, the buzzing of insects, the patter of rain as it slid down the leaves and trunks of the trees. The rain reverberated, resembling the steady sound of drums.

"Atl," he said.

She hacked through the jungle, her machete swinging back and forth, opening a path. She paused for a moment, raising her head, as if someone had called her name. She smiled. Almost immediately she pressed forward, sinking into the endless greenery of the jungle.

The chatter of birds spread, as if they were welcoming the girl.

In dreams, he smiled too.

VAMPIRE CLANS, THE EZZOHQUEH

The Aztec word for vampires is "ezzohqueh," the "bloodthirsty ones," but vampires are not unique to the Americas. Ten vampire subspecies exist nowadays, though if you believe certain rumors, there might be one or two secret vampire subspecies that have evaded detection. Not every human culture encountered vampires through history, though modern airplanes and ships have made it easy for them to migrate.

Vampires share broad similarities. Vampires are territorial, hierarchical, have a tendency to display ritualistic, violent, and volatile behavior, and their main food source is humans. They are organized around tightly knit clans. (See **Revenant** and **Imago** for the sole exceptions.) Though vampires may have a variety of powers and abilities that eclipse those of humans, they are outnumbered by humans, a fact that can place them in a precarious position. Humans are also more adaptable and creative than vampires, who are set in their ways. Vampires have sponsored or admired the work of great inventors, painters, and poets, but these have all been invariably human. This, however, may be a cultural taboo rather than a biologically determined quality. The vampire emphasis on tradition, for example, may discourage more subversive expressions.

A number of clans may eschew modern clothing and dress and live as though they were still in a different century. As a result, when you enter a vampire abode, you may suddenly find yourself talking to men in livery and women in corsets. In recent decades many vampires have found themselves increasingly thrust into a modern world they may not enjoy.

Vampires are not immortal, though they can have much longer life spans than regular humans. Revenants and Imagoes are especially long-lived, though other vampires whisper they can grow confused in their old age, developing a type of dementia.

Despite stereotypes disseminated by popular media, not all vampires are wealthy and aristocratic. Certain vampire families have managed to amass considerable wealth, but constant in-fighting means numerous vampire clans have also fallen from grace and lost resources. Others have never managed to gather resources in the first place due to the highly stratified nature of vampire culture.

ASANBOSAM

Native to West Africa. The Asanbosam possess very sharp teeth and were originally tree-dwellers, something that can be easily ascertained by looking at their feet with their long claws. They are able to shape-shift and when they do they resemble gigantic bats. In this form they have the capacity for flight.

IMAGO

The origins of the Imago and details about them remain hazy. They are likely Egyptian. They can adopt the guise of any human or vampire they come in contact with, concealing their true form, which is more batlike than human. However, an Imago's real face will be visible if you take a photograph of it or look at its reflection. Like the Revenants, they are solitary creatures, preferring to stay away from other vampires. Their name derives from the fact that they periodically "cocoon" themselves during their lifetime in order to rejuvenate, a process that requires an extensive "feeding." They like to burrow and sleep in the earth.

JIANGSHI

Native to China. Popularly called "hopping" vampires, the Jiangshi earn their name due to their arthritic limbs, which make it hard for them to walk or run. Their mobility diminishes as they age. The Jiangshi relies on its highly developed telepathic powers of suggestion for sustenance. They can "suggest" that a human offer their own blood willingly to them or control them by inducing a trancelike state. An adult Jiangshi can maintain dozens of humans under its suggestive powers, puppeteering them in a more refined fashion than the Necros. Jiangshi can also transfer their consciousness into human vessels and interact with the outside world while they remain in their chambers. Jiangshi can tolerate sunlight, but in order to engage in their telepathic manipulations they must stay in a dark room, hence they prefer to spend their lives in inner chambers, often underground. A Jiangshi's hair is generally white, even at a young age, a distinctive trademark that makes them easy to spot though they may wear wigs or dye their hair.

NACHZEHRER

A European subspecies, likely Teutonic in origin. The Nachzehrers greatly resemble the Necros, possessing their resilience and ability to feed off almost any blood source. They display a preference for carrion rather than live humans, a trait that sets them apart from other vampires who despise "cold" blood. Like the Tlāhuihpochtli or the Wendigo, the Nachzehrer shape-shifts. It can appear in the form of a wolf. They are hirsute, and the men generally sport beards and wear their hair long.

NECROS

This Central European vampire variety most closely resembles the vampire found in traditional media, with sharp teeth, pale skin, and a strong aversion to sunlight. They are organized around a patriarchal clan structure. They are very agile and can dislocate their limbs in order to get into hard-to-reach places—for example, to gain access to a house. Necros are very strong, resistant vampires. Unlike other vampires, the Necros can consume any kind of blood, even if it comes from a sick human. They also enjoy human food and alcohol, which several vampire subspecies cannot consume. Sexual or blood contact with a Necros will cause a human to come under the influence of the Necros, allowing them to manipulate the human's actions. Unlike the other vampires, who hold on tight to tradition, the youngest generation of Necros are brash and bold, and disregard many of the old precepts.

OBAYIFO

Native to Western Africa. They glow in the dark and this property might have been useful for them to find their way, to hunt for prey, and to attract their prey, as their glow is said to be hypnotic, drawing humans to them. The Obayifo can conceal their glow by manipulating the perception of those around them, just like certain marine organisms deploy flaps of skin to hide glow-spots. They are not as physically resilient as the Necros and other subspecies and thus are more vulnerable to attacks. They sleep in shallow water.

PISHACHA

Native to India. They are gaunt, have sharp claws and teeth, and are completely nocturnal. Pishachas, like the Imago, are able to alter their form and take on the appearance of others. They may also become "invisible," camouflaging themselves. They can be identified by their red eyes, which, no matter what shape they take, remain visible, though savvy, modern vampires can utilize contact lenses or sunglasses to disguise this. They are said to live near burial grounds and burrow beneath the earth.

REVENANT

Unlike other vampires, Revenants tend to live in solitude. Males are especially prone to living alone. While other vampire subspecies may interact due to trade or warfare, all vampires fear the Revenant because of its particular feeding mechanism. Revenants feed by absorbing the life force of creatures around them, generally humans, but they can feed on vampires. Revenants are capable of reading the minds of others. Unlike the mild telepathy displayed by other vampires, their mindreading powers can be quite refined, making them an extraordinary foe. However, Revenants have a number of physical ailments. They usually develop bone problems, which gives them their distinctive "hump," and can suffer from diminished lung capacity—the breathless quality of the Revenant's voice truly does indicate they are out of breath. Revenants are also very sensitive to light, sound, and smells. Revenants have extremely long life spans, though it is often hard to gauge their age because they can "rejuvenate" after a feeding, displaying unlined and unblemished skin. However, no matter how much a Revenant rejuvenates, he will never be able to straighten his bones or completely diminish the other physical ailments he suffers from, and which increase as he ages. Revenants possibly originated in Russia.

TLÃHUIHPOCHTLI

Plural, Tlãhuihpochtin. Original to Mexico. The name "Tlãhuihpochtin" is applied only to the women of this subspecies. Males cannot shape-shift and have shorter life spans. They are called Ichtacãini. These vampires follow a matriarchal clan structure. They can consume only the blood of young humans, and like several other vampire subspecies they are allergic to silver and garlic. The females are able to sprout wings and fly, a detail that might have given rise to American legends of flying witches who drink the blood of babies. They can walk in the daylight but are stronger at night. They are very private and prefer to reveal few details about their existence or their practices, though it is known they speak Nahuatl and hold in great esteem a number of ancient Aztec traditions, including the art of warfare. Before the arrival of Spaniards to Mexico, the Tlãhuih-pochtin were a high caste of priests and priestesses, dressing in bird feathers and wearing jade necklaces. Their flesh was considered sacred and they were an earthly manifestation of the god of war. They remained celibate while serving in the temple, but when they concluded their religious duties, which usually encompassed two decades, they married and could beget children. These Mexican vampires made their way to the Philippines during the colonial Spanish period, giving rise to stories of the manananggal, supposedly a flying witch who sucks the blood of humans.

WENDIGO

Native to Canada. A voracious subspecies that prefers cold climates. Very tall, with skin that is icy cold to the touch. They are active in the winter and slumber during the warmer months. They have sharp claws and their eyes are said to glow in the dark. They were said to live in caves or mounds before the arrival of Europeans, but the modern Wendigo has had to adapt to the presence of new humans and new vampires, just as the Tlāhuihpochtin did. Nevertheless, they remain highly rural. The cities with the largest number of Wendigos are Winnipeg, Toronto, and Montreal. Vancouver is too warm for them and it is dominated by the Chinese Jiangshi. They can shape-shift, acquiring the characteristics of a ferocious bear. In this shape they are very strong, but in their natural form they are considerably weakened. Their height draws attention to them, so they can't easily pass as human.

VAMPIRE HEALTH

Human diseases do not affect vampires, though a vampire will stay away from unhealthy humans because they will invariably vomit and reject tainted blood. Through their more advanced senses they can usually identify if a human is ill and avoid them as a food source. There are such things as vampire diseases, though, and they can grow ill if exposed to these.

Vampires heal at a faster rate than humans and can tolerate pain very well. Some vampires can even regenerate limbs. This means the most effective way to kill vampires is not using the mythical stake through the heart, but by burning them or cutting off their head. Vampires are highly sensitive to certain triggers, such as silver, garlic, and sunlight, which can incapacitate them far more easily than by employing a regular bullet.

Vampires can quickly be identified by looking at their blood, which contains a higher iron content than human blood, allowing for rapid coagulation. Vampire blood has a darker coloration than human blood.

Despite what the legends may say, humans cannot become vampires if they drink vampire blood.

CRONENG'S DISEASE

A disease that makes humans hemorrhage from the nose and gives them sores, transmitted through bodily fluids (saliva, sweat, semen, blood, etc.). Vampires are very sensitive to diseased blood and abhor Croneng's because it spoils their food supply. Even a Nachzehrer won't feed on someone with Croneng's. Urban legends say Croneng's disease is a designed disease, created to exterminate vampires, but it did not work the way it was intended to. Other urban legends indicate the opposite: that vampires gave humans this disease.

VAMPIRE RELATIONSHIPS

The sexual practices of vampires vary greatly depending on their subspecies. The idea of Dracula and his "brides" is likely based on the sexual practices of Necros: the Necros male does take several mates. But this is far from a universal practice. The Imago and Revenant are solitary and a male generally does not cohabit with a female.

Vampires follow strict clan rules and traditions, and many of them could appear old fashioned to modern humans. For example, many vampires follow elaborate courting processes. Vampires often marry to strengthen alliances, to solidify their place in a hierarchy, and for a number of other practical reasons. Arranged marriages are common.

Bisexuality and homosexuality occur among the vampire clans, though in specific and sometimes ritualized contexts. For example, though the Aztecs executed homosexuals and lesbians, lesbianism was allowed among the Tlāhuihpochtin. Nowadays, a high-ranking Tlāhuihpochtli will pick an appropriate and equally high-ranking male as her consort. She will be expected to mate only with this male but may keep female lovers.

Because vampires are less fertile than humans, reproduction is encouraged, even demanded, especially among the high-ranking classes.

Vampires—except for the Necros and Nachzehrers—shun humans as sexual partners. Vampires are seldom interested in sexual relations with vampires of a different subspecies. Certain vampire subspecies, such as the Imago, go as far as to encourage incest among their clan rather than mingle with outsiders. Vampires do not consider humans as viable sexual partners, which is logical since they cannot reproduce with them and humans do not provide vampires with any sociopolitical benefits.

RENFIELD

Slang, used to refer to a vampire's human companion. Any high-ranking vampire has a human companion who can carry out tasks for him, such as guarding the vampire's lair during the daytime. A vampire's assistant is generally well treated by the vampire.

Renfields should not be confused with the "puppets" created by Necros, humans bent to their will through sexual or blood contact. Renfields also differ from the Jiangshi's human avatars or shells. Renfields retain their autonomy, but choose to serve vampires. Most vampires can maintain a noninvasive, mild, telepathic bond with their Renfield.

One important task carried out by Renfields is to serve as emissaries. The Victorians had calling cards; vampires have Renfields.

TLAPALĒHUIĀNI

A vampire's human companion. (See **Renfield** for more details.)

XIUHTLAHTŌLLI

A word utilized by the Tlāhuihpochtin that means "precious speech." It is the crude telepathic bond that joins together a human and certain vampires. Other vampires have different names for it, such as "blue note" or "resonance."

VAMPIRE RELIGION

There is no one vampire religion. Originally, vampires followed pagan traditions, but nowadays almost all Necros follow the Christian faith, albeit in a modified form, and other groups have followed suit, taking up different religions. Nevertheless, many vampires do still follow pagan traditions. The Tlāhuihpochtin continue to celebrate Aztec festivities and pray to Aztec deities, even if they do not do so in the same way their ancestors did. The most important god in their pantheon is Huitzilopochtli, a deity of war, the sun, and human sacrifice. Just as in the old days they will lance their skin and offer their blood to the gods or engage in ritual combat. In comparison, Wendigos practice an animistic and shamanistic religion.

VAMPIRES IN THE MODERN ERA

For most of human history vampires were regarded as nebulous myths and legends, their existence remaining unconfirmed. Technological advances, however, forced the vampire from the shadows. In 1967 a joint task force organized by the governments of the United States and Great Britain revealed to the world the existence of five subspecies of vampires. Microscopes, X-rays, and other modern medical advances were used to identify them and later served to reveal the existence of the other five species.

The discovery that vampires were real prompted a variety of reactions from governments around the world. Some countries, like Spain and Portugal, deported vampires. Most countries adopted either a "vampire-free zone" policy or a "vampire-occupied zone" policy. A country that favors the vampire-free zone policy will designate neighborhoods or entire cities as off-limits to vampires. Mexico City, Vienna, and Prague are three large vampire-free zones. On the other hand, the vampire-occupied zone restricts vampires to specific neighborhoods or cities, which they may not leave without special passes. The United Kingdom, France, and Germany follow this policy.

Most governments track vampires, require special identification papers for them, and request that they regularly stay in contact with a sanitation unit. Some governments have established highly restrictive policies that bar vampires from working in certain occupations, such as law enforcement or medicine. Anti-vampire bias has generated resentment in several cities. Vampire and human clashes were not uncommon in Europe and the United States in the 1970s. In 1981, vampires led by Pierre Antoine Bellamy murdered more than two dozen Parisian police officers and declared that a "new world order" was at hand. Similar murders were repeated in London and New York. Eventually, elders of the most prominent vampire clans signed the current treaties with humans that establish rights and restrictions for vampires.

Not all vampires have fared poorly in the past couple of decades. Mexican vampires face relatively few restrictions, though a number of them have acquired their prominent positions through the formation of cartels.

DEEP CRIMSON

One of the large, human-organized crime groups in Mexico City. They do not trade with vampires and regard them as a scourge. Members sport red clothing and/or red tattoos.

Horror author Silvia Moreno-Garcia has a true body of work: intricate, mysterious, and full of surprises and scars. Whether she's winning the World Fantasy Award for editing the very first all-woman anthology of Lovecraftian horror fiction or penning gothic novels so evocative they get snapped up by Hulu after bursting onto the *New York Times* Best Seller list, Ms. Moreno-Garcia gets her readers' blood pumping. I recently had the privilege of speaking to her about her inspiration and creative process behind this novel.

Let's start with the most important question. Arithmomania was such an interesting common affliction for you to give all vampires, why did you settle on that?

Vampire folklore is full of tidbits that nowadays seem silly and antiquated. It's laughable to think you could stop a vampire by throwing a bag of rice at it, but I thought it actually made perfect sense if vampires tend to be obsessive-compulsive. Bernardino is a hoarder, which also seemed like a natural trait.

Your love of crime and noir shines in many elements of *Certain Dark Things*, but especially the idea of the city as a character. What were your inspirations for this version of Mexico City?

Mexico City is very interesting. First of all, because it's huge. It has nine million people in the city proper, but it has extended outside of those limits so you can't see where it begins and where it ends. To picture it as something walled and separate is a wild idea, but also makes sense because it feels like its own thing. And if you go back a few centuries, there really was a very clear border between the outside and the inside of the city because it was built on a lake and bordered by water. Therefore, some of the city's history helped me project the "what if."

Another thing that inspired me were Mexican noir films, which tend to be a bit different from American noir because they are often concerned with class differences and economic inequality. Cabaretera and rumbera films, for example, are a combo that is part musical, part melodrama, and part noir. It's hard to explain, but there's a lovely texture to some of these films and especially their femme fatales, that made me want to create a femme fatale who was literally a devourer rather than the metaphorical man-eaters like María Félix or Ninón Sevilla, who appeared in several noirs. And in these noirs, the city just looks amazing. It's all shadows and stark lighting and smoke. When I was talking about this reissue, the editor asked me what I wanted to see on the cover and I said I wanted it to look "neon-noir."

✂✂✂✂✂✂

It seems like Domingo's life on the street prepared him for becoming a vampire's assistant; in fact, a lot of the book touches on how predators like vampires could take advantage of the cyclical nature of poverty and the ability of people to make things feel normal. What inspired you to make that such a major motif?

My neighborhood in Mexico City was a kind of bizarre combo. It wasn't a rough area. But right near my home there was a pool hall where I'd go and it was filled with smoke and young men drinking. And I met a few street kids that lived nearby. I had a family and I was okay, but I knew people who were very vulnerable and it's a tough thing to live like that, because people live just for each day. You can't be making plans for the future. So, you sort of grab what you can and just run with it.

I wanted Domingo to be a character who makes bad choices but he actually has a good reason for them. Because, I mean, why wouldn't you become a vampire's assistant if that's your best option? Atl may be bad, mad, and dangerous to know, but she looks like a great option to Domingo.

✂✂✂✂✂✂

Certain Dark Things **seems explicitly a postcolonial vampire novel; the colonizing of Mexico by vampires is tied to historical colonialism thematically as well as in terms of its effects on the world of the novel. Please tell us a little about your idea to use vampires as a lens to focus on colonialism?**

I wanted to touch upon class, not really colonialism, but it just seeped into the book uninvited, so that you have European vampires versus local Mexican vampires, and it's as if a natural balance has been wildly disrupted. And then, of course, one thing that happened was that I've been chasing the idea of colonialism and what happens in its wake through several other books, including *Mexican Gothic*. It's just this thing that keeps coming back.

⬦⬦⬦⬦⬦⬦⬦⬦⬦⬦

I liked the idea of the chaos being a result of the disruption to the vampiric ecosystem—which you touched on a little by invoking the plagues brought to the Americas by European colonial powers. I think it's fascinating that the colonial angle "seeped in." Has that ever happened before, with any of your other projects?

Yeah. Writers are always having conversations with their subconscious. Sometimes you realize that's what's going on early on, sometimes it takes a while to catch on. Intelligent dialogue with your subconscious is, of course, the best recipe for success, but sometimes it's messy dialogue.

⬦⬦⬦⬦⬦⬦⬦⬦⬦⬦

Nahuatl words figure prominently in *Certain Dark Things*. Did the language help create any elements of the novel?

Atl, the protagonist of the novel, is a tlāhuihpochtli. A tlāhuihpochtli is a creature from central Mexico which belongs to the tradition of witches in Latin America and the Caribbean. My great-grandmother spoke of witches menacing the countryside, casting spells on men and performing mayhem. The tlāhuihpochtli is a type of witch that is able to transform into an animal, often a turkey. It drinks the blood of small children during the night. It can glow in the night (my great-grandmother spoke of balls of fire in the trees, which cackled). A tlāhuihpochtli is born with this condition, which manifests when they become teenagers. Evil is therefore a genetic gift or ailment.

In transplanting that idea from folklore into a modern novel, I made changes. And as I made changes I tried to create a mythology that made some sense, so I overlaid certain pre-Hispanic concepts onto the book and the Nahuatl started appearing.

⬦⬦⬦⬦⬦⬦⬦⬦⬦⬦

Let's talk about sexiness for a moment. The sexiness in *Certain Dark Things* is alloyed with awkwardness and dread, which I like. But I actually want to ask about sexy wing-reveal scenes in other media. They're just the best, aren't they? My favorite as a teen was in this weird 90s anime called *Vision of Escaflowne*. What's yours?

I don't remember seeing *Escaflowne*, but in the 1980s *Wings of Desire* had these angels in trench coats and at one point you see their wings. It's just briefly there, and the film is beautiful, and quiet, and it goes from marvelous black and white to color. *The Prophecy* came out in 1995, and it's an imperfect movie with some perfect moments, and some of the perfect moments involve angels perching like birds atop chairs. There's something birdlike when Christopher Walken is moving around. It makes perfect sense, he used to be a professional dancer, so he has this great physicality. I'm pretty sure *Constantine* used that film as inspiration and it also has a great, winged moment with Tilda Swinton. So . . . yeah. People with wings! Not used enough in literature these days, probably.

⬚⬚⬚⬚⬚⬚⬚⬚

What do you think has changed about the horror field since the initial publication of *Certain Dark Things*? What's stayed the same?

God, a lot seems to be changing. For decades, since the 1990s, horror has been a marginal genre. We had the big implosion of the genre with the demise of the Dell Abyss imprint, and horror became a category nobody wanted to publish, so people either changed genres, going into crime writing, or went with small presses. Now suddenly there's Tor Nightfire, several horror books are selling well, and even vampires—which I was told were dead for all eternity—are popping up, as you can see with this reissue.

⬚⬚⬚⬚⬚⬚⬚⬚

What's the scariest book you've read recently?

I'm writing this in 2020, and it's been a really good year for horror! *The Only Good Indians* by Stephen Graham Jones was really quite great, and very creepy at times, and it manages to feel like classic 1980s horror but it's also fresh. There's also *Tender Is the Flesh* by Agustina Bazterrica, which is about a dystopia in which we now consume human meat. There's a lot of great horror coming out now.

⬚⬚⬚⬚⬚⬚⬚⬚

For readers coming to *Certain Dark Things* after reading *Mexican Gothic* and *Gods of Jade and Shadow*, what will they find familiar? And what might surprise them?

I love dialogue and I love characters that are complicated, so I think that's something that remains consistent across my books. But there are many more shades of gray in *Certain Dark Things* than in some of my other books because it's a noir. I write a lot about Mexico and I hope people can read my books without looking for exotic thrills, and that they understand that I'm trying to construct a polychromatic view of my country. I like the mundane, I like the fantastic, I like horror, but I also like fantasy and science fiction and noirs. I want to tell many stories, not just one.

⬙⬙⬙⬙⬙⬙⬙⬙

So, what are you working on now? What can your readers look forward to?

My second crime novel, *Velvet Was the Night*. It's set against the backdrop of the repression and massacre of student protesters in Mexico City at that time by the government. And then it follows two characters on the hunt for a missing woman. The other book that is on the horizon is *The Daughter of Doctor Moreau*, which is set in the 1800s in southern Mexico. People can always look forward to me writing something completely different the next time.

"We are our hunger."

That's how the revenant Bernadino describes vampires to street kid Domingo. Vampire fiction should be sensual, and Silvia Moreno-Garcia's prose is satisfying in its own right—but for a certain sort of person, there's nothing that enhances a good read like a thematic beverage. So here, for your delight, are two potential potations for you to savor as certain *other* things on the page are being sipped—or guzzled for that matter.

—Recipes by Molly Tanzer

THE REVENANT

Citrusy and smoky, this take on the Corpse Reviver No. 2 may not bring the dead back to life, but it'll certainly awaken your palate.

> 1 ½ oz mezcal
> 1 ½ oz Lillet Rouge
> ¾ oz Cointreau
> ½ oz lemon juice
> 8 drops absinthe

❋ Combine all ingredients in a cocktail shaker or pitcher with lots of ice and stir until cold. Strain and serve in a coupe glass with a flamed orange twist, or with a Luxardo cherry in the bottom of a cocktail glass.

TENAMPA PUNCH

This virginal offering is no sacrifice to drink. Based in part on the Barbadian punch-making rhyme, "one of sour, two of sweet, three of strong, and four of weak," serve this in small cups, or over crushed ice. This fancy little mocktail is a thirst-quencher in hot weather, but it's also delightful with sparkling wine in place of the seltzer water. Serves 4 to 6 victims.

> ¼ cup chia seeds
> 1 ½ cups pomegranate juice
> 1 cup fresh basil leaves
> ¼ cup honey
> 3 cups boiling water

2 limes, freshly squeezed
Several healthy dashes of rose bitters
Seltzer water to taste

❋   Several hours before serving, bloom the chia seeds in the pomegranate juice by mixing them together well and chilling in the fridge. Make the basil-honey tea by putting the honey and the basil leaves in the bottom of a heat-safe bowl or pitcher, and pouring the hot water over it. Stir to mix completely, let steep at room temperature for an hour, then discard the basil and chill the mixture well.

❋   Combine the pomegranate-chia mixture and the basil-honey tea, add the juice of two limes, and a generous dashing of rose bitters. Do not add the seltzer (or sparkling wine) until the moment of serving. Punch is for drinking over time, so I suggest being fussy with the service to ensure it's always perfectly cold and fizzy. Here are a few ideas:

❋   For a more formal presentation, serve in a punch bowl. Make sure to freeze an ice hemisphere (they melt more slowly than an ice ring) by filling a bowl with water and freezing it solid. Thaw a bit by running under warm water to easily remove, then place that in your punch bowl. Pour half the tea mixture over the ice ball and top with 2 cups seltzer water. Taste and add a bit more pomegranate juice if you like. Refresh with the second half of the mixture and seltzer when it's running low.

❋   If you'd like to serve more casually, mix up the base in a nice pitcher and chill it well (no ice—it'll get watery), and set it out it beside a fancy bottle of sparkling water in a bucket full of ice. That way, people can mix up their own cups as they go.

DISCUSSION QUESTIONS

1. What are the advantages and drawbacks of being a Tlāhuihpochtli vampire? In what ways is Atl's identity distinctly different from all of the other characters in the novel?

2. Does Domingo's ability to fall in love cause him to become stronger or more vulnerable? How does his sense of purpose change when he meets Atl, even when she is exploiting his poverty? Would you be willing to serve as a Renfield?

3. Near the end of chapter 14, Elisa tells Atl, "Most governments consider you a plague." What similarities did you notice between attempts to eradicate vampires in the book and attempts to eradicate a pandemic in real life? In the novel, how successful were government responses (passports, a walled city-state) and human nature in managing a threat to the community?

4. Ana's forensic skill makes her a tough opponent against Atl. Though the two women are equally determined and courageous, their purposes are at odds. Were you rooting for one or both of them?

5. Headlines link vampires to the drug war, but Atl's hunger for blood is tied to her survival, not to addiction. How does the novel reinvent our assumptions about the drug trade?

6. In the novel, which has greater power: violence, money, or wisdom? What other powerful forces determine who survives?

7. Atl recalls her family legacies and the days when her ancestors were priestesses. How does she keep this noble status alive in her own sense of self? Why is it appropriate that her name means water as well as war?

8. Describe the ways in which Mexico City is presented as if it were a character, from the ancient Zócalo where the Aztecs gathered to the modern nightlife of the Zona Rosa. How does the city reflect the people who inhabit it? How has it evolved alongside the characters in the novel, at once weary and formidable?

9. What drives Atl to succeed where her mother (Centehua) and her sister (Izel) couldn't? If you were Elisa, would you have been willing to assist Atl?

10. What would it be like to exist alongside supernatural creatures that view humans as inferior? Did you see any metaphorical truths in Aztec beliefs regarding the origin of strength and the nature of evil?

11. As you watched Rodrigo try to manage the junk-food-addicted Necro vampire Nick Godoy while they pursue Atl—while Ana pursues them all—what distinctions are drawn between male and female characters in the novel?

12. How did you react to the epilogue? What does it say about the potency of memory and imagination?

13. Discuss the ten subspecies described in the Encyclopaedia Vampirica. How have they adapted through centuries of change? Which subspecies would you want to serve (or be)?

14. How does *Certain Dark Things* enhance your experience of other novels by Silvia Moreno-Garcia? What is unique about her visionary storytelling?

Guide written by Amy Root Clements

ABOUT THE AUTHOR

Silvia Moreno-Garcia is the *New York Times* bestselling author of the novels *Velvet Was the Night, Mexican Gothic, Gods of Jade and Shadow, Untamed Shore, The Beautiful Ones,* and *Signal to Noise.* She has also edited several anthologies, including the World Fantasy Award–winning *She Walks in Shadows* (a.k.a. *Cthulhu's Daughters*). She lives in Canada.